Marion McLeod lives in Wellington. She writes a new fiction column for the New Zealand *Listener*. She is the editor (with Bill Manhire) of *Some Other Country* (Allen & Unwin, 1984), a collection of short stories written in New Zealand.

Lydia Wevers taught Women's Studies in New Zealand before moving to Australia where she now teaches at the University of New South Wales. She is the editor of *New Zealand Short Stories* 4 (Oxford University Press, 1984), *Selected Poems of Robin Hyde* (Oxford University Press, 1984) and is currently working (with Elizabeth Webby) on a collection of short stories from the nineteenth century to 1950 by Australian and New Zealand women.

One Whale, Singing

and Other Stories from New Zealand

Selected by Marion McLeod
and Lydia Wevers

The Women's Press

First published in Great Britain by
The Women's Press Limited 1986
A member of the Namara Group
34 Great Sutton Street, London EC1V 0DX

First published as *Women's Work* by Oxford University Press, New
Zealand, 1985

British Library Cataloguing in Publication Data

One whale, singing and other stories from New Zealand
    1. Short stories, New Zealand   2. New
    Zealand fiction—20th century
    I. McLeod, Marion   II. Wevers, Lydia
    823'.01'089931 [FS]   PR9637.37.S45

    ISBN 0-7043-5006-8
    ISBN 0-7034-4014-3 Pbk

    Printed and bound by
    Hazell Watson & Viney Limited
    Aylesbury, Bucks

899.31

Contents

Acknowledgements

For permission to reproduce copyright material grateful acknowledgement is made to the publishers and copyright owners of the following:

Janet Frame, 'The Bull Calf' and 'Insulation'; Amelia Batistich, 'All Mixed Up', from *An Olive Tree in Dalmatia* (Longman Paul, 1963); Susi Robinson Collins, 'A Day at Hot Creek'; Joy Cowley, 'The Silk' and 'God Loves You, Miss Rosewater'; Linda Scarth, 'The Funeral'; Fiona Kidman, 'Flower Man' and 'A Strange Delight'; Margaret Sutherland, 'Codling-Moth' and 'Loving'; Helen Shaw, 'The Gipsies'; Yvonne du Fresne, 'Christmas (Shirley Temple is a Wife and Mother)', from *The Growing of Astrid Westergaard* (Longman Paul, 1985); Phyllis Gant, 'The Revolver'; Patricia Grace, 'Mirrors' and 'Kepa', from *The Dream Sleepers and other stories* (Longman Paul, 1980); Keri Hulme, 'One Whale, Singing' and 'Kiteflying Party at Doctors' Point'; Stanley Roche, 'Structurally Sound'; Rosie Scott, 'Diary of a Woman'; Rowan Metcalfe, 'The Cat'; Edith Campion, 'Good Morning, Wardrobe'; Annabel Fagan, 'In a Bamboo Garden'; Kathleen Crayford, 'Duncan'; Jean Watson, 'Princess!'; Violet Coalhouse, 'The Mask'; Daphne de Jong, 'Vagabundus Vinea' from *Venus, Vagabonds and Miscellanea* (Kara Press, 1984); Shonagh Koea, 'Meat'; Jennifer Compton, 'One of my families'; Jessie Feeney, 'A Married Woman'; Fiona Farrell Poole, 'Airmen'.

Foreword

The last two decades have seen a marked increase in the amount of short fiction published by New Zealand women. This may be due to a change in editorial attitude as much as to an actual increase in the number of women writing; but the upsurge of the women's movement cannot be coincidental. The point is not that a sudden burst of feminists began writing (though this also happened) but that in a climate of thought stimulating to women whatever their individual reactions to it, a great many more women began appearing in print.

Phoebe Meikle has discussed the relative proportions of fiction published by men and women in New Zealand. In an article in *Landfall* 130 (1979) she pays tribute to the strength of 'women's eye' views in our early literary history (Lady Barker, Blanche Baughan, Katherine Mansfield) but goes on to note that between the mid-twenties and the mid-sixties there was an almost complete absence of women's voices.

Lyndahl Chapple Gee was writing then. In his autobiographical essay 'Beginnings', Maurice Gee wrote:

> My mother was a writer. When her day's work was done and her husband and children in bed she sat with her feet in the range oven and wrote stories and poems in exercise books. She had natural gifts, but her circumstances were wrong. She needed to write hard, she needed practice. There was never sufficient time. She could not discover what it was she wanted to say. . . . Now and then she came near to her subject. Frank Sargeson included her story 'Double Unit' in his anthology *Speaking for Ourselves*. One can see she would have been a writer. There should have been other stories, better ones. But she did not have time. Her family swallowed her.

The mid-sixties proved a turning point. As Meikle noted in 1979, women had published in the preceding decade at least three times as many stories as in the whole of the previous ninety-odd years. Leaving aside the complicated question of gender and the differences it may or may not make in art, the fact remains that more women are expressing themselves publicly, and this fact is related to feminism, though the expression itself may not be.

We have read all the stories published by New Zealand women since 1963, or at least all that we could find. (Some may have remained invisible behind male pseudonyms or the genderlessness of initials.) Reading women's stories chronologically for an anthology such as this affords a fascinating exercise in sociology. It would be possible, for instance, to chart the rise of the 'suburban neurosis' story, to trace how comic stories of domestic chaos which wryly accept the female lot give way to a much less jolly picture of domesticity. In part this was due to a more general trend towards introspection — male writers did it too — but there is a clear emergence of feminist awareness. Some of the stories are raw, but they are opening up new ground. As Marge Piercy has said, women are 'unlearning to not speak'.

Writing about Sylvia Ashton-Warner in 1969 Dennis McEldowney commented:

> It has been remarked before that in the writing of New Zealand novels many of the barriers have been broken by women novelists. . . . Their discoveries have been made not so much through intellectual contemplation as through intensity of feeling. This has exposed them not only to the dismay and hostility of their contemporaries but to the danger of overburdening their writing to the point of breakdown with emotion. The central problem . . . is that of embodying emotion in an acceptable form, or any form at all; as it were, of grounding it.

Some, maybe, prefer to fly. But it's too easy simply to claim that male critics could not understand or appreciate the writing of women. McEldowney is generous and sensitive. Unlike many others he appreciated Ashton-Warner and his response to her does not just dismiss a way of writing that is unconventional by accepted male criteria. It is a difficult area; the question of conventional male response and its limitations involves all of us who have been educated in their 'school'. Feminist journals like *Broadsheet* and *Spiral* and the various women's publishing collectives which have mushroomed around the country are publishing stories which explore the traditional roles and conditions of men and women, and which deal with subjects previously taboo. They are not all perfect stories, but they are pushing at the barriers.

This book is not a selection of feminist writing, though such an anthology could be compiled and might result in a more unified volume. Our choice as editors has been subjective. We did not set out to illustrate any thesis on the nature or development of short story writing by women, nor have we opted for an even spanning of the years, though all the stories were first published during roughly the last two decades. Though predominantly from a female point of view, the stories here are not exclusively so. In 'Airmen' Fiona Farrell Poole deals overtly with the question of women writing about men: 'I shall write about three things I do not understand: a man, a motorbike, and an aeroplane . . . . It will be a challenge (think of Ibsen with Nora at his elbow in her blue dress, Hardy and his secret red-lipped Tess).' Again, most but not all are set in New Zealand: Annabel Fagan's 'In a Bamboo Garden' is about an Anglo-Indian woman, and is set in India. Though most of the writers are still writing and publicly known, some are not; some have moved away. There is a wide range of ages, and there are, perhaps most importantly, writers who are not European and whose experience leads to a fundamentally different perception of our society.

All these stories can stand alone; none needs to shelter under a 'women's' umbrella. There are many more which we would have included had there been more space; our problem was not what to include but what to leave out. This anthology is intended as a celebration of the excellence of recent short story writing by New Zealand women, and also as an encouragement to those women who are just beginning to discover what it is they want to say and to risk finding their own way of saying it.

Marion McLeod and Lydia Wevers

Janet Frame
The Bull Calf

'Why do I always have to milk the cows?' Olive said. 'Couldn't the others do it for a change?' But no, it is always me. Up early and over the hills to find Scrapers. At night home from school and over the hills again to find Scrapers, to bring her down across the creek (here it is difficult; I tie a rope over her horns and make my leap first; she follows, if she is willing) through the gate that hangs on one hinge, into the cow byre with its cracked concrete floor. Pinning her in the bail. Putting on the leg rope. Day after day rain shine or snow.

'I'm tired of milking the cows,' Olive said. 'Beauty, Pansy, and now Scrapers who is bony like bare rafters and scaffolding. One day I will refuse.'

Sometimes she did refuse, in the early morning with sleep gumming her eyes, her body sticky with night, her hair tangled.

'Milk your own cows!' she cried then, retreating to the bedroom and sitting obstinately on the bed, chanting rhymes and French verbs which her Mother could not understand because she had left school at sixteen to go to service. . . .

But the thought of Scrapers waiting haunted Olive, and soon she would get up from the bed, clatter to the scullery, bumping furniture on the way to show her resentment of everything in the world including corners and walls and doors, take the bucket with a swill of warm water in the bottom for washing the teats and climb the hill in search of Scrapers who, if her bag was full, would be waiting mercifully not far away.

Olive went to High School. In the morning she worried about being late. And every morning when the teacher called suddenly, 'Form Twos, Form Twos,' Olive worried in case no one formed twos with her. Very often she found herself standing alone. Is it because I stink? she thought. Then she would press the back and front of her uniform, down below, to smooth away the bulge of the homemade sanitary towel, layers of torn sheet sewn together with the blood always leaking through. The other girls used bought towels which were safe and came in packets with tiny blue-edged notices inside the packet, WEAR BLUE LINE AWAY FROM THE BODY. The other girls did not seem to mind when in Drill, which was later called Physical Education to keep up with the times, the teacher would command sharply, 'Uniforms Off, Come on Everybody, Uniforms Off!' Why should they mind when they were using towels which did not show, or even the new type where the advertisement had a picture of a woman in a bathing suit, shouting with rapture from the edge of a high-diving board, 'No Belts, No Pins, No Pads!' But on the days when Olive wore her homemade towel she would ask, blushing, 'Please can I keep my uniform on?'

'Oh,' Miss Copeland said. 'Yes.'

And Olive and one or two other girls with their uniforms on would huddle miserably on the end seat, by the bar stools, out of everybody's way.

Olive and her sisters had hickies on their chins and foreheads. The advertisements warned them never to wear 'off-the-face' hats. Whole pages of the newspapers were devoted to the picture-story of the disasters which befell Lorna, Mary or Marion who continued to wear off-the-face hats in spite of having hickies on their chins and foreheads. Lorna, Mary, Marion were lonely and unwanted until they used Velona Ointment. Olive and her sisters used Velona Ointment. It had a smell like the oil of a motorcar engine and it came off in a sticky grass-green stain on the pillowcase.

But mostly Olive was tired. She stayed up late working on mathematical problems, writing French translations and essays, and in the morning she was up so early to go over the hill and find Scrapers. There were so many trees and hollows on the hill, and often it was in these hollows where the grass was juiciest, nourished by the pools of yesterday's rain or the secret underground streams, that Scrapers would be hiding. Sometimes Olive had to walk to the last Reserve before she found Scrapers. Then there was the problem of tying the rope across her horns and leading her home.

Sometimes Scrapers refused to co-operate. Olive would find her dancing up and down, tossing her horns and bellowing.

'Scrapers, Scrapers, come on, be a good cow!'

Still Scrapers refused, Olive could not understand why. I'll be late for school, she thought, after struggling with and trying to chase the entranced cow. But it was no use. Olive would hurry down the hill, across the creek, through the broken-hinged gate and up the path to the house where the family, waiting for breakfast, would ask, 'Where's the milk?' while Olive in turn confronted them with her question, 'What's the matter with Scrapers? She's dancing and tossing her horns and refusing to be milked.'

Her Mother received the news calmly. 'Leave the cow. She'll be all right in a few days.'

Nobody explained. Olive could not understand. She would pour stale milk on her Weet-Bix, finish her breakfast, brush the mud from her shoes, persuade the pleats into her uniform, and hurry away to school.

It was always the same. She stood alone in Assembly, concealing herself behind the girl in front who was taller. Captain of the 'A' Basketball Team, Holder of a Drill Shield. Olive did not want the teachers on the platform to see her standing alone, hiding behind the girl in front of her.

> *Peace perfect peace in this dark world of sin*
> *the cross of Jesus whispers Peace within*

she sang, sensing the mystery. Her heart felt heavy and lonely.

When she climbed the hill in search of the cow she always stopped in the paddock next door to pat the neighbour's bull calf which was growing plumper and stronger every day. Everyone knew what happened to bull calves. They were taken to the slaughterhouse while they were still young, or they became steers journeying from saleyard to saleyard until they grew old and tough and despised, without the pride and ferocity of bulls and the gentleness and patience of cows. If you were caught in a paddock with them and they attacked you it was in bursts of irritation which left them standing as if bewildered, half-afraid at their own daring. They did not seem able to decide; they panicked readily; they had no home, they were forever lost in strange surroundings, closed in by new fences and gates with unfamiliar smells, trees, earth; with dogs snapping at their heels, herding them this way and that, in and out, up and down. . . .

Olive knew that one day Ormandy's bull calf would be a steer. 'Calfie, calfie,' she would whisper, putting her flattened palm inside the calf's mouth and letting it suck.

Night came. The spotted grey cockabullies in the creek wriggled under the stones to sleep, and soon the birds were hushed in the willow trees and the hedge and the sighing pines. This evening Olive was late in fetching Scrapers. She was late and tired. Her best black stockings, cobbled at the back of the leg, were splashed with mud, there were no clean ones for tomorrow; her stockings never lasted, all the other girls bought their stockings at Morton's, and theirs were cashmere, with a purple rim around the top, a sign of quality, while Olive's were made of coarse rayon. She was ashamed of them, she was ashamed of everything and everyone. She kicked her shoes against a clump of grass. Toe and heel plates! Why must she always have toe and heel plates on her shoes? Why must they always be lace-ups? She yawned. Her skin felt itchy. The pressure of her tight uniform upon her breasts was uncomfortable. Why hadn't Auntie Polly realised, and made the seams deeper, to be let out when necessary? Olive's sisters wore uniforms made by real dressmakers. Her sisters were lucky. How they teased her, pointing to the pictures in the *True Confession* magazines, digging their elbows slyly at each other and murmuring, 'Marylin's breasts were heavy and pendulous.'

'That means you,' they said to Olive. 'You'll be like Mum with two full moons bobbing up and down, moons and balloons and motor tyres.'

Yes, her sisters were lucky.

'Why don't they help with the cow?' Olive asked. 'Why don't they milk the cow for a change?'

She walked slowly up the hill, keeping to the path worn by herself and Scrapers; it was rucked with dry, muddy hoofprints and followed along the edge of the pine plantation. When she reached the top of the hill and there was still no sign of Scrapers she went to the fence bordering the native plant reserve and looked out over the town and the sea and the spilled dregs of light draining beyond the horizon. The silver-bellied sea turned and heaved in the slowly brightening moon-track, and the red and green roofs of the town were brushed with rising mist and moon. She identified objects and places: the Town Clock; the main street; the houseboat down at the wharf; the High School, and just behind the trees at the corner, next to the bicycle sheds, the little shop that sold hot mince pies and fish and chips at lunchtime. Then she gazed once more at the sea, waiting for the Sea-Foam-Youth-Grown-Old to appear. It was her secret dream. She knew he would never reach her. She knew that his bright glistening body became old, shrivelled, yellow, as soon as he touched the sand; it was the penalty. She sighed. The grieving hush-hush of the trees disturbed her. Their heads were bowed, banded with night. The wind moved among them, sighing, only increasing their sorrow. It came to her, too, with its moaning that she could not understand; it filled the world with·its loneliness and darkness.

Olive sighed again. What was the use of waiting for the Sea-Foam-

Youth-Grown-Old? What was the use of anything? Would the trees never stop saying Why, Why?

She was Olive Blakely going to milk Scrapers. She was Olive Blakely standing on the hill alone at night. The cutty grass and the tinkertailor were brushing against her black stockings; there was bird dirt on the fence post; the barbed wire had snapped and sagged.

That evening she milked Scrapers on the hill. What a miracle! The cow stood motionless for her and did not give those sudden sly kicks which she practised from time to time. Scrapers was an expert at putting her foot in the bucket.

Olive patted the velvety flank. Scrapers was standing so calmly. Why was she so calm when a few days ago she had danced, tossed, bellowed, jumping fences and running with her tail high in the air? Now she stood peacefully chewing, seeming to count the chews before each swallow, introducing a slight syncopation before returning the cud to her mouth which she opened slowly once or twice in a lazy yawn releasing her warm grassy-smelling breath on the cool air. Her teeth were stained and green, her eyes swam and glistened like goldfish. She let down her milk without protest.

Leaning to one side to balance the full bucket with its froth of creamy milk, Olive walked carefully down the hill. Damn, she thought. I will have to iron my uniform tonight, and sponge it to remove the grass stains. And damn again, I have trodden in cow muck. Cow muck, pancakes, cowpad. . . .

She mused on the words. The Welsh children up the road said *cowpad*. They were a compact, aloof, mysterious family with the two girls going to High School. They had a cousin called Myfanwy. Olive wished that she were called Myfanwy. Or Eitne. Or anything except plain pickled Olive.

She crossed the creek. The milk slopped against her legs, dampening her stockings and staining the hem of her uniform.

'Damn again,' she said. She would have to look in Pear's *Dictionary*, 'Household Hints', to find how to remove milk stains; she never remembered.

Then just as she was approaching the gate she noticed two men leaning over the bull calf in the corner of the paddock, near the hedge. 'Mr Ormandy, Mr Lewis,' Olive said to herself. 'Old Ormandy.'

He had been named *Old Ormandy* when he stopped people from picking his plums but there was no law against picking them, was there, when the tree hung over the fence into the road, inviting anyone to take the dusty plums split and dark blue with pearls of jelly on their stalk and a bitter, blighted taste at the centre, near the stone.

Old Ormandy. The girl Ormandy picked her nose and ate it. Their uncle had been in court for sly-grogging.

Olive watched the two men. What were they doing to the bull calf? It was so dark. What were they doing in the dark? She waited until they had left the bull calf before she went over to say good night to it.

'Calfie, calfie,' she whispered. It was lying outstretched. She bent over it, seeking to pat its face and neck. Its nose felt hot and dry, its eyes were bright, and between its back legs there was blood, and a patch of blood on the grass. The calf had been hurt. Old Ormandy and Lewis were responsible. Why hadn't they noticed the calf was ill? Or perhaps they had deliberately been cruel to it?

'I wouldn't put it past them,' Olive said aloud, feeling strangely satisfied that she was expressing her indignation in the very words her Father used when he became suspicious. 'I wouldn't put it past them.'

She trembled and patted the calf.

'Calfie, calfie,' she whispered again. 'Sook sook. Never mind, calfie, I'll get someone to help you.'

But her heart was thudding with apprehension. Supposing the calf were to die? She had seen many animals die. They were not pampered and flattered in death, like human beings; they became immediate encumbrances, threats to public health, with neighbours and councillors quarrelling over the tedious responsibility of their burial. Or were dead human beings — in secret of course — regarded in this way also, and was their funeral procession a concealment, with flowers, of feelings which the living were afraid to admit? Olive's thoughts frightened her. She knew that all things dead were in the way; you tripped over them, they did not move, they were obstacles, they were no use, even if they were people they were no use, they did not complain or cry out, like sisters, if you pinched them or thumped them on the back, they were simply no use at all.

She did not want the bull calf to die. She could see its eyes glistening, pleading for help. She picked up the milk bucket and hurried through the gate to the house and even before she reached the garden tap (she had to be careful here for the tap leaked, the earth was bogged with moss and onion flower) she heard her Father's loud voice talking.

His friends, the Chinese people, had come to visit him, and he was telling the old old story. His operation. He had been ill with appendicitis and while he was in hospital he had made friends with the Chinese family who came often now to visit him, filling the house with unfamiliar voices and excitements, creating an atmosphere that inspired him to add new dimensions of peril to his details of the operation.

'Going gangrene . . . they wheeled me in. . . .'

Almost running up to the house, fearing for the life of the bull calf, Olive had time only to hear her Father's loud voice talking to the visitors before she opened the kitchen door. She was almost crying now. She was ashamed of her tears in front of the visitors. She tried to calm herself. Everyone looked up, startled.

'It's calfie, Ormandy's bull calf, it's been hurt, there's all blood between its legs and its nose is hot!'

Olive's Mother glanced without speaking at her Father who returned the glance, with a slight smile at the corner of his mouth. The Chinese visitors stared. One of them, a young man, was holding a bowl with a flower growing in it, a most beautiful water narcissus whose frail white transparent petals made everything else in the room — the cumbersome furniture, the heavy-browed bookcase, the chocolate-coloured panelled ceiling, the solid black-leaded stove — seem like unnecessary ballast stored beyond, and at the same time within, people to prevent their lives from springing up joyfully, like the narcissus growing out of water into the clear sky.

'The bull calf, what will we do about it?' Olive urged, breaking the silence, and staring at the flower because she could not take her eyes from its loveliness and frailty.

Her Mother spoke. 'It's all right,' she said. 'There's nothing the matter with the calf.'

Olive stopped looking at the flower. She turned to her Mother. She felt betrayed. Her Mother, who took inside the little frozen birds to try to warm them back to life, who mended the rabbit's leg when it was caught in the trap, who fed warm bran to the sick horse that was lying on its side, stretched out!

'But it's bleeding! The calf might die! I saw Mr Ormandy with it, Old Ormandy and another man!'

She knew the man had been Mr Lewis, yet she said 'another man' because it seemed to convey the terrible anonymity which had suddenly spread over every person and every deed. Nobody was responsible; nobody would own up; nobody would even *say*.

'The bull calf's all right, I tell you,' her Father said, impatient to return to his story of the operation. 'Forget it. Go and do your homework.'

Olive sensed embarrassment. They seemed ashamed of her. They were ashamed of something. Why didn't they tell her? She wished she had not mentioned the bull calf.

'But I saw it with my own eyes,' she insisted, in final proof that the calf was hurt and needed help.

Again everybody was silent. She could not understand. Why were they so secretive? What was the mystery?

Then her Father swiftly changed the subject.

'Yes, they wheeled me in . . . going gangrene . . . I said to Lottie, I said, on the night. . . .'

Olive was about to go from the room when the young man in the corner beckoned to her. He smiled. He seemed to understand. He held out the bowl with the narcissus in it, and said, 'You have it. It is for you.'

Gratefully she took the bowl, and making no further mention of the sick calf she went to her bedroom. She put the narcissus on her dressing table. She touched the petals gently, stroking them, marvelling again at the transparency of the whole flower and the clear water where every fibre of the bulb seemed visible and in motion as if brushed by secret currents and tides. She leaned suddenly and put her cheek against the flower.

Then she lay down on her bed and with her face pressed to the pillow, she began to cry.

Amelia Batistich
All Mixed Up

Mama comes from Dalmatia. She is round and rosy and her skin is white as white. Not like Daddy's and mine and Rudi's. We are the dark ones. Tina is like Mama. She has the same blue eyes and her hair is gold as the sovereign on Daddy's watch chain.

In the boarding-house where we live Mama rules like a queen. The men, all Dalmatians like us, respect her because she is Mrs Parentich, and that you know is something quite different from being Mrs Anybody Else.

Mama is always busy. Work is what she believes in. It's her religion like some people's is going to church. God loves people who work, Mama says, and she makes sure of His loving her a lot. Work was what Mama came to New Zealand for — and to see America. In the old country, she explains, all the new world is 'America' not just America on the map. 'Everyone wants to go there,' says Mama. 'I used to listen to them talking about it and I would say to myself: "I will see this America, too!" '

Of course, Mama was no ordinary person, even in Dalmatia. She was Milka Filipova there, and the way she says it it's like saying she was a princess or something. She had four sisters and four brothers, three of them in the real America, in New York. Her mother, our *Baba Manda* (Grandmother Manda), was left a widow when she was only as old as Mama now, and she had all the children to look after, and the inn where they lived, and the vineyards and olive trees and the sardine boats as well. The inn was a big, white stone house, years and years old, right by the sea. *Three* floors it had, and flower-painted walls. *And* a Spaher stove.

'Having all that and being poor?' I wonder.

'It's a different kind of "poor" from here,' Mama says. 'In Dalmatia you have everything but money.'

I like Mama's stories about Dalmatia. It is such a lovely place there. You have lots and lots of grapes and the sun shines a lot and they ripen till they're black and you go out with all the other children and pick them and press them into wine.

'How do you press the grapes?' I ask.

'With your feet,' says Mama. 'You go down to the sea and wash them and the children with the cleanest feet stamp out the wine.'

I would like to press grapes with my feet. Sometimes I wish Mama had stayed in Dalmatia. Then we could live in the story too. 'It is better for you here,' says Mama. 'And what about Daddy? Would you like to be without him?'

No, I would not. I like Daddy. I like the way he laughs with his eyes and his mouth together. I like the way he looks at me, and I like his wonderful black moustache.

Daddy found Mama when he went back to Dalmatia. He didn't go to stay but to see his father, our grandfather Petar.

When Daddy went to New Zealand Mama was only a little girl. Their families were friends and he remembered her. The men who had come out later used to talk about her in the gum camps. 'She has grown to a lovely girl,' they said. 'But she is very proud. She will not marry just anybody.' So when he went back he thought: 'I will have a look at this girl who is too proud to marry just anybody. Maybe she will marry me.' And she did.

Mama did not like New Zealand when she came here first. It was nothing like 'America'. She was homesick and lonely and she cried for her home. But she got used to it. And when she saw how you could get on here like you never could in the old country she was glad she came.

Daddy and Mama have different ideas on lots of things. Money, for instance. Daddy thinks it is for spending. Mama says it is for saving. She scolds him when he gives us the pennies from his pocket for lollies. 'Spoiling the children,' she says. 'They should put pennies in the money-box.' But I like spending them at Martin's better. 'Making the shopman rich,' says Mama. 'What about us?'

What about us? I think we're all right. We live in a good house. We wear good clothes. We never go barefoot to school like some children do. Sometimes I have a dream and in it I am sitting in school and I look down at my toes and there are no shoes there. I am poor, like Minnie Thompson, and no one wants to play with me, either.

That's one thing I'm glad I'm not. Poor. But I am Dalmatian and that's different from everybody else, and when they want to, the other girls can say; 'Poof! You're only an Austrian squarehead anyway.' Just like we all say to Minnie that she's poor.

But why I'm Austrian I don't know. I don't properly know what

'Austrian' is. When I ask Mama she says, 'You are not Austrian. You are Dalmatian New Zealander. Tell them that.'

And now I have become a new thing. The boarders are always talking about it like a word they have just learnt and can't say often enough. It's a *Yugoslav*.

I don't like this new word. It's got the sound of being poor. Dalmatian is fine. It has a rich, poetry sound. I like the way it looks on the map: D-A-L-M-A-T-I-A spread out in a lovely long line.

But I do like the picture we have just got of the new Queen. She is young and pretty and she is wearing a lovely necklace, but no crown. The King is by her. He hasn't got a crown either.

Susi Robinson Collins
A Day at Hot Creek

All through the Hot Creek Valley there was the folding and unfolding of tobacco leaves. All along the yellow lanes of earth, between the tobacco plants, the sun made its way — falling on the surface of the leaves and parching the throats of the workers. There appeared to be no shade anywhere, not even in the foothills that lay sprawling, fold upon fold, blue and yellow and as dry and brittle as parchment. Only a yellowness wavered before the eyes and splintered the air.

It was a yellow day, alright.

'Laurie and I love each other,' said Jenny-May from her drooping, loose mouth where the flesh appeared to dangle uneasily. She stooped to pick a yellowed leaf.

'What do you mean? What are you talking about? You're trying to be funny, surely, Jenny-May,' I said. 'Why, you hardly know the man. Do you feel alright?' These words tumbled in surprise from my lips as I looked up at the slim figure from my stooping position in the tobacco row. She didn't appear to hear me.

'We knew it from the first moment we looked at each other. He wants me to go away with him.'

'What! And leave this tobacco rotting in the rows. And leave Sealy and her boys — and us in the lurch. Why, Sealy will kill you. She's that kind of woman. Not to be played with, I tell you.'

'Sealy only *lives* with him. He can't shake her off, he says. And the boys are old enough to look after themselves.' She straightened her body. There's a girl who doesn't worry enough, I thought. I felt sick. I saw the world go black and leaden as an icy night. I had never before been told anyone's intimate feelings. No one had poured their love-life in my ears. It was as embarrassing as people who stood on street corners and called out the name of Jesus and asked if you were *prepared* and *ready*. I turned away from Jenny-May, who stood fragile and pink, the shape of her figure making neat rounds here and there.

She was an acquaintance of my student friends, and had talked herself into accompanying us when we decided to go South to the tobacco country for the season. She had made little contribution to our talks and discussions, but had melted about on her own. I turned toward her and looked into her eyes. They were like big velvet pansies. They had abandoned all thought and reason except the fact that she was riding on air because of this feeling of love for Laurie Hemmings, who owned the small farm where we worked. But I was not prepared to carry on this conversation about love, in the tobacco rows, in the yellow light, with blushes and embarrassment flooding through me. The day that had begun with so much felicity had already disintegrated too far.

'What's for tea tonight, Jenny-May?' I said. It was her turn on as cook. This question dissipated her thoughts of love.

'Tinned beef and semolina pudding — and more *talk*,' she said. With the 'and more talk', her voice took on a somewhat sarcastic ring. This girl with the pink carnation skin bursting with love, stood smoothing her fingers up and down her thighs.

And from my surprised mouth the extraordinary conversation I had had with Jenny-May escaped in a frenzy of words to my friend, Queenie. 'Something's happened to Jenny-May — or did I dream it? She says she and Laurie *love* each other. Terrible! God, what's happened to her, Queenie?'

Queenie pulled at the ripening leaves with her gloved hand keeping a steady rhythm. Queenie was a calm and experienced one, we felt. Her husband had been killed in the desert and she was now back at the University completing her degree. She appeared to be full of good sense, calmness, and a solidity that made her presence a positive thing. But occasionally her calmness deserted her when she began thinking about the boy who was killed in the desert, running and hooting toward the enemy. Her little wound would open.

I hung on to my frenzied words and waited for Queenie to look up at me and offer some words of wisdom and healing that would take the fear from my spine and reconcile me again with the yellow day.

'This valley, this new life,' she said, 'has given Jenny-May a set of new values. Yes, that's it. She sees Laurie as she feels she should see a country man. Big and strong and smelling of the good earth — all that sort of thing, you know — a little different from the travelling salesmen gents about whom she occasionally drops hints. Yes, she's magnified him.' She paused and poised her gloved hand in the air. *'Magnified* him,' she repeated in a whisper.

But I had no wisdom and little things worried me. I could feel the pressure of the tobacco leaves and the yellow sun. And already, in my mind, the figure of Sealy with her big bare arms, intent on killing, was lunging into the quiet of our cottage down in the valley.

'We must warn Jenny-May. Sealy's a hard nut. She's mad about that spindly idiot. She'll allow no one on her territory. Oh, I'm *frightened*, Queenie.' Queenie gave me a look I could not interpret at the time. Then she said: 'Don't worry about Jenny-May. Everything will turn out alright, you'll see.' And she continued the quick rhythm of her picking.

It was about this time that big, henna-haired Sealy, with her slapping great arms and legs worked her way toward where Queenie and I were passing words and working hard at the picking. She made a noise with her body like a large animal crashing through the bush.

'I like you girls, but let that Jenny-May make one false move and I'm warning yer — she's for it.'

There was no veneer on Sealy. She was tremendously natural and real; it seemed to me that she was prehistoric woman still, and had never grown a covering of the conventions and habits of the societies man had lived through. But we liked her. She could laugh. She was kind. And she had no secrets disturbing the lining of her thoughts, but she, too, had magnified the spindly man and filled his flesh and bones until, in her eyes, he was a god strutting the tobacco rows and pacing the Hot Creek hills. And his breath was fire. We, in fact, only saw him as Laurie the thin, sheepish, bloodless dolt who never smiled nor looked you in the eye. And who had no summers at all.

I looked at Sealy through the leaves. 'I think you're wrong, Sealy,' I sniffed. 'Jenny-May won't hurt you.'

'She better not. I've met her kind before: the creeping lilac kind — roots all over the place.' Sealy spat out a spume of spittle that vibrated with hate.

'We'll have a talk with her,' Queenie said, 'but I don't think you've got anything to worry about, Sealy.'

'I'm not so sure; not so sure,' she said. I could not answer the angry female look that hung over her face. She smacked her voluminous thighs, sucked in her lips, and padded away with a full bin against her belly. The belly rippled with her walking steps.

All that day a tremor ran through my spine. At lunch-time I whispered the news to Delores and Teeny, our other student friends. They were not surprised, for they had seen sly smiles and fingers touching and a brushing against hips when Jenny-May and Laurie passed each other in the rows. They were surprised, however, by Jenny-May's attraction for Laurie Hemmings. But then they hadn't known about the magnifying.

For the remainder of the day there was a secret furtiveness abroad in the tobacco paddocks, the paddocks that were hugged in by the hills, with meandering Hot Creek running its tired course to the flats below. Jenny-May was wrapped in mystery. She appeared to float among the rows, the carnations bursting from her skin. I don't pretend to know what thoughts passed through her mind for she neither talked nor sighed, only floated and floated and bent and picked and used her handkerchief. I saw her once stoop to pick a dandelion and blow at its fluffed petticoats. And they too, floated.

Five o'clock and the day came to a halt. We packed our lunch things, drank a mug of Sealy's oatmeal water, and left the paddocks for the cottage. Instinctively we kept close to Jenny-May, talking as naturally as we could of the hot day, the number of bins we had filled and tried to laugh at our self-conscious jokes hoping, of course, that all these actions would take the anger from Sealy's breast. Until we got away from Laurie's property, anyway. And then we would speak to Jenny-May and try to make her see some reason.

Delores and Teeny had fallen behind a little. They were intense, studious types and had removed themselves so far from Jenny-May that her problems only skimmed the surface of their minds. Right now they were arguing about Nietzsche's epigraph, that one must chaos within to give birth to a dancing star. They were completely engulfed by their own proclivities; miles away from chaos, it would seem. And it appeared to me, at that moment, that all the dancing stars were in Jenny-May's breast.

'Jenny-May, I hope you've changed your mind. I hope you're only fooling about going away with Laurie Hemmings. What will the authorities say, who paid our fare here? Have you a mother, Jenny-May?' Fear put these words into my mouth. And a soaring wind took them away.

'You all don't understand,' she sighed. 'No one will understand.' And she began to float. The sounds of the day had run down to a whisper, even in the wind. And now Queenie asked why we didn't understand. Jenny-May's mouth smiled and smiled and said we were all *green* and hadn't lived; that we only read books and argued about impossible things; that if we had *lived* we would now be helping her. She then told us to keep quiet anyway. And thank God she wasn't being pushed into the University to boost her parents' *ego*. And then, when she had breathed all this, her love sealed her off from us and we walked away down the valley.

That night, when it was black outside, there came a heavy banging on the kitchen door of the cottage. We were all in our night clothes except Jenny-May, who had finished fastening her hair into metal curlers and was now slapping cream on her face with the slow and measured movements of a Balinese dancer in a trance. Her eyes were held in the mirror and looked back at her from remote pools. And then a voice.

'Youse inside — send out Jenny-May!' It was Sealy's voice, cracked and hoarse like an old trumpet. Jenny-May's fingers jumped inside the jar of face-cream. The pansies in her eyes were trapped by fire. No one spoke. Our mouths were open and gaping ridiculously. The banging continued. It grew louder.

'Youse inside, send out that Jenny woman or I'll break in the bloody door.' The broken trumpet had shattered to fragments. The trapped pansies looked from one to the other of us. A festering fever of the spirit had overwhelmed us, even Delores and Teeny. Then our eyes turned on Queenie who stood tugging at her nightdress. We felt sure she would know what to do. But Queenie couldn't speak. The banging became more violent. Outside in the black night Sealy was god-damning and bitching Jenny-May. And all the while she looked from one to the other of us, appealing wordlessly for help. And none was forthcoming – not even from Queenie!

What thoughts passed through Jenny-May's mind we shall never know, but suddenly she tilted her metal-fastened head and walked toward the door, opened it and disappeared into the night — and Sealy's hands. In the imaginative embodiment of our fear we were all rooted in the floor.

The short silence that followed was as shocking as death.

And then came muffled words and thuds, and time was a terrible, sickening electric current that took us and shook us and sucked our minds of all coherent thought. Then presently the door opened and Jenny-May stood there with her hand clasped weakly on the handle, an astonished look in her eyes. We all peered into the night, past Jenny-May's bruised face and flattened curlers. Beams of light from the rooms fell on the ground as far as the barbed-wire fence. On the other side of the fence Laurie Hemmings was lighting a cigarette. He looked up. Jenny-May had caught his eye. For a fleeting moment their gaze was held. Then Laurie cast down his eyes and blew out the match. Jenny-May passed into the kitchen.

'I told yer there was no life in that one. Now come on. . . .' Sealy was rolling down the sleeves of her cardigan as she walked toward Laurie. Soon they were sealed in the night.

In the morning, when we awoke, we found Jenny-May's bed had not been slept in. A crumpled piece of paper fluttered from under her pillow. It read: *Goodbye you green lot. Don't come after me, I'll be too far on my way.*

We crawled into ourselves.

I could see, in my mind, Jenny-May walking along the yellow dust road, casually swinging her patent-leather bag in one hand and her suitcase in the other. The pansies would be quite dead now.

And for Jenny-May nothing was magnified any more.

Joy Cowley
The Silk

When Mr Blackie took bad again that autumn both he and Mrs Blackie knew that it was for the last time. For many weeks neither spoke of it; but the understanding was in their eyes as they watched each other through the days and nights. It was a look, not of sadness or despair, but of quiet resignation tempered with something else, an unnamed expression that is seen only in the old and the very young.

Their acceptance was apparent in other ways, too. Mrs Blackie no longer complained to the neighbours that the old lazy-bones was running her off her feet. Instead she waited on him tirelessly, stretching their pension over chicken and out-of-season fruits to tempt his appetite; and she guarded him so possessively that she even resented the twice-weekly visits from the District Nurse. Mr Blackie, on the other hand, settled into bed as gently as dust. He had never been a man to dwell in the past, but now he spoke a great deal of their earlier days and surprised Mrs Blackie by recalling things which she, who claimed the better memory, had forgotten. Seldom did he talk of the present, and never in these weeks did he mention the future.

Then, on the morning of the first frost of winter, while Mrs Blackie was filling his hot water bottle, he sat up in bed, unaided, to see out the window. The inside of the glass was streaked with tears of condensation. Outside, the frost had made an oval frame of crystals through which he could see a row of houses and lawns laid out in front of them, like white carpets.

'The ground will be hard,' he said at last. 'Hard as nails.'

Mrs Blackie looked up quickly. 'Not yet,' she said.

'Pretty soon, I think.' His smile was apologetic.

She slapped the hot water bottle into its cover and tested it against her cheek. 'Lie down or you'll get a chill,' she said.

Obediently, he dropped back against the pillow, but as she moved about him, putting the hot water bottle at his feet, straightening the quilt, he stared at the frozen patch of window:

'Amy, you'll get a double plot, won't you?' he said. 'I wouldn't rest easy thinking you were going to sleep by someone else.'

'What a thing to say!' The corner of her mouth twitched. 'As if I would.'

'It was your idea to buy single beds,' he said accusingly.

'Oh Herb — ' She looked at the window, away again. 'We'll have a double plot,' she said. For a second or two she hesitated by his bed, then she sat beside his feet, her hands placed one on top of the other in her lap, in a pose that she always adopted when she had something important to say. She cleared her throat.

'You know, I've been thinking on and off about the silk.'

'The silk?' He turned his head towards her.

'I want to use it for your laying out pyjamas.'

'No Amy,' he said. 'Not the silk. That was your wedding present, the only thing I brought back with me.'

'What would I do with it now?' she said. When he didn't answer, she got up, opened the wardrobe door and took the camphorwood box from the shelf where she kept her hats. 'All these years and us not daring to take a scissors to it. We should use it sometime.'

'Not on me,' he said.

'I've been thinking about your pyjamas.' She fitted a key into the brass box. 'It'd be just right.'

'A right waste, you mean,' he said. But there was no protest in his voice. In fact, it had lifted with a childish eagerness. He watched her hands as she opened the box and folded back layers of white tissue paper. Beneath them lay the blue of the silk. There was a reverent silence as she took it out and spread it under the light.

'Makes the whole room look different, doesn't it?' he said. 'I nearly forgot it looked like this.' His hands struggled free of the sheet and moved across the quilt. Gently, she picked up the blue material and poured it over his fingers.

'Aah,' he breathed, bringing it closer to his eyes. 'All the way from China.' He smiled. 'Not once did I let it out of me sight. You know that, Amy? There were those on board as would have pinched it quick as that. I kept it pinned round me middle.'

'You told me,' she said.

He rubbed the silk against the stubble of his chin. 'It's the birds that take your eye,' he said.

'At first,' said Mrs Blackie. She ran her finger over one of the peacocks that strutted in the foreground of a continuous landscape. They were proud birds, iridescent blue, with silver threads in their tails. 'I used to like them best, but after a while you see much more, just as fine only smaller.' She pushed her glasses on to the bridge of her nose and leaned over the silk, her finger guiding her eyes over islands where waterfalls hung, eternally suspended, between pagodas and dark blue conifers, over flat lakes and tiny fishing boats, over mountains where the mists never lifted, and back again to a haughty peacock caught with one foot suspended over a rock. 'It's a work of art like you never see in this country,' she said.

Mr Blackie inhaled the scent of camphorwood. 'Don't cut it, Amy. It's too good for an old blighter like me.' He was begging her to contradict him.

'I'll get the pattern tomorrow,' she said.

The next day, while the District Nurse was giving him his injection, she went down to the store and looked through a pile of pattern books. Appropriately, she chose a mandarin style with a high collar and piped cuffs and pockets. But Mr Blackie, who had all his life worn striped flannel in the conventional design, looked with suspicion at the pyjama pattern and the young man who posed so easily and shamelessly on the front of the packet.

'It's the sort them teddy bear boys have,' he said.

'Nonsense,' said Mrs Blackie.

'That's exactly what they are,' he growled. 'You're not laying me out in a lot of new-fangled nonsense.'

Mrs Blackie put her hands on her hips. 'You'll not have any say in the matter,' she said.

'Won't I just? I'll get up and fight — see if I don't.'

The muscles at the corner of her mouth twitched uncontrollably. 'All right, Herb, if you're so set against it — '

But now, having won the argument, he was happy. 'Get away with you, Amy. I'll get used to the idea.' He threw his lips back against his gums. 'Matter of fact, I like them fine. It's that nurse that done it. Blunt needle again.' He looked at the pattern. 'When d'you start?'

'Well — '

'This afternoon?'

'I suppose I could pin the pattern out after lunch.'

'Do it in here,' he said. 'Bring in your machine and pins and things and set them up so I can watch.'

She stood taller and tucked in her chin. 'I'm not using the machine,' she said with pride. 'Every stitch is going to be done by hand. My eyes mightn't be as good as they were once, mark you, but there's not a person on this earth can say I've lost my touch with a needle.'

His eyes closed in thought. 'How long?'

'Eh?'

'Till it's finished.'

She turned the pattern over in her hands. 'Oh — about three or four weeks. That is — if I keep it up.'

'No,' he said. 'Too long.'

'Oh Herb, you'd want a good job done, wouldn't you?' she pleaded.

'Amy — ' Almost imperceptibly, he shook his head on the pillow.

'I can do the main seams on the machine,' she said, lowering her voice.

'How long?'

'A week,' she whispered.

When she took down the silk that afternoon, he insisted on an extra pillow in spite of the warning he'd had from the doctor about lying flat with his legs propped higher than his head and shoulders.

She plumped up the pillow from her own bed and put it behind his neck; then she unrolled her tape measure along his body, legs, arms, around his chest.

'I'll have to take them in a bit,' she said, making inch-high black figures on a piece of cardboard. She took the tissue-paper pattern into the kitchen to iron it flat. When she came back, he was waiting, wide-eyed with anticipation and brighter, she thought, than he'd been for many weeks.

As she laid the silk out on her bed and started pinning down the first of the pattern pieces, he described, with painstaking attempts at accuracy, the boat trip home, the stop at Hong Kong, and the merchant who had sold him the silk. 'Most of his stuff was rubbish,' he said. 'You wouldn't look twice at it. This was the only decent thing he had and even then he done me. You got to argue with these devils. Beat him down, they told me. But there was others as wanted that silk and if I hadn't made up me mind there and then I'd have lost it.' He squinted at her hands. 'What are you doing now? You just put that bit down.'

'It wasn't right,' she said, through lips closed on pins. 'I have to match it — like wallpaper.'

She lifted the pattern pieces many times before she was satisfied. Then it was evening and he was so tired that his breathing had become laboured. He no longer talked. His eyes were watering from hours of concentration; the drops spilled over his red lids and soaked into the pillow.

'Go to sleep,' she said. 'Enough's enough for one day.'

'I'll see you cut it out first,' he said.

'Let's leave it till the morning,' she said, and they both sensed her reluctance to put the scissors to the silk.

'Tonight,' he said.

'I'll make the tea first.'

'After,' he said.

She took the scissors from her sewing drawer and wiped them on her apron. Together they felt the pain as the blades met cleanly, almost without resistance, in that first cut. The silk would never again be the same. They were changing it, rearranging the pattern of fifty-odd years to form something new and unfamiliar. When she had cut out the first piece, she held it up, still pinned to the paper, and said, 'The back of the top.' Then she laid it on the dressing table and went on as quickly as she dared, for she knew that he would not rest until she had finished.

One by one the garment pieces left the body of silk. With each touch of the blades, threads sprang apart; mountains were divided, peacocks split from head to tail; waterfalls fell on either side of fraying edges. Eventually, there was nothing on the bed but a few shining snippets. Mrs Blackie picked them up and put them back in the camphorwood box, and covered the pyjama pieces on the dressing table with a cloth. Then she removed the extra pillow from Mr Blackie's bed and laid his head back in a comfortable position before she went into the kitchen to make the tea.

He was very tired the next morning but refused to sleep while she was working with the silk. She invented a number of excuses for putting it aside and leaving the room. He would sleep then, but never for long. No more than half an hour would pass and he would be calling her. She would find him lying awake and impatient for her to resume sewing.

In that day and the next, she did all the machine work. It was a tedious task, for first she tacked each seam by hand, matching the patterns in the weave so that the join was barely noticeable. Mr Blackie silently supervised every stitch. At times she would see him studying the silk with an expression that she still held in her memory. It was the look he'd given her in their courting days. She felt a prick of jealousy, not because she thought that he cared more for the silk then he did for her, but because he saw something in it that she didn't share. She never asked him what it was. At her age a body did not question these things or demand explanations. She would bend her head lower and concentrate her energy and attention into the narrow seam beneath the needle.

On the Friday afternoon, four days after she'd started the pyjamas, she finished the buttonholes and sewed on the buttons. She'd deliberately hurried the last of the hand sewing. In the four days, Mr Blackie had become weaker, and she knew that the sooner the pyjamas were completed and put back in the camphorwood box out of sight, the sooner he would take an interest in food and have the rest he needed.

She snipped the last thread and put the needle in its case.

'That's it, Herb,' she said, showing him her work.

He tried to raise his head. 'Bring them over here,' he said.

'Well — what do you think?' As she brought the pyjamas closer, his eyes relaxed and he smiled.

'Try them on?' he said.

She shook her head. 'I got the measurements,' she said. 'They'll be the right fit.'

'Better make sure,' he said.

She hesitated but could find no reason for her reluctance. 'All right,' she said, switching on both bars of the electric heater and drawing it closer to his bed. 'Just to make sure I've got the buttons right.'

She peeled back the bedclothes, took off his thick pyjamas and put on the silk. She stepped back to look at him.

'Well, even if I do say so myself, there's no one could have done a better job. I could move the top button over a fraction, but apart from that they're a perfect fit.'

He grinned. 'Light, aren't they?' He looked down the length of his body and wriggled his toes. 'All the way from China. Never let it out of me sight. Know that, Amy?'

'Do you like them?' she said.

He sucked his lips in over his gums to hide his pleasure. 'All right. A bit on the tight side.'

'They are not, and you know it,' Mrs Blackie snapped. 'Never give a body a bit of credit, would you? Here, put your hands down and I'll change you before you get a chill.'

He tightened his arms across his chest. 'You made a right good job, Amy. Think I'll keep them on a bit.'

'No.' She picked up his thick pyjamas.

'Why not?'

'Because you can't,' she said. 'It — it's disrespectful. And the nurse will be here soon.'

'Oh, get away with you, Amy.' He was too weak to resist further but as she changed him, he still possessed the silk with his eyes. 'Wonder who made it?'

Although she shrugged his question away, it brought to her a definite picture of a Chinese woman seated in front of a loom surrounded by blue and silver silkworms. The woman was dressed from a page in a geographic magazine, and except for the Oriental line of her eyelids, she looked like Mrs Blackie.

'D'you suppose there's places like that?' Mr Blackie asked.

She snatched up the pyjamas and put them in the box. 'You're the one that's been there,' she said briskly. 'Now settle down and rest or you'll be bad when the nurse arrives.'

The District Nurse did not come that afternoon. Nor in the evening. It was at half-past three the following morning that her footsteps, echoed by the doctor's sounded along the gravel path.

Mrs Blackie was in the kitchen, waiting. She sat straight-backed and dry-eyed, her hands placed one on top of the other in the lap of her dressing gown.

'Mrs Blackie. I'm sorry — '

She ignored the nurse and turned to the doctor. 'He didn't say goodbye,' she said with an accusing look. 'Just before I phoned. His hand was over the side of the bed. I touched it. It was cold.'

The doctor nodded.

'No sound of any kind,' she said. 'He was good as gold last night.'

Again, the doctor nodded. He put his hand, briefly, on her shoulder, then went into the bedroom. Within a minute he returned, fastening his leather bag and murmuring sympathy.

Mrs Blackie sat still, catching isolated words. Expected. Peacefully. Brave. They dropped upon her — neat, geometrical shapes that had no meaning.

'He didn't say goodbye.' She shook her head. 'Not a word.'

'But look, Mrs Blackie,' soothed the nurse. 'It was inevitable. You knew that. He couldn't have gone on — '

'I know, I know.' She turned away, irritated by their lack of understanding. 'He just might have said goodbye. That's all.'

The doctor took a white tablet from a phial and tried to persuade her to swallow it. She pushed it away; refused, too, the cup of tea that the District Nurse poured and set in front of her. When they picked up their bags and went towards the bedroom, she followed them.

'In a few minutes,' the doctor said. 'If you'll leave us — '

'I'm getting his pyjamas,' she said. 'There's a button needs changing. I can do it now.'

As soon as she entered the room, she glanced at Mr Blackie's bed and noted that the doctor had pulled up the sheet. Quickly, she lifted the camphorwood box, took a needle, cotton, scissors, her spectacle case, and went back to the kitchen. Through the half-closed door she heard the nurse's voice. 'Poor old thing,' and she knew, instinctively, that they were not talking about her.

She sat down at the table to thread the needle. Her eyes were clear but her hands were so numb that for a long time they refused to work together. At last, the thread knotted, she opened the camphorwood box. The beauty of the silk was always unexpected. As she spread the pyjamas out on the table, it warmed her, caught her up and comforted her with the first positive feeling she'd had that morning. The silk was real. It was brought to life by the electric light above the table, so that every fold of the woven landscape moved. Trees swayed towards rippling water and peacocks danced with white fire in their tails. Even the tiny bridges —

Mrs Blackie took off her glasses, wiped them, put them on again. She leaned forward and traced her thumbnail over one bridge, then another. And another. She turned over the pyjama coat and closely examined the back. It was there, on every bridge; something she hadn't noticed before. She got up, and from the drawer where she kept her tablecloths, she took out a magnifying glass.

As the bridge in the pattern of the silk grew, the figure which had been no larger than an ant, became a man.

Mrs Blackie forgot about the button and the murmur of voices in the bedroom. She brought the magnifying glass nearer her eyes.

It was a man and he was standing with one arm outstretched, on the highest span between two islands. Mrs Blackie studied him for a long time, then she straightened up and smiled. Yes, he was waving. Or perhaps, she thought, he was beckoning to her.

Lynda Scarth
The Funeral

I'm thinking about prayers. The most recent prayer — for me and others — that I remember was at the christening. I was sitting beside my mother. I remember thinking these thoughts: 'I wonder if Mother remembered to bring me some brown eggs.' (She lives in the country and does not often come to the city, but when she comes she often brings eggs from these brown hens she apparently has.) 'If she did, how shall I carry them home? They won't fit in my handbag, and if she has them in a paper bag, as usual, there'll be no free paper, as usual, to twist at the top of the bag and so carry it in the one hand I shall have free, after my handbag. So I must have another container of some sort, and I haven't, and I don't imagine she has, and my sister won't lend me one as she believes I shall never return anything I borrow, though what I should do with yet another string bag I can't imagine. . . .' The prayer ended. We raised our heads, and my mother whispered to me: 'I may forget to tell you later. I brought some eggs for you. I put them on the table in Elizabeth's kitchen. But I don't know how you'll carry them home in the train.'

So this was the last prayer before my sister's latest baby was christened, and this must have been some weeks after the funeral. My mother's only brother's funeral. The christening had its novelties, but the funeral was more deeply interesting, not so much for the prayers as for the interior monologues imaginable. The funeral was altogether like a conversation when at any point one of the participants might have said, 'I don't know what we're talking about', but there were no defections, and all continued to toss the ball desperately to and fro. . . .

No one expected that mother's brother might die on the Sunday night he chose, and I was of course unprepared for the telephone call to tell me of his death. Then there were so many things to think about. Clothes, for instance. Did one really wear black to a funeral? My best suit happened to be black, and very well cut. And of course I had a black handbag and gloves and shoes and a hat, because one has these things for most occasions and I did in fact wear this black suit with these black etceteras almost every other day. But to a funeral? Well, I would. I thought I would. So one little decision was taken, and that was a start. I did rather resent the need to take so many over so many details, but once I felt the swing of the situation I was pleased by the range of it, and I was resolved to make a thoroughly personal and the best possible job of it all.

I imagined that Mother would come to make the arrangements for the funeral itself, but she thought that there were good practical people like myself and my sister on the spot and not five hundred miles away; so why should she come? This was, of course, quite the correct attitude from her point of view. Naturally she would want just to keep going and not interrupt her pattern of events too abruptly, for then the full significance of the death of her brother might dawn on her, and she might be overwhelmed by grief, and so not be useful anyway.

My sister had given birth to her third son only a week before mother's brother died, and it might appear that she would not be in any condition to face a funeral. Much less, arrange one. From her point of view an interruption like death to the pattern consequent upon birth might be unthinkable. No, not at all unthinkable, but suitable only as a subject on which to reflect generally, rather than to act practically. You can imagine how my sister might be disposed to reflect upon the consecrated continuum of birth and marriage and death but you could not reasonably expect her to neglect the practical consequences of birth for the sake of involvement with the practical consequences of death.

Will the funeral ever be arranged? Ah, you don't know much about how things really happen, do you? You don't know much about my sister, or my mother, or myself. For my sister, the death of her uncle was a considerable happening, and she was inclined to be Totally Involved. Now I don't quite know how she did all that she did, but the progress of the funeral arrangements indicated her stage management of the whole affair. She alone had visited the part of the world where my uncle was born and had lived for most of his life, and she knew the people to whom all the information she had should be given, so that it would be taken into account at the funeral. Hers were the little touches everywhere. . . . Why, the funeral made him come alive. All the little grace notes made something quite whole. It seemed that he had indeed quite *consumed* his life, so that all the falsities and truths he had encountered had been in all manners of expression remarked upon and absorbed. At the end of his life there was this effect of shape and style and totality although in the course of his life none of us had noticed his progression towards it. If it had not been for my sister, this glory might not have been revealed.

On the morning of the funeral I had, in my own way, prepared myself for it. At least, I had repositioned my own life.

This had been the situation. I was, as they say, casting off a lover. Naturally I meant to do this in a deep, meaningful and total way.

The single thing for which I had taken responsibility was the preparation of flowers for the funeral. You can imagine that I didn't wish to hand the business over to a florist. One likes to add a personal touch when the death is the death of a relative. I wanted to do one last, special thing for my uncle. Of course it crossed my mind that it would be rather less expensive were I to do some of the work myself.

However, during my lunch hour the day before the funeral I ordered six magnificent carnations from the florist whose shop happened to be beside the place at which I worked. They were magnificent carnations because on that particular day there were only magnificent carnations to be had. I must make quite clear that I didn't ask for the most magnificent carnations available. They simply happened to be there, and there were no scrawny, cheaper ones. Well, I think I might have overlooked scrawny cheapness in favour of magnificence had I been faced with the problem of choice, but there was no such complication.

I often went to my lover's apartment . . . my lover! Absurd words. Siva. His name was, is, and always shall be Siva. I want to say *was* because I was so intent upon casting him into my past, and the effect is quite reinforced by references in the past tense. His name was Siva; he was an Indian; he was a student; he was handsome; he was very good to me and he persistently said he loved me. Naturally, I said I loved him too. However, recently another man had quite horizontally topped off this rather vertical proposition, and although Horizontal would never know — never see — would never be told of the perfection of the repositioning, I meant to make a profoundly satisfactory resolution of it all.

Siva lived in a lovely house, in a lovely room. In this room there were beautiful paintings of me on the walls and the walls were a glowing cream colour, and in the morning I would wake to see perfect moving patterns of light and leaves on the walls, and a flash from the gold chain Siva wore as he turned to me.

Gold and light and leaves and peaches and doves. Yes, doves. They came down to the garden in the evening, and in the morning they flew away, and you might think that this is somewhat obvious and so perhaps not true, but it is true. Doves in this infinite garden, and the leaves were beautiful with rain, and lilies came and flowered and disappeared. Roses would be suddenly glowing. One expected nothing and there would be violets and ivy and an extraordinary cactus, and daffodils and snowdrops.

At the time of my wishing to leave Siva almost a year of knowing him, and knowing the garden, had passed. I knew the flowers to expect at all times. October, and these great white mysterious lilies began to flower, springing from nowhere. One expected nothing, and this splendour came . . . lilies blazing white and crushing from sight all there was beside them.

Early one morning I left the bedroom and walked through the garden. The first lily had flowered, and it kept me there. There seemed to be ripples and ripples of lilies and light which held me . . . and I had this rather common feeling that every manifestation of life and change must somehow prove that I was alive and changing.

I picked seven lilies and went back to Siva's room.

I looked at myself in the diamond mirror between the paintings of myself, and I looked beautiful. Beautiful in a way which makes a critic indecisive . . . tantalizing. Say I'm arresting on first sight. Then I begin to talk, and my expressions create an illusion, so that my beauty seems to be just a fraction beyond me. If I pause I feel that whoever is in the desperate state where he must decide for himself now, and once and for all whether this girl is or is not beautiful, begins to think, 'Now, with that nose, *is* she beautiful? Can anyone with a nose which is not quite straight be beautiful? Isn't that tilt a defect? Isn't that lower lip too full, and the jaw too square or is that an extraordinarily beautiful square jaw?' I'm happy for him when he looks at my eyes because my eyes are on any analysis beautiful, with all the characteristics. Deep but not sunken. Wide, but not too wide set. Wonderfully green and swept with lashes perfectly long and upward-curving. . . .

Stuff that. I know that I'm beautiful because men — not to mention women — are continually trying to decide whether I'm beautiful or not. Notwithstanding my cleft chin and my short nose and my high eyebrows and the lines under my eyes and the little shifting hollows in my cheeks . . . all this which is nothing to do with beauty.

So I looked at myself and remembered my theory and didn't look for too long. I sat down in a chair by the bed and I took a cigarette from the table. Siva always kept a box of the cigarettes I liked though he smoked others. I lit the cigarette and I thought about myself, and about death

and life and beauty, and the possibilities for so many little perfections.
I thought about how I must attend to details, and how I must make my
private progression through the events of this day and the next, and I
saw how the drama of the funeral would dramatize my life, and I would
move on and leave all in order.

I finished the cigarette and thoughtfully I put it out. Have you noticed
— of course you have; why else does one smoke — how cigarettes make
the way from thought to deed? In a movie of my life I might credit
Continuity to Cigarettes. The time is just right. One lights the cigarette,
inhales, taps, looks upward and beyond where there should be a window
or a photograph with lost but lingering associations on which to gaze . . .
feeling that little loneliness as the filter approaches, then action. What
else? You cannot light another cigarette without very real frustration.

No. I stood up. I ran my hands over my breast and down to my
waist. Yes. Good. I walked to the door and down the stairs and I made
my way, as they say, to the garden.

Seven more lilies. I picked them all, and around me I felt some sort
of sensuous consternation. The wind rose and fell quite wildly, and the
rain drenched my shoulders as it dripped from the trees, and I thought
the vines pulled at me and tripped me. I took the lilies and trailing ivy
and I walked back to the house — up the stairs and through the door,
and I threw the lilies and the ivy on the bed with the other flowers, and
I sat on the chair and took another cigarette.

I'd made one little gesture. I'd felt, seen, experienced and finalized
one more of the multiplicity of details of which my life was made, and
more continuity was required. The cigarette made me feel slightly sick.
I'd not been in the garden for so very long. Too much continuity and
not enough action, perhaps.

I took the flowers up, and I laid them down again. I was about to
arrange the flowers for my uncle's funeral. I was about to make this perfect
wreath on the bed in which I'd slept on golden nights and many not so
golden with my first, only, now-grown-tiresome, beautiful misleadingly
and too enduringly skilful lover.

How else to conclude with perfection that which had become
imperfect? The final gesture must have more finesse than anything that
had been before. I had to cancel out life with death . . . simply because
I'd been frightened to find myself thinking, when I slept with my hand
on his shoulder, that nothing could compare with this exclusive experience
of life. How much room left for the deep, delicate and endless discontinuity

of life *out of bed*. Huh? How much room for *becoming*? None whatsoever. A hand closed over my soul.

I pulled the fingers apart. I made the wreath and it lay glowing very white on the bed.

Siva surprised me by coming in. Siva said did I get the carnations from a stall. No? Well, how foolish. They would have been far less costly there. I began to be scornful. The very thought was indelicate. My Uncle. Dead. My God! And this idea of petty economy. . . . We stared at each other.

Siva asked where should we sleep. For one thing, the flowers were on the bed . . . but the real question was whether or not I was planning to go back to my apartment. This was not awfully ugly, but nor was it particularly fine. There were often sternly practical reasons for my return. Perhaps I couldn't for another day wear any of the clothes I kept in his house without appearing to be choosing a suspiciously sequential and limited number of outfits — suit, dress, suit, dress — and that was it. My apartment was miles away, and I hadn't been there for weeks. Often in the morning I telephoned the girl downstairs and tried to arrange delivery of more clothes, but such arrangements usually fell through. I worked all day, and this pattern of night-time living with Siva had developed. Still, I must soon make one of my periodic returns to collect letters and burn the evening papers and pour milk down the kitchen sink — you know the sort of thing.

Honestly — do you see how thin and ugly the affair had become? And deceit was to be piled upon deceit. I can hardly bear to tell how much. I was to say to Siva that because of the events of the moment I must go, but I would return very early in the morning and take the flowers and go. I was to say that the death of my uncle had affected me beyond words, and I wanted to be alone. I felt that I couldn't live anymore as I had been living, and I must leave.

Remember that the truth was only that I wanted another lover . . . wanted to be alone to think about him . . . wanted to be alone to dream and to plan . . . wanted more than the small world of my hand on his shoulder and this sleepy, sleepy love which had not perhaps been so very great at any time.

Siva had no time for grand visions, and wasn't inclined to see how death and the death of love must become one. He had no belief in the symbols I set up. As I left I felt that my interrupted vision of life at that moment was large and wonderful, but I was very aware that he had not played the part in it I assigned to him.

I crossed the city and I was at last back in my apartment. As I walked in the door, the telephone rang. My mother. Was everything all right? Yes, well, she would be there in the morning. I should meet her at the airport. Very well. Goodbye.

Obviously the drama would have been too far-flung had she continued to call me and I hadn't come home. The thought hadn't occurred before, but if it had I wouldn't have wanted to make use of it as an excuse to leave Siva. For him it would have been a straw to clutch at. I wanted a deep, severe and final detachment.

Good. The symbols were ordered, and their meanings clear to me. Me, Me, Me. I moved slowly and elegantly from place to place. I prepared all there was to prepare for my appearance at the funeral, and I went to bed.

The next morning I was awake very early. Swiftly, I dressed. Click, click, click very softly as the doors closed behind me. I walked through the grey wonderful windy sorrowful air . . . the quality of light like arrowheads . . . and I left the flowers by the coffin.

I told my employer I must take bereavement leave, and he seemed to notice that there was nothing unprecedented in my funereal air — and I remembered a conversation he overheard which I had had with a girl who worked beside me and who took an unjustifiable number of days of medical leave, so that she had almost none left — and she began to tell me of a number of mysterious elderly relatives for whose affairs she took responsibility; relatives who lived in distant parts of the country and who might die at any time. We might conclude that she'd been called away to arrange a funeral if on any day she didn't come to work. Remembering this, I felt sorry for my employer. Inhumanity was for him an occupational hazard. He had to be suspicious of death, or regard it, if proved, as a ploy even so. But this was the truth on this occasion and I had to go to the funeral, and I would be back at work the next day.

So I called a taxi and I went to the airport to meet my mother and my uncle's brother and my father to whom my uncle had been brother-in-law.

My timing was perfect — all part of the dignity I preserved — and I was waiting in the concourse when my father and mother entered. I was poised to watch every detail. This was death, remember. A funeral. My uncle lying in his coffin and lost and alone for ever.

My mother wore the gold suit she'd worn for my other sister's wedding. This sister had been married the previous autumn. Well now, autumn is autumn and late spring is late spring or perhaps early summer. And weddings are weddings, and funerals funerals, one would suppose. But this is superficial, isn't it? If it's tidier not to allow one's ideas of one institution to slop over into one's ideas of another . . . is it right? The gold suit was probably all very well. Father wore his city suit and his serious city face, because whenever he came to the city he came for a conference or some consultation with others on serious matters. So his expression was serious but not necessarily distinctively and funereally serious.

They came forward and kissed me. I kissed them back. This was for-a-long-time-I've-not-seen-you kissing.

I was inclined to feel some pride in the fact that I was somehow more conscious of the events of the moment than they, but I had to remind myself that the fact of my uncle's death, and my conduct in the face of it was stylized for my own ends. For me it was a lucky fresh wind, and I was trimming my sails and impelling myself onward in terms of it. I was riding high on the crest of the wave of feeling I might — or might not — have had over it. It was convenient to feel deeply and to act as if I did.

Mother talked about how it had been for her, and the details seemed unimportant. It was clear that the event had not had for her the personal utility or value it had had for me. For her it had been an interruption, merely, to the pattern of days and events established, and she didn't want an opportunity or a justification for slithering out of a situation which threatened to engulf her. She didn't want a disguise. I did. I suppose it's foolishly egocentric to imagine that I might have willed the death, but it's also foolish to pretend that I hadn't seized on it as an opportunity to restructure my life.

Mother had been in the middle of goodness knows what consecrated sequence of ineluctable seasonal events in the country. So she had the cable and she'd wept a little and then she knew she must do one mundane thing after another. And of course she loved this work which was her life, and I should not describe her work as mundane for it wasn't so to her. The point is that she had no wish or no need to see herself writ large in this event, and this reluctance affected her conduct. She wasn't inclined to carry herself through the day magnificently, as I was. She didn't have to underline the depth of her feelings. She wanted only to get things settled in an orderly and conventional manner.

Nevertheless, she was admirable. So were we all. There wasn't any absence of emotion; there were only the variously hand-tailored ways of making use of it. At least none of us acknowledged defeat in the absence of it — which is surely the most corrupt posture of all. Everyone knows the person who has no soul to show, or heart, but knows he ought to have. Some quality or tone or line of character of which he's dimly aware as a part of the self-possession of others. He's so afraid he knows nothing of the infinite ways of translating emotion into action. He's tortured in his awareness of the privacy of the sorrows of others. So he finds himself demonstrating: 'Watch me. I suffer. I feel deeply. I am in pain. I weep — look at me weeping. I scream . . . I cry . . . I suffer . . . I *feel*. Say something to me.'

Just the same, Mother seemed to have no funeral manner, though she must have been to funerals before. I was amused to see that she greeted the people quite as she did at weddings — and remember that I'd been critical of her wedding manner, as I thought it too fulsome. So she didn't have the personal style which one admires. But what did this prove? I was more confused, and perhaps I made as many mistakes. Perhaps I spoke too little. If it seemed to me that silence was more significant than effusions over commonplace affairs; so what if her small talk seemed so obvious an evasion of the issue in which she ought to have been involved.

For some reason she wished to take some of the flowers with her, and this seemed to me to be another confusion of symbols. Flowers were not necessarily festive. These were white flowers. This was death. It was macabre that the wreath I made was the one she chose to take with her, to brighten up the dining room. My God.

But I can't bear personal dishonesty. On a level of feeling I don't much care to acknowledge that I was glad and proud and felt rather special. I felt profoundly misunderstood, and perhaps freed of the guilt I felt for having so deviously tried to leave a mark to declare my subtlety on this which was not mine but death's day. So she took my flowers and swallowed my little act.

After the funeral we went to the little house where my uncle lived, and we found it to be quite without personality. There wasn't a whisper nor a shadow of a thought which had been his alone. He was an engineer, and he hadn't been acquisitive. I didn't expect a valuable collection of somethings — paintings or carvings: I wasn't looking for expressions of taste, but surely there would be something to reveal what it had meant to him to be quite, quite alone — as he had been. But there was nothing, nothing, nothing at all. Not even a book which it would have been a surprise to discover he cared to read. There was nothing personal at all. The thing most sadly like and unlike the thing I sought — while Mother mused over the suit which had never been worn, and the underwear still in paper parcels — was an ashtray on which he'd signed his name with a strangely defiant little squiggle beneath. I hadn't seen such a squiggle before. I'm probably investing it with an absurd significance. It was a little curved line which led nowhere. I took the ashtray for the sake of the little nowhere-leading line.

After the funeral I went home. Mother and Father entered the communications system at some point which would lead to their return; and my sister with the new baby was I suppose happily in her hospital bed with her baby beside her. I went home, to do the thing I often did; a collage of events. A little fur from somewhere — I might go to Russia with my new lover. A photograph of Siva cut into inconsequential shapes. Ivy leaves. Nightshade berries because they were there. In black silk cording, a little curved line which led nowhere.

Fiona Kidman

Flower Man

The magnolia tree towered high above the church hall casting skeleton shadows in the winter, and providing deep green shade in the summer. In the late spring foliage, blooms could just be seen, heavy and exotic, the colour of whipped sour cream.

From where we lay in the coarse kikuyu grass at the end of the school playing fields, we could glimpse the tree. It was November, the air stripped clean ready for a Northland summer, and the sea not far away, sang promise.

There were four of us, Phyllis, Geoff, David and myself, who they call Magog, though my name is Marguerite. The nickname is apt though, for I have a peculiar mockery of a face, Grock-like, but it's never been the hindrance it should have been.

Geoff smiled at me and I rolled over to hide my face in the scratchy claws of the grass. I adored his pale, ugly face with its receding forehead and stubbly red eyelashes. Perhaps it was because neither of us were beautiful, but I thought he was brilliant too. I was right. Now a well-known surgeon, he is a very clever and extraordinary man.

'What's the matter, Magog?' he said. 'Is it maths again?'

'Yes,' I lied.

'Poor old Mag-nag,' he said, twisting my name still further, so that I ached, because I loved the way he said it so much. Phyllis and David would be smiling indulgently, I knew, even though they liked each other a lot, so I kept my face down and let them think what they like. Phyllis has always been like that, rather cynical, but now a superior sort of woman, who men like because of her brains and her dry intelligent humour, and thin, magazine cover looks. But she never gets involved. Yesterday she came to see me, with a present for my latest baby, and seeing her is what brought me to thinking about all this. I felt a mess when she came, because I was dripping milk through my blouse, like a fat animal, but she looked at me intensely over a cup of coffee which she had brewed for herself in my impossible kitchen, and said through the smoke between us, 'God you're lucky, Magog. Bloody lucky, bloody lucky, lucky, lucky,' repeating everything as she always had.

'Why not you?' I said, and she had muttered something which was supposed to be sharp and modern, but didn't quite come off, about always wanting to talk business when she was supposed to be doing bed drill. That about sums Phyllis up though, and neither of us laughed because it was awful for her, us both knowing it was true.

'You should quit worrying about maths,' said David. This was his way, quieter than the rest of us, and reassuring. He had deep-set eyes and crinkly hair, from his mother, the woman they called 'the mad Dally'. I never thought of her that way. Once I called on David on a Saturday morning to collect some homework, and she was sitting by the fire, rocking gently, her great bulk heaving and sighing, and her black moustache rippling over a smile every time David turned to speak to her. When he passed by her chair her hands would reach out to touch him, his arm, his hand, his body, with love. A big, broken-hearted Yugoslav who had never been accepted by her husband's solid, third-generation New Zealand people, and rejected by her own. No wonder she loved David.

I sat up and we all stared at each other gloomily. To quit worrying about maths was so clearly ridiculous, despite the soothing nature of David's remark, that we did not bother discussing it.

It was, of course, an unending dilemma for us. No students had ever been so haunted by the desire to pass exams, or so we thought. We were at a district high school which served a small farming community on a northern reach of sea coast. Little talent flowered in Waituna, certainly not academic, nor, to any great extent, pastoral. The area had been established by pioneers, whose descendants saw small value in change, and latterly, inadequately financed dreamers had moved in with them, occupying small pockets of land which the others had considered too rough to bother about. David's parents, as I have said, belonged more or less to the first category, mine wholly, and Phyllis's to the second, while Geoff's father ran a wayside store outback, between the village and the next major shopping centre. They had a few cows as well which Geoff milked before and after school, putting out a billy of cream each day, which annoyed the truck driver and brought little return.

The four of us believed, with the immense satisfaction of the young, that we were special. Although the school had prepared University Entrance candidates for many years, no one had ever passed the examination, nor had anyone ever hoped that they would do so. This year, the four of us were thought to be good, and we were nurtured and cherished by our teachers like beings apart. It was this feeling of being

different from the rest of the school which threw us so constantly together.
Our conversation became too precious to share with other people, and
I think we were passably disagreeable.

But we were also unusually high-spirited, and this was not surprising
either. We believed in ourselves, and longing to leave this indifferent
countryside, we saw too, within ourselves, the means of our escape.

Each morning we left from homes between the hills, places of love
without aspiration, sometimes, as with Phyllis's parents, inhabited at first
with hope, later with despair. A few of the young people had had the
internal resources to leave, a School Certificate, hard-won, almost
inevitably allowing them to pass thankfully into the shelter of teachers'
hostels, where they hung indifferent careers upon this convenient refuge.
But University Entrance offered more, the bigger chance, the better
prospect, and we thought we had it made. Well, most of the time, unless
afflicted by the doubts produced by mathematical formulae or French
verbs.

Until the advent of Rad Barclay, that is, who had solved many
things.

Take French. Before he came, we had sat in a long room, with an
ageing French mistress, a relic of some long-ago girls' school, who made
us sing *Claire de Lune* each morning before the lesson began. Geoff's and
David's voices were breaking and Phyllis and I would weep helplessly
with uncontrolled laughter, and the old mistress, teaching only to
supplement her pension in seaside retirement, would suck her false teeth
so that they clattered on her gums. At winter's beginning she left to tend
her geraniums through the cold, and in her place came Rad, bringing
with him visions not of a gaunt moon in an echoing room but a France
of wine, sun, indelible blue skies and Scott Fitzgerald. Verbs became our
catch tunes.

He was always in our thoughts, and when we thought about him
he usually appeared, which meant that he was usually with us.

So that while we sat there, looking at each other, he did appear.
I lifted my head and saw his trousered leg.

'What's the matter, Magog?' he asked me, too.

'Nothing,' I said, hugging my breasts, and my body full of spring
fever, and longing and the need for everything to be over and I on my
way, yet confused with wanting them all to be with me for always.

'There is,' said Phyllis. 'She's worried about maths, and she's mad,
mad, mad.'

Rad knelt beside me. 'Poor Magog,' he said. 'You want a cloudburst, and much colour, and a palette and easel upon which to express it all, and instead you see rows and rows of figures, and little three-sided boxes, and spotted algebraics. It's not fair.'

This was his appeal to us, a kind of multi-hued way of talking, and a capitalization of the most obvious parts of our natures. He was very clever.

It didn't seem fair either. As he knelt beside me, he ran his fingers on the ground, his flesh digging through the grass, to brittle dirt, scratching his nails against jagged pebbles. His hand looked oddly out of place there, against the earth, he was not of our place, or our origins. He might stand against a curved horizon, and walk on salt-soaked marshland near the sea shore with us; he might go to the sea, and peer at the violet smudges of the islands on the edge of distance, but in doing so, he reminded us rather, that he was not at home here.

He was from the city, a student teacher, which made him very young, maybe not many years older than any of us. His skin was pale sepia, and his lips, warm and full, betrayed his beginnings, or some of them. He hated them bitterly, deeply, believing that to be neither one nor the other, was a sin of parents against children. Yet his Maori ancestry was very slight, and it was to it that he owed his looks. Of all of us, it might have been expected that he and David would be the closest, sharing a bond of mixed race. It was not so. David, the quiet one, trusted him less than the rest of us. Well, neither Geoff, nor Phyllis, nor myself mistrusted him at all. With our French at his command, and our English splendid but orderly, we had much to thank him for. Teachers had to be versatile at Waituna District High, and so he taught us history as well. We thrived and that pleased the Head, and relieved him, for though bright, and precious in our hopes, we were also a burden on the system.

So we saw a great deal of him, and he, being lonely, turned more and more to us, talking, always talking, full of ideas, and hate too. Hate for systems, hate for tradition and, quickly, hate for the rural class strait-laced little township, trailing through the valley towards the hills where the farmlands lay.

It was hot enough to swim at Labour Day that year, and all five of us had gone to the sea. On the sand, by sunlit feathers of the silver spinifex, we lay, and Rad gave us coconut oil to rub on his back, then we rubbed it on each other and the liquid turned to golden globules in the midday sun. Rad talked about girls he had been with, and books he had read which were banned and should not be.

We listened peeling oranges, sucking the pips, and Geoff flung peel on to the sand. I jumped to retrieve it, and Rad said sharply, 'Leave it.'

'Why?' I had said, stopping on my knees, to look at him. 'It's untidy here.'

'I know. Leave it.'

'It spoils the beach,' I argued.

'That doesn't matter,' he said, beginning to get angry. 'It will rot, or the gulls will take it away. Tonight, tomorrow, a week, it will be gone.'

'So what?'

'So you jump up when we sit talking, enjoying ourselves, thinking naughty, naughty, someone is spoiling the view. You expend energy on things that don't matter.'

I had picked up the peel and wrapping it placed it back in my bike satchel. He watched me, coldly, and turned on his stomach, away from us, silent. The others looked at me, then him, not knowing which one of us to resent.

That was when it really began, the continual tug between us, between the things that we had been taught to believe did matter, and that which Rad said did not.

As he knelt beside me in the school grounds, splendid in his mustard pants and corduroy jacket, he said, 'You have to pass maths, Magog. Try, won't you? It's the only way. You must get through them. You'll fly through the rest. You only have to get a thirty per cent pass and the rest of your subjects will carry your average.'

'If only you taught us maths instead of Tweedledum,' said Phyllis, referring to the headmaster.

'I'm good but not that much,' Rad said, mocking, with false pride.

'It's all right. They're not so bad,' I said, for maths seemed to be an indifferent subject to talk about, when all I had been doing was loving Geoff.

A cloud of elegantly cool perfume assailed us, and without looking up, we knew that Danny Ferry was on his way. An old man, he ambled towards us, his arms full of magnolia blooms, with petals as wide as our hands.

He stopped at the school fence and nodded.

'It won't be long now,' he said.

We smiled agreement.

'I'll have a flower for you,' he murmured. 'Here take one now,' and he handed us each a magnolia, the boys smiling sheepishly — except Rad, who pretended to look the other way.

We smiled again, understanding. He walked on up the street, to his house, with its open door and dim interior.

'He's a dreadful man,' said Rad, savagely.

'He is not,' I said, sharply. 'He's kind and good, and he's never done us harm.'

'God, you're sentimental, Magog,' he said. 'You're just a great wet flabby emotional mess. Why don't you try to grow up?'

I threw stones viciously against each other on the ground, trying not to cry.

'What's so good about him?'

'He believes in God,' I said childishly. 'Do you?'

'Oh for Chrissake — ' he started, and grinned at himself. 'That's not much good is it? He's a lucky old bastard, isn't he then, eh?'

We were silent.

'Damn you all,' he said. 'Damn you. Of course it would be good, wouldn't it? Wouldn't it be good to believe in God and pick flowers to give to people, like he does? Sure, I'd like to be like that, oh yes, I would. It would be comfortable, relaxing oh yes.'

'I'm sorry, Rad,' I said. 'Don't be mad at us.'

'It's all right,' he said.

We watched the old man out of sight. He was a legend in those parts, Danny the Ferry Boat Man. For years no one had ever called him anything but Danny Ferry. What his real name was I have forgotten, but so long had he been known by the other, that it didn't matter any more. And it was through him that that magnolia tree had staked out a special claim in our lives.

He was a man of great learning, and while he had plied the old ferry each day down the edge of the coast in years past, picking up a little cream, delivering some mail, carrying a bit of cargo, he had his books there too. They said he could tell you anything. I think he probably could.

He never locked his house, though it had been burgled twice, and he had lost a great deal. Keeping open house for his friends was more important than the value of his possessions, Danny had said, and nothing so trivial as what had happened to him was going to make him change his habits.

He loved children, and he loved that magnolia tree. He had tended it when he was a child, and it was a little tree, and he had watched it grow. It was on public property, standing just outside the church fence, but of course people in our district never thought of it that way. It was Danny Ferry's tree, and he made sure that it gave more pleasure to people by being his tree, than if everybody had laid claim to it, and expounded the policies of 'keep off the grass' usually accorded to communal vegetation. If any of our people were sick in hospital down at Whangarei when spring came, then Danny sent them magnolias on the bus, and paid for a special delivery from the depot. Everyone could help themselves, and there would still be more magnolias than you could count in a year. They would be inside the church, as well as outside, each Sunday, overflowing it with branches of great luminous petals, and a magnificent powerful scent, which made the senses gasp and flutter. The magnolias had travelled down the coast each Monday morning aboard the ferry, in years past, and at each stop they would be unloaded to eager farmers' wives.

In time Danny became too old for the ferry, and he retired to grow flowers, and each year to supervise the School Certificate and University Entrance for the district high school, taking the pupils in the seclusion of the church hall.

He had never done any teaching, but the authorities who had given him the job were glad to have him, and kept him on year after year. The first morning of the examination, on each desk there would be placed a large bar of chocolate and a magnolia, the last November ones, from the lowest branches. Danny could not let an opportunity pass to give his magnolias away. They became a link between his love for the children, and that tree.

Once, long ago, one of the pupils had placed his magnolia in a bottle of ink. Each vein, each delicate thread of life, had taken the colour of the ink, so that the bloom was a pale translucent blue. From that year on, it became a symbol, a talisman. The blue flower held proudly after the exam, set you apart, the little select band, who held the school's hopes, the parents' fears and earnest desires, the children's gateway to a world beyond.

I looked down at the flower lying in my hands. 'The flowers though, they're beautiful, Rad.'

He looked at them grudgingly. 'You're not going to stick them in the ink are you?'

'Who told you that?' David asked.

'Oh, I heard it in the staff room. It made me puke.'

'Don't you see,' said David, 'that he wants for us the same things you think we should have? Don't you know that he wants us to pass those damn' exams too?'

'Yes, go off on a cloud of sentiment and tradition. Follow my steps, devout disciples, be good sweet maids. Ugh, nonsense. Do you mean to tell me you'd come out waving a bit of ink-soaked vegetation to show you'd sat an examination?'

They were good days that followed though, in spite of these odd bouts of scratchiness and dissent, and even these served to excite our senses and make us more aware of the profound changes which were taking place in our outlook.

In this mood of excesses and delights, we saw November inch forward. School Certificate was sat by a few younger pupils. We watched them spending miserable days between the church hall and school, exhibiting the ink-stained petals of their magnolias, and munching left-over chocolate bars.

Then it was nearly our turn, and right in the last days, things started to go wrong. Influenza struck; Geoff and Phyllis's parents, whose properties backed each other, started losing cows with bloat which was disastrous, as they both had so little to begin with, and a flash flood went through our farm one night, taking stock with it before I and my father and young brother could make it to the lower paddocks. As if that wasn't enough, David's father got drunk and beat up his mother who was twice as big as he was and broke his arm by way of retaliation. We were all dead beat and our spirits were way down low.

Rad would come over to the patch by the fence where we spent the lunch hour, and shake his head when none of us responded to him. By the last day I think we could all four of us have thrown in the whole thing. When Rad came I was leaning my head against the worn rock at the back of the shelter shed and the others were lying on the ground, snuffling the last of their colds into handkerchiefs.

'What are you doing, Magog?' he said. 'Praying?'

'As a matter of fact I was,' I replied coolly. 'Any objection?'

He burst out laughing, took a last drag on the cigarette he was smoking, and threw it on the ground, then squatted alongside of us, rocking on his heels, his hands on his knees. 'Oh you're funny, you're priceless, you kids.'

'You can laugh,' I said stiffly. 'You've passed your exams. What do you know about us? You can laugh at us if you like, but we're kids and you're grown-ups. That's what it says in the record books anyway.'

He looked at me sombrely. 'You're in a bad way, aren't you? So you think it was easy for me to pass exams?'

'Well, you were in the city. It was a bit different to this, wasn't it?' I replied.

'Some day, Magog, I'll take you past where I lived in the city. Rusty roofs and tumbledown fences, corrugated iron in the windows and broken steps, great dollops of dirt and fish an' chips papers everywhere and the old man's puke on the veranda from where nobody had cleaned up the night before when he was drunk. Inside, no, I can't tell you about the inside really, but I can tell you about the place where I did my homework. Broken electric light bulb, had to buy new ones out of my pocket money, that's if I got any, and if I didn't I pinched it. And the noise, all night the noise, the trains shunting.'

'Rad, I'm sorry,' I said. 'I'm sorry.'

'My father, last time I saw him, he called me a lousy little punk 'cause I wasn't following in his footsteps, and doing a decent job of work, a man's job, he called it.'

'Rad, please stop,' I cried to him. 'Please.'

'And you kids wonder why I question tradition. Blind faith. Do you have blind faith in what everyone tells you is right — because it's what your fathers did?'

He was silent, and so were we. I felt the others looking at me, accusingly, yet it didn't worry me, because I knew they were accusing themselves as much as me. I had only said the things they were thinking. It was for him I was worried.

A muscle flickered round his beautiful mouth. 'You kids made it good for me here. I wish I could have done something for you. I'd like to have seen you . . . do something.' He stood up.

'Rad,' I said, tentatively. 'If there was something we could do — ?'

'Pass your exams,' he replied shortly.

'We could have a milkshake tonight after school.'

Rad smiled at last. 'Okay, see you tonight.'

He turned to leave. It may have been coincidence that, at that moment, Danny Ferry approached down the street again, but thinking back, it can not have been. I remember now that his sister came over from where she kept house for an old couple on the other side of the village three times a week to prepare a meal for Danny, so on those three days, he would have to be home at one, from his walks, or whatever he happened to be doing, for his sister was a strict woman, who vowed the Lord only listened to their Grace before meals at an appointed time, and that time was Monday, Wednesday and Friday, at one o'clock.

Danny stopped to talk and his arms held magnolias. Always neat, he seemed sprucer than usual, possibly because it was examination time. The tufts of hair in his ears had been neatly clipped, his white hair and moustache shone silver and the gold watch-chain across his chest was polished brightly.

'Tomorrow, only till tomorrow,' he said. 'Here, I was taking flowers home for my sister, but you'll enjoy them more.'

He held out the flowers. I looked at him, from where I sat, and doing so, I intercepted Rad's cool stare.

'Thank you,' I said, 'but no, they would wilt before I reached home.'

Nervously, the others looked at me and then at Rad, and then at Danny.

'Not today, thanks,' said Geoff.

'I think I'll leave them for now, too,' Phyllis said.

David looked undecided. For a moment he wavered, then seeing our eyes on him, he said, 'Another time perhaps. But thanks anyway.'

The old man looked at Rad, then looked away. I experienced sudden sharp pain deep inside. He withdrew the flowers a little awkwardly, but his smile only flickered for a moment. 'Yes, well,' he said, cheerfully, 'my sister would have been sorry to have missed her ration I expect. Goodbye, then, till tomorrow.'

We muttered, and he moved quickly down the street, towards his house, with its cool understated light and old portraits staring grimly down from every wall, and his sister, their replica, at the head of his table.

The four of us got up, for the bell was ringing. Together we mooched towards the school building, not caring much to look at each other, or talk. Only Rad seemed buoyant and careless, and by the time we reached the classroom his mood was beginning to infect us, so that when we sat down defiance was growing in us. We looked around again, surreptitiously at first, then boldly, and already our spirits had picked up on the last few days of misery we had had.

The afternoon seemed endless. The teachers were handling us like eggs. The last period of the day, the whole school sang together. We assembled in two classrooms between which the doors swung open to make

one big room. This room served as our assembly hall, and overcrowded
it was too. We huddled in, while November turned on one of its hottest
afternoons.

A cow outside our window roared painfully in a late season calving.
We watched fascinated, the juniors making callow remarks and sniggers,
though, heaven knows, they had witnessed the spectacle often enough.

'Ta-ta-te-teh,' warbled the headmaster, who was also our singing
teacher, and thought well of himself as such.

'Ta-ta-te-teh,' we bellowed back, dutifully.

Then we sang some dirge while the temperature rose steadily in the
room, and at that point the woman from the office came in with a
telegram. She went down the back of the room where Rad was standing
and handed it to him. Everyone wanted to turn around, but in a minute
he walked up the front and spoke to the Head, who had stopped the music.

Rad's face was white and hard. He spoke to the Head, and you
couldn't hear what either of them said, until they were nearly finished,
when, as Rad started to walk to the door, the other looked at his watch,
and said, 'You've got about half an hour to catch it, if you hurry.'

As he turned back to us, Rad looked at us near the front, very briefly,
and I may have imagined it, but his hands seemed to gesture vaguely
as he held the telegram.

When he had gone, the Head said, 'I'm sure you'll be sorry to hear
that Mr Barclay's father died earlier in the day. It's nearly end-of-term
so I don't expect he'll be back this year.' The singing lesson proceeded,
and that was that.

Stunned, we gathered in the dusty milkbar after school. None of
us really believed what had happened, that he could have gone so quickly
and left us without a word.

'We have to do something,' I said at last.

'I can't get through the next few days if we just leave things like this,'
said Phyllis.

The boys agreed.

Then someone did think of something, and this is what has worried
me so often. Just who did think of this plan. At first it seemed ridiculous,
then it took hold of us, and before any of us realized just what was
happening, we were committed.

Late that night, we met in the village. We quietly stowed our bikes
away behind the church fence, hot after long rides, for none of us lived

less than two miles away and David and I had come nearly five, all of us still scared by our flits from sleeping homes.

It was just after midnight when we congregated under the tree, a very quiet, black midnight, the sort of languorous spring into early summer night that only the north can provide. Beside the stifling bump and thud of our own hearts, we could hear no sound.

It was a big tree, that magnolia, and an old one, but it did not have a great girth. The magnolia has slim branches, and the wood is not unduly hard. David and Geoff had a two-handled saw, which they used unskilfully but with results. It was surprisingly soon that the tree gave a sickening lurch. The boys tore out from underneath and we girls, stationed to watch for interruptions, leapt with them. We were on our bikes almost before it hit the ground.

Within moments we were speeding along the metalled road, gravel flying up and hitting our legs, a slight breeze suddenly zipping up against us, seeming like a howling gale trying to slow us down; and our breaths like sobs in our chests. We glanced back when we reached the top of the hill; below us at the policeman's house, and at the Manse, lights had come on. They wouldn't know in which direction to even start looking.

We got off our bicycles and started to laugh, shudders of hysterical laughter, until at last we collapsed on the bank by the road. It still seemed early, and we had come out to grow up that night, but the breeze had developed a chill quality. We lay on the grass in couples, and made a little rough and untender love, during which we all remained virgins, but the hysteria in our actions kept returning, and the magic which might have been in it for me, vanished as I lay close to earth, while Geoff whispered in my ear something which might have been 'Magog, oh Magog,' but was, more likely, 'My God, oh my God.'

Before long we left and, parting with Geoff and Phyllis, David and I rode slowly towards our homes.

When morning came, the night seemed remote. It was like something we had heard on the radio, knowing it had happened, and that it was important to somebody, but not to us. That is until we got to the church hall, straggling up from school, the four of us not looking at each other.

Round the fallen tree there was a knot of people, children, storekeepers, just standing, not saying much. There were old women there, crying, not so you'd notice, but inside them all beat up, with just an odd tear on the outside. The old man, Danny Ferry, he was there too, not looking at a soul. He was using a pair of secateurs to pick the last flowers off the tree, and as he cut them he cast aside the crushed and broken ones, choosing the best and placing them in an old flax kit.

He straightened up when we approached. I didn't want to look, but his eyes held fascination. I wanted the reassurance that he didn't know who had done this thing to him. He dwelt on us for only a moment, but what I sought was not there. It was an imperceptible flicker which betrayed none of us, except to each other.

He went on ahead of us and in a few minutes called us in. On each desk there was a magnolia bloom, the very last ones of the season, or of any season.

I looked at my paper, mechanically realizing that it was a good one, then picked up my pen and started to write, forcing my hand across the page. The words I had written stared back at me, meaningless. Glancing around, I saw that the others were having the same difficulty.

And still our eyes kept straying towards Danny. His eyes looked back, not at us now, but rather, beyond. The hands, veins swelling along their backs in blue cords, quietly threaded finger over finger. Then he would stop and the stillness was frightening. But worse, as the motion began again, the fingers binding, binding together, faster, taking on a methodical rhythm.

The hours in that room stretched ahead of us like forever.

After about half an hour, Danny got up and walked towards us. Still the eyes looked beyond, but when he spoke it was in the quiet, courteous voice we had always known.

'I cannot go on today,' he said. 'I cannot go on.'

He left us, drifting aimlessly out into the morning. We sat on in uneasy silence, tense and mindful of the fact that the rules forbade us to leave the room during the examination. We just waited, waited for something to happen. Something big, something momentous, I suppose, maybe retribution.

It didn't. Not really. Soon the minister came over from the Manse to continue our supervision. The four of us looked at each other for long moments, until we could no longer bear it. I picked up my magnolia from the desk, and placed it in the ink bottle, watching as the slow process of osmosis began. The others nodded, following me, then came the release, hands and minds moving, really moving at last, pens racing, breaths fluttering with the effort to regain time; flying, nothing but clear space ahead of us.

We never saw Rad Barclay again, and I have not presumed to judge him, because to do so might be, at once, both more and less than he deserved. As for all of us perhaps.

But as for me, sometimes, in dreams, bad dreams, like last night after Phyllis had been here, I dream that I was the person who was responsible. In waking, I fear that it may be so.

Fiona Kidman
A Strange Delight

He walked across the morning, trampling a welter of shadows, a tidy, hard man, pushing the sunlight ahead of him. Carefully dressed down in too perfect casuals, Peter still felt uncomfortably aware that he was clothed as if going to a company barbecue. It had taken him a long time to decide what to wear, and though at last the garments were chosen, the Italian shirt even bought specially, he knew, as he walked along, that he could not achieve by any means the casual disregard for them which was really the way Bethany liked to see clothes worn. And, for that matter, the way she wore clothes so effectively herself.

It was a walk he might have enjoyed had he chosen to make it, but as it was he would have preferred not to have been seen abroad in that street. Still, the airport bus had put him down at the end of the way, just a few hundred yards distant, so there he was. The street was wide and tree-lined, well established now, though that was not the way it had been when he bought the section and had the house built for his wife. But he had known then what it would be, that road; a broad band of green and middle-class where he would be able to sell well when he could afford a still better move. The neighbourhood had turned out just that way, with silver birch grown up and neat block walls, even a tennis court or two stretching down to the fencelines bounded by shasta daisies and michaelmas. The painted letter boxes stood in line with wrought iron numerals fixed on them, and by common agreement of all in the street, camellias were planted uniformly along the edge of the grassed verges, apple blossom sasanquas to cast a glimmer of pale pink ice in winter. And the people were right too, not wealthy enough to afford the luxury of public squabbles, and certainly too well off to do the same things in poverty. No one talked about the Vietcong, or abused God except in swearing which was different, or made love on the lawn as Bethany had suggested they should do and hadn't. Oh yes he had chosen well.

And it had seemed to him that Bethany too would grow with, and as, the flowers and the shrubs. True, her style was her own and not inherited, but then neither, too much, was his. She had worked in a laboratory where she had had to use her brains; there was some standing with the job, and it contained her exuberance enough to make it charming when it did show. So why, so why then, had she not mellowed and moulded with the years into the shape of the street and its inhabitants?

More strangely still, why, despite her incongruity amongst the coffee parties, and club bazaars, and the jumble sale pricing, the cashmere and Munro spun tweeds, did they tolerate her, and not him — he who had tried so hard?

For though they might appear to ignore conflict, the people did feel here, and care — and, most of all, they wondered. Right now, eyes would be watching him, eyes that knew him, that would consider his movements with memory and knowledge, and the pursuit of drama. Eyes that would wait hungrily for developments. Ears that would listen. Children who must suddenly be still. A surreptitious phone call. Peter is back.

So at last he came to his house, and knew instinctively that if the woman was there at all, she would be on the porch at the back on a day like this.

As he rounded the corner he felt a sudden knot collecting in his stomach. Up until that moment this visit had not assumed reality. Carefully considered, yes. The possibilities planned, most certainly. But the emotions carefully contained, because one knew that, deep down, they were waiting there, ready to rise up out of a lost stratum, there to engulf him if he was unwary.

He shut his eyes against the sunlight, and panic, for an instant, paused just long enough for the knot to subside, then walked briskly forward.

The yard was much the same as when he and Bethany had lived here together. Only the fence leaned at a droll angle towards the neighbour's vegetable garden now and lank weeds struggled with the glowing colours of summer flowers untended. Bright water lily dahlias, perennial phlox and a wild dream rose, the one they called First Love, grew raggedly, falling across the edges of the proliferating grass. In one corner sunflowers propped themselves indolently against the garage, and in another a plum tree spread enormous branches laden with ripening fruit. He would have thinned the sunflowers long ago, and he knew that the plum would lose half the fruit because the tree was too heavy.

And there was Bethany, as of old, seated on the steps, baring long, golden legs to the light. Her dress was of heavy orange and brown linen, too hot for the day, yet the colours somehow right for it. Its skirt was tucked into the legs of her panties. Her shoulders were slumped against the pillar of the veranda, so that her breasts were thrust forward, and the top of her dress too was pulled down into her brassiere so that there also she could soak up the warmth.

She opened her eyes when she heard his footstep, and with a quick involuntary movement pulled up her top with one hand, and her skirt down with the other, fumbling so that the book which had been in her lap fell to the ground.

He nodded. 'Hullo,' he said, and sat down beside her on the step. 'Hullo,' she said.

They smiled briefly, preserving the habits of civility, then simultaneously shrugged and turned away.

'Gerald's out,' she said.

'I guessed he would be.'

'Of course. You would have known.' Simple flat statements.

'Cigarette?'

'Thanks.' She took it from him, and he lit it for her, noticing, as he used to, how her unlipsticked mouth was a soft pucker around it, a ripple in yielding flesh; not tense little corrugations like most women offered. He had a quick vision of her entire body and imagined sex, cursing himself as he did, knowing she would know.

'I thought I ought to see you,' he said sharply.

'Thank you,' she said, resting her head on her hand, and not looking at him. 'That was gracious of you.'

This was better, he thought, the old familiar needling; it helped at times.

'I haven't seen the children for a long while.'

'There's nothing to prevent you,' Bethany replied. She gazed into distance, or at a sunflower, he could not be sure, and her remoteness irritated him, as a moment before her nearness had disturbed him.

'I've been offered a job with the firm in Australia,' he said. 'When the divorce goes through Patsy and I thought that we might go — that it would — perhaps — be best for us. So — I thought — ' he spread his hands awkwardly. 'Oh I don't know.'

'You thought that you should see that Gerald didn't beat me, and that your children loved him like a father, and that we would get ourselves safely married so that you'd be free from any more responsibility to us, and that your conscience would be quite clear as you sailed — sorry, jetted — off into the blue, with Patsy.'

She paused and glanced sideways. 'Your conscience always gave you hell. Funny.'

He wanted to defend himself, but couldn't. He wanted to say — I didn't leave you for Patsy, she came after — after when I was lonely and I wanted to come back and I couldn't, because you had found someone else. Which I should have known. Which was fair. But it hurt. Picking someone up with ease, like a flower from the roadside, like — plucking a man, any man, out of nowhere, out of inspiration.

Any man? Not Gerald, he wasn't any man. She wouldn't make the same mistake so easily again.

'Can't you make it with Patsy when your conscience is troubling you? You were always susceptible to outside influences.'

He flushed and she laughed, a short, dry noise deep in her throat, like static.

'Still you never could leave well alone,' she remarked further.

So he said nothing, resting his elbows on his knees, letting his hands hang down between his legs, trailing blue smoke from his cigarette. Words, he thought, always words, and a surfeit of quick answers and cool laughter. Did they laugh, iced water laughs, when they thought of him? Crisp sprinkles of derision, remembering him, after love. Or worse, did they remember him at all?

Whereas he thought of them often. Imagined their bedroom, a jumble of clothes and bedcovers, and her nut coloured hair, thick and uncombed on rumpled pillows. And Gerald — but no he couldn't really think of Gerald. So then he would talk to Patsy about the untidiness of the lives of people like Bethany and Gerald and she would agree and be comforted with the sense of his own orderliness. For wasn't it Bethany who had resisted the flat lawns and bevel edge hedges and the new wallpaper in the hallway each spring where she had let the children put their dirty hands, and the kitchen repainted annually because the fat splashed over and her cigarettes burned holes while she read books?

Which he and Patsy would never stand for. And he would know that he couldn't have stood it any more and had been right to go, and there was no need to justify it all over again.

He turned over her book which she had dropped. Lines of poetry sprang out of it —

Love is blankets full of strange delights
Love is when you don't put out the light
Love is —

And do they laugh when the bed is warm?

Love is you and Love is me.

'How are the children?' he said at last.

'They're fine. You've no need to worry,' she said carelessly. 'They really do love him like a father.'

Love is a prison and Love is free.

She shrugged again at his look. 'Well that's good isn't it? Isn't that what you want. For them to be happy?'

'And the neighbours?' Again he felt the watching eyes.

'Look,' she said impatiently. 'Look really.' She flung her hands open protestingly. 'After all, you did leave me.'

'You don't seem to care a lot about it all,' he remarked, bridling.

'Why should I care?' she cried out. 'You — left — me,' spacing each word so that it became weighted with meaning.

'You're all right then?'

But she only arched her throat and let the laughter out again, only more gently. He looked at her, wondering, almost hoping.

'Would you like some coffee?' she said.

'Have you tea?'

'Oh of course.' Bethany grimaced at her forgetfulness, caught out that she had forgotten the habits of their lives together. Tea for breakfast, tea at the mid-morning, for lunch, and every time they sat down to eat, except after dinner when, for her sake, they made coffee.

'I've got China tea,' she said wrinkling her brow with vexation, 'but that's awful with milk and you won't have it without. Some cordial then? It's very hot.'

Peter nodded. 'Yes, that would be nice.'

She went into the house. His house. After a while he followed her in, wanting to see her in it again.

His house. It was the same, they hadn't changed the furniture. But his eyes were screwed up from being in the sun and the interior of the kitchen was frazzled with the red spots in his vision, so that it was a time before he saw that the house, though his, was not his. That there were shaggy flowers in a jam jar above the sink, that there were books lying open on the refrigerator and that, on closer inspection they were about communism, which made him suddenly frightened as if he were being watched; and that Gerald's shirt was lying on the floor.

'What do they really say?' He jerked his head towards the houses across the road.

'What about?' she said, pouring orange liquid into glasses.

'Us.'

'Us?' She shook her head as if trying to grapple with an alien concept. 'Us? Nothing much. Not to me. To each other? Depends.' She smiled at him, really warm all of a sudden. 'Nell Parker. What do you think?'

He smiled back tentatively.

'It's a bit off, you'd think she'd take her fancy man off somewhere away from decent folks and their children,' she said, mimicking. 'Of course,' she added, lowering her voice conspiratorially, 'you've got to be charitable, it was him that took off, most likely it's affected her mind, poor thing.' She tucked her chin and rolled her eyes. 'You know how it is?'

'I know.'

'The rest — well, they forget, or they seem to, and if they don't — do you care?'

'No, no,' he said, turning away from her. 'I never think I do — until I'm here. Then it seems to matter and I always think it must to you — and yet I know it doesn't. I care about you not caring. I can't explain,' he said despairingly.

'Yes, I understand.' She spoke slowly, as she always did when her understatements carried more meaning than he was prepared for. 'I understand that — when you're here — we're in it together again, aren't we?'

She picked up the tray on which she had placed the drinks. 'I'll take these outside.'

'I'll go to the bathroom,' he said, resisting the temptation to ask her permission.

In there, he was reminded again that this house of his wasn't his. After he had relieved himself, he washed, more meticulous than the average man, and sat on the edge of the bath, suddenly tired and flat with the morning, and saw that the bath was dirty and that sticking in the dirt were curly brown hairs. There was a sickly smell in the air and lying at his feet was a small wet bundle. He was filled with premonition and thought to go through the house, but she was calling him, to say it was hot and would he come because the drinks were suffering.

He went out and sat down with her.

'You've put on weight,' he said. 'It suits you.'

She glanced at herself.

'I suppose I have, it's the baby.'

'The baby?'

'You didn't know? No I suppose you wouldn't. One forgets — how long it is.'

'You — and Gerald — you have a baby?'

The ripe flesh, the gold and the laughter, took on new meaning. She got to her feet and went inside and in a minute came back to him with a child wearing a napkin and singlet, in her arms.

'She's nine weeks.'

'A girl?'

'Yes.'

'Like Gerald.'

'We think so.'

We, we, we think so.

'You always wanted us to have a girl.'

'I know,' said Bethany. 'So did you.'

So I did, he thought. Together we wanted. At breakfast we would make pointed jokes about it being the right day for conceiving girls, by afternoon the jokes would be more general, and by night time conception would be forgotten entirely and it would simply be wanting. It was in those days that they had seemed to have the permutations of forever.

But later breakfast times were too acrimonious for jokes and whatever it was that they had wanted at all had been forgotten.

The baby snuffled at her mother's hand. 'She's hungry,' Bethany said, and unbuttoned her dress and unhooked the protective shield over her nipple. It sprang out from under the cloth, dark and strong, surrounded by the white, blue-veined breast. The child seized it in its mouth, sucking avidly.

'Mmmm, darling, there, there, darling,' Bethany crooned, cuddling her baby, and forgetting him.

He leaned his head back against the veranda, consciously shutting his eyes this time, shutting her out, shutting out Gerald.

'Having babies always suited you,' he said, harshly.

'Yes,' she said simply.

'Gerald — ' he began.

'Yes?'

'You looked lovely feeding the boys like that.'

'You always said so.'

'And Gerald — ?'

'Of course. Of course he likes it. Don't all men?'

'Of course — I always said — the bottle was better — in the long run — '

'Oh you did, I know.'

'Do you take your calcium tablets?'

'I try to remember. You know what I'm like.'

'Yes, I know what you're like.' He waited, choosing his words carefully, though their meaning was plain enough. 'You're happy then?'

After a while, she said, 'A baby makes a difference doesn't it?' Avoiding his question.

'But you wanted it? You and Gerald, you wanted the baby?'

Her laughter, a little rueful now. 'Oh we never not wanted it.'

'What do you mean?'

'We forgot. One night. We forgot. I forgot.' The old Bethany, laughter peeling out now, the old careless Bethany with her mouth opening, her legs uncovered, her breast shaking in her baby's mouth laughing at something beautiful beyond the range of the fat yellow sunflower cushions, somewhere he couldn't see. 'But it was lovely,' she gurgled. 'That night, at least — it was lovely.'

His stillness penetrating at last, and she looked at him again, watching silently as he got to his feet.

Two steps away from her, and she said, 'You're going?'

'Well,' he said stiffly, 'a baby does make a difference doesn't it?'

At the corner of the house, he turned around again to look at her. She had put the baby down and pulled up her dress. As he turned, she got to her feet, and stood shaking and strangely white in the bright day.

She clenched her hands at her side. 'Why didn't you make it better?' she called after him. 'Why didn't you make it better for me?' And the tears had started to stream down her face.

Keep on walking he told himself. Keep on and don't look back. The eyes will watch and know me for the bastard I am, and soon it will be all right for her again. She won't ever change, that's right too, and I won't ever forget her the way she is.

Note
The lines of verse on p. 54 are from Adrian Henri's 'Love is', reprinted here, with acknowledgement, from *Penguin Modern Poets 10*.

Margaret Sutherland
Codling-Moth

We talk about it a lot. It is as unattainable, as desirable as beauty. In secret we crave it; cynics, we talk about it as we sit together under the gum trees at lunchtime, eating peanut butter sandwiches.

'It's ridiculous, the way they go on about it all the time,' says Mel, tossing her crusts to the predatory gulls. We aren't supposed to feed them but we do. 'I mean, it's one thing in the pictures and books and poetry and that stuff, but take real life. Take my parents. Or yours. They love each other but you don't see them slopping all over each other and going on as though that's all there is to think about. Do you?'

'No, you don't,' I say. When my father comes home he kisses my mother, or rather he kisses the air by my mother's cheek, and if he's late, as he often is when shift work or his mates at the pub delay him, my mother, rattling plates, says 'Your dinner's in the oven and if you don't hurry up and eat it it'll be dried up to nothing.' I suppose they love each other.

'Of course they have been married a long time,' Mel says, thinking. You know when she is thinking. Her eyes go away from you, like a blind person who, in following the direction of your voice, misses and looks past your shoulder. 'It's probably different when you're married. Romeo and Juliet never got married did they.'

I think of Romeo coming in late from work and Juliet rattling plates and saying 'Your dinner's in the oven.' It makes me feel sad. Mel and I saw the film. I cried at the end. Mel's more sensible than I am. She doesn't believe in crying, as a rule, but she didn't want to look at me when we came out.

'It's different, being married,' I say, to bring her back to sitting under the trees and feeding the seagulls. 'It must be. I've never seen any married people who love each other so they'd rather die than stay alive if the other one died.'

Mel bites into an apple — glossy, red, perfect. 'Ughff, look at that,' she says, spitting out the words and the apple together, and showing me the core. A dull greyish powder spreads from where the worm has tunnelled.

'Codling-moth,' I say. Mel has a quick look round and shies the apple at the bossiest gull, which lumbers into the air, settles a few feet away, and regards us with the icy outrage of our headmistress objecting to complaints of behaviour on the buses with the boys from St Pat's.

A thought has just occurred to me. 'Maybe they make it up,' I suggest. 'I bet there's no such thing as love. That kind anyway. Maybe people know there isn't and wish there was, so they make it up and write books and compose songs and all the time it isn't true.'

That makes us silent. I wish I hadn't had that thought. I hope I'm wrong.

'I think you're right,' Mel says suddenly. When she's finished thinking, she's back with you, snap; quite startling if you've gone away into your own thoughts while you've been waiting for her. 'There's no such thing. Jolly good thing too. Who wants to go all sloppy and slushy about some idiot with sweaty hands and pimples. It's absolutely disgusting when you think about it. It makes you sick.'

'But they're not all like that,' I say quickly, trying to unthink my thought. 'What about Jolyon Townsend?'

'You certainly see a lot like him,' says Mel, who can be sarcastic. 'At the school ball the floor was littered with boys like him, wasn't it. You tripped over them at every step. Or they tripped over you more likely.'

'Well . . .' I say.

'Well?' she says. Mel likes to be sure she's won the point.

'Well,' I say, 'they can't help it. They might look better when they're older.'

'Like twenty years older.'

'Anyway what about us?' I've remembered the photo of Mel and me, in flocked nylon dance frocks and long mittens, standing in front of the artificial gladioli. 'What about that photo of us?' There is nothing to say.

I try again. 'How about Mr Krassmann then?' I ask in a very insinuating way. I think Mel has a crush on Mr Krassmann, who tutors her privately on Saturday mornings in German. When she came round to my place after her lesson last week her face was quite pink, and *Heute und Abend* isn't the sort of thing to put roses in anybody's cheeks. Mel is giving nothing away.

'Mr Krassmann?' she says, drawing it out as though I've suggested old Harry, the school caretaker, who is about seventy and smells of tobacco. He spits too. 'You must be joking.'

In *The Importance of Being Earnest*, our play for English Lit, this term, Mel has the part of Lady Bracknell. I concede. 'OK,' I say. 'Love's an illusion.' I've heard that somewhere. To agree with Mel is the best way to call her bluff, sometimes. She looks at me. It's her other look, the opposite of her far-away one. She has unusual eyes — flecked, the iris blue and green and grey and gold and each colour distinct; the white part is very white. Mel's eyes are her best feature. But when she looks at you this way you stop noticing her eyes, as though you can see past them to a small secret place where the real Mel lives. She doesn't let you in very often, which is only natural.

'Gabriel? You don't really think that's true, do you?'

'I hope it isn't true,' I tell her honestly.

'I hope it isn't too,' she says. The game is over. We're in agreement, which we usually are though we like to pretend. We go down to the pool for a swim.

The pool is new. For two years we've had raffles and class fund-raising contests and limp fudge cake from the school tuck-shop, sixpence the piece. And now we have a swimming pool. Mel and I stand beside the steps that lead down to the water, eau-de-nil water that reminds me of polar seas, lapping on smooth tiles white as ice floes. My bathing-suit is regulation black and my skin is very pale.

I tried to tan last year when Mel and I went camping with her cousins. The tan stayed for two days and peeled away, like dirt. All that stayed in my skin was the smell of sunshine when I breathed on my arm. We kept to ourselves in our ten-by-ten canvas world and waited for sunburnt boys to pay court. We wore eyeshadow, and four changes of beachwear every day. The boys went by our tent and we noticed that the girls beside them looked like Ann, who never wore eyeshadow, and said 'somethink'. We were not grateful to Ann for taking us camping, in the same way that we were not grateful to our parents for conceiving us in their middle age. We did not think about it. Mel and I did not talk about the boys. We bought chocolate-dipped ice-creams, and walked along the beach with our heads close together to hear over the wind and surf.

The light went quickly one evening when we were still on the beach. The two boys came silently out of the sandhills so that at first we were startled. We walked, the four of us, towards the rocks at the end of the beach, together at first, later in pairs, Mel and her boy ahead. His walk was almost a shamble; his arms, before he put one round her shoulders, swung loosely. Smugly, I felt sorry for Mel. The boy beside me was tall and his hand felt firm and warm. It grew dark, and I could have walked on to the rocks for ever.

Mel and her boy drew further ahead as we turned back and went towards the dunes. I wished that Mel was following to notice that my boy didn't shamble and was tall. The juice of the succulent plants, closed now against night, ran out between my toes as he turned me to him and kissed me. His lips, like his palms, were dry and warm. But then his tongue was terrible, slithering wet, strong, a dark eel belonging under stones in the river. He held me tightly but I pulled away and ran back, on and on, to the camp, to the tent. My chest hurt with fright and running. I waited for Mel and was angry because she hadn't stayed with me.

She came back soon. I was curious to know if she had been kissed by her boy but she didn't say and I didn't like to ask. Nor did I tell her about the kiss that had made me afraid. I knew I had not behaved with sophistication, although my eyeshadow was silver and glistened under light. We went to bed soon, on the double mattress that Ann had brought on the trailer for us. Mel's warmth, her solidity, the faint spicy smell of her hair near my face comforted me and I fell asleep against her.

Holidays end; school brings back the pleasures of challenge, approval, Mel's company. We vie in class. While other girls form friendly circles at lunchtime, Mel and I sit apart. In wet weather the shelter sheds smell of sour milk and sandshoes, and wasps hang around the overflowing rubbish tins. When it's fine we sit under the gum trees, and sometimes after lunch we go for a swim.

I look at the pale water, and think that I'm not a good swimmer, that I don't like cold water, that I don't want to go in. Mel, beside me, reaches out and touches a finger behind my shoulders. 'You have such a smooth back,' she says, sounding surprised as though she's just noticed something. Compliments are unusual: from adults who are watchful of praise, from Mel, who tries as I do to be adult. Her words sink like smooth pebbles to the bottom of my thoughts; later I will take them out, turn them over, fondle them. I am flattered. I am happy. I leap suddenly into the water and without a single rest I swim a full width of the pool.

After school we catch the bus to town. It is Friday afternoon, the first Friday of the month. Mel and I are making the Nine First Fridays, in honour of the Sacred Heart. When we have finished we shall be certain of going to heaven; as promised to St Margaret-Mary by the Lord Himself we shall be allowed the grace of final repentance on our deathbeds. Death seems beyond us, as impossible as the committing of horrible, mortal sin, but then one never knows. The Nine Fridays may save us in the final count. Mass and Communion for nine consecutive First Fridays of the month is a little price to pay for heaven. Besides, before Mass at seven o'clock, there's afternoon tea and a five o'clock session of the pictures. We never see the end of the film because we can't be late for Mass. It doesn't matter a lot. We make up our own endings.

Mel's watch is fast. We are early for Mass. Men and women tread quietly past the confessional boxes into the great cave of the church. Confessional doors open and close; voices too muted to understand exchange private words as Mel and I, kneeling together, examine our consciences. HailHolyQueen. HailOurLifeOurSweetnessAndHope. ToTheeDoWe Come. BeforeTheeWeStand. SinfulAndSorrowful. Sinful. Even the just man falls seven times daily. Why so hard to put together a respectable list for Father who waits gravely in there, in the small cave smelling so strongly of old planed wood? His profile beneath the dim bulb appears as the window slides back. Latin phrases of absolution switch suddenly, like light, to the patient, 'Yes, my child?' My child? Can he see me? How does he know this is not an old woman, a murderer, a sinner come to repentance after thirty years? Oh, to have the choice of thirty years' wickedness from which to pick sins like cans from a supermarket shelf; oh, how disappointing a display of sin. Disobeyed Mother. Several times. Told lies twice. No. Not harmful to anyone. Not calumny. One about the music practice. One about the chocolates. Mother knew anyway. 'And anything else?' Anything else, anything else. . . . Surely, surely, *something?* Answered back, but she deserved that. I answered back, Father. Impure thoughts? Had an impure thought. 'Yes, my child. I see. And anything else now?' Anything else anything else Father I'm almost wetting my pants because it's so dark and there's nothing else so please give me my penance — a thought only, unspoken. Would that be a sin, to do that in Confession? Surely not, not even there. Has anyone ever? . . . dear child, pray for help, Our Blessed Mother, temptation is no sin, remember that the Devil tempted Christ Himself in the desert. . . . Yes Father. Pray my child. Yes Father. You do remember your prayers always? Mostly Father. 'I see, my child. And nothing else?'

When I was small I used to clutch when I felt I couldn't wait and

Mother would say don't, Gabriel, don't do that. Nice little girls don't do that. I do it now, praying that Father can't see, praying there won't be a little trail of wetness left behind on the brown linoleum when I emerge, absolved, into the light.

For your penance three Hail Marys, and now a good Act of Contrition. OhMyGodIAmVerySorryThatIHaveSinnedAgainstThee. BecauseThouArtSoGood. AndIWillNotSinAgain. Amen. *Te absolvo.* Thank you, Father. The window closes.

I open the door, go back to the church and the faces looking up from their conscience-stricken hunting. Have I been a long time? Too long? Fall gratefully, blushing, into any pew. Disappear. A light-headed feeling of freedom like the last day of term. Sin all gone. Sorrowful? Happy. Bury eyes down on to clasped hands. Three Hail Marys, one, two, three. A soul now, round and white as a peppermint, the smuts of sin rubbed out. Gabriel shriven.

Most people leave as soon as Mass is over. Mel and I stay behind, kneeling side by side. The church is a great high cave where we are together, lost, alone. The candles sparkling on the side altar remind me of glow-worms high up on the caves at Waitomo, cold caves, dark, with lapping black water sensed more than seen. 'My, now *this* is *something*!' the American woman says, impressed again. I think of black sky, no moon, the death of a star, and I am glad to climb the rickety wooden steps up to the light again. Caves are sinister places, running back to no-exits of darkness and dripping water. Mel isn't afraid of caves. She is practical. She will be saying the fourth decade of the rosary and planning her weekend essay. Her beads move, tapping lightly the polished pew cut with the initials J.B., rayed round with lines like a child's sun.

The church smells warmly of flowers and incense. I ease my weight to one knee, to the other, and rest my face against my bent arms. It's no good. I give in and sit down, tracing through the lisle stockings the deep indentations that mark each knee. Mel's back rises straight and rigid as the brown-robed St Joseph who gazes past us from his niche. His head does not wear a beret, but clustered curls and a plaster beard, set stiffly on his chin like old spaghetti. Looking at Mel I am ashamed. I kneel down again, notice the blunt renewed ache in my knees and the warmth of Mel beside me. Her blazer filters a musky smell like faded incense. HailHolyQueenMotherOfMercy. HailOurLifeOurSweetnessAndOur Hope. ToTheeDoWeCome. BeforeTheeWeStand. SinfulAndSorrowful.

Grateful when Mel's nudge comes, I stand up stiffly, like the old women who wear headscarves and chew on their prayers without caring who listens in to their conversations with the Lord. How sad, I think, how impossible to ever be old like that. I follow Mel down the side aisle, my legs forgetting their stiffness, my callous soul ignoring the sad dimmed oil paintings of the Way of the Cross. Dip, splash, the holy water font an ivory shell. Catholic Truth Society pamphlets, red, blue, purple, on the rack in the church porch. *Have you a vocation? Sacramental Grace. Youth and Problems of Purity.* I cannot go and take that title out of the rack, not with Mel or somebody to see me and wonder why I'm buying that one; but it sounds more interesting than *Fallacies of Jansenism.* We pass the pamphlets and go outside. It is March and by eight o'clock night has settled down cosily. I was sleepy in the warm church. Now, feeling the thin cold air trickle through my nose, I am suddenly wide awake, and pleased with myself.

'Well, that's eight,' I say.

'Eight what? Oh, you mean Fridays,'

'Only one to go. Did you think we'd really do it, Mel?'

'We haven't yet. There's one more, remember.'

Sometimes I find Mel's precision annoying, but I don't mind tonight. What does it matter? Mel is coming to stay the night and I am happy.

We have never been less tired than we are now, at bedtime.

'Straight off to sleep now,' Mother says firmly, hopefully. In the darkness I sense Mel in the other bed. We talk in whispers, muffling giggles in our pillows.

'Mel? You know when we were up at the beach last summer, and you went down to the rocks with that boy?'

'The one with the acne? The friendly monster from outer space?'

'He wasn't *that* bad.'

'He was. You were jolly pleased the other one picked you.'

'I was not.'

'Yes, you were. He was a crumb.'

'Yes, but did he . . . did you . . .?'

'What?'

'Oh *you* know.'

'For heaven's sake!'

'Did you, well, kiss him?'

'*He* did. I didn't.'

'Didn't you like it?'

'No. I don't think so. It was wet.'

'Was it? So was mine. All sloppy. He just about stuck his tongue down my throat.'

'Mine didn't do that. He kind of chewed, like those old men who don't wear their teeth.'

'Ugh.'

'Yuck.'

Exquisitely funny. We scream silently into our pillows.

'Licking ice-cream.'

'Slurping soup.'

'Gob-stoppers in your mouth. *Two*.'

Excruciating. We roll on our stomachs, hysterical. We have forgotten that Mother, in the next room, is tired and is trying to have an early night. Bang of the wall. Bangbang. Stop that noise, girls. Off to sleep. At once.

Silence.

'Gabriel?'

'Ssshh! She'll hear. Come over here.'

Mel in blue pyjamas brings her incense smell into my bed. We arrange ourselves together, bump to hollow, hollow to bump. 'Gabriel? What do you think about it? You know what I mean. Did your mother tell you or what?'

'She told me. Did your mother?'

'She gave me a book. Last year.'

A whole book! My information had been received in the five minutes between rosary and night prayers.

'What was it like?'

'Awful drawings.'

'Like biology class?'

'Worse. There wasn't much about it. The actual part. It had a lot about getting pregnant and how not to and diseases and that.'

Disappointing. I thought there might be something Mother had forgotten about. What she had told me had seemed really rather pointless.

'Mel? Didn't you think it sounded silly? I mean, don't you wonder why people *do* it?'

'It sounds mad, I think. Don't ask me. You'd think they'd have a better system, wouldn't you? An incubator plant or something.'

'Yes. I think it sounds awful.'

'Well I'm not going to do it anyway. Ever.'

'Neither am I.'

Is it incense, powder, faint sun-on-skin perspiration, this special warm smell that is Mel? The winceyette cloth of her pyjama coat has rubbed into tiny balls under my fingers. I am alive. I quicken with awareness like the vibration of a single hair when we sit, heads not quite touching, in the pictures. I will change my mind and be embarrassed, so I say it quickly before I have time to think. 'Mel,' I say, 'I do like you.'

She turns her head back as though she hasn't heard me. The toothpaste on her breath reminds me of the pink smokers we buy in cellophane packets as she answers.

'Well I like you,' she says. I am happy. I find her lowest rib and tickle. We have forgotten again. Bang. Bangbangbang.

'Get to SLEEP!'

Silence.

'Mel?'

'What?'

'I thought you were asleep.'

'No.'

'Oh.'

At the back of her neck, in the hollow, the hair is fine, like a baby's. I feel it for an instant, lighter than a touch on my lips, and wonder if I imagine its softness.

'G'night, Mel.'

'Mmhmm. G'night.'

Then it is morning and Mother is standing by the bed, wearing her least-pleased expression. We stumble up from sleep and go in dressing-gowns to the kitchen for breakfast. The air is thick with Mother's bad mood and fumes from the kerosene heater. Our plates are whisked away, dealt ferociously into the sink. The silence trembles with crashes. I ask with guilt if I can dry.

'Don't bother yourself,' Mother says, passing the tea-towel to me. 'You go and enjoy yourself with your friend. Don't think of your mother.'

'Didn't you have a good night?' I ask foolishly. Mother snatches her trump.

'Good night? Good *night*? The pair of you talking and giggling half the night. . . . My word, wait till you're my age. Young people are selfish today. Very selfish.' I dry in silence.

'Is it all right if Mel and I do some homework now?'

'Do as you like. Don't bother to ask me what you can do or can't do. You'll do what you please. You're just like your father.'

I go back to the bedroom. Mel is dressed. 'What's the matter with your mother. Isn't she feeling well?'

'Oh,' I say vaguely, 'she gets like that. She didn't have a very good night or something.' It does not seem reasonable that Mother's sleep is dependent on my own. A heavy burden.

Homework is done. Mother is ironing.

'Mel wants me to go over to her place. Can I?' I ask.

'You and that girl are always in each other's pocket,' Mother says with resentment. 'If it's not her coming to our place it's you wanting to go there. I don't know what her mother thinks, I'm sure.' It hasn't occurred to me that Mel's mother thinks at all. She is a doing person, never still, always washing, ironing, busy in the kitchen. She uses the weekends to catch up on the week when she's away at work.

'We have to finish this project on pollution by Monday, and Mel's got a book about it.' (BlessMeFather, I told one lie.)

'Go if you must,' says Mother, branding Father's shirt with a vicious stab. 'Please yourself. If her mother can put up with your nonsense and carrying on, go. It makes no difference to me. What I'd like to know is, where are all those nice little friends you used to have to your birthdays, that nice little what's-her-name, Rosemary, Mary Rose, what's-happened to her?'

I am patient. 'Mother, that was years ago. Absolute ages. She's gone all stupid now. All she talks about is boys.'

'There's worse than boys,' says my mother, thumping the iron fast. 'A lot worse. You want to think about that, my girl.'

'What d'you mean?' I ask. The damping-bottle flies, sprinkling me with drops, like holy water from the Benediction procession.

'I'll tell you what I'm talking about; you see far too much of that girl, that's what I'm talking about. In case you don't know it there are some funny people about, very funny men, and funny women too, and no girl of mine is growing up into one of them. That's what I'm talking about.'

'I don't know what you mean,' I say. 'I don't understand you.'

'I hope you don't,' she says, and says no more, for she has looked at me and seen my face and I think she is sorry that she let her tiredness and her oldness make her say that, that way. But I think also that she is glad it has been said. At least that is what I decide, later on. As I turn and run away out of the kitchen, into the bathroom, lock the door, sit on the edge of the bath, let the hot hot tears run down, I understand nothing, and everything, and I feel sick to my heart. A grey web of guilt is spinning itself about me. For the first time in my life I learn what it is to be quite alone.

Mel and I go to town. We have afternoon tea. We go to the pictures. We go to church, and kneel side by side. The doors of the confessionals open, close; inaudible words murmur a thread of melody. Mel leaves me and closes the door behind her.

Bless me, Father, for I have sinned. Anything else, my child? Anything else? Sin unspoken makes a worse sin, the sin of deceit, for the priest is the ear of God. Have I sinned? I remember the softness of old winceyette, the fineness of young hair at the back of the neck, in the hollow.

Mel comes out, composed as always. 'I'm not going,' I say. And I turn my back on her surprised face and walk up the church away from the confessionals.

The Ninth Friday. Nine consecutive First Fridays and nine communions and heaven is a promise. This is My Body. And This is My Blood. Mel goes up to receive communion. I do not go. I stay in my seat, kneeling very straight, and I try to concentrate on the pain in my knees and not think of the other pain. I have not made the Nine Fridays and I am trying not to cry.

Helen Shaw
The Gipsies

'Great-grandfather Rosa shared in the building of this house. He was its architect. The stained-glass window you'll see up on the second floor was all his own workmanship. Great-grandfather Rosa was an artist by profession. He painted the old pictures you'll find still hanging around some of the rooms. He was a teacher of art, back in the nineteenth century, and held his own school in some of the rooms. The Rosa Academy of Art it used to be called. His pupils were young ladies and no doubt would have been driven here up the old carriage-drive in horse-drawn conveyances.'

So Angelo Colquhoun sums up the run-down old residence that once was the home of his ancestor Paolo Rosa.

There are twenty rooms in the pillared house with its stone portico and verandas and balconies. Most of the rooms are occupied by itinerant young people, some of them students. The atmosphere is transitory. The tenants come and go, each in a world of his or her own, where life once flowed quietly and in harmony with the work and ideals of Angelo Colquhoun's great-grandfather, Paolo Rosa.

In surviving Victorian portraits and still-lifes hung in some of the rooms, students sense the past even while they themselves struggle with the urgency of their own personal problems.

Elfrida Smith is looking at herself in a mirror, at her long dead-straight yellow flaxen hair. She has only recently moved into a room in the house and finds Angelo's manner of thinking unexpected, different, exciting; and yet — after all, he is attractive, has a touch about him of his great-grandfather, something of a gipsy in his looks. She remembers having heard her grandmother sing to her, when she was a child, *My mother said I never should play with the gipsies in the wood,* but Elfrida Smith had left those simple days behind her. Before she made up her mind to throw in her lot with Angelo Colquhoun he told her that if she came to live in one of the rooms at the Colquhouns' house she would be regarded as one of the 'family'. He told her the old conventions were dying, perhaps already were dead, had lost most of the vitality that once animated them. He said that seeing beyond *things* mattered much more than some people believed. At the age of twenty-one, he had woken up to find himself with a house large enough to be able to invite his friends and casual acquaintances to come to live in it, that is, all those with whom he had a natural affinity. An unusual situation for a young man to be in. But of course the condition of the house would make some people open their eyes. Inherited by Angelo, it had for many years been totally neglected. It was only when Angelo came of age that he had been entitled to claim the house. It had been left to him by his grandmother, Christina Colquhoun, Paolo Rosa's daughter. She had left the house in trust for her grandson having refused to leave it to her son, Shawn Colquhoun, who may be summed up as having been a penniless drunkard who had even more debts to his credit than his father, Maurice Colquhoun, the poverty-haunted tenor who had married Christina Rosa. — *never should play with the gipsies in the wood if I did she would say naughty little girl to disobey.*

I am twenty years old. Elfrida thinks, old enough to decide for myself. In the beginning Angelo's ideas startled Elfrida, until she came to see with his eyes, until she began to think his philosophy for herself, as though it were her own. Until Elfrida Smith met Angelo Colquhoun she had never known any man, either young or old, who believed in the philosophy of sharing a common house and a common belief. This is how Angelo's attitude to life may be described. He wants everyone to share his belief, wants all those who choose to live in the house he has inherited to practise the same philosophy of a common pool he himself practises. For one thing all the hens wandering about in the overgrown orchard are everyone's property, are held in common just as is the house. All tenants feed scraps to the hens while Angelo supplies them with some wheat. One young couple living in a glassed-in porch on one of the balconies keep an ancient car down in the orchard. The red dented body is mottled all over with pink blue and yellow daisies. Everyone, at times, makes use of the flower car. The hens walk lethargically about, sometimes are to be seen under the car, scratching the ground looking for what they can find. Often they walk along the long verandas, a rooster in their midst playing his strutting rôle of emperor. Angelo is a believer in love but considers that only where an actual struggle for its discovery is taking place can it be said to exist. 'Living in this way,' Angelo often says, 'we are making our own love which has a potential to cure the problems. Let us take in our friends to live

with us and share this new and wonderful life which my great-grandfather
Paolo Rosa sensed, as he worked, might be possible, and so has handed
on to us.'

'Did your great-grandfather give you your original ideas, Angelo?' Elfrida
asks. She is leaning over a banister talking down to Angelo as he comes
up the stairs, rather awkwardly for he is carrying one very large painting.
Forgotten for many years it had been hanging in what had once been
a maid's bedroom, a small dark room opening off the scullery. 'I am
bringing up this picture to you. My great-grandfather painted it of
Christina Rosa, one of his daughters. Study it, Elfrida. Her face is radiant,
as though she became aware of the immaterial side of life while she sat
for this portrait. She must have found happiness in pleasing her father.
You can see clearly on her face that she must have become illuminated
while Paolo Rosa was painting her. Do you see how the painter has
conveyed the impression that his model's flesh has a lustre over it, a
physical illumination, we might say, Elfrida.'

They go into Elfrida's room. Angelo Colquhoun stands up Paolo
Rosa's painting on Elfrida's bed, a single brass bedstead with a red and
white cotton cover. He leans the framed portrait against one end of the
bed. 'I think great-grandfather Rosa saw on his daughter Christina's face
the innocence of inexperience. He conveys this in the painting. I have
brought it up from the cave-like room where it had been discarded,
Elfrida, for you, because this is the painting I regard as Paolo Rosa's
best, even if after his death they did shut it away where no one ever looked
at it. I want to let you live with it for a while in order to find out for
yourself the secret of Paolo Rosa's example to us today.'

The portrait of Christina Rosa, the painter's daughter, has a
gleaming, lavender sheen over the face neck and arms. The same sheen
shines over the chiffon, swathed and fastened in the front of the pale green
bodice, by a white rose attached. The dark, harvest-red colour of the
loosely-draped hair creates a romantic effect with a touch on it reminiscent
of the art of Rossetti. The picture radiates its own light. The artist's
signature is simply *Rosa*.

'How beautiful she must have been, your great-grandfather's
daughter,' Elfrida says.

'You too are beautiful, almost as beautiful as was grandmother
Christina, Elfrida. Probably I have told you that she married a poor opera
singer, Maurice Colquhoun, convinced that she had been brought into

the world to save his soul. He was a persuasive man, who lived on his debts. Women found it difficult to resist him although he soon tired of them. Rather than have his soul saved by Christina, on the contrary he gave her a son, Shawn Colquhoun, an unhappy man, my father. My grandfather's and my father's failings were more plentiful than their virtues. But without Christina having had to bear with these, Angelo Colquhoun would not be talking to you now. My grandmother, this lovely soulful girl, grew very plump indeed, yet retained a benign nature all her life, so the story goes. But his daughter, as Paolo Rosa has depicted her in this picture, was probably an interpretation of his particular dream of what a perfect young woman should be, a pure type of girl, the virginal young woman some men dream about. He set her up on a very high pedestal.'

'How you talk, Angelo. You are trying to tell me something. I'm not clever enough, am I?'

'Why must you be clever? You are beautiful, instead, like Paolo Rosa's daughter. There's a soft light over your hair, as on *Christina*'s in the painting. But of course you haven't red hair. All the Rosas have red hair, my blonde Elfrida.'

'Shall I change the colour of my hair?'

'It would be a deception. You'd be a kind of impostor. I might lose interest in you. You must bewitch me with your true self. You have your own beauty, Elfrida, and you have the personality that belongs to you. Don't change the colour of your hair. I have the Rosa red hair. Do you want to become a mere mirror, a reflection of Angelo Colquhoun? We aren't brother and sister, after all, are we?'

Elfrida Smith laughs. She is not really embarrassed although a certain shyness in her nature might suggest that she is. Angelo says, 'You're at the same radiant time in your life, Elfrida, as Christina Rosa must have been when her father painted her portrait. Now that I look at you more closely, a little more intimately, I see that you are very similar, you and Grandmother Colquhoun, even though she was a red-head and you are blonde.'

Together they look closely at the painting that has survived from the last century. After a while Angelo says he will hang it on the wall opposite the head of Elfrida's bed, so that she can see it when she opens her eyes, each morning.

'Paolo Rosa's paintings are all the same. They are painted to give love,' Angelo says. 'I keep on talking to you about my great-grandfather

Paolo Rosa but he was a considerable artist. What is more to the point, I consider he is still walking about in spirit in this many-roomed old house of the Colquhouns.'

The tenants refer to Angelo's mother as the 'prima donna' when she is not in their hearing, and to her face they call her Fanny. Fanny Colquhoun spends hours singing, sometimes for as long as six hours daily. Her faithful companion is her borzoi, in whom she constantly confides, telling the elegant creature her most intimate revelations and needs. The borzoi, named Boris, follows after Fanny Colquhoun quite submissively yet with a loping authoritative bearing, as though at some time having been familiar with artistic high circles. Angelo's tenement house, which had once taken in Paolo Rosa's young pupils, boasts a flight of steep, twisting, narrow stairs up which the painter must often have climbed, to a room he had used as a retreat; from its windows to observe the surrounding landscape and rather distant buildings of the city before descending again to give tuition to his young ladies. In this 'observatory' as they call it, built in the shape of a hexagon and enclosed with fixed windows of royal blue white and ruby glass and opening leadlights, Angelo's mother sings arias from favourite and lesser known operas, in a coloratura voice of no small volume. The sound gloriously goes spiralling down the staircase to travel on through all wings of the house, sometimes carrying as far as to the orchard.

'Fanny Colquhoun has sung major parts in Grand Opera. Now she has given up that life. Yet she told me she feels she must keep her voice in good form, for what else would there be in life to live for! Sometimes Fanny, whose father was a touring actor, Bliss Dickens Wilkes if you please, is asked to fill a minor rôle, and so for that reason if for no other keeps up her daily practice. When I moved in here,' Bernadette says, 'and heard Fanny singing up in the observatory I thought, Is it possible to stay here, Bernadette Mulloy, with those arias competing with the blackbirds. But I have become used to them. I hardly hear Fanny, now.' Elfrida Smith and Bernadette are drinking coffee together, in the old kitchen that serves all the tenants.

At present Bernadette Mulloy is studying rather unconventional philosophies. She reads reads reads. She wears large, very round glasses. Although she has an overwhelming thirst for delving into the most obscure books she can dig up relating to orthodox and unorthodox philosophy from every part of the world, nature has not provided her with ideal eyes for intensive studies. She is a plain, mentally animated, extremely short-sighted girl.

'Fanny Colquhoun is what I'd call eccentric. I have never met up with anyone quite like Angelo's mother,' Elfrida says. 'Yesterday I overheard her accusing the borzoi of being heartless, in his behaviour to her, of showing a total lack of feeling for his kind, devoted mistress. She actually said — I'm not making this up Bernadette — "Boris, you know how much I crave for some show of gallantry, a little courtesy and civilized attention, in return for all those sacks and sacks of meat and bones you so enjoy. I am a woman, Boris. I want to be admired. But there is no such delightful satisfaction to be derived from you, Boris. Do you present me with flowers? open doors for me? make flattering remarks when I am in good voice? murmur soothing phrases to me when I am in a depression?" What do *you* think of the "prima donna", Bernadette?'

'Yes, I've heard it all. "Dear Boris, tell me I thrill you. Tell me my singing reminds you of Madame Patti's. Flatter me, Boris. Call me the queen of song." Mad crazy mad, but you sound so patronizing, when you call her the "prima donna" Elfrida, and you wouldn't say it to her face. If you love, you don't jest about a person when he or she is not there to hear you. And love is the absolute in-thing, today,' Bernadette says. 'Love is adorable. Love is mod. Love it must be — at all times.'

'You've been talking with Angelo, Bernadette.'

Excitedly Bernadette replies, 'Have I? Elfrida, I have hosts of ideas. They are all my own. Fabulous ideas, some of them are, without appearing to be conceited I say this. Don't let yourself be mesmerized. My ideas don't come from Angelo, not all of them. I believed in love before ever I moved in here with the Colquhouns. Love was always romantic. And even if Angelo does succeed in influencing me, I don't have to defer to him on *all* points with favour. Angelo Colquhoun is a charmer, darling Angelo, one of the wide-awake ones, but I do not need to be convinced by him, not in a personal way, that love — just *is the* great modern invention. Since we seem to be talking about Angelo, tell me, what is your opinion of him, Elfrida? In my view Angelo is a very modern type of romantic who sets love before everything else, which is daringly innocent, or smashingly provocative!'

Elfrida's Kate Greenaway frock of violet and rose paisley-patterned print, enhanced by frilling round the neck and round the hem of the long skirt, adds to her wistful appearance. She takes her empty cup to the sink, dreamily rinses it under the cold tap. 'Angelo claims Paolo Rosa was a

fabulous artist,' she says. 'He considers his great-grandfather Rosa is still
walking about in spirit upstairs and downstairs in this old house. I agree
with Angelo, Bernadette. Look at the way Angelo himself talks, and the
way he dresses, purple corduroy trousers, and cream woollen tunic,
sometimes a fur cape, and then he wears a rosary, and look at his thick
waving red hair. I think Angelo wants us all to live in tune with the artistic
mana, as he called it the other day, of his great-grandfather. I do begin
to feel I am being influenced by Paolo Rosa. Have you asked yourself
if *you* are, Bernadette?'

'Take it from me, it is Angelo who is influencing you. Great-
grandfather Rosa may still be walking about "in spirit",' Bernadette says.
'But, after all, Angelo whose eyes smoulder as he talks to you, Angelo
with rich gorgeously flowing hair, the mark surely of a *Renaissance,* is
walking about the house "in person". He's exciting to contemplate. Surely
he is rather vitally significant in the pattern of your life, Elfrida. In a
word, love is dynamic in Angelo. But it is unwise, I don't recommend
it, to refer to his mother as the "prima donna". These Colquhouns are
independent, and don't ask to be patronized. Of course this is only
Bernadette Mulloy speaking from her limited experience of twenty years.'

Elfrida puts away her cup in a cupboard where an odd assortment
of chipped cracked crockery, no two pieces matching, is kept. 'Angelo
has hung up one of his great-grandfather's paintings on the wall opposite
my bed,' Elfrida says, 'a portrait of Paolo Rosa's daughter. Angelo thinks
Paolo Rosa sensed the power of love while he was painting. You know,
Angelo has lovely thoughts about the art of Paolo Rosa. And I share his
ideas.'

'You're even more romantic than Angelo,' Bernadette says, rinsing
out her cup. 'Not so surprising. Everyone's at heart romantic, must be,
who flouts convention to dare living with the Colquhouns.'

Sometimes, after singing for half the morning, Fanny Colquhoun will
open a pair of doors in the room at the top of the house and step out
on a little balcony. It has a curved balustrade and a pair of fluted stone
columns to support it. Up there she looks as though she is in a genuine
setting for a scene from an opera. But, instead of singing for a great
auditorium, she looks down on a neglected garden and orchard where
a number of wandering hens and one rooster are straying about. There
too, stands, permanently parked it seems, the ancient car, with daisies
painted over it, for devilry or joy, perhaps a mixture of both ingredients.

Beyond the garden Fanny Colquhoun from her balcony observes the tall buildings of concrete rising higher, higher, the city nearing the dense boundary of indigenous and European trees, some of an immense height, around the old orchard. This is the house that, in the day of Angelo Colquhoun's great-grandfather, was occupied by the Rosa family, although even then it was a refuge for the young ladies, sent to the artist to be instructed in how to paint gentle water-colours in their albums. Some perhaps benefited more than others from Mr Paolo Rosa's talent; but, on the whole, the prime reason for being sent to his Academy of Art for Young Ladies was in order to learn how, in a civilized manner, to employ leisure hours.

'He was a gifted artist, one of those Victorian seers, my great-grandfather Rosa — they were all artists in the family — his father John Maria Angelo Rosa was also a painter — his mother was a goldsmith's daughter, and his wife, great-grandmother Amalia Chloe Cottonfold Rosa, told fortunes and painted on velvet. Paolo Rosa's influence lives on, Elfrida. Sometimes he goes walking through this house, in that old tiled passage out there. He still walks along, as I see him, pausing at the south door, just as he must have done way back in the last century. He'd be reflecting there. Perhaps one of his young lady pupils, waiting for the door to open, might have looked through and seen her teacher's thick chestnut hair, silk cravat, and velvet jacket dyed emerald royal blue or scarlet depending on which coloured pane of glass she happened to be peeping through. All his young lady pupils are said to have admired him. A few fell in love with him. I have a psychic sensation that my great-grandfather Rosa is here in spirit. Perhaps his unconventional life is conditioning my thinking.'

Angelo has invited Elfrida Smith into a recessed, and pillared room, at the front of the house downstairs, which had served as a schoolroom in Paolo Rosa's day.

'You know, Angelo,' Elfrida says, 'I do feel your great-grandfather Rosa is here in spirit. Quite often I sense it. You don't have to believe me but I feel that he is here now. It seems, Angelo, he is trying to tell me something. Can you guess what he is saying to me, Angelo? Your great-grandfather wants you to be a painter. He believes in you, I guess he does, Angelo. That's why he's telling me I should persuade you that you are meant to be an artist, and follow him.'

Angelo is overtaken by a wonderfully buoyant mood.

'You don't know it but I do paint, it so happens,' he tells Elfrida.

'Isn't that romantic and fabulous, Angelo. Then probably your great-grandfather Rosa *is* here, and is persuading me to tell you his wish for his great-grandson.'

Angelo's face looks as though he feels light-headed. As Elfrida talks to him he calls out, 'I see hundreds of creative ideas for paintings crowding in on me.' He is only afraid they will fly away before he has a chance to record even one of the many abstractions of future works. 'Here is one of great-grandfather Rosa's little-known works,' Angelo says. He waves his hand towards a large oil, gilt-framed in an old-fashioned style of decorative scrolls. The painting depicts a triangular space of olive green against a brownish, gold-encrusted background. Within the triangular area a richly moulded bunch of grapes is resting among vine-leaves placed on a high-standing golden dish. The grapes have been portrayed, each one, with a glimmering bloom. They are richly lifelike, as though each grape has a life of its own, interior to itself from which comes its lustre. The painting suggests that Paolo Rosa loved to paint the living quality, the realistic essential truth of his subject, whether this was a young woman or a still-life. As he looks at this painting Angelo becomes convinced that Paolo Rosa has directed Elfrida to come and live in one of the rooms at the Colquhouns' house, and share the life of Angelo Colquhoun. She understands him and responds to him and she is intuitive.

'Yes, I paint sometimes, Elfrida. I've done about six paintings. After a while I usually ask myself, Why am I painting? This is the explanation for my indecision. At other times I believe I'd prefer to be a thinker. Or if I discovered my own source a new Hermann Hesse. I plunge into reading up all the philosophers and prophets. But aren't they perhaps mesmerizing me? I must find out for myself. You have given me a new starting point, Elfrida. My next painting will portray you. But it will be an abstract, a black rectangle filled up with rows and rows of grapes ranging through many shades of grey and lavender to purple. It will be called *Spheres of Affection*. Of course,' Angelo says, '*Spheres of Affection* will have a secondary, inner meaning, the secret of ourselves that we share, Elfrida.'

Angelo has given Elfrida a new, fabulous feeling. The very sight of the blackbird down on the balustraded terrace below her window, quietly folding its wings as it alights on the lip of a stone urn and with long grass and geraniums growing up round it, fills Elfrida with awareness. She feels in tune with the nature of the blackbird. How urgent its dark feathers become, so living, so poignant and almost hurtfully beautiful that the blackbird represents her new coming-to-terms-with-life since she has been living with the Colquhouns.

Angelo is painting *Spheres of Affection*, determined to show or prove in the work that, although he paints in a modern technique at the same time it should not be assumed that he is blind to his debt to the past; to the spirit of Paolo Rosa's work. On a black background, shaded from grey to black in four panels, Angelo has painted in regular rows the spheres or grapes. Every row builds up in tension, after being pale at the beginning of the line of spheres, to a deep, black-purple evocative of love perhaps also of protest. The canvas is so large as to fill almost one wall. Elfrida sits watching Angelo working on *Spheres of Affection*. While he paints she feels her own ideas coming to life. She thinks that this is a similar happening to dreaming with one's eyes wide open. An idea slowly then faster faster turning, breaks up into colourful images. She wonders if Paolo Rosa drove in a carriage, and before her enchanted eyes sees the smallest carriage to be imagined galloping in space drawn along by a pair of white horses. Elfrida is enchanted. Scenes are continually arising, blue fields of waving gold flowers, cloudlike herds of silver deer climbing snow mountains through stars to the moon mountains, the moon a spinning crystal of all colours, on the moon one red poppy glowing beckoning. There seems no limit to such phenomena as Elfrida experiences.

Angelo has asked Elfrida to climb up those twisting stairs with him, to the room at the top of the house where Fanny Colquhoun sings. Today Fanny is not in the room which means they have it to themselves. An apple-green folding screen has many time-curled-and-stained photographs of opera singers pinned to it, some signed with bold flourishes and extravagant declarations and claims of love. Among these is one of Fanny herself, in a wrap-over coat and immense fluffy fur collar, several ropes of pearls falling in loops from her neck. In this room, propped up on an old bureau, is an oil-painting, the head and shoulders of Paolo Rosa, his self-portrait. Elfrida Smith stares for long at this portrait, and asks herself, Hasn't Paolo Rosa a romantic face? Of course he isn't beautiful she thinks. His is not a handsome face. His features are quite irregular, rather heavy. She sees something coarse, yet at the same time refined about this face of the artist. Like Angelo. A gipsy? *I never should — with the gipsies —* but that was wrong. An old wives' jingle. Dark red hair in

an undisciplined mane ripples round Paolo Rosa's head. The blue-white
eyeballs are prominent, the eyes black and staring with a certain boldness,
but the expression on the full lips suggests to Elfrida that Angelo's great-
grandfather must have been sensitive to feeling.

Angelo touches Elfrida's hand. 'Do you love me, Elfrida?' he asks her.

Later he says, 'Great-grandfather Rosa believed in work. What would
he have to say of us, of the way we live? But he looks out at us, Elfrida,
as though he does have some understanding for us. We're different from
all he loved. But we must build on what he has given. We have some
of his paintings. If we forget them, and always prefer the masterpieces
of Europe, we may betray our own destinies. We must learn to love the
works of Paolo Rosa the artist.'

Does she love Angelo? Elfrida wonders. As she looks into the self
portrait of Paolo Rosa she sees that Angelo resembles him.

'Are you going to kiss me, Angelo Colquhoun?' she asks him.

'We are in love then,' Angelo says.

'Fanny Colquhoun's mad crazy. If dogs could talk, her borzoi might agree
with me. Listen to her saga, Elfrida. The story of her life is forever
changing. Poor husband Shawn Colquhoun seems to have spent his life
following his wife from opera house to opera house. It seems he courted
Fanny in Spain or was it in Dublin? And married her in Paris where
he gave her the furs he pawned at St Petersburg to pay debts he incurred
over roulette in Monte Carlo. Angelo was born in Copenhagen, on a
night of traditional storm, but I have also heard Fanny say she gave birth
to Angelo while singing in a gondola in Venice. Colquhoun was much
given to indulging in extravagances as they seized his imagination, such
as the time he rode through a village at midnight in evening dress, on
a borrowed horse without permission from the farmer, and rang all the
church bells. The climax came when he followed Fanny on stage,
absolutely drunk, and the audience taken by surprise clapped and cheered
believing he was part of the opera. After that, they sailed for Australia
where Colquhoun seems to disappear from the scene. In New Zealand,
Fanny and Angelo waited for a dream to materialize, that is for Paolo
Rosa's house to come to them when Angelo came of age. He may have
told you the saga himself?' Bernadette Mulloy says. She and Elfrida Smith
are talking in a corridor running through the second floor of the house.
Near them is a high-reaching stained glass window. Heavy curtains,
originally a mixture of purple green crimson and blue now faded almost

to lavender-grey, are draped on either side of the figures and scenes that glow in the glass.

'She may overhear you, Bernadette.' Elfrida casts her eyes over the tapestried curtains framing the window's patchwork of colours. Everything in the house of Paolo Rosa has its own beauty, she thinks. The soft pattern of shepherds and shepherdesses formal trees peacocks fountains and sheep and lambs woven into the old curtains adds to the appeal they hold for her.

'No, because I saw her go up the golden stairs to the observatory, followed by Boris, to sing — it's Lucia just at present — and does she make any distinctions between parts played in opera and those she's called on to play in real life?' Bernadette says. 'Crazy mad Fanny, she's an actress, an exhibitionist. Always acting. And Angelo's a modern romantic. Less romantically inclined young men might feel they were on the way to bankruptcy. He lives here on almost nothing other than a romantic conviction about love. We are all trying valiantly to keep his ship afloat which has I understand a debt quite fantastic. We all approve of Angelo but how can you be quite so carried away by him?'

'Do you know what is best for me, Bernadette? Think of these.' Impulsively Elfrida touches one of the curtains. 'One day in the last century someone saw this fabric, fell in love with the design, had it made up into curtains, and hung them up there on the bamboo rod. All these years they've been here. Do you think whoever was responsible for choosing the fabric, it might have been Paolo Rosa himself, would have dreamed the curtains would play an active part in the lives of people who were not even born then? These old curtains are so beautiful, I am sure they do affect my thoughts.'

'You've come under Angelo's influence Elfrida, so strongly you are talking like him. You are thinking Angelo's thoughts.'

'I hadn't begun to think, before I met Angelo. There is something quite fascinating about finding you're in love. It revolutionizes your outlook, Bernadette.'

'So with you it is a case of conquest by love. That did not take long, though longer than some take, today. In love with Angelo Colquhoun? with his philosophy? So he convinces you?'

'Angelo's philosophy is mine now. The spirit of Paolo Rosa, that's Angelo's idea, is in this house.'

Bernadette smiles, as Elfrida looks dreamily at her.

'But what will you do, when they demolish the house?' Bernadette asks, 'when the bulldozers come to change the shape of things?'

'I'll follow Angelo, Bernadette. But they mustn't. Angelo won't let them.'

'Do you live in the world of today, or in a daydream, Elfrida? This morning Fanny and I collided, in the orchard. We were out on an egg-hunt, looking under the agapanthus. "Bernadette darling," Fanny said, "don't you always think, when you find a newlaid egg, of the sweet little bundle of fluff that might have come cheeping into the world! But has Angelo told you? I call it a threat of vandalism. We must all protest. They want to take this house and garden, Bernadette, for their motorway. *There's no love to spare for art Fanny* as my father Bliss Dickens Wilkes used to say. I shall put on deepest black and appeal for mercy. A house steeped in the art of Paolo Rosa — why this very house?" But it seems certain a motorway *will* pass through here, on the very spot where the house stands,' Bernadette Mulloy declares.

'Through Angelo's house?'

'And incited by his mother, mad crazy Fanny, Angelo will protest. Although they say there's such a debt on the estate it can hardly be held to belong to him. For Fanny Colquhoun, this is drama! life! a plot out of Grand Opera.'

'But Paolo Rosa!' Elfrida cries. 'The spirit of Paolo Rosa.'

'In the eyes of the law a motorway is of prime necessity — although admittedly it does go against the grain to say so — more important, Elfrida dear, than the spirit of great-grandpapa Rosa.'

Bringing the conversation to an end with a quizzical glance, given through her large, round glasses, Bernadette walks away along the wide tiled corridor. She wears a bottle-green silk shawl, yellow fringed, and black satin trousers. Elfrida gazes into the translucent segments of the stained glass window, asking herself if Angelo will save the house, once Paolo Rosa's Academy of Art for Young Ladies.

Yvonne du Fresne
Christmas (Shirley Temple is a Wife and Mother)

We are on our Christmas journey, north, home, at the end of term. Sometimes I have been able to think of the car, the dog and me like the Three Wise Men, journeying on in noble simplicity, but heat, petrol stations, ice-cream wrappers, etc., render this nearly impossible.

This Christmas will pass like all the other Christmases. With a brisk infant mistress's trot I make for the car. The dog collapses on the footpath and pants desperately, eyeing me shrewdly. There is no water anywhere. I rehearse: Could I have a drop of that water you have in that handy can behind that petrol-pump there? No, I haven't got a saucer, perhaps you have an old bucket, an old fish-tin, perhaps I could soak my hanky and squeeze some moisture into that poor dehydrated mouth?

How do mothers cope? I bite one piece off a warm Wellington tomato and place it neatly by the dog's front paw. Lovely, juicy. *Eat it*, I say. The dog stiffens, and pathetically removes both paws from dangerous contact.

OK, I say heartlessly. No water from here to home.

We take off, and soon float rather than drive into an alien world of paper-thin leaves and grass in the cruel sun, as if they have been pressed between the pages of a Bible — an old, black, long-ago Bible.

As we drive, a forgotten memory almost jabs through. Some routine I learned last Christmas to fix all Christmases to come, for ever. I must have been very tired last Christmas to have to learn a *routine*.

Now I remember. The first hairline crack in the placid mirror of my year is suddenly here. No husband. No child. Christmas is coming. The Festival of the Mothers and Babies is about to begin.

Daddy, Daddy — she's here. Our little girl.

All right — all right — don't tell us all the punctures you had.

Daddy, she's only just arrived and you are at her the *minute* she steps in the door. The dear little dog, then. Look at her frisking about. Not a bit ruffled by the long trip you've had.

Well, how many broken hearts did you leave behind? Any exciting visitors suddenly dropping out of the skies — unable to bear your absence a moment longer? Any mysterious male voices on toll for this Christmas?

Now leave her alone, dear. Don't nag her the minute she's stepped in the door.

Still, Daddy — our girl — home at last!

Can you still be their girl at forty-five?

The only toll call I'll get will be, 'Madam, we regret to inform you that your house burned down last night. The fire appears to have been started by two six-year-olds.'

We have had tea. The dog has had two biscuits and is lying — freed from terror at last — log-like under my father's chair. There is no news except interesting titbits about my house.

Did I tell you that the geraniums came out after all? I got twenty-three cuttings off that bush I found and now I've got twenty-three geranium bushes all exactly the same colour. All sisters — well — brothers and sisters I suppose you'd say.

There is a short silence.

Nancy has new slip-covers, says my mother. Dark. It'll keep Clara's children from dirtying them. Just fancy — two children and there, Nancy is a grandmother already.

Entering very dangerous ground here.

We say to them, don't we, Daddy — grandchildren! Wouldn't be bothered with them. Upsetting everybody. And the furniture! This way we've got you every Christmas. Come next year and Nancy and Bob will be cooling their heels — an empty house — he'll have *his* parents and off they'll go. Clara wouldn't think twice about the loneliness here.

It is my turn.

Clara's *young* isn't she! She hasn't any proper job qualifications has she? Not like you, dear — with all those exams you've got. We look at them and we say Huh, don't we, Daddy? Keep your grandchildren. We wouldn't be bothered with them.

Clara was nine when I was twenty.

Clara is a wife. Clara is a mother.

Shirley Temple is a wife and mother.

And Princess Margaret is a wife and mother.

It is very hot. But I go to the library to get out Stone and Church and *Aspects of the Gifted Child's Development*, etc. so that I will go back to work remembering the meaning of dichotomy and so on, when I am using them in spirited conversation in the staffroom.

I am getting out Stone and Church and *The Gifted Child*, etc. to show the librarian, my parents and any visitors picking up a book after I have carelessly strewn the lot about the house, that I have a mission, almost a vocation, to teach. The word will go around again. Oh, no — she has a vocation for teaching. Not marriage for her — she is a brilliant teacher, they say.

The high soft singing is beginning. 'What Child Is This?', 'I Wonder As I Wander'. I check the defences. No secret photograph album full of little godchildren and cousins. No desire to linger by other people's prams. A thankful getting out from under at end of term.

Ho, I say. Bring on anything you may have in your bag. Even a lost Child in the snow.

I see myself unguarded in the bathroom mirror, a dangerous Lorelei wreathed in steam, luring the traveller to his death.

I don't want to feel like the Lorelei.

I don't want to meet any more travellers, all brave as bulls, and running to their mothers at the most desperate moment. When do we stop thinking we are princesses in disguise? There I am, rather fat, sitting at the breakfast table drinking coffee in the early-morning sun with my dear love, rather lined, rather fat. Who was it who said I'll build you a little sod house by the Waimakariri, I'll build you a little slab house by the Manawatu? Someone who said Let us seek the wild cattle in the scrub when the sun is high, let us sit and sing lullabies to our sheep when the sun sinks in the west.

Oh, we would have been honoured as the most famous pioneers in all of New Zealand. You for the invention of a revolutionary shearing shed. And me for general excellence in the management of the camp-oven.

Tonight is the night of the lighting of the Christmas tree. The Christmas tree is thin and going brown. We closed the deal at fifty cents with the Minisuper Market. Now Father is draping the vigorous green fairy light cord over it and tying everything down strongly. The tree seems to give no more heartbeats under this last burden. Father switches on the lights and there they are as if new. Once again I am swept over by the pink light. It is terribly pink. You should have outgrown me, it signals.

Is ours the prettiest tree in the street? Mother goes out into the dark garden to judge. There are no lights anywhere in the discreet house over the street — shrouded in sensible trees. They probably wrap all their rubbish carefully in newspaper over there. No nonsense with fairy lights for *them*.

The anonymous battered State houses still have their front curtains tied in knots and half a car by their front doors. Father, coming back from his observation post in the kitchen, reports that the Mayor's house on the hill has not only a Christmas tree that switches on and off by itself but an extra row of coloured light bulbs lining the downstairs windows. Confusion reigns and out of it Mother's voice says clearly that of course he would have access to the city decoration equipment and has just used some illegally on his own house. She judges our tree the most natural — lights in clusters here and there, and not artificial rows of coloured light bulbs making a vulgar show and nothing else. We eat supper, observing our tree narrowly. The pink light still signals to me.

Christmas is just a new problem in each year, and I've licked it, I think. I've got over the lullabies, we've got over the Christmas decorations with babies in. I've got over the neighbour's children's excitement; I've got over the dog's trusting eyes, as if he too wanted me to take him to town to see Father Christmas. Please God, we'll get over Christmas. The house, when I go outside, looks just the same ranch house set in browning Christmas grass as it ever did, except I am no longer riding my bike round and round the lawn to stem my dangerously rising excitement.

Today I took twenty minutes to make my bed. Tomorrow I'll take even longer, sitting around mooning at my two feet. So now, all right, it's the day of Christmas Eve. The shops are telling us that soon they're shutting, and are we ready? Never ready, me.

We look anxiously at the sky all morning. What's it going to do? Is it going to rain or is it going to blow?

Oh Cecil, we can't have a blowing Christmas. I couldn't bear that. Can you think what it would be like now? Hmm? Can you just imagine it with all that wind blowing and the back lawn muddy and nowhere for the dog to run? All of us cooped up inside? All fighting. Do you think I should bake some more little cakes — some Nutty Chews?

The telephone rings. It is my younger aunt. She asks How are we getting on? Are we tired yet? She is very tired. She has been working all morning and now she just thinks she'll do out the cupboards. Do we think it would be a good idea if she tidied the cupboards? We urge No, think of all your visitors coming, be bright for them, Nancy. Yes, she says, she must be bright for them, and not exhausted.

Over the road some children are starting to run senselessly in and out of one of the houses. It is a very dirty house with curtains knotted at the windows, not new-washed, new-ironed for Christmas. They look up at the sky almost as if they're going to run into their mother any minute now with the signal, He is here, Mother; just the hoofs of the first reindeer we can see, coming over the sheep at the top of the hill.

Now, are we going to make some Nutty Chews? Where did we find that last good recipe?

I have a new recipe, here it is in my glossy new book of Kiwi Cooking that I brought all the way from Wellington just for you to bake Nutty Chews from for us all.

But that's not the same recipe, dear, that hasn't got condensed milk in it. They must have hundreds of recipes for Nutty Chews by now, all different. I know I have the right one. Think of the Nutty Chews, think of them when we had them years and years ago, when they always tasted better four days after they were made. It's the condensed milk makes them like that.

I go into the sitting-room and check just once more to make sure we haven't forgotten one tiny little thing, and to see if the Christmas tree is looking slightly different. Nothing's going to happen to that tree. The lights are going to come on and that's going to be all. But I still go into the sitting-room just to check up. The room is so clean that it threatens us. It says, I am waiting for the signal that tells me that the moment is about to begin. What are we going to do? I think All right, we are going to come in here, and the TV announcer is going to tell us Merry Christmas, and we'll smile back and then we'll look at the Christmas tree and the pink light is going to save me again by making me see in my inward eye the 1933 pink striped pencil, the 1939 candy floss. And I will think, happily, This is the world's birthday, then I think No, only two thousand years of birthdays, and I think back to the Greeks and the Egyptians before that, and the thought catches me by the throat again, What is going to happen when we all die? Where are we going to go? Where are all those slick smooth answers I knew when I was fifteen and playing Chopin? They've temporarily gone. I must go to the library and

look up P for Plato and A for Aristotle, and no skipping, read right
through them, so that I can shelter behind those great men. And I think
O God, here I am *wanting to stay* for the first time in my life, and now
I have to think of shuffling off this globe with a calm and happy heart.
And I may never find the shoulder of my dear for my weary head.

The phone rings early. It is my older aunt. And she says How are we
all getting on with The Work? We reassure her that we're just bearing
it. After all, she says, even though you have only got one child coming
home for Christmas you still have *something*. Oh hell, here we go again.
I frown at my cup of tea. When I see the next crib I will think OK,
there you are a baby, but you'll be mine when you're five. You'll be in
my room and I'll teach you reading and when I'm feeling especially strong
I'll pick you up in my arms, and say Whose girl are you? or Whose boy
are you? All forty-three of you.

It isn't only lullabies that come thick and fast on every radio — but
lullabies for a *lost* child outside on a snowy night. The feelings of the
parents at birth I dare not even think about. Peace, peace, after this
tremendous moment. How would I drift into sleep with my dear one's
shoulder protectively *there*, not bolting away.

I am *useless* at self-discipline about dangerous thoughts.
         Oho, I rage.
         What about that picture long ago in *The Family of Man* of a pregnant
woman a still centre in a street that was a blur of rushing cars and people?
Only herself at peace? What about that years-ago pregnant woman in
a grey pinafore holding a woven bag and her children's hands peacefully
waiting for the lights to change by Kirkcaldie's? Why did I witlessly
imagine her home and the children playing and her dear coming home
from work and their both having the secret look of love that she had by
that traffic light?
         Why, why, why did I put myself there, keep those pictures in my
mind, *let myself drift*?

Hide me O my Saviour hide me — hide me hills — make a thick blanket
of folded hills around my unpainted house. And let the rooms be soft
and warm — and the windows frosted over with salt so that a parchment
glow warms the plants in their pots, and me. I will never complain again,

oh Lord — even if you unleash the strongest northerly gales and we can't see out of the sea windows for weeks. I start a helpless imaginary wander through my house, mooning out of windows at blonde summer grass, sheep lying in the hollows for their afternoon nap. I have lost myself. *Who am I?*

> *Miss Taylor — he has taken my pencil.*
> *Who has taken your pencil Helen?*
> *That Richard — he has taken my pencil and licked my name off.*
> *I didn't take no pencil Miss. This is my pencil, my pink pencil.*
> *Helen, wasn't your pencil* green?
> *My* old *pencil green Miss Taylor — not my new* pink *one. . . .*

I'll have to concentrate on busily writing new ideas for Social Studies and Language in Action when I get back, if I ever get out of Christmas.

And why haven't I new ideas for Social Studies and Language in Action written down in fat bursting notebooks? I've been lazy. I haven't covered acres of pages daily with little ideas, nitty-gritty slog. I'll have to do it — spade by spade. I can see my pen slowly moving like an ant on a plain.

There, the neighbours will say. Do you see that woman in the sunporch of that house on the hill? It's her holiday really, but she sits down regularly every afternoon and you just see her writing page after page. Never nibbling fattening toast and spying on her neighbours with binoculars. Just working.

And *here* is the Queen. Mother gets right down in front of the screen — crouched like a worshipper — but only to give Her Majesty's carved chair a raking inspection. Father gives a helpless vulgar trapped snore. But I sit dully on, recollecting that we were girls together. Both of us wore tweed coats, felt hats, long socks and stout walking-shoes. But — ah me — she has had four children and one husband. I have had forty-three children a year, and no husband. We both look worn out. And still only half-way to senility. I think of the stream of workbooks I will have to invent before then. She is thinking of all the luncheons and smiles ahead. She clears her throat and sets her lips in a way that tugs at my memory. She is not pleased, she tells us severely, with the situation in Ireland. I feel guilty that we have caused her such worry. Then my memory clears. It is my old head prefect giving us a wigging. We have not *worked* hard enough, we have not pulled together. We politely sit. A Merry Christmas to you *all*. The very same vowel sound. I remember with shame the many

merry occasions when I did my successful imitation of her broadcast to
the children of the Dominions at the beginning of the war. Higher and
higher — like piglet's voice — over all that gunfire of static.

How lovely, says Mother. She looks *so* nervous. And tired. Still.
Never mind.

Tired, scoffs Father. If she were out, holding down a decent job
somewhere, or just democratically biking through the streets.

Mother bridles with imperial languor. You don't understand, I hear
as I bolt to the kitchen, and soothing cups of tea for all.

The visiting to all the family starts. My old, new country house is dragged
up. It sounds, says my uncle solemnly, like a good place for a homicide.
An old house like that perched on a hill by itself and only the sea in front.
Did you, he asks Father, as one who never neglects these things for *his*
children, did you consider that when she took it? I presume there is thick
cover right up to the house?

A tiny picture flashes into my mind. I see a white-haired sixty-year-
old child of nature, me, come wavering up my path. She talks to birds
hopping ahead of her; she brings in the escaped convict she finds shaking
with fever behind the spare water-tank. The birds and the convict stay
with her for ever. Thunderbolts never fall on that house ever again.

Well, bluffs Father, she's a big girl now, Henry. She should be able
to ring the police by herself. He bares his teeth in a hostile smile at me.

It's so *lonely*! cries my younger aunt.

She could be hit on the head, shrills my older aunt, and left for a
week! She only has that dog, and that useless cat! cries Mother. And
they don't need much money to hit anyone on the head for these days.
Just the thrill. A loud whistle — a loud whistle's the thing! shouts Henry.
Just one blast.

The gentle little old lady of the first pictures turns into a tough little
old lady dressed in a track suit and tennis shoes, crouching behind the
spare water-tank, gripping a whistle.

What does homicide mean again? (Say lady, ring Homicide — there's
been a —) Ah yes, now I recollect.

The visiting to the old family friends begins.

I should swallow my fright and go. I should be able to keep my head
at my age and not smile too much, not talk too quickly, and sit,
occasionally smiling with that old wing of silver-blonde hair sheltering
my gently experienced face, and lean against a veranda post, not the

shoulder of my dear. For will he be there? Not anywhere there, I fear.
I will speak with the fed-up husband and his wife, answering me with
their eyes searching for their missing children. Oh yes, they will gladly
cry, we know Wellington! Did you ever know Dustin Crescent in
Wadestown? A little house with a dear little plum tree? The usual death-
sweat breaks over me. I was in the next street to them, those days. *I must
not ask them*: Did you ever see a man and a woman walking down your
street — amazed and silent with love — and see a lamp go on, and hear
Mozart, and see even the outside of that awful green concrete house on
your corner grow solid with midnight love and constancy?

And how is your little house? they all ask vaguely, handing the plate
out to my father with a merry smile, while he pops his eyes and blows
his cheeks out at yet more rich Christmas cake.

All right, I'll tell you, I rage, biting cake.

It has peaceful white walls and a solid floor. I have almost forgotten
it! Then my alarm ceases. I can see a streak of winter sun lying across
its stone hearth. A fire is burning. There I am, writing on my very own
writing block in my very own armchair. Very settled. Then *who* is this
nervous woman eating fruit-cake and smiling too much?

I go to the library to take back Stone and Church and *The Gifted Child*,
etc., from where they have been lying under my bed, eclipsed by all the
news about how to eat more and weigh less, and ways to redecorate a
mews cottage, from my mother's magazines. The sad tourists and I
lethargically pass each other in the sun-scalded street. O Lord, I say,
as I see a cross-section of all of our faces in Woolworth's regrettable street
mirror. It is not mothers and babies we should be thinking about at
Christmas — it is all of us — all shot to pieces by shovelfuls of damaging
Christmas.

Oh, I hadn't planned all this at all. Not having to think about life
and death. I just wanted to lie in a warm chair and dream over comforting
Christmas magazines, full of paintings and diagrams of galleys and
Victorian trains.

How could we plan a new Christmas next Christmas? Have trees
in our streets laden with our gifts for each other? Manage to lure out
the invisible gentleman with the stiff leg and his silent housekeeper from
their lair behind the trees that shroud their windows and say Happy
Christmas my dears to us all? And then sit and talk and touch each other's
hands for comfort against the year to come? In the library the word

'Depression' on a magazine catches my eye, as it has over the past few days. My wet fingers leave clumsy dark marks over all that clean organized print.

> This is the time of the year in many parts of the world when the affliction of depression cuts deepest. Psychologists are so familiar with the phenomenon of Christmas depression that they have given it a name — The Holiday Paradox. There are a number of obvious reasons why the depression occurs. The season inexorably stirs up deep-seated childhood and family traumas.

It wasn't me, just me. It wasn't me alone!

> Christmas celebrations stimulate a desire to regress to childhood innocence and normal expectations in life. And when this is contrasted with painful realities, psychic crisis results. . . .

Thousands of us, reaching for the telephone for a psychiatrist, praying for one to appear at the other side of the table, ready and waiting, and paid for by Social Security.

> Even the most well-adjusted personalities suffer the pangs of the Holiday Paradox at one time or another — and then go on to an uneventful recovery. . . .

And soon, with all the other well-adjusted personalities, I find my Holiday Paradox is over. The endless summer world arches over our blonding hair. We stray through long dry grass, staring and dreaming. The summer clicks and hums about us. Soon we are specks, dots, lost in the long, droning summer afternoons. O Lord, if not a dramatic conversion to religion this Christmas, in place of a family could you not give us — the newly-ageing — a space before we have to go; a little more time to sit and talk and be together, in the tender evening light by the sea?

Phyllis Gant
The Revolver

Ted had not yet missed the revolver. Helen dreaded his looking for it, at some time of crisis, perhaps — a prowler in the house, a more than ordinarily savage quarrel with her — and finding it gone. What would she tell him? What *could* she tell him? She pictured the face he would wear, appropriate to these situations: the blank disbelief of finding the weapon gone, of her professing to know nothing about it; of his being overwhelmed, momentarily, by helplessness. If it were a quarrel, his rage at such a pitch that, unarmed, he would attack her physically, perhaps kill her. Less likely, though, than with that bloody gun — revolver, Helen corrected herself; Ted hated this kind of inexactitude; he was scathing about people who lumped all firearms under the term 'gun', called unfired cartridges 'bullets'.

Helen discovered the revolver soon after they were married. Ted told her she was to keep quiet about it; no one must know. It was not registered; nor was there sufficient reason, under law, that would allow him to keep it. Later, when there was an arms amnesty, Helen asked him to turn it in; he looked at her, amazed, and said, 'Don't be silly — I can't do that.'

'Why not?'

'One is safer, that's why not.'

'*Safer*? — any number of people don't have one of those things tucked away in a drawer. Why should you feel that much more threatened?'

He explained, with exaggerated patience, that his parents had always kept firearms of one sort or other in the house; this was seen simply as a matter of self-preservation in those parts of Africa where they'd lived, as necessary as food and drink and shelter. It was something he had grown up with. By the time he was eleven he was hunting with his father and as good a shot with a .22 as any man. His mother, too, had her regular practice; the old man would get her out there with the target board set up and she'd blaze away like a champion with this very weapon — it was a few years old, but none the worse for that. He showed her where the cartridges were: they were never to be moved; there were just six; he would not be able to replace them.

Every now and then Ted took the revolver out and cleaned and oiled it. 'Where is it? — my God, where is it?' he would say, finding it gone, his tone signalling rising panic. 'Helen — where the hell are you? — did you shift it? The revolver!' — his voice, now, barely more than a whisper — 'and the cartridges.'

Yes, that would be when it was likely to come out, when he set about giving the revolver routine attention, with the doors locked, the bedroom door closed, the curtains in place, allowing enough light but no chance of any passing glimpse of his activity.

Helen twitted him about his caution; he made such a fuss about secrecy, was so preoccupied with security; you'd think he had a body stowed away in the house. 'I suppose you realize,' he said, 'I'd be for the high jump if this were found out — what's more, the weapon would be confiscated.'

Anyway, apart from the cleaning, he did take it out occasionally; when there were unidentifiable noises outside, he put the bloody thing under his pillow. 'You took it out yourself — don't you remember? I do. Don't go blaming *me* for your negligence!'

It was worth a try, thought Helen. She just couldn't see him buying it, that's all; Ted could be accused of many things, but negligence wasn't one of them.

Helen weighed up which would be the more dangerous situation for her. The greater risk posed by a major threat from outside would deflect his wrath, meantime, at least. A really bad scene between them would make his temper worse, but in all probability would cost her less than her life. *Would* he kill her? The comparative calm of the routine situation would be the more demanding.

Where would she go from there? She could deny all knowledge of it — 'I never go to that drawer. They're all your papers and things' — he wouldn't believe her, but if she continued in her denial, what could he do? He would have to accept it. Would he? 'If you didn't, who did?' Who, indeed!

He would question her, asking, insistent, persistent, over and over; bullying, striking her, probably, then, afraid — she felt the cold on her own brow — cajoling: 'Do try to remember, sweetie. Did you go out at some time and forget to lock up?' And if she said yes, what then? He couldn't inquire; he couldn't go to the police.

That, on the whole, seemed to be the best course. 'Yes, I'm so sorry.

One day when I went to the shops — I don't suppose I was away more than ten minutes. It must have been then. I'm usually so particular about locking up.'

'Careless bitch!' He would slap her, hit her about the head, perhaps punch her arms and chest, kick her; then, spent, he'd be as helpless as ever. He'd work out what he would say if he were accused of having had possession. He would think of something.

But it would recur. His not knowing would always confront them. Helen doubted her ability to stand up to it; one day she would break, and tell the truth.

She could tell the truth now. Now, literally? Before he found it was missing? Or not until? Some time when things were good between them. One Sunday morning; as they lay, not having to get up, kidding about who was going to get whom a cup of tea, she would say — No; she simply could not hear herself saying it. There'd be stops and starts. 'Yes? — go on.' And, once embarked, she would have to go on.

Could she ask Bob to tell him? 'Are you mad, woman?' Any scenario she liked to think up included that; she asked it of herself — the idea of putting forward Bob. . . . That's what he said when she turned up with the revolver in her bag. Couldn't he have been simply someone she went to for help? Oh, come off it! — it was out of the question.

But — the truth! Simply to tell him. . . . Attack! — that was the answer. She was being defensive: why should *she* be defensive? — put *him* on the defensive; he was the one that was in the wrong. He shouldn't have had the bloody thing.

And apart from the present matter (since truth was the subject), he was a bastard and she ought to leave him. If she told him the truth she'd be leaving him, all right. She would make her plans to go, then tell him.

Tell him? Why? If she went, why tell him?

Because he would follow her when he found out. She'd give no address. He would find her. She would tell him to go; he was trespassing; if he didn't, she would call the police. She would not argue. 'I have nothing to say to you,' she would say, and shut the door.

It wouldn't work like that. She would ask him in. Before she could remember to *say nothing* they'd be in the thick of it. Ted would think she had the revolver with her; it would make him the more determined; he would see that he took her by surprise.

Bob would not go away with her. He made that clear from the start. 'I made that clear from the start,' he said. She couldn't go to him. He would launch into ponderosities that began, 'My wife — ', 'My wife and I — '; these would founder, high and dry on the shoals of his inadequacy.

He wasn't inadequate, however, when he took the revolver away from her. He said, after, he had dropped it from the bridge into the river. Appalled, he told her that the cartridge she had so idiotically inserted was in the next chamber to be fired. He demanded that she bring the other cartridges to him, and she did; these, too, he dropped into the river, going at midnight and taking heaven knows what risks. He hammered her about her intention: she asked herself that. She didn't know. Nothing. There was no intention. She was no worse off than usual, rather, perhaps, the contrary: the sun shone, birds sang; Ted, mowing the lawn, playing home and garden, strode up and down, looking more or less content, behind the racketing mower.

Helen couldn't imagine leaving him, not after ten years together. It was a long time in habitude — but that, surely, was *all* it was? 'At the same time, I was fascinated by it. I was making the bed, and it occurred to me to — '

It was absurd that a grown man should be so dependent on having a gun — oh, stuff him! — in the house. Bloody childish. 'I took it out and held it between my hands. My heart pounded because I knew Ted — you — could have come in at any moment.

'I used to read *True Detective Stories* when I was a kid — I knew John Dillinger, Pretty Boy Floyd, Ma Baker and the rest as well as — better than — I knew the neighbours. I wondered what it would be like to have — a gun in my hand.'

Yes, she could hear herself saying it; it would be a relief. And, after all, what could he do?

Once she started there'd be no stopping her. 'I flicked the cylinder aside and it seemed only logical to put something in it. So I put a cartridge in one of the holes. I didn't choose; it was random — I was curious, that was all. Then I couldn't get it out. And I couldn't put the revolver away, loaded. I couldn't tell you what I'd done. I pressed the muzzle into the pillow and I squeezed the trigger — yes! I can scarcely believe it myself; I was in a dream. Nothing happened. I squeezed the trigger again; and again, panicking. I stood there by the side of the bed, terrified, thinking, oh, for about half an hour. Then I thought of taking it to Bob.'

No — she must keep Bob out of it. That omission wouldn't trouble her conscience — no question of conscience if she could get away with it; the certainty of discovery forced her to these projections.

She would say she was afraid with it in the house; it was safely out of the way, now, in the mud at the bottom of the river. No one would find it.

Ted would be relieved. She would wait until he went to the drawer. Why precipitate the crisis? He might never clean and oil it again — too true!

She would leave him one day. She could not imagine spending the rest of her life — or his — with him. How does one do these things? 'Bye now, I'm off.'

'Off where?'

'I'm leaving you.' *Que sera, sera.*

'You must be joking.'

She *could* be decisive. In buying clothes: she'd put it off for months. Then she'd go out to buy shoes, a dress, a hat. It never happened that she came home with just one; she ended up with two or even three pairs of shoes, two or three hats, any number of dresses. All had suited her; it was too hard to choose; she had taken the lot. *This* was decisive?

It was strange, sitting here, silence between them, the room full of chat from the television; strange to think she could get up, turn off the set, speak. 'There is something I must tell you.' How corny!

Her voice; that mere vibration: the difference between speaking and not speaking. A breath away.

They watched, without fail, the current affairs programme. She would gain his attention if she switched that off, that was certain. Even then, of course, she could change her mind. She would not have committed herself. 'Why did you do that?' He would look up, annoyed. Wait for it to finish.

Then her voice. Just testing. 'Ted. . . .' No.

'I was just wondering if I could have the car tomorrow.'

'Did you have to turn the bloody telly off to ask me that?'

The sense of fascination was on her, that detached curiosity. Would she speak? Would she tell him?

Helen got up and went to the set. She paused, standing aside so as not to block Ted's view. She drew in her breath and reached out.

Patricia Grace
Mirrors

So out under a hanging sky with my neck in danger from the holes in
my slippers. Hey slippers. Watch out now, we've both seen younger days
remember. Hurry me down to the end of the drive for the milk. Milk.
Then turn me and we'll scuff back inside together to where the heater's
plugged, pressing a patch of warmth into the corner where I'll sit with
my back to the window, drinking tea. By gee.

Woke early this morning into shouldered silence with light just
signing in, and thought how it was, how it could be, to sit silent in a
silent house, in a warm corner drinking tea. Just me.

Or instead, I thought, I could as usual sleep. And wake in an hour
to the foot thuds and voice noise. Doors and drawers, and perhaps with
his arm reaching to turn me towards him. But my feet made up my mind.
Poking from under the covers ready to find the floor, dangling. Two limp
fillets of cod. How did you get like that feet? That shape, that colour
— haven't seen you since the summer and don't know you lately. We
found the floor and poked you into these two grinners, or gaspers. Shuffled
to the wardrobe for a gown and then to the bathroom to wash.

Six drops no more, and only to keep the record straight. Because
I nag them in the mornings. In the mornings I issue lists — to flush the
toilet, to wash, to comb. Not to swing on chairs, to grab, eat like pigs,
fight. But none of that this early morning. No lists, no nagging. This
next half hour's mine. Only six I promise, a quick flick is all.

Into the kitchen. Plug the heater, plug the jug. What shall it be,
coffee or tea? What do you say slippers? — your tongues hang out like
mine.

Yes tea, but you see, no milk.

Can't spoil the cup for want of. Milk. And it'll only take a moment,
unplug the jug. Step quietly, sleep has ears remember. Trip me and it'll
be the end of you two I promise, trippers. Turn handle and out. Out
under a sky filled and sagging.

Dog next door is up before me and in a bad mood this morning.
Anyway I don't want to talk to him, I'm hurrying. He turns his back
and huffs, snuffing the ground, big footing through silvered grass and

scaring a bird. That was perhaps finding a snail to take and knock on stone. Leaving little specked brown shell pieces splintered on rock, and the morsel gone.

And cat prints ahead of me too. Cautious stars in the soft soil where the garden begins — she's dug a hole there perhaps, somewhere among the rusting silver beet and the holed cabbages. Somewhere in the early hours she excreted precisely, covered, and walked away. Perhaps. After roaming the darkness, pressing out soft stars on to the whole length and breadth of the night, that's right. Eyes specked like cut onion.

Quickly now. And remember I've come only for want of a few drops. Of milk. So I'll keep my mind on it. The corner waits warm and quiet. A nudge of a switch will set the jug uttering. So go. No time for star gazing. Get flapping, flappers, it'll rain. See how the sky reaches down. See its uncertainty — there a rinsing-water colour that's not the telly ad kind with *diamanté* bubbles rising and good enough to drink, but which is the real kind, yes. From the tub full of jeans, or load of jerseys and socks — and there, shot through with green, brown, black and purple. Growing and shrinking. Pocked and pimpled like mould. And I will sit warm listening to it, alone, the rain plunging, if I hurry. In a warm corner with my throat scalded by the flowing of hot liquid.

Here now, and I can reach into the box. For milk. Turn my back and go. No need this morning to look past the gate, over the road to the sea, to see, to determine its mood, find out about the island. They'll both be there mid-morning, tomorrow, next year, so go. But no, the gulls rise screaming.

See how they beat their wings into the wind this morning, their legs dangle useless like shreds of red or yellow balloon before they tuck them out of sight.

And now my eyes are spiked, winkled out from their sockets on bright pins, and swivelling. See how the horizon is buckled by the waves' leaping, and how the waves ride in bumper to bumper each side of the island, then forget which way to go. Face each other snarling. Pounce and fall back, chop and slap.

Kung Fu Fighting,
Yes, Yes,
Kung Fu Fighting,
Yes, Yes.

The island like the old dog grouching, in a bad mood this morning.
But nearer to shore the waves remember and reassemble, find the

right curve and come gnashing in like great grinning mouthfuls of teeth. Heaping wads of weed on to the shore and tossing out white sticks. And further along they climb stacked rocks and splinter into marbled drops, wind hanging, then slow motion falling. Fingering in over ledges and into crevices, then evacuating as small stones roll and spin.

And this afternoon the children will walk there, take up the white sticks and stir the weed heaps to spark the small firework displays of leaping sand fleas.

They'll turn the tessellating stones for sticky fish which will play dead even after being pressed quite firmly with prising thumbs. They'll look into the rioting water for new things because once there was a netted glass ball from Japan, and once a bag of drowned cats, and once a corked bottle which could have contained a message but didn't. Once there was a condom floating, rim upward, which didn't look so out of place really and could have been a herring or a cod, open mouthed, coming to the surface to feed.

And they'll yell out over the water I wish it was summer.

I want to come in.

Wish it was summer.

I wish.

Summer.

I want I want.

I wish.

And they'll see their words curl in under the waves' furl and watch the words hurled back fragmented at their feet retreating.

And now there is the first drop, on the back of my hand as I turn. Hurry now. Safely do you hear. Next door's plum has one white flower and twig ends groaning. She'll be home tomorrow with her new baby and a bagful of black knitting.

I'm going, she'd yelled. But I came back for my knitting. And she had waved a plastic bag of needles and black skeins. So this minute while others sit in bed making white shells and fans, and loop up row upon row of holes in two-ply on twelves, she turns out an enormous black jersey cabled and twisted, for her husband who will be ashamed to have anything so wonderful. He will give it away and she will be pleased about the story she has to tell. There will be two flowers tomorrow perhaps, or more.

The next drop now, and there look. Damn dog. Hurry. I'm going to hit him hard with a bottle of milk. He sets himself at the top of the path, by the front door. He closes his eyes, hunches his shoulders and lowers his hind quarters as the stool elongates from under his tail. Hangs, as I come yelling, my neck in jeopardy. Slowly drops, coiling back on itself like a suicidal scorpion. He doesn't look at me, doesn't hear, but lowers his tail, lifts his head and walks off. His morosity parcelled away.

And all I wanted was a half hour I tell you, not great rain bullets fired at me as I look for a spade, not skin lumping from the cold and a mess to clean. Only a warm few moments and breathing in and out, drinking tea. Time to look at the folds in the curtains and to watch the grey reels of darkness rotating in the room's corners and growing paler. A time to be you see.

But now they'll be up. Opening and closing. Peeing, washing. Dressing. And he'll be on the march, opening windows. Letting fresh air in, instead of warm in bed. And I could have, if I'd thought, stayed. I'd have been warm right now and still asleep perhaps. Could have turned to him and we'd have coupled quite lazily. Warmly. Shared a quiet half hour, if.

But instead I make a vee-shaped hole with two thrusts of the spade while the rain assaults and the flesh bulges. Damn dog. Sat and shat. Then walked away, quite simply that.

Now look you've trodden in it, you'll feed the fire true you two. You're done for. I shunt what's left of dog into the vee and cover. I whip you two off and run with you under the despatching sky and throw you into the incinerator. Goodbye. Then hose the wretched feet blueing under the sudden slam of water.

And now I step in on to the mat, gasping, and they have come to look at me.

Why?

Did you run round in the rain?

Barefooted?

In a dressing gown?

In pyjamas?

And leave the heater on?

And a cup. Waiting?

I'm in a mood, like dog — and island — and won't answer.

They stare, then the boys go back to their hunt for football jerseys. Two diving in the washing and the other hanging from a shelf in the hot-water cupboard. And I won't help them, won't say folded on the top shelf. Up there. The two little ones will not take their eyes away from my mood. They stare.

So at last I tell them grumpily I trod in it and had to hose my feet. And throw my slippers in the incinerator. Dog bog.

Dog bog? Their faces flower.

What colour was it?

We found a white one once.

On the footpath outside the shop.

We took half each.

To draw with.

On the road.

But it broke.

And fell into crumbs.

They want me to laugh but I'm flinging off clothes and rubbing my hair. Why should I laugh? Why don't they leave me alone? Pickers. Naggers.

And the other two will get up soon and yell about the noise that's going on. They'll turn on their music and grumble.

In the kitchen and lounge the back windows are open and fresh air pours in. He is striding, but stops to look at me, and at the mood I'm in.

Your feet, he says. Put something on them. Slippers.

She burnt them.

She trod in dog shit and now her slippers are in the incinerator. For burning.

Burning.

He is all washed and combed and vigorous looking; the jug steams and he has made the porridge. His eyes are full of what he will do this morning zipped into an oilskin and booted to the knees. Mirrored I see two barrow loads of seaweed for the garden, forked out, spread and reeking. A trench for the kitchen scraps and two new rows of cabbage plants.

Now the three boys are in, geared for their games.

Burning?

Your slippers?

Why?

Waiting for me to break silence, to cry perhaps, or laugh.

He has gone out and returned with a pair of his socks, his fingertips touching over the ball that the socks have been rolled into.

Put them on. We'll feed these ones and have a cup of tea before the other two get up. Grumbling. Turning their songs up loud.

And along with the seaweed and the scrap trench and the planted cabbages, I see mirrored I missed you this morning. And could have had a half hour quiet, together.

We play at ten.

The three of us. At ten.

If the rain stops.

And this afternoon I'm going down the beach.

To see.

To find something from Japan.

I wish I saw.

The dog.

Bog.

So I pull the socks over the two fillets of feet, purpled, and shut two windows.

On the plum tree. Next door, I say. There's one new flower. And twig ends all ready to heave.

Keri Hulme
One Whale, Singing

The ship drifted on the summer night sea.

'It is a pity,' she thought, 'that one must come on deck to see the stars. Perhaps a boat of glass, to see the sea streaming past, to watch the nightly splendour of stars.' Something small jumped from the water, away to the left. A flash of phosphorescence after the sound, and then all was quiet and starlit again.

They had passed through krillswarms all day. Large areas of the sea were reddish-brown, as though an enormous creature had wallowed ahead of the boat, streaming blood.

'Whale-feed,' she had said, laughing and hugging herself at the thought of seeing whales again.

'Lobster-krill,' he had corrected, pedantically.

The crustaceans had swum in their frightened jerking shoals, mile upon mile of them, harried by fish that were in turn pursued and torn by larger fish.

She thought, it was probably a fish after krill that had leaped then. She sighed, stroking her belly. It was the lesser of the two evils to go below now, so he didn't have an opportunity to come on deck and suggest it was better for the coming baby's health, and hers, of course, that she came down. The cramped cabin held no attraction: all that was there was boneless talk, and one couldn't see stars, or really hear the waters moving.

. . .

Far below, deep under the keel of the ship, a humpback whale sported and fed. Occasionally, she yodelled to herself, a long undulating call of content. When she found a series of sounds that pleased, she repeated them, wove them into a band of harmonious pulses.

Periodically she reared to the surface, blew, and slid smoothly back under the sea in a wheel-like motion. Because she was pregnant, and at the tailend of the southward migration, she had no reason now to leap and display on the surface.

She was not feeding seriously; the krill was there, and she swam amongst them, forcing water through her lips with her large tongue, stranding food amongst the baleen. When her mouth was full, she swallowed. It was leisurely, lazy eating. Time enough for recovering her full weight when she reached the cold seas, and she could gorge on a ton and a half of plankton daily.

Along this coast, there was life and noise in plenty. Shallow grunting from a herd of fish, gingerly feeding on the fringes of the krill shoal. The krill themselves, a thin hiss and crackle through the water. The interminable background clicking of shrimps. At times, a wayward band of sound like bass organ-notes sang through the chatter, and to this the whale listened attentively, and sometimes replied.

The krill thinned; she tested, tasted the water. Dolphins had passed recently. She heard their brief commenting chatter, but did not spend time on it. The school swept round ahead of her, and vanished into the vibrant dark.

. . .

He had the annoying habit of reading what he'd written out loud. 'We can conclusively demonstrate that to man alone belongs true intelligence and self-knowledge.'

He coughs.

Taps his pen against his lips. He has soft, wet lips, and the sound is a fleshy slop! slop!

She thinks:

> Man indeed! How arrogant! How ignorant! Woman would be as correct, but I'll settle for humanity. And it strikes me that the quality humanity stands in need of most is true intelligence and self-knowledge.

'For instance, Man alone as a species, makes significant artefacts, and transmits knowledge in permanent and durable form.'

He grunts happily.

'In this lecture, I propose to. . . .'

> But how do they know? she asks herself. About the passing on of knowledge among other species? They may do it in ways beyond our capacity to understand . . . that we are the only ones to make artefacts I'll grant you, but that's because us needy little adapts

have such pathetic bodies, and no especial ecological niche. So hooks and hoes, and steel things that gouge and slay, we produce in plenty. And build a wasteland of drear ungainly hovels to shelter our vulnerable hides.

She remembers her glass boat, and sighs. The things one could create if one made technology servant to a humble and creative imagination. . . . He's booming on, getting into full lecture room style and stride.

'. . . thus we will show that no other species, lacking as they do artefacts, an organized society, or even semblances of culture. . . .'

What would a whale do with an artefact, who is so perfectly adapted to the sea? Their conception of culture, of civilization, must be so alien that we'd never recognize it, even if we were to stumble on its traces daily.

She snorts.

He looks at her, eyes unglazing, and smiles.

'Criticism, my dear? Or you like that bit?'

'I was just thinking. . . .'

Thinking, as for us passing on our knowledge, hah! We rarely learn from the past or the present, and what we pass on for future humanity is a mere jumble of momentarily true facts, and odd snippets of surprised self-discoveries. That's not knowledge. . . .

She folds her hands over her belly. You in there, you won't learn much. What I can teach you is limited by what we are. Splotch goes the pen against his lips.

'You had better heat up that fortified drink, dear. We can't have either of you wasting from lack of proper nourishment.'

Unspoken haw haw haw.

Don't refer to it as a person! It is a canker in me, a parasite. It is nothing to me. I feel it squirm and kick, and sicken at the movement.

He says he's worried by her pale face.

'You shouldn't have gone up on deck so late. You could have slipped, or something, and climbing tires you now, you know.'

She doesn't argue any longer. The arguments follow well-worn tracks and go in circles.

'Yes,' she answers.

but I should wither without that release, that solitude, that keep away from you.

She stirs the powder into the milk and begins to mix it rhythmically.

I wonder what a whale thinks of its calf? So large a creature, so proven peaceful a beast, must be motherly, protective, a shielding benevolence against all wildness. It would be a sweet and milky love, magnified and sustained by the encompassing purity of water. . . .

. . .

A swarm of insect-like creatures, sparkling like a galaxy, each a pulsing light-form in blue and silver and gold. The whale sang for them, a ripple of delicate notes, spaced in a timeless curve. It stole through the lightswarm, and the luminescence increased brilliantly.

Deep within her, the other spark of light also grew. It was the third calf she had borne; it delighted her still, that the swift airy copulation should spring so opportunely to this new life. She feeds it love and music, and her body's bounty. Already it responds to her crooning tenderness, and the dark pictures she sends it. It absorbs both, as part of the life to come, as it nests securely in the waters within.

She remembers the nautilids in the warm oceans to the north, snapping at one another in a cannibalistic frenzy.

She remembers the oil-bedraggled albatross, resting with patient finality on the water-top, waiting for death.

She remembers her flight, not long past, from killer whales, and the terrible end of the other female who had companied her south, tongue eaten from her mouth, flukes and genitals ripped, bleeding to a slow fought-against end.

And all the memories are part of the growing calf.

More krill appeared. She opened her mouth, and glided through the shoal. Sudden darkness for the krill. The whale hummed meanwhile.

. . .

He folded his papers contentedly.

'Sam was going on about his blasted dolphins the other night dear.'

'Yes?'

He laughed deprecatingly. 'But it wouldn't interest you. All dull scientific chatter, eh?'

'What was he saying about, umm, his dolphins?'

'O, insisted that his latest series of tests demonstrated their high intelligence. No, that's misquoting him, potentially high intelligence. Of course, I brought him down to earth smartly. Results are as you make them, I said. Nobody has proved that the animals have intelligence to a degree above that of a dog. But it made me think of the rot that's setting in lately. Inspiration for this lecture indeed.'

'Lilley?' she asked, still thinking of the dolphins,

'Lilley demonstrated evidence of dolphinese.'

'Lilley? That mystical crackpot? Can you imagine anyone ever duplicating his work? Hah! Nobody has, of course. It was all in the man's mind.'

'Dolphins and whales are still largely unknown entities,' she murmured, more to herself than to him.

'Nonsense, my sweet. They've been thoroughly studied and dissected for the last century and more.' She shuddered. 'Rather dumb animals, all told, and probably of bovine origin. Look at the incredibly stupid way they persist in migrating straight into the hands of whalers year after year. If they were smart, they'd have organized an attacking force and protected themselves!'

He chuckled at the thought, and lit his pipe.

'It would be nice to communicate with another species,' she said, more softly still.

'That's the trouble with you poets,' he said fondly. 'Dream marvels are to be found from every half-baked piece of pseudo-science that drifts around. That's not seeing the world as it is. We scientists rely on reliably ascertained facts for a true picture of the world.'

She sat silently by the pot on the galley stove.

. . .

An echo from the world around, a deep throbbing from miles away. It was both message and invitation to contribute. She mused on it for minutes, absorbing, storing, correlating, winding her song meanwhile experimentally through its interstices — then dropped her voice to the lowest frequencies. She sent the message along first, and then added another strength to the cold wave that travelled after the message. An ocean away, someone would collect the cold wave, and store it, while it coiled and built to uncontrollable strength. Then, just enough would be released to generate a superwave, a gigantic wall of water on the surface of the sea. It was a new thing the sea-people were experimenting with. A protection. In case.

She began to swim further out from the coast. The water flowed like warm silk over her flanks, an occasional interjectory current swept her, cold and bracing, a touch from the sea to the south. It became quieter, a calm freed from the fights of crabs and the bickerings of small fish. There was less noise too, from the strange turgid craft that buzzed and clattered across the ocean-ceiling, dropping down wastes that stank and sickened.

A great ocean-going shark prudently shifted course and flicked away to the side of her. It measured twenty feet from shovel-nose to crescentic tailfin, but she was twice as long and would grow a little yet. Her broad deep body was still well fleshed and strong, in spite of the vicissitudes of the northwind breeding trek: there were barnacles encrusting her fins and lips and head, but she was unhampered by other parasites. She blew a raspberry at the fleeing shark and beat her flukes against the ocean's pull in an ecstasy of strength.

. . .

'This lecture,' he says, sipping his drink, 'this lecture should cause quite a stir. They'll probably label it conservative, or even reactionary, but of course it isn't. It merely urges us to keep our feet on the ground, not go hunting off down worthless blind sidetrails. To consolidate data we already have, not, for example, to speculate about so-called ESP phenomena. There is far too much mysticism and airy-fairy folderol in science these days. I don't wholly agree with the Victorians' attitude, that science could explain all, and very shortly would, but it's high time we got things back to a solid factual basis.'

'The Russians,' she says, after a long moment of non-committal silence, 'the Russians have discovered a form of photography that shows all living things to be sources of a strange and beautiful energy. Lights flare from fingertips. Leaves coruscate. All is living effulgence.'

He chuckles again.

'I can always tell when you're waxing poetic.' Then he taps out the bowl of his pipe against the side of the bunk, and leans forward in a fatherly way.

'My dear, if they have, and that's a big if, what difference could that possibly make. Another form of energy? So what?'

'Not just another form of energy,' she says sombrely. 'It makes for a whole new view of the world. If all things are repositories of related energy, then humanity is not alone. . . .'

'Why this of solitariness, of being alone. Communication with other species, man is not alone, for God's sake! One would think you're becoming tired of us all!'

He's joking.

She is getting very tired. She speaks tiredly.

'It would mean that the things you think you are demonstrating in your paper. . . .'

'Lecture.'

'Work . . . those things are totally irrelevant. That we may be on the bottom of the pile, not the top. It may be that other creatures are aware of their place and purpose in the world, have no need to delve and paw a meaning out. Justify themselves. That they accept all that happens, the beautiful, the terrible, the sickening, as part of the dance, as the joy or pain of the joke. Other species may somehow be equipped to know fully and consciously what truth is, whereas we humans must struggle, must struggle blindly to the end.'

He frowns, a concerned benevolent frown.

'Listen dear, has this trip been too much. Are you feeling at the end of your tether, tell us truly? I know the boat is old, and not much of a sailer, but it's the best I could do for the weekend. And I thought it would be a nice break for us, to get away from the university and home. Has there been too much work involved? The boat's got an engine after all . . . would you like me to start it and head back for the coast?'

She is shaking her head numbly.

He stands up and swallows what is left of his drink in one gulp.

'It won't take a minute to start the engine, and then I'll set that pilot thing, and we'll be back in sight of land before the morning. You'll feel happier then.'

She grips the small table.

Don't scream, she tells herself, don't scream.

. . .

Diatoms of phantom light, stray single brilliances. A high burst of dolphin sonics. The school was returning. A muted rasp from shoalfish hurrying past. A thing that curled and coiled in a drifting aureole of green light.

She slows, buoyant in the water.

Green light: it brings up the memories that are bone deep in her, written in her very cells. Green light of land.

She had once gone within yards of shore, without stranding. Curiosity had impelled her up a long narrow bay. She had edged carefully along, until her long flippers touched the rocky bottom. Sculling with her tail, she had slid forward a little further, and then lifted her head out of the water. The light was bent, the sounds that came to her were thin and distorted, but she could see colours known only from dreams and hear a music that was both alien and familiar.

(Christlookitthat!)

(Fuckinghellgetoutahereitscomingin)

The sound waves pooped and spattered through the air, and things scrambled away, as she moved herself back smoothly into deeper water.

A strange visit, but it enabled her to put images of her own to the calling dream.

Follow the line to the hard and aching airswept land, lie upon solidity never before known until strained ribs collapse from weight of body never before felt. And then, the second beginning of joy. . . .

She dreams a moment, recalling other ends, other beginnings. And because of the web that streamed between all members of her kind, she was ready for the softly insistent pulsation that wound itself into her dreaming. Mourning for a male of the species, up in the cold southern seas where the greenbellied krill swarm in unending abundance. Where the killing ships of the harpooners lurk. A barb sliced through the air in an arc and embedded itself in the lungs, so the whale blew red in his threshing agony. Another that sunk into his flesh by the heart. Long minutes later, his slow exhalation of death. Then the gathering of light from all parts of the drifting corpse. It condensed, vanished . . . streamers of sound from the dolphins who shoot past her, somersaulting in their strange joy.

The long siren call urges her south. She begins to surge upward to the sweet night air.

. . .

She says, 'I must go on deck for a minute.'

They had finished the quarrel, but still had not come together. He grunts, fondles his notes a last time, and rolls over in his sleeping bag, drawing the neck of it tightly close.

She says wistfully, 'Goodnight then,' and climbs the stairs heavily up to the hatchway.

'You're slightly offskew,' she says to the Southern Cross, and feels the repressed tears begin to flow down her cheeks. The stars blur.

> Have I changed so much?
> Or is it this interminable deadening pregnancy?
> But his stolid, sullen, stupidity!
> He won't see, he won't see, he won't see anything.

She walks to the bow, and settles herself down, uncomfortably aware of her protuberant belly, and begins to croon a song of comfort to herself.

And at that moment the humpback hit the ship, smashing through her old and weakened hull, collapsing the cabin, rending timbers. A mighty chaos. . . .

Somehow she found herself in the water, crying for him, swimming in a circle as though among the small debris she might find a floating sleeping bag. The stern of the ship is sinking, poised a moment a moment dark against the stars, and then it slides silently under.

She strikes out for a shape in the water, the liferaft? the dinghy?

And the shape moves.

The humpback, full of her dreams and her song, had beat blindly upward, and was shocked by the unexpected fouling. She lies, waiting on the water-top.

The woman stays where she is, motionless except for her paddling hands. She has no fear of the whale, but thinks, 'It may not know I am here, may hit me accidentally as it goes down.'

She can see the whale more clearly now, an immense zeppelin shape, bigger by far than their flimsy craft had been, but it lies there, very still. . . .

She hopes it hasn't been hurt by the impact, and chokes on the hope.

There is a long moaning call then, that reverberated through her. She is physically swept, shaken by an intensity of feeling, as though the whale has sensed her being and predicament, and has offered all it can, a sorrowing compassion.

Again the whale makes the moaning noise, and the woman calls, as loudly as she can, 'Thank you, thank you', knowing that it is meaningless, and probably unheard. Tears stream down her face once more.

The whale sounded so gently she didn't realize it was going at all.

'I am now alone in the dark,' she thinks, and the salt water laps round her mouth. 'How strange, if this is to be the summation of my life.'

In her womb the child kicked. Buoyed by the sea, she feels the movement as something gentle and familiar, dear to her for the first time.

But she begins to laugh.

The sea is warm and confiding, and it is a long long way to shore.

Stanley Roche
Structurally Sound

Amid so much genial good neighbourliness, the Hartmans' house seemed
deeply reserved. It was built of brick and concrete in a street where
weatherboard and plaster prevailed. But had it been built of mud or
alabaster no one would have been the wiser, for it was completely covered
in creepers so that all that could be glimpsed of its surface was the upper
parts of the chimneys where they rose above the roof, and a smear of
brick at the window sills. Children's hands scrabbling sometimes through
the leaves encountered a certain roughness of texture, an odd sense of
falling away. The house perhaps was crudely finished — the creepers
a face-saver. Even in winter it was leaf-encrusted, for the base cover was
ivy. On the sunny back face bougainvillaea competed with this and
jasmine wreathed the porches.

It was not a large house (1380 sq.ft) and it was set far back on the
quarter-acre section. Between it and the front hedge (taupata) there were
eight large trees — an elm, two silver birches, a Japanese maple, a plane
tree, two kowhais and a tarata. Most suburban houses in this town were
visible from the street, and this gave them a clean well-adjusted look.
No dark corners or cobwebs, you thought, no corruption even in the
cupboard under the sink. Some of the neighbours envied the Hartmans
their privacy and summer shade; others felt that house would give them
the heebie-jeebies, being so dark and maybe damp and full of insects.

Kevin Hartman, married, two children, wages-clerk for the City
Council, liked it for he also was reserved and inclined to be secretive.
He had bought it when he was twenty-seven with a small down-payment
and a twenty-year mortgage. His own dark corner, unrevealed but not
to himself frightening, hid an obsession with mortality. He had been
orphaned young and walked always with the knowledge of death beside
him.

This private intimacy expressed itself outwardly only in a tendency
to buy more life insurance than most young men — who naturally believe
they are immortal — and a fondness for wandering in cemeteries and
reading (for hints? or portents?) the gravestones of the dead. Old

cemeteries are best for that; self-conscious moderns leave deadpan statistics behind them.

The house reminded him of the nicest kind of cemetery — the rich and quiet odour of vegetable decay, afternoon sunlight lying on placid or stirring leaves, the mute marriage of life and death.

His wife, a still gentle woman named Lillian, liked it too, and the children, if they were occasionally embarrassed by it ('Do you live *there*? Hell, it's spooky!'), had a peaceful childhood.

When he was forty-four, Kevin Hartman, reaching for an old file on the top of the cabinet by his desk, heard an unidentifiable noise behind him and swung round to find himself eye to eye with his secret friend. At which shock, he fainted and died some hours (three hours twenty-seven minutes) later in the intensive-care ward. His wife grieved for him but after the first shock was not altogether surprised.

The children, almost grown when Kevin died, finished their schooling and left, leaving their trail grown cold behind them. An old gym-tunic, comically nostalgic, in the wardrobe, rollerskates rusting in the wash-house, a pile of textbooks that would now never be returned. They were good children. They had played their records loud in adolescence and reluctantly tidied their rooms, but they didn't take drugs or beget bastard babies and their hair was usually trimmed and brushed. Ross, a quiet thoughtful boy, became an economist (he was good at figures like his dad), went to Canada for post-graduate study, married there, and stayed. Celia, a dutiful daughter but inclined to be bossy, became a high-school teacher. Twice a year she came back, walking through the quiet house with heavy-duty footsteps, bringing her mother up-to-date on muesli and political awareness and militant feminism and fondue cooking. When she had gone, the silence flowed back.

It was very quiet in the house under the trees. The window-panes all fringed with undulating leaves, made the light palely green, and tree shadows moved on the walls and carpets like underwater patterns. Alone, but not lonely, Lillian lived out her days, feeding and sleeping, a quiet creature in her quiet cave. She wrote once a week to each of the children (a stray tabby came to the back door last Tuesday, such a thin miserable thing, but Timkins chased it away. Mrs Howley, you remember Mrs Howley down at the corner, she's crippled with fibrositis but as cheerful as ever. The leaves on the maple are turning already — they're early this year).

The leaves fell in deep dry drifts on lawn and path and rotted to humus and the trees quivered back to green again. A grandson was born to her in Canada. 'The darling!' she wrote, and knitted cardigans and leggings, but could not quite imagine a Canadian baby — sophisticated? fur-wrapped? Friends came to talk and knit and drink tea from her blue-and-white visitors' cups. Widows they were mostly — men are so delicate. She enjoyed the company but sometimes, sitting sipping with the shadows moving tremulously on the walls and the conversation desultory and bleached because the little there was to say had been said, she felt embarrassed by an appearance of pathos — two widows drinking their lonely late-afternoon tea. She enjoyed more the robust afternoons on her knees hunting and slaying the devious couch-grass and flushing out coveys of oxalis.

The widows discussed their nightly nervousness, that disease of lone women, and clung to TV, relishing even the advertisements (at least it's a voice in the house, dear, and you know they *are* clever). But Lillian was not afraid and rarely lonely. Coming from town or the neighbourhood shops — ritual how-are-you and cold-again talk — she saw the house, all wrapped in leaves, as a deep cube of peace. More and more often she sat in the afternoon on the sitting-room sofa, hands clasped on her blue skirt, and listened to the remote swell and ebb of the traffic waves on the through street three blocks away. Pale hands, palely blotched, and a sound like the sea.

And suddenly one day said the words aloud without knowing she had been thinking them.

'I am sitting here waiting for death.'

It was not a complaint; she was not pained or outraged. It was a fact, just that. She drowsed on gently in the calm light.

Later that winter the plughole of the sink became slow and reluctant, gagged when it was fed and breathed out a seeping halitosis. She phoned the plumber.

He came in a Volkswagen Kombi, with a flourish swishing up to the back door along the leaf-lagged drive, a big man with thick forearms and a well-padded arse. He crouched at the cupboard below the sink wielding powerful tools and she noticed the thick vitality of his grey springing hair.

Later she made a cup of tea and they drank it together at the kitchen table. He admired her leafy house — 'I like a bit of privacy myself.' Did he really, she wondered. He walked outside in a deliberate way, stood with feet apart looking up at the creepers, swished his breath through his teeth and pronounced. She'd have trouble with the gutters, look they were overgrown there, and there too. Probably blocked all the way. He didn't know anyone could let them get into such a state. They did leak, now didn't they? She admitted it; felt guilty, exposed, stupid and — obscurely — flattered. She'd been meaning to have something done about them.

'Well, there you are then,' he said not noticing her guilt. Pleased it seemed at this simple demonstration of cause and effect.

Inside again, he softened, asked her if she knew the house out on No. 3 Line — big brick place covered with — what was it? — turned red in autumn. Virginia Creeper? That was it. 'You want to get your husband to take you out there — it's quite a sight this time of year.'

She said in her soft voice, 'My husband's dead. He's been dead six years.' And her voice went on as it had when it told her she was waiting for death, without orders, without emotion. 'He died of a heart attack. He was only forty-four. There wasn't even any warning.' The voice which spoke without her consent trembled, for effect it seemed, on the last word. She stacked the cups not looking at the plumber.

He said, 'You get over it. They say it takes you seven years.'

'I wouldn't know about that,' she said. 'He used to see to the gutters.' It was this, she realized, that accounted for her outburst. He should have been around to see to the gutters.

'I'm alone too,' he said. She was shocked. He seemed so unshaken. You could usually pick the initiates.

'I'm sorry,' she said turning. He was squatting again by the pipes. Thick haunches, the moleskin pants straining over them, furred forearms.

'They went over the bank in the gorge. Poor old Nita! She always said she wouldn't drive anywhere with Barry if it was the last thing she did.' He barked a laugh that was somehow shocking. 'Well there you are then.'

'That's awful!' she said.

'Every day there's someone killed. Buggers like Barry, they never learn.'

He came back two days later on the pretext of checking the pipes. Also to ask her if she'd like to drive out in the weekend and take a look at that house on No. 3 Line. Passive, but interested, she agreed. 'We'll pick you up about two,' he said. She wondered who 'we' were and found out next Sunday.

Karen was big like her Dad — fourteen, bulky girl but wholesome, blunt blonde features, emphatically innocent. No secret life behind her eyes. She played her transistor loudly in the back seat (request session) and thrust it at intervals between the ears (one each) of her father and Lillian Hartman. So that they could better hear her favourites. The leaves on the house on No. 3 Line had succumbed to winter. It was a relief to get home. Lillian refused an invitation to a spot of tea at their place and, though she knew they expected it, didn't ask them in. She doubted that she would hear from the plumber again, but found herself mildly aggrieved and defensive when, at the end of a fortnight, she hadn't.

It was Karen who came ringing her doorbell on a still afternoon. What on earth did she want, fat-thighed and grossly innocent on the doorstep in her swollen gym-tunic?

Nothing it seemed. She sat heavily in an armchair and talked, drank a cup of coffee, slurping slightly between sentences. 'Then Carol, that's my girlfriend, she's a dag, she said we'd go up town and there's this shop up Main Street. You know that shop up Main Street?'

'I know some of the shops on Main Street.'

'You know that shop, it's up Main Street. It's got these fabrics. . . .'

It was simpler, Lillian found, to nod where the voice seemed to rise for confirming punctuation. Lillian had put a plate of biscuits within reach. Karen's hand went out seven times. Her voice plodded through mufflings of chewing and crumbs. '. . . and then Steve — Steve's my boyfriend. . . .' Boyfriend? Was the child leading up to some confession of pregnancy? Motherless child. It seemed not. She was leading nowhere. She lumbered to her feet at five o'clock, said, 'I have to go. Dad raves on if I'm not home. . . . I could ring him up. . . .' As though she was being pressed to stay — but went at last.

Rather irritated, rather amused, Lillian vacuumed the crumbs from carpet and armchair. As she peeled her single potato, washed five flowerets from a head of cauliflower, the sweet melancholy peace of evening did not return. 'Does she think I've nothing better to do . . .?' Had she anything better to do?

In the next week Karen returned three times. The last time she hauled a parcel out of her satchel and spread a length of material over the sofa — satiny, poppies on a silver ground. 'Do you think it'll do?'

'What for?'

'You know.' Then registering for once a blank failure of response, 'You don't remember much these days, do you?' And continued with deliberate clarity, 'The party. That Steve and me are going to.' She was away again. He said she didn't need a new dress but she hadn't got anything, Dad didn't have a clue. There was this fabric in this shop in the Square but. . . .

'You don't think it's a bit old for you?' Lillian said, and was annoyed with herself. She had given up feeding the child coffee and biscuits. A stray may miaow round you for a week, but if you don't feed it it'll give up in time. This one was too big for Timkins to chase away.

But Lillian had been a mother for twenty-six years. Her habitual patterns of response had betrayed her.

Karen reacted with an overtone of aggression. What did she mean, too old? Steve's friends were in a flat. He had a job in a garage but the others didn't work (was that, thought Lillian, the new criterion for maturity).

'They smoke dope,' cried Karen big-eyed now with frustration and anger. She had won. Lillian was shocked.

'Do you? Does Steve?'

The child's face assumed an absurd, deadpan expression. She turned and began shoving the material, all crumpled up, into her satchel.

'Do you?' Lillian tried to make her voice light and registered her own transparent falsity.

'No, of course not.' Karen's rather loud voice sounded thin. Embarrassment? Humiliation? Fear? Struggling with the zipper on her satchel she said 'Shit!' as though tears were close. Big behind in a gym-tunic with the hem riding up. One shoe split at the back.

Lillian said very carefully, 'Would you like to make me a cup of coffee before you go? I'm a bit tired.' Caught.

'All right.' Drinking it, Karen said suddenly, 'Are you going to tell Dad?' She emphasized the 'you' in an aggressive, insulting way.

'About the . . .,' an odd self-consciousness made it impossible for Lillian to use the word 'dope'. The wrong dialect — ludicrous. 'About the drugs? I think you should discuss it with him.'

'You tell him and I'll kill myself.' Tree shadows like water on the walls. Go away you stupid melodramatic girl. Go away and leave me to the trees and the widows and the gentle cups of tea.

'It's not my business to tell him anything. I think you should though. It's a foolish habit.'

'There's nothing wrong with it. What's wrong with it? Everyone does.'

Lillian stood up. 'Look, I'm not going to argue. What you do is your business — yours and your father's.' She wanted her voice to say, 'I don't know why you've been coming to see me but it's clear that we have very little in common. Perhaps you should find someone to visit nearer your own age and interests.' But this time her voice, which seemed more and more to be assuming independent life, did not relay the message. Karen graceless, but managing to exude an impression of dark power, lumbered away.

That evening for the first time in months Lillian longed for someone to talk to. There was no one. She turned on TV and watched warily as though there might be transmitted from some remote source of wisdom a message in the code of an advertisement in the pattern of jokes and laughter in a comedy half-hour.

If such a message came she failed to decipher it. She went to bed late and slept badly, woke, put on the light to read and fell asleep again with it still burning. She dreamed she was walking through a cemetery carrying jonquils to put on her husband's grave. (In fact Kevin had been cremated — the scene had no equivalent in life.) She found the grave and read the headstone (but could not remember afterward what it said). Sorrow poured over her in a sweet profound tide and she swayed and rocked with it, relinquishing her will in an ecstasy of tidal grief. Later it seemed she was cleaning a jar that was green-stained from some grave. It smelled — the intimate corruption of decaying flowers. She was using not a tap but a pump. The water gushed and splashed on to the ground and she began to worry in case she was recklessly wasting some rare and vital elixir of limited quantity that her efforts were drawing up from the earth.

Then it seemed she saw a lumpish figure she knew to be Karen stuck ludicrously on a grave on all fours like a cow. She became very angry and afraid and cried, 'Get up! Get up!' for it was obscene that the child should be there as a cow. Cow-Karen reared up and glared at Lillian with a look that was stupidly cunning and hatefully secretive and Lillian saw that her underside, her udder-breasts, were smeared and dripping and stained all over with thick dark blood.

The dream was still potent, underpinning her waking thoughts with a kind of horror when seven hours later she saw the plumber walking up her path through a blessing of mid-morning sunlight. It was the first mild day of spring. He had left the Kombi at the gate. She felt both nervous and relieved. Thickset and rolling slightly, he looked capable and kind and he greeted her heartily. Karen had been dropping in on her he heard. 'I'm served up Mrs Hartman for breakfast, dinner and tea,' he said and laughed, finding this, it would seem, genuinely extraordinary.

She laughed too at his tactless laughter and protested, 'But I don't say anything. How could she quote me? She does all the talking.'

'Well,' he said, 'there you are! I'm grateful for anyone at all that takes an interest in her.'

The way he puts things, she thought. But was relieved and with the relief, light-hearted. Whatever Karen had or had not told him, this much was clear — the responsibility was his. Her dream seemed a shameful act of hysteria that his mere presence, his dense solidity, had utterly dispelled.

They drank a cup of tea together sitting outside for the sun. Like his daughter he found conversation no burden, took her interest for granted. Told her about shortages that frustrated his work and the complications in laying pipes for a house raised on a solid concrete slab, finished his tea, rolled a cigarette and stood up.

'D'you want to come to the game on Saturday?'

'What game?'

He grinned. 'You're a bit out of touch, aren't you?' Genuinely amused and pleased that I don't know, she thought. Flattered somehow too. Well, well, it's all safe ground with this one.

'The shield?' she said, shattering his illusion. 'Are you inviting me?'

'Should be a good game! I've got tickets.'

Why not, she thought, why not!

'We'll have a spot of tea at home afterwards,' he said, stating it, not asking. 'Karen and me can knock up a meal all right.' Then seriously, 'That's one thing I stuck to after poor old Nita copped it. Good solid meals. None of this bread and butter and eggs bit!' With Karen's bulk in her mind, she agreed solemnly that good solid meals were important.

The game was, after all, exciting. I'd forgotten, she thought — forgotten how to take a holiday from myself.

Yet when she returned that night, after the tea, plate hugely piled, and their noisy cheerfulness, she had never loved so much the leafy silence of her own home. She put on the heater and sat in the dark, watching the trees moving outside her window, with a passion that was like pain.

Whatever sulkiness Karen had manifested was over. She arrived as before, two or three times a week. The plumber dropped in for morning tea almost as often. No weekend passed without the swish of the Kombi on the drive and cheerful elemental cries from the door — 'Get on your gladrags — we're off!' To the football, to a concert at Karen's High School, to the construction site where he was working.

It seemed there was no element of choice; for them a blind compulsion, for her a compelled acquiescence.

He asked her to marry him as she knew he would. 'What say you and me team up, Lil? I know we're both of us a bit long in the tooth, but I reckon we've got a bit of go in us yet.'

'But I couldn't leave my home!' she cried.

'That's all right,' he said cheerfully, 'wouldn't expect you to. Karen and me'll move in.'

The image of this astounded her. But it rang with authority. Like an alarm clock sounding off through a seven o'clock dream.

'Do you think we'd make a go of it?' she said doubtfully.

He was cheerfully confident. 'Bound to. We hit it off all right and you and Karen get on like a house on fire.'

A fortnight before they were married the plumber decided to clear the gutters. The spring growth had carried the ivy half-way up the roof.

'You won't take more than you have to, will you?'

'Not to worry,' he said. 'Just knock them back a bit.'

Indeed she didn't worry. Creepers as strongly rooted as these would recover quickly whatever was done to them. It would be masochistic, all the same, to watch the attack. It was a Saturday afternoon, warm for November but overcast. Karen, in stretch jeans and T-shirt plonked herself down on an upturned box under the trees to watch her Dad get things under control. The plumber mounted the ladder. A pleasant domestic scene. Lillian took herself off to visit one of the widows.

She found two there. They greeted her with cries of affection. In the past few years there had been comfort for all of them in the knowledge of each other's existence. They were losing her and would be that much more exposed. Drinking her ritual cup of tea it struck her, not for the first time, that one of the things she was leaving behind her was a particular brand of peace. But again a sense of ludicrous pathos touched the edge of her consciousness. The withered bride and her withered maidens. We're all a bit long in the tooth. Or was it a sacrament she was taking, a last supper?

This perhaps was what they felt. One took her hand at the door and said mournfully, 'It'll be a comfort to you to have a man in the house, dear.' The other, more robust, looked her in the eye. 'Are you sure you know what you're doing, Lillian?' In all her life she had never been sure of that, was less so now, but did know for sure that what had been still water was flowing again. She did not answer the question but, unusually demonstrative, kissed the widows' soft cheeks.

When she got home the house was half denuded. It was no more than she had expected, and it was not this that appalled her. The shock lay in what was revealed. At first she saw only that the house was unusually structured. The wall revealed was a series of large concrete corrugations, big circular rods of concrete set together horizontally from ground to roof.

Karen and the plumber, with slaughtered ivy round their feet and trailing from their hands, turned large flushed faces to her. The plumber said, 'Well, what d'you say to that?' and Karen cried, 'It's a log cabin. Bet you never had a clue, eh?'

It was indeed. A house constructed of solid trunks of concrete, each scored with identical round scars to represent sawn branches, placed at exactly uniform intervals. The protruding ends of the logs were marked by regular concentric circles to represent the rings of growth.

She had no words for this. With enthusiasm the plumber began to explain the process of construction. 'This is the way they've cast it, Lil. . . .'

Karen interrupted with her gasping cry, 'Isn't it *neat*! What a dag — living in a log cabin!'

'No! No!' Lillian cried, as though she had been hit unfairly. 'No!' The same cry had come from her when she had first been told of Kevin's death. The pain of her protest punctured the enthusiasm the others had raised.

Blushing angry for her deflated joy, Karen wailed, 'You never understand us young people,' and furiously tore out yet another handful of ivy.

The plumber said, 'Well, there you are, Lil. It's a character of a house and well-built, too.'

She turned to him, her voice out of key as though it had not been used for years, 'Who made it like that? They must have been mad. It's so silly! That's what the creepers were for — to cover it, because it's so stupid and silly!'

'Come to that,' he said, 'the ivy'll be up again in next to no time. Good as new this time next year. You'll never know the difference.'

She turned from him and walked into the house. She was surprised to find it intact. It was true the creepers would grow.

But what made her legs tremble and her heart thump as she stood in the unchanged living-room was the realization that she had lived there for so long without ever knowing the nature of the house she inhabited.

Rosie Scott
Diary of a Woman

i

And living in this muddled, gloomy, dirty, peeling house with its knowing walls which defy any form of taming — a great mass of brown, dark and dirty shapes and tainted with maybe a death and certainly a long and indecipherable life littered with all sorts of fears and last sordid and sad relics. A feeling of being placed right in the middle of the vortex, no escape, or any of the escapes prepared are only hollow and pathetic appeasements. With the wicked traffic zooming past and walking out on to the dirty, sad, unloved pavements. And the mess within, centre no longer there, a sweet attempt to have a last sincere dialogue above the continual frenetic record-player, or in between the faceless women flitting in and out, or the varied job hours. The six of us continually returning to this room because it is dark and womb-like and a little bit sad and very safe. Fleetingness of our together pleasures, meals prepared with care and eaten quickly because the joy was in the making, a smoke then silence, wine flagons staining the table, still wrapped in paper, a gentle argumentative drunkenness pervading the room. Late night sessions in which the joys and fears are paraded; among the three old friends a strong feeling of quiet and secret love, a peaceful supporting and accepting, half-irritated, brotherly love. A home of all sorts of subterranean desires and disappointments, the feeling of communality often a joyous one, the wanting to expunge a certain part of their life now gone, a sort of uneven recovering where all sorts of ghosts and monsters are still flitting around and fed or discarded as you listen to them. In spite of itself, something strong and not destructive struggling out of it, too many lifegiving elements, more strong and enduring than could be found in a blander place, born of being a long way down and still daring to explore the scene of the crime, rather than escape any of it. Grapefruit-flower smell, white, waxy, in a jar on the bench, wet-sack smell of beer brewing, fragrance of love and lust and joyous heartsinging of the Stones and the bathsinging in the next room. Summer afternoons sprawling half-naked on the grass in the hot sun at the back of the house, reading talking with beer and transistors and a bowl of salad — children crying and traffic behind the rickety wooden fence. And me all alone in this darkdeathshouse and feeling sharp as a fox and clean, and watching everything with great attention and listening. This aliveness part of a life and me trying to set impressive scenes with me as centre — my deep and abiding sense of eternal order being necessary — really as if one could mimic certain rhythms of the universe and by doing so be safe from the sort of chaos which stems from despair.

ii

For Mike has been in Australia for two months and I am soon to follow him; in his absence I can begin to feel dimly that we are drifting apart in a way unprecedented in our seven years together — with his novel finished and having worked at nights for months now, he is ready for something different. From his letters, which are uncharacteristically brief and impersonal, he hints at a new lifestyle. After years of working on his own, he is now in the hub of things again. He feels no regret at leaving New Zealand, and I begin to wonder whether he misses me, as part of his old hermit life, his discarded self. I am afraid, from past experience, and write to him asking if he wishes to break things off from this point, more because I crave reassurance. He writes back remotely, that of course he wishes me to come, but it sounds like another person politely insisting, and I know I have to go. I say goodbye to friends and family as if I shall never see them with the same eyes — I feel as if I were preparing for some great ordeal. The last few weeks are passing in a haze of unreality, as if I were withdrawing into misery, drawn to Australia though I do not wish to go. I am sad to leave my job, I feel all the roots being slowly and painfully pulled up. I realize in this leavetaking and the future unknown, how much I love New Zealand and my life here. In all my daydreams I am an incredibly lustful whore, translated by my middle-class inhibitions in real life, into a great zeal for my work in those last weeks. Thus, throwing all my desires into really trying to understand people and loving them in a remote way — like Stephen, the gentle and suicidal boy who watches his world go by in an almost catatonic walking dream, the women passing briefly through my sight who are dying and who want to die, the gentle eccentrics, the helpless old, the woman who can only speak in surrealistic jumbles, and who gazes above her moving mouth with kind old sane eyes — she says looking over at the flower garden out the window and the quiet hospital — it's really very brutal, I'm waiting for the wake and it's sad really. And looking at me she says softly, you look beautiful, lovely sweet, so I felt like a shower of roses. Social work is an elaborate way for me to have people love me I know — is it partly because my husband whom I love as much as I am capable seems not to love me? For often there is so little to give, except vague promises about a world which holds very little promise — only my own self and my hand to hold, to those who probably have so much more wisdom than me.

iii

Only Peter can really see this schism in my personality: our relationship is my own self in miniature, and only he can understand Mike's need to escape from me and also to return. For Peter loves me, he finds me beautiful and sympathetic, he tells me he will remember me for the rest of his life. But because he himself is slightly insane, a manic-depressive perhaps, he has increased perception into my soul, and sometimes he despises me for my falsity. He tells me I am a twitchy and immeasurably sad woman, he tells me with great venom that I am nothing but a nuisance to Mike, that I am always trying to score because I am so hung-up, I need the reassurance of putting people down.

It is the nameless dread that I fear most of all, the fear I felt even when my life was just beginning in the kind arms of David, which Peter too feels all the time, the flying statues which Sartre describes. The externalities do not come into it, it is then a combination of the known and the unknown; can I absorb both into my being and not break in half denying either one side or the other, or, as I am now, poised for decisive action of some sort — denying both, the ultimate sterility? Elaboration — we three, young, false, shining with beer, youth, facing Peter in a semi-circle and no one to care, the wounded lion, crazydrunk, do we have to be so personal said one of them. And fuckofffuckofffuckoff till all were uncomfortable because the creeping paralysis affecting his brain affected theirs, his agony had all the despair of a person with no hope left, and he would have wounded all he could, drunken poet with sad pug face and crawling skin, blond rake with the face of an innocent and debauched child — no more *bodsittvas* now, and me, I don't want to say anything about me because it was to me most of his anger was directed and I felt only like shrinking into a shell of absolute immobility. Only he was not uncomfortable, with a horror of his probable and most feared destination, he mentioned the padded cell and the poet told him to stop this posturing morbidity. They all remembered moments of intimacy with me and talked of them, grimacing, because none of them could hope to guess what I thought, being the placating angel with nothing to say (so they thought). It was all quite farcical, only he was in earnest and ready to kill someone, immolate his tortured soul, he did really want to strangle someone because it seemed to be the only way for him to find any peace with himself, forever feed his self-contempt.

iv

And now to transplant all this into that brash, brainless sprawl of a country under those hot blue skies, red dust in the streets of Sydney, to face Mike again with this growing fear, to try and live yet another ordered life, patching as I go in the endless shuttle of new and unwelcome impressions. I can hardly face it. It is the last acting out of our mutual fantasies, and as it is I feel so fragile, that I wonder what strange new forms my self will take after this new furnace. And yet I am longing to see him again and be there with him, I long for his drawling voice and his desire, the focal point of my existence.

v

The first day in Australia with Mike — no one to meet me at the airport. One of those technicolour blue, sweltering, alien days of an Australian summer — driving through the brick suburbs of Melbourne chatting to the friendly young taxi-driver, my heart heavy with impending disaster.

Leaving New Zealand — waving to the little knot of people at the airport gate who looked somehow forlorn as if I were already dead. Weeping on the plane as I see the last soft green coast slip into the sea. Arriving. An old terrace house of the uninteresting kind next to a vacant lot, weeds, rusting cars. Mike appearing at the door, looking remote, to take my suitcases. The gay, French, striped singlet, brown skin and blue jeans absurd, like an offering which has been ignored. My husband. Weeping in bed after making love. I don't know him at all, he is forever in his own world. Meeting the young students in the house and feeling old and blasé about going through the familiar hassle of sharing houses, they had not known of my existence. Feeling humiliated.

Mike's only salvation is his own inviolateness; my presence is disturbing his peace and making him doubt himself again. His presence with all the familiar no touches and barriers through which our relationship has to try to function is of no value at the moment — I only feel the lack of being loved by him. Living on blindly with him for the last seven years — with no ability to stem things and make a stand. I do not have the will to impose my views on others, however close, I am always on the outer, no haven for all my contradictory desires. I sit at the window alone in this small room feeling the huge grinding of the city below and beyond. It is still hot at eight o'clock and I can hear a strident rock band from the university. I have a brief vision of Stephen in hospital, Alan in prison and I free. My freedom is a mockery, for my mind is churning in closed channels. I have been despairing and depressed for the last two days, and feel so alone, all I can do is sleep, read, walk around the city, daydream a little — I can't think too closely about myself.

vi

With no one, and nothing to do — a sort of mindless limbo — I find it is a long time before I can stir up whatever was there long before I became a sentient being, life is so filled with being and no time to allow certain phantoms to haunt at the darkest and most alonest recesses of my soul, to only escape by worry or sleep or work or friends, to attempt to grapple with the innermost things which cloud my self, with my very rationale for existence. Is it such a sunshine thing or a subtle revenge to inspire guilt in others? Do I really feel such beneficence towards people or do I find the world a frightening, hostile and baffling place which I can only propitiate by soft words spoken from a hard heart? (Like the animals who deliberately show their most vulnerable spot to their adversary, so that it is only kicked ritually, being passed with contempt — a humility based on hostility and fear.) I wonder how many of my actions are based on the desire to be loved rather than to love, but I am encompassed with so many self-made traps which forbid understanding I cannot change my responses — looking at the world as if only I existed, wanting everything to be an affirmation of me. Maybe I have stayed with Mike so long because he will never approve of me fully. I feel that surely, since we have been together all this time and I have given so much of my precious self to him, he cannot disdain such a gift. . . . I cannot accept the totality of my being as it has been for twenty-seven years, but do not do anything to change it. I keep banging my head against the wall which I myself have constructed with such loving care, the walls which I have analysed and pondered over for years and keep building and strengthening unable to break away from certain conventional patterns of life. Perhaps the gift of my marriage has been that I cannot be happy and therefore cannot allow myself to be immersed in trivia, but must fight to stay alive — I am alive and responsive as a hunted animal.

vii

I go to bed out of sheer boredom, for Mike is never home, just me in this small room, wrestling in my mind whether I am being unkind, justified, behaving as I wish to, proud or unclear, or too intense, or adding up things merely to support my own idea of the universe. I am so tired of my face in the mirror, through introspection and unlovedness, it is tight and hard and small and unbeautiful. I begin to feel claustrophobic, I cannot control the desire to smoke, to brood, to keep my mind on certain obsessions concerning people in my life whom I feel wronged by, to see the unchanging pattern of streets, cars, corner dairies in my life as an ugly trap which my being with Mike has placed me in. A small sour flowering in the dark, so many bad dreams.

viii

Lying in my room, listening to records, smoking non-stop, my self bare and empty as a swept-out room. When he comes home at 10 p.m. I begin to weep and he looks at me with resignation, busy, preoccupied with work. He says that our relationship is dead, there is nowhere to progress, our relationship has lost its innocence, nasty strangers quarrelling, only avoidance. Yet how many times have we said that to each other hard-eyed and still could never part, or when I left, he wanted me so to come back? Is it different this time — with a fuck a week and no communication? He is the only person I could ever really communicate with; I remember sadly after a separation that we sat talking on a park bench for five or six hours, unaware of the time until it became dark, and we went home to make love. I lie on the bed and sometimes allow myself to think of the past with him, a self-indulgence which often is too painful. All those places of farewell far more sunlit than any other, music and common regret and morning rooms. Bread and coffee for breakfast, dusty carpets and peeling prints on the walls. Lying in bed together not touching, in the middle of the afternoon, gazing up at the stained glass window and tapestry pattern on the wall, in your big untidy room, a record playing Bob Dylan (so long ago, it was 'Boots of Spanish Leather', thinly nostalgic), talking as if our hearts would burst with closeness. And Sunday mornings when we lived together, getting languidly out of bed, bodies hot and stale with making love all morning, frying eggs in the kitchen, talking to the cats. There were two of them both black-and-white; you were writing a novel in the sunroom. We were always poor then; we used to go to the movies all the time, our arms around each other in the dark, and buy potato crisps at interval, or go to the pub and drink beer with our friends. . . . We have separated so many times before, but there is a hardness in us both this time. I can see in your eyes that I am just a tiresome reminder of the past, that I am in your way, and though I know you will tire of the women as you always do, and will find the freedom largely illusory without me, there is no going back.

ix

I am trying to get a part-time job, and it seems rather difficult — any New Zealand training seems not to count here, but as yet I don't feel even urgent about that. There is a concerto playing in the next room; the shy blond student who watches me when he thinks I am not looking, trying to work out why I am here and whether I am mad sitting in this room all day long. . . . I am typing facing the mirror with the red flag curtain behind my head in the background. My skin looks translucent in the gloom, my hair tied back severely, and enormous round tortoise-shell spectacles. My lipstick matches the curtain and my face is small and unsmiling, small rather intense vague eyes, my own self as I write, ponytail of coarse-looking brown hair on my shoulder. The clock ticks continually — this moment of riskily-based peace, the ephemerality of myself going down into the kitchen and talking to people, dressed in purple slacks, barefooted, making tea and smiling, being happy about music, the nice young people here — we are older and do not set a very good example I fear. And these actions can be repeated a hundred times, a thousand times of listening to a harpsichord in a dark house and preparing food, or waiting or hoping in the dark, a needle in the groove, being given things and surrounded by the familiar. A chance to see life stripped of everything but mere existence; watching the wall, not useful, failing every test set however slight, watching things go by with indifference, discounting anything at all in my past life as quite irrelevant to me, knowing that my own special life has just begun, not to force myself, but see where my directions lie if it takes me years. I would ideally get myself into a tight corner of self-doubting and aloneness just to achieve this purity, go mad if need be, forgo a normal life like the one I have been leading, forgo children, love, family, become old and withered andmad, but such *angst* is for a stronger person — I can only flounder in my ordinariness and weep that my husband does not love me.

x

An escape before the jaws close. We all have to leave our house because there are too many people living in it: such a rabbit warren with its worn passages and lino, the anxious Italian landlord. So we have settled for a tiny cottage quite near to the university for Mike. In spite of myself I hope that something will happen there. I have looked for a new place for a long time. And I will not be too alone for one of the young girls is coming to live with us, as she has nowhere to go. So on the last night we all went to see Ginsberg and Ferlinghetti at a poetry recital — at least ten years after it is all over, they come to the provinces! But it was the first time I had really enjoyed a poetry recital, listening to Ferlinghetti's poems as a quiet gentle beginning, and then of course Ginsberg with big short body and a flashing humorous face, reading out 'Howl' with all the intensity of an accrued twenty or so years — all those enormous images pouring out fresh and sharp, one of the beginnings of it all, a sort of apocalyptic manifesto in language so precise and spectacular that it was impossible not to be excited and stirred, a rediscovery of what poetry means, and how it can encapsulate, define and point to a new direction with a seemingly effortless beauty — read with so much life and belief still, it felt like a rush of ice-cold water. And he also sang Blake's 'Nurse's Song' — and the little ones leaped and shouted and laughed — a reincarnation of Blake's energy — the pure force of love — the acceptance of all things — sung with a joy that was immediately transmitted. He sat behind his glasses and squat hands, howling and moving every part of his body in sheer delight, it was amazing how much joy, energy and humour were radiating from him — it was the sort of intensity which made me want to grin. Three glorious hours — a beautiful relief where reality was intensified to an unbearable degree.

Ginsberg was one of Mike's first heroes, who opened the gates for him to that new world, now so dated and so exciting then, of Burroughs, Kesey, the Merry Pranksters, madness, peace signs and marijuana, and he found it equally moving I think. I watched his handsome baby face with those weary knowing eyes, and he looked relaxed for a change. I thought — he is suffering too, and on the way home we talked about it with pleasure, and there were no quarrels or silences.

xi

I had a dream that night that Mike and I were walking along in a park-
like place, and we passed a group of people who were sitting around.
Mike suddenly said it was a tutorial he had forgotten about — he had
to hand in an essay, which he accordingly did. The professor was a grey-
haired big man who looked intelligent and rather fine. I sat at the edge
of the group waiting until it was over and someone handed me a sugar-
scoop. I demurred saying I did not want it, but the person thinking I
was a student, said, but it's part of the tutorial, so I took it unwillingly.
Then snow started to fall, little soft flakes which changed into water the
instant they touched the ground, fairy flakes, and I saw that we were
in the grounds of Auckland University, and Mike was nowhere to be seen.

xii

It is so bad to have so much running through the mind in a never-ending,
glorious stream of feeling and ideas half-expressed in thoughts, yet so
rich all the time. And there is a horrible ache in not being able to pull
them down out of the air and clothe them with words befitting, and what
emerges is watered-down, shabbied, indescribably paled, cliché-ridden,
worn-out misty quarter-truth and the tapestry keeps unwinding and loses
itself in time and distance. Far worse — and leading to pretension,
frustrated ambition, dissatisfaction — leading a useless life, and trying
to ignore the thoughts that burst like beautiful, bright and gauzy balloons
when pricked by sheer relentlessness and inability. But then to be happy
on top of this and still not accept it is the cruellest blow of all; far better
to die in a gutter with no pain (as Bob Zimmerman might have said and
did). But in the corner clothed in grey cobwebs and sitting in perfect peace,
Krishnamurti waits and counsels by silence. Once he has entered the
room, he probably never leaves it, but there are no reproaches for often
he understands everything. A lot of other things come and go including
mortal love, ambition, beauty, peace, security, and then there is nothing
bright left, only the greyness of absolute truth. Why is it that I have to
posture and mouth and never come out with it? My husband writes good
poetry and thinks me shallow and probably there is little I can reply to
that except that I try and am self-pitying to quite a deep extent. To write
'my husband' distances the whole thing. It also shows up the odd trappings
of marriage. I keep things very clean, pluck my eyebrows and buy food
and cook and eat it and also dream of misty purple-tinted sex and being

loved, and am always alone. I can hear TV playing schmaltz music next
door and can also catch occasional snatches of tinny dialogue. I will switch
the heater on, and relish the nasty and cigarette-y taste in my mouth,
and maybe I will go to bed unwashed, unsung, to sleep another unloved
night, and dream of bacon and eggs in the bed of bricks and the man
of straw. Oh I have realized that I am too passive and should rape some
willing man, the flesh can only stand so much, but there you are, I have
no sexual initiative and the days go by. This is the picture: in the purple
bedroom, half-lit and the shining (and strong) body of a man fucking
me into complete silence so that my own body is completely satisfied and
sweatshining, and then I can have an adult cigarette in the gloom and
we can laugh in a friendly, mutually respectful way and talk only about
nothing and so on till at last he takes his leave with a general feeling of
warmth and joy and I can turn over and sleep with no dreams and have
no ache when I awake. I feel so proud of my body and eyes and my mouth
and would so like to feel no shame. How can I start? I can only stay in
the shell of myself and feel my stomach turn over with lust and that is
all. My mysterious vagina has had such a hard time of it recently with
the growing thing ripped untimely and no one to love it. . . .

xiii

My childhood has come back to me in a rush after a chance meeting in
the street with an old school-friend — we sat in the kitchen and talked
of the past which rose up before me in bewildering detail, as if I had
blocked it all out. She said that she remembers Harold turning cartwheels
in the dunes at Muriwai his glasses flying off exuberantly and all the glories
of our teenage life. And then I remembered walks through the bush with
David and Joshua, still summer afternoons with woodsmoke filling the
air with nostalgic fragrance. And sitting unknowingly on the lawn at Piha,
reading our diaries in the sun in front of the little white tent; my first
kiss, that abiding sense of innocence and wonder still. And growing up
now, with broken marriages of our own, and babies and confidence, with
the little germ of childhood still there in our apprehensive eyes, the
smoking problem, and responsible jobs, but it is still there and in the
sharing of what has been, the ensuing time seems to disappear and a little
corner of our minds still seems to operate on that groove. It made me
happy to meet a bit of my past, and glory in it all — all the absurd
grotesque and innocent happenings of our life when we were thirteen!
Fourteen years after in a kitchen in Carlton facing each other with those

emotions! Gwen, well-groomed, poised in a bright, wool suit and career woman mannerisms, me rather woolly in jeans and a tight polo-neck jersey blundering about making tea in pottery mugs. I am still the same as then though, and maybe deep down still have that joy. It's so fine for me to be here, in this situation and think that. The great skein of glowing memories, of what went into me — the people and the places woven forever into my memory and body and face. After she has gone, some coffee and records alone, revelling in my unaccustomed lightness of heart. When the wind hangs heavy on the borderline remember me . . . she was a true love of mine . . . it's good to see you too, Joe. Conferences in endless kitchens, cups of coffee in lounges, bottle-clinking in the backs of old cars at midnight — yippee. Almost overpowering to think of it all. Air quite heavy with memories. . . .

Long ago and so far away I fell in love with you . . . your guitar it sounds so sweet . . . but you're not there to hear, it's just the radio. . . . Don't you remember you told me you loved me baby, said you'd be coming back this way again baby. . . . Me just listening to music and seeing the future and the past in one great gentle present. I might die tonight. Today I thought of the mammoth woman who controlled our destinies — sitting gleefully in her little gloomy office and asking unanswerable questions which you don't want to try and answer, laughing and smoking, she had you. I know a lot of fancy dancers, people who can glide you on a floor they move so smooth but have no answers when you say why did you come here for. Your guitar it sounds so sweet. I love your little house, won't you come in? I'm yours. And the moon was enormous and yellow and there was a gigantic witches' ring around it and we stood there and laughed in the dark. Do you have dreams about me too, love? Your body in the dark is all I crave for, sweet enough to think of it, a dilation of the nostrils, tensing of the spine as the shiver goes through and your teeth in the dark. Only to think of it. For it's sad to be married to a man who does not want you; sly caresses in the bath and stale cigarette air. Saying hello and the empty walls only, and the little ones leaped and shouted and laughed and all the hills echoed, Ruth stood in tears amid the alien corn. Hello I'm here, look at me. Am I beautiful to you? And I will have three geraniums in earthenware pots on the sill, and the sun will shine. Do you want milk, cheese, and oranges. I have them all and more. Breasts shining in the bathwater, and cool walls glimmering in the steam, quiet as a cleanflagged dairy with only the water splashing and the slippery soap. There are so many beds you never dreamed of, with sheets gold as the sun. Well, I hit the rowdy road . . . I listen to the robin's song, saying not to worry. . . .

xiv

Feeling a burst of melancholy — grey Sunday afternoon, meaninglessness of my life here, reading my diaries full of all the vivid and intense ramblings of the alive, sexually obsessed and sincere nymphet that I was then, battling through all the problems which still perplex me now, and trying so valiantly to make some sense of the life around me. I suppose that I'm being sentimental waiting for time to pass here with our relationship slowly crumbling into nothing and me bored and miserable. Fluffy cumulus clouds in the dusk sky, and the golden trees are almost bare of leaves now, they look quite wintery and sad. All today I have been thinking that this house is a dreadful mistake, and that I could never people it with happy ghosts as I secretly hoped. And when I am alone here? I have not been able to find a job yet, so I have not been able to sort out all the financial worries. But it is difficult to say for certain and I will just have to give it a bit of time. I feel sometimes as if my life were hanging on a single thread, and I will have to treat things with great gentleness, the Great Dread is too close again, I must keep moving mentally. Maybe it is frightening to me that Mike has become a stranger, and therefore my only index of the familiar has altered, to feel unloved in a strange city and try to keep things going. It is very autumny, lots of dry leaves everywhere, dying trees, crisp melancholy twilights, listening to children's voices playing in the street. Now I only want peace from this incessant thought.

xv

What can I possibly write about that hasn't already been written? Who am I to say that I have anything to say? Words, words, words, (as He said). All alone in the busy world with no one to love. Maybe the brooding about sex is more exciting than the real thing. It only lasts for a moment and think of all the worries — am I pregnant, am I pleasing, have I offended someone? Body odour. I wonder if it is possible to love something like a faithful, green, old typewriter, a little bit rusty and dirty which sits there in silence to everything and copies it down for my private joy. How many hours have I spent clacking on these old keys and dropping ash into it, and drinking coffee, and looking out how many windows. It is a long story, but this little machine just is there as part of my life and far more lasting, it goes where my mind goes and writes songs for me, and I feel as if it loves me too. And sitting on my small arse and watching the shadows of people as they pass unendingly in front of the white curtain.

xvi

I dreamt that we (the social workers) were going in a car on an important mission to find a fugitive. Yet I felt alienated from the search because I knew the fugitive was on the right side. Then just we women were wandering over a gloomy German hill in grey light; below was a dreary concrete pool — narrow, two wings, with dark unshining water. And then I saw Margaret — a really old grey spectral figure standing there in misery by the pool. I ran down to her unbelieving, calling her name and knelt down to her, she looked so sad and saintly I could not stop weeping. We mentioned David and Joshua but only in broken words and I could feel the other women gazing down in pity at our sadness. To wake with my cheeks wet with tears.

xvii

A person stripped of everything, facing himself and the universe is like a newborn baby, shivering and naked, still shining with the grease of his mother's body. Learning how to make his way in a world hostile, threatening and ugly. It is not the obscurity so much as the fact that things are seen for themselves and are almost unbearably mis-shapen — colourless, stripped of breadth, association, things *per se*, nothing to relate to nor are they related to one another, just there, hanging in their dreary little aura, things that are not even dead because they have never been alive. And one can only be a part of this, like a baby, one's own self cannot be detached from these horrible surroundings, and one can see with a clarity that is more frightening than illuminating at the time the you of your own precious self, the objective you, nothing can be done against all these close and formless forces which are twisting and suffocating you into submission. This *angst* is probably insupportable for any length of time, because all the defences put up with infinite care and self-protection are being ruthlessly stripped away, revealing their pathetic inadequacy, their sad little attempt to shield yourself against the artificially contrived problems — ignoring the real and dreadful one that lurks beneath the bland exterior. In any major upheaval each of a person's small previous acts which have anchored him more firmly to life are swept away by the enormous forces which are impossible to appease in any way.

xviii

The night draws on and the approach of the terrifying stranger who shares my bed, and seems to silently deride my very presence, and little pink Sara with her soft and wavering mouth and clear eyes disappearing like a ghost as the record-player pounds out Joe Cocker — there is a kind of humour in that, beleaguered here, we await the crack of doom when the clock falls off the sideboard, and Mike's watch shivers to pieces on his wrist, and there is silence and our unclothed faces. Oh, yes, quite gone, with the muscles of our cheeks and the red strings of veins hanging off the bone and clots of eyes staring at the door. Yes, how dreadful it would be, so we tiptoe and eye the door nervously.

The coffee will hide the smell of smoke, but alas there is a pall snaking through the hall, there are so many ways the truth will out. He arrives with his grey and sad-eyed mistress, stringy; I will look up and seem surprised but deeply underneath I will feel a great suck of pleasure — at last the drama has come, and we can play the last bit, and then leave satisfied that we have paid our due to posterity and down will go my head on the typewriter and anxiously a cigarette will appear to be lit with shaky fingers. Most satisfying except for the loneliness after, the laughing ghost of six good fucks on one grey afternoon, and the images conjured like smoke. It is all very sad and maybe better than nothing. The electrician with amazing legs and brown hands who sits on the floor in the corner fixing the fuses, and looking at me with blue blue eyes as we talk about the American Indians' religion.

Melancholy falling like a cloud, same place, same time. Reading old diaries — the old self blossoming and eager — in a Chinese restaurant and Mike saying that he will start looking for another place soon, and only weariness and desire for him to get it over and done with. A sick headache and a glass of wine, if I can rise from the ashes then it's all right, maybe, maybe. What am I doing here, can I begin anything? My headache precludes all serious thought, and only dizziness, not happy. So few things I can really say, I have said them all already, but in apathetic compulsion. Drown it all in sleep. . . .

xix

Things are definitely going beyond control, a nightmare that thugs broke down our flimsy front door, and when I ran into the bedroom to get Mike, he was my father asleep. The Freudian significance was lost in the horror of it. I woke shaking and sweating. So tired of hassling for jobs, houses, love; being lonely and feeling a failure; cannot cope with too many things at once, so become passive and still between these four walls, gazing at the street and weeping at night, my brain and body at the edge of something I cannot explain away, and Mike moving out tomorrow.

xx

I only want my private world of communing, the external world is beginning to fade for me, and I am beginning to feel more and more alarming disgust about other people, my earlier optimism about the redeeming value of love or beauty or spirit has slowly given way to a kind of nausea, a desire to withdraw — whom do I respect or love or admire wholeheartedly? — people are so flawed and demand so much — there is so much ugliness and cruelty and hatred in the human soul that I cannot believe in it anymore. The bloodbath with Mike, the sheer turbulence of my friendships, love, men and jealousies, the hopeful child I was lost forever. All those years, things were lost and destroyed, I begin to understand how people's lives atrophy and how they live without knowing why. Now looking back, how could I say this blighting was a necessary part of growing up and that to be an adult one must lose this sense of urgency, of the here and now and the wonder of it? I used to think that I must never lose this; a spring day, a person's face, an idea so immediate that one could never forget. But I did, and the days merge into one another so that nothing is real or immediate anymore. My whole life unchronicled, bare, so unconnected that I am like a wound-up toy suddenly stopped in the middle of a crowded street with no more of that strange bright energy to propel me. My surroundings alien and me feeling as if I have suddenly been put here by a giant unfeeling hand. Now ship-wrecked on my rock in the middle of this sea, it is all almost a dream, as if I passed through it all in a trance and have not awakened till now. All those people swarming through my life mean nothing to me now, only Mike — through ties of blood.

xxi

Dreamt that I was hanging almost by the nails to the edge of a grassy and fairly innocuous-looking cliff. In the dream I knew that to fall was the end, but did not really see what was below me. Some people I knew hovered above me — my mother was one of them. Although they looked sad for me they did not help. When I woke my back was aching with the strain of keeping myself there, poised.

xxii

The house suddenly bleak and bare with all Mike's things gone; a cold Friday night and me all alone. A woman came round to take Mike's furniture in her car and looked at me as if I were a monster. I could only stare at her in bewilderment. No shoulder to cry on, and I have never felt so desolate. And the hot-water system is broken; it is all a nightmare. Oh cheerful me, sitting here with nicotine-stained fingers, sweating nervously, hungry cold, with my shorn hair and pink face, the water coming singing cold out of the tap and so dirty I am; I have become so thin. And the Friday night traffic zooming outside, and cold as cold the dusk falling around my icy ears. It would be good to have a bath, that's just what I need — steaming hot and fragrant with soap everywhere and someone to sit on the edge and talk to me as I wash. It's horrible to be so cold, I will never get warm now. The night before I woke up with my hair cut and Mike saying he hated my face, and I knew that if by any chance there had been a loaded shotgun by the bed, I would have reached down and in an idle moment shot myself through the head.

xxiii

Walking back from my last interview, no job, a gardener raking leaves in the park, misty cold sky, ragged trees. Sitting in the fish-shop waiting for my tea, raining and growing dark outside. The shopman with shining muscular elbows, warm smell of floury greasy chips, sizzling fat, wet bodies. Felt panicky about returning to the cold dead house, pushing aggressively past the ghosts as I enter the front door. Each night I dreaded Mike's key in the lock, his big boots stumping down the passage, his stiff unloving body slipped in beside mine, his curt and cold words, our brief uncaring quarrel, but he is all I have.

Rowan Metcalfe
The Cat

Lena Sherman lay back on the pillows on her bed in the big front room. She lay back and felt her head pushing into their soft white folds and the cool touch of fresh pillowslips pushing up round her face. She heard the tiny rustling of hair, crushed between scalp and pillow, and the tick tick tick of her little bedside clock, which was made of glass, with all the little turning clicking wheels twinkling through it. She lay back and listened. She thought she heard a bird in the guttering, another hopping on the iron roof. A mina maybe. She didn't care for minas so much. Such mean, shifty birds, and arrogant too. She listened, and felt sure it was a mina, to make such a loud, bold noise.

At half-past one she heard Nurse van Roon turn on the television in the living-room. There was music, and a murmuring of voices. A shower blew over, and brushed the garden with wetness and more birds came to the guttering, sending big, silvery drops of water splashing down over the edge, past her windows and down into the hydrangeas. Up in the dark wet branches of the silver birches the little darting silhouettes of birds showed black against the white, winter-white sky. Sparrows, hundreds of sparrows. She watched them darting in and out of the branches, coming and going on their little sharp snipping wings. There was always food for the sparrows in her garden. She had Nurse van Roon throw out the stale bread, every day. She had had a dish hooked into a branch of the empty almond tree and filled each week with good dripping. The sparrows knew to come every winter to her garden. And the thrushes and blackbirds and the little polished waxeyes, like jade. Even a tui now and then. And the gloating, strutting minas, of course. On warmer days she had the windows thrown open to hear them all as she lay in her bed.

At two o'clock she heard Nurse van Roon coming down the hall on her brisk rubber soles. 'Almost time for your programme, Miss Sherman,' she said, wheeling a trolley with a portable television on it up to the bed. 'Last episode next week,' she said. She stood back as the picture showed and looked sideways at it critically, with her mouth drawn in. 'It's the aerial, always the jolly aerial,' she said. 'Now let me see.' She fussed about with the aerial on top of the set, twisting it round and lifting it up and down. 'There. There. Now, I'll just prop it up with a book. All right? Ah, yes, that's better.' She stood back again and surveyed. 'Have you been all right? Do you want anything? Are you all tucked in?'

'I'm fine, Nurse van Roon. Nothing, thank you,' said Lena. But Nurse van Roon tucked in the sheets anyway, and propped up the pillows, and did some thumping and primping and fluffing with her small, quick pink hands. 'There,' she said. She looked sideways approvingly, with her hands tucked into her big white pockets. 'You know, your hair *does* look nice like that, Miss Sherman.'

'Thank you, Nurse van Roon,' said Lena. 'It's just the way you do it. I don't know what I'd do without you, as I've said before. That'll be all now. I'll call if I want you.'

Nurse van Roon left the door a little ajar. She went down the hall to the living-room and sat down on the sofa. She loosened her shoe-laces and, with a sigh, she propped her feet up on her footstool and took up her knitting. Her hands moved very fast, back and forth, back and forth, and the tiny, complicated lacy pattern fell from her needles like magic. She watched the television and she knitted and now and then she gave a little gasp or a sigh, or even a laugh — a small, pleased guffaw. And she knitted and knitted and by afternoon tea-time she had made a sleeve, a very small baby's sleeve. She held it up and looked at it, and she pulled at it so the pattern stretched open and she could see if maybe she had made a mistake somewhere and missed it. She looked at it very closely, back and front, but there were no mistakes, and she laid it out carefully over the arm of the sofa and went to make the tea.

Nurse van Roon and Lena always had their afternoon tea together. Nurse van Roon stacked up the pillows against the bedhead and Lena sat back into them with the sheets pulled up round her waist and her long, fingering hands clasped on the sheet, waiting. Nurse van Roon drew the big chair up next to the bed and poured the tea. She offered Lena the sugar, in its round, silver bowl, and the plate of biscuits, which were afghans today, with sprinkles of coconut. She took two sugars, but to the biscuits she said, 'Not today, Nurse van Roon. Just my cup of tea.'

Nurse van Roon began casting on stitches for the second sleeve. 'My niece is having her first,' she said.

'Is that so?' said Lena. 'Fancy, Nurse van Roon. A great aunt!'

'A great aunt,' said Nurse van Roon. She sighed.

'I remember our Great Aunt Alice,' said Lena. 'We were always

frightened of her, Bart and I. She was terribly stern, and she had a stick.'
Lena leant back in her pillows and took a long, slow swallow of her tea.
'You know, that's where the sugar-bowl comes from, Nurse van Roon,
from Great Aunt Alice. She left it to me. The sugar-bowl and my silver-
backed brush. And Bart's got all Great Uncle John's war medals. From
the Boer War, you know. He was killed there. She kept them in the
sideboard and she showed them to Bart every time we visited.'

'I never had a great aunt,' said Nurse van Roon, thoughtfully.

'Mother's aunt,' said Lena. She took another sip of her tea. 'That
was for best, that sugar-bowl,' she said. 'Fancy her leaving it to me.'

'Must have had a soft spot for you,' said Nurse van Roon.

'And I think one or two of those medals are quite valuable too,' said
Lena. Nurse van Roon nodded. She had already knitted an inch. 'Do
you like the pattern?' she asked, holding it up.

'Very nice,' said Lena, 'I've never been a knitter myself, as you know.
Perhaps I should. It would certainly keep me busy, wouldn't it?'

'Never too late to learn,' said Nurse van Roon, taking another afghan.
'Sure you won't have one?'

'Not today. Not that I don't like your afghans, Nurse van Roon.
Just I don't seem to feel the need today, you know.' Nurse van Roon
nodded. She brushed a crumb off her smock. 'I like the baby clothes
myself,' she said. 'I always feel inspired by baby clothes. So *dainty*.'

Lena set her cup down with a nice, chinking, bone china sound,
and looked past Nurse van Roon, through the windows into her garden
and suddenly, 'Oh, look!' she cried. 'In my garden.' And such a shudder
went through her that her teacup tipped over on its saucer and the last
of her cup of tea spilt all over her clean sheet. Nurse van Roon dropped
her knitting and leapt to rescue the teacup. But Lena was pointing out
into the garden with her long, quivering arm. 'Look, look! Can't you see
it?' she cried.

'Where, where? What is it?' said Nurse van Roon.

'A *cat*, Nurse van Roon. There's a cat in my garden!'

'So there is,' said Nurse van Roon. And sure enough, there it was.
A cat, a great, plump, rounded grey cat, was sitting on the lawn between
the camellia and the lilac. He sat very still, on his haunches and his head
was lifted up, and his ears pricked and he looked all about him, alertly,
and as the two women looked at him he turned and seemed to look right
back at them, completely unafraid, almost cunningly, as if he would eat
them too, given half a chance.

Nurse van Roon crossed to the window. She was about to throw it open and give a shout, when the cat got up and, quite slowly, he walked across the lawn and through the azaleas, looking very intent, not looking back, and was gone.

Lena leant back on her pillow. 'What an awful thing,' she said. 'What an awful thing to happen in my garden.' She closed her eyes at the thought.

'There. You mustn't upset yourself,' said Nurse van Roon. 'Just lie back now.'

'But do you think it will come again? What a terrible thing. My poor birds.'

'No, no. Now lie back and I'll change your sheet. You mustn't worry.'

'But if it comes back. . . .'

'You only need to call, and I'll shoo him away,' said Nurse van Roon. 'The cheek of him. And I only changed your sheets this morning.'

Bart Sherman was not the sort of man to announce himself at doors. He didn't come stomping in, calling out and banging things down like some men. He slipped in quietly. He drew the door closed behind him with hardly a click of the latch. Sometimes he found his sister dozing and surprised her creeping up and waking her with a kiss. Sometimes she saw him coming up the path and called, 'Hello, Bart!' as soon as he had come in the door. Today when he pushed open the door to her room there she was, sitting up waiting, her hair brushed into frail, downy curls, like a baby's, wearing a duckling coloured bed-jacket, but looking very stern about something, all the same. 'Bart,' she said, as soon as she saw him. 'The most awful thing has happened. There was a *cat* in the garden. A big tom-cat.'

'Was there?' said Bart. 'What a fright you must have had.' And he clasped the hand which she stretched out for him to take.

'It was awful,' she said. 'You've no idea. You could *see* how greedy he was. A great big tom, after my birds.'

'And did he catch any?' asked Bart.

'No, but he wanted to. You could see he was after one. Ask Nurse van Roon. She saw him too. She was here with me.'

'Well, as long as he didn't catch one,' said Bart.

'But what if he comes back, Bart?'

'I'm sure Nurse van Roon will come and frighten him away for you, if you call.'

'It's the very thought though, Bart. The very thought. A *cat* in my garden. It makes my blood run cold,' said Lena. She pressed her head back into the pillows and she closed her eyes. For a moment there was quiet. The little clock tick, tick ticked. Her long knobbled hand lay cool and moist in his own. He looked at her face, which was still soft, like a girl's, at the soft pinkish dabbings of powder she had put over her nose and cheeks, at the frail baby-curls put in by Nurse van Roon. Then she opened her eyes, slowly, as if she were waking. 'Bart,' she said, 'if ever I see it again I want you to get out the gun and shoot it.'

'The cat?' said Bart. 'But I couldn't, Lena.'

'Why not?'

'It's against the law. You aren't allowed to shoot in a built-up area. You know that.'

'But I want you to shoot it, Bart.'

'Lena, how can I? It's against the law.'

'I will not have a cat in my garden, Bartholomew,' said Lena. 'I will not lie in my bed and watch a cat come after my birds. I want you to shoot it.'

Bart and Nurse van Roon ate together at the dining-table. Nurse van Roon had turned on the radio, to dinner music. She had changed out of her stiff smock and her fluffy red-blonde hair was fanned out on either side of her face, freshly combed. She ate very busily. Her hands went back and forth between plate and mouth very quickly, they stretched out over the table for more sauce, more salt, more peas, they busied themselves sawing and slicing the food on her plate. Not until she had finished her dessert and the spoon and fork lay neatly side by side on her plate, did Bart speak. 'Lena mentioned a cat,' he said.

'Oh, yes,' said Nurse van Roon. She patted the edges of her mouth with her napkin. 'Yes, yes. She was terribly upset. We were just having our cup of tea this afternoon when she happened to look up and see it. She got such a fright she spilt her tea. All over the clean sheets. It took quite a bit to calm her. A big cat too, and he didn't give a hoot for us. You'd have thought he owned the whole garden, the way he sat there looking at us.'

'She wanted me to shoot it,' said Bart.

'Shoot it!' cried Nurse van Roon.

'But of course I couldn't anyway,' he added quickly. 'It's an offence to discharge firearms here.'

Nurse van Roon reached out to take his plate. 'Is that right?' she
said. 'Well, I just hope it doesn't come back, that's all, because I don't
know what she'll do if it does. It's not good for her to be upset like that.'

'No,' said Bart.

Nurse van Roon pushed back her chair and stood up. She picked
up the plates with one hand and the custard jug in the other, and then
suddenly, with the look of a conspirator, she leant over nearer to him.
The big, soft puffs of her hair seemed astonishingly close to his face. 'To
tell you the truth, Mr Sherman,' she said, in a hushed voice, 'I've seen
that cat before. Only yesterday, as a matter of fact, round the back, but
I didn't say anything. I didn't want to upset her. Do you think I should
have said something?'

'No, no, don't worry about it, Nurse van Roon. Perhaps it won't
come again,' he said.

'P'raps not.' She straightened up. 'Cup of tea?' she asked him.

Bart took his cup of tea to his bedroom and closed the door. He
straightened out the bedclothes and sat down on his bed with his feet
on the small square rug beside his bed. With only his bedside lamp on
the room was quite dark and there was the warm rough smell of dust,
which he liked, and would not let Nurse van Roon come in and clean
away, poking among his things with her brooms and dusters. It was his
room and he would not have a woman in among his private things.
Sometimes he wondered if he ought to lock the door when he went out
in the morning. Perhaps it wasn't quite as private as he thought. Once
there had been fingerprints, two or three, very faint, on the top of his
bureau, but he had let it pass. It was only once, and a woman is naturally
curious.

He finished his tea and lay back against the pillow with his hands
behind his head, to relax. He looked at the ceiling, which was always
the same, and he crossed his ankles and wriggled his toes inside his socks.
There was a coldness though, coming up round his calves, under his
trouser legs, so he got up and went quietly, in his socks, to the kitchen
to get the two-bar heater, and he reached into the dark cobwebby space
under his bedside table to plug it in. It made friendly pinging noises,
warming up, and glowed nicely red. He felt warmer straight away. It
was raining again, quite heavily, making a comforting drumming on the
roof. In the corner opposite his bed, standing between the wardrobe and
the wall, was the gun, which had been his father's. It had not been used
for years. In fact, when he thought about it, Bart could not remember

the last time it had been fired, although now and then he took it out and brushed the dust off it, and maybe gave it a quick oil. He had always meant to sell it, but Lena said not to, because one day he might need it. 'Need it? What for?' he had asked.

'Well, to *shoot* something,' she had replied. 'You never know Bart, when the need might arise.'

So it was still there, and he wished now that he had sold it.

The room was warming. He let one arm fall over the edge of the bed into the hot beam of the heater, and he felt his fingers becoming warm, hot, growing large and loose with warmth. The rain rushed past the windows and the heater ping pinged and a trailing loop of dusty cobweb, high up above the bed, wavered gently, like a seaweed, rising and falling on the tide of warm air. How safe his room was, how safe and comforting after the office, with the silly girls tap tapping on their typewriters, dashing about on their high, clacking heels, talking and chattering all day, brushing their hair and cleaning their nails and fussing with themselves like a lot of little twittering squirrels. How safe and still here. Nothing moving but the high loop of web, rising and falling, rising and falling. And yet he was uneasy and after a while he got up from the bed and he took the gun from its place in the corner. He lifted it, rather gingerly, and ran his forefinger along the barrel. A black, rather oily dust stained the tip of his finger and he wiped it carefully on his trousers. On the top of the wardrobe he found the box of rags and a little black bottle of oil, and the long rod, with a twist of oily rag at its tip left from the last time he had done the job. He sat down on the bed, arranging himself comfortably so his feet were in the warmth of the heater and took the gun between his knees. With the prongs of the fork that he kept in the box specially, he prised the cork from the oil bottle. He ripped off a new piece of rag, dabbed it with oil, and threaded it through the loop at the end of the rod. Then, holding the rifle tight between his knees, he took the rod and forced it, quivering, down, down, into the tiny, dark round slot of the barrel.

'Like to go and sit out on the porch a bit?' asked Nurse van Roon when she'd cleared away the morning-tea things and shaken the crumbs off the counterpane. 'It's cleared up lovely. Only the occasional cloud now,' and without waiting for an answer she was off into the hall to fetch the wheel-chair and Lena heard it making little surprised squeaks as Nurse van Roon unfolded it, and then into the bedroom she came, pushing it as proudly as if she were bringing in a shiny new perambulator with a brand new baby in it. Neatly she swung it round on its big, silent, ballbearing wheels. 'Ready to go?' she said. 'Got your book, got your specs?' And little as she was, she bundled Lena up in her arms as if she were made of concertina paper and swung her into the chair in one perfect arc.

'Oof, you always take me by surprise,' said Lena, with one hand to her heart.

'Never you worry, Miss Sherman,' said Nurse van Roon. 'I've been a nurse now for what, nearly twenty years, and never dropped anyone yet. There you go. Cushion. Rugs.' With a shake of the big rug and a thump of the pillow she'd tucked Lena in. She arranged her book and her glasses on her lap as if it were a little table, she fluffed her fingers through her hair, and out they went.

'You know,' said Lena, when they reached the porch, 'you know, I might just like to go right out on the grass this morning.' She leaned forward, sniffing the air.

'Well, if you're sure you won't be cold,' said Nurse van Roon. 'Another blanket maybe. . . .'

'I'm as warm as toast,' said Lena. 'I've never felt the cold. You know that.'

'I wouldn't want you to catch a chill though,' said Nurse van Roon. 'Now whereabouts. Just there by the lilac?' She wheeled her down the ramp, which Bart had specially built in place of the steps, and along the path and she arranged her on the grass as if she were going to be the subject of a painting.

'There's spring in the air don't you think?' said Lena.

'There certainly is, Miss Sherman. Another month or so and you'll be wanting to be out all day every day I expect. Now, are you comfy?'

'Comfy,' said Lena.

Nurse van Roon went to finish the washing. 'I'll be back just as soon as it's on the line,' she called when she reached the porch and as she looked back her eye caught, for just a moment, the sunlight sparking off the chrome of the chair, and the glowing red blanket, like a fire, consuming the little pale stick of Miss Sherman as she sat there in her garden.

The sky was a tender, silvery shade of blue and daubed with small, wet-looking clouds that melted away at the edges. And there was the sun at last, glittering and winking up above the birches. Lena tipped up her face. She closed her eyes to feel the white light of the sky pressed upon her lids and the dark lacework pattern of branches and leaves and twigs,

printed upon the light. She felt the cool, moist air flowing over her face
and through her hair. The birdsong pressed on her as if it were a solid
thing, a ringing, vibrating wall of pure sound. She breathed deep and
the air went rushing down into her lungs, into her blood, like a liquid,
and it was so perfect, so exquisite, that she felt about to burst out of herself
and unfold, like a flower breaking out of its bud. And when she opened
her eyes again it seemed the whole garden was alive. The trees yearned
quivering upwards to the sky, the plants almost trembled in the earth,
the big wet lily clumps under the trees seemed full of life, dark and secret.
The whole garden was stretching, straining, reaching up and out of the
wet earth into the sky and the sunlight. And on every branch were her
birds. So many that the very air vibrated with their song and the beating
of their wings. Among the branches their little pert, bobbing silhouettes
showed dark, they set the fine, drooping twigs of the birches all moving,
they came and went — up into the light then back again, they sat watching
and listening and waiting, they cocked their heads and shook their
feathers, and it seemed as if, with their rising and settling, they were
making music, as if each bird, with every movement struck a note, and
the sounds soared up on their wings and the trees were great reed pipes
to carry the sound, and it was the music that made the plants all tremble
and each limb and leaf and stalk to reach lovingly towards her, as if to
bear her up with them, up and up, up through the treetops and into the
sky.

But it was only for a moment, for suddenly, with a strange, pattering
rush of wingbeats, the birds were going, going. In dismay she saw them
fly up at once, through the highest network of branches, scattering into
the sky and gone. And there was nothing. The garden seemed to hold
its breath and there was silence. Then, from the dark shrubbery down
near the hedge, came the little shrill, cutting cry of a captured bird.

'But it's only a cat,' Bart had said. 'I don't think you ought to be getting
yourself so *upset* about a cat.'

'Only a cat!' Lena had cried. 'It's coming murdering my birds,
frightening my birds away! Don't you care that it's coming killing my
birds?' And the very thought seemed too much and she shut her eyes
and leaned back.

'Of course I care, you know I do, Lena,' said Bart, and he looked
down and saw that her hand, lying in his own, was a limp, broken white
wing and her pulse tapping at his fingers was the heart of a little broken

bird, unable to fly. And yes, he cared, he cared, he was overcome with sorrow and he stroked the little limp hand. 'But what can I do?' he said.

She sat up, she almost sprang at him. 'You can shoot the cat!' she cried.

'Lena, I *can't*,' he said. 'I can't break the law.'

'Then you're a coward,' she had said, leaning back again. 'Nothing but a coward. You were a cowardly little boy and you're a coward now.' She folded her hands on the sheets and closed her eyes. She closed her whole face. He was a coward.

Nurse van Roon, coming down the hall with the dinner tray, had heard it all, but she kept her face quite straight and said nothing until Miss Sherman asked her what she thought. And then she said it wasn't her place to take sides but if she had to say one way or the other she'd be inclined to agree with Mr Sherman. 'After all, it *is* only a cat Miss Sherman,' she said. 'And if it'll make you feel any better I'll go to the neighbours tomorrow and enquire. It must *belong* to somebody, and it wouldn't be right to kill somebody's pet would it?'

'But it kills *my* pets,' said Lena.

'Well, it's natural for a cat to be a hunter,' said Nurse van Roon.

'But not in *my* garden,' said Lena. 'I won't have it hunting in my garden, natural or not.' And when Nurse van Roon set out the dinner tray she only sniffed at the chops that Nurse van Roon had grilled so nicely and said she didn't have an appetite tonight, thank you all the same.

'Well, you please yourself, Miss Sherman,' said Nurse van Roon, 'but it won't do you any good to go without your dinner.'

There was a certain sympathy between Bart and Nurse van Roon that evening at the table. 'Quite personally, I'm rather fond of cats,' remarked Nurse van Roon. 'I always think there's nothing like a cat to make you feel cosy.'

'Well, that's odd, Nurse van Roon,' said Bart. 'I never thought of you as a cat lover.'

'Oh yes,' said Nurse van Roon. 'I'm very fond of cats.'

'Myself, I don't care one way or the other about them,' said Bart. 'But between you and me, I've always rather fancied having a dog.'

'A dog!' said Nurse van Roon. 'Well, why *not*, Mr Sherman? It'd be company for you, wouldn't it. A nice spaniel. . . .'

'Yes, but it's a bit much trouble really, isn't it?' said Bart. 'And it wouldn't be very fair on Lena, having a dog barking and frightening the birds. I don't think she'd like it at all.'

'No,' said Nurse van Roon.

'And I do try to please her you know, when I can,' he said. 'But this business of the cat, Nurse van Roon. I couldn't break the law, could I? You understand?'

Nurse van Roon laid down her cutlery, and gently she touched his hand across the table. '*Quite* understand, Mr Sherman,' she said. '*Quite* understand.'

The sky was stretched above the trees, taut and bright as the skin of a blue balloon when, after Saturday lunch, Nurse van Roon came down the front path with a bundle of glinting garden tools and her biggest apron on. Business-like, she set to work, down on her knees by the iris beds, her hands in among the stiff blades of iris leaves, down into the still, dark, wet soil, turning out the weeds, tugging out their white roots and tossing them behind her. The little trowel glittered in the sun, her soiled, white-pink hands went in and out among the leaves and the soil and the soft rotted layer of old leaves that lay on the surface, tugging out the weeds and tossing them behind, and the gold coloured fleece of her hair bobbed above her bent little body, springing out fine and soft into the sharp air. From the back of the house came the sound of digging, the chunking sound of spade driving into earth, the occasional ring of a stone against the metal, as Bart cleared the plot for this year's tomatoes. Half-way along the iris bed Nurse van Roon lifted her hair from her forehead with one of her soiled hands and sat back on her heels to look back at what she had done. The new-turned earth glistened dark and moist and clodded along the bed and the weeds lay back behind where she had moved in a long row, their thin white roots tangled on the grass. Nurse van Roon gave a little sigh and pushed back her hair again. She looked back up the other way where she still had to clear, and then behind again and then, as she was about to take the trowel in her hand again, she saw it. She saw it move silent and sure-pawed between the bushes and step out on to the sunlit grass like a dancer on to the stage. The cat. She saw it stop, sit down on its strong rounded haunches, with its tail lying twitching out on the grass beside it. Its ears pricked up, its head lifted, watching, its back curving straight to the earth, fur licked with silver, ears up twitching, prickling with energy. And he sat there, prickling with stillness, a part of the earth, and Nurse van Roon too, sat rigid and electric, speared for one moment to the earth, as if *she* were the prey he had come for. And then she laid down her trowel, and the cat was looking at her, holding her with his sharp eyes. For a time they sat motionless, and then she called, quietly, 'Puss, puss.' He pricked his ears, watching her. 'Pussy puss,' she called again. And he stood up. He came towards her. She saw his strong, silver grey legs coming silently, one in front of the other, across the grass to her, his green gold eyes, unblinking, the long, soft white tufts at the tips of his ears. 'Puss,' she whispered, as it dropped down by her and rubbed its back against her knees, as it turned over and showed its long, thick furred belly, its eyes closed, rolling with pleasure under her hands. And she felt how warm it was, how warm and living under her hands, and how its fur slipped through her fingers and the light slid liquid over it and how gentle were its round satiny paws, like a kitten's. So when Bart came round from the back of the house he saw her bent over something and came to see. 'The cat!' he said. Nurse van Roon lifted up her face to him and sunlight sparked gold in the soft mass of her hair and lit up her face and her soft woman's lips. 'Yes,' she said. 'It's him. But look how playful he is, Mr Sherman. Look, feel how thick his fur is, and how gentle he is.' And Bart went down on his knees with the cat between them, to feel its silvery fur, but he saw, too, Nurse van Roon's little plump, sugar coloured hands, dirtied with earth, and her face washed clean by light and her spangled hair and in one strange quivering moment, with the sun warm on his back and humming in his head, he put out his hand and laid his fingers among the springing red gold curls, as she had laid her fingers through the fur of the cat.

At that moment Lena, who had woken earlier than usual, let out a strange little howl, a shriek of anger.

On Sunday morning when Nurse van Roon had gone away, Lena lay alone in the big front room, and the glass clock tick tick ticked, and the white counterpane lay unsmoothed, hills and valleys and a long, white horizon, across her. Half-past twelve had already gone and the lunch tray had not come, with the squeaking of Nurse van Roon's soles, the little rattle of plates, the bobbing of her brushed-out hair, the quick, touching, pink-white hands to smooth the bed, brush the crumbs. Oddly empty the house lay. And Nurse van Roon was not there. She had gone, first thing in the morning. She had said she would not stay in any house where she was called a traitor and a liar. Bart had asked her, begged her to stay. For Lena's sake. But how could she stay, even another day in a house where she was called a traitor. 'After all I've done for your sister, Mr Sherman, and when I think that it's all this trouble over a cat.

No, I'm sorry, Mr Sherman, but it's all arranged.' And she had not even let him carry her bags down to the gate. She got the taxi-driver to come up for them. And Bart, though he knew it was past lunchtime and Lena would be waiting, silently, for him, would not go to her. He stayed quiet in the house and he watched from the windows, the birds flicking in and out of the branches in the garden. He looked at the iris bed, still only half weeded, and the branched stems among the leaves with the new, tight rolled wettish buds of iris flowers, and the row of shrivelled weeds lying along the grass. He saw the fat, orange-pink rosettes of leaves breaking from the withered stems of the climbing rose along the porch rails, and all morning he watched, silently, how the birds came down to the almond tree to peck at the lumps of lard.

Lena did not call. The house was quiet and he waited, watching the birds flick between the branches.

Until at last it came. On its light silver feet treading over the grass. It came walking through the shadows, round and heavy and strong, but weightless, gliding. Bart took the gun from its place. He slid a cartridge into place and cocked it and gently he pushed open the window. And the cat was there on the grass, looking at him, so sharp, so bright, so real, that it was as if something locked between them, they became locked into one strange pulling current, he and the cat, as if the same blood ran through them, through the earth and through the air. But gently, gently he raised the gun and aimed, and the very green of the grass seemed to dazzle him and the birdsong roared through him like the pulse of blood, and he fired. With the sound of the shot the garden seemed to shatter up and out, breaking into a myriad sharp pieces, the birds rose shrilling in waves from the trees, and the cat leapt, fell, and was still.

Edith Campion
Good Morning Wardrobe

'I'll wear the beige.' Mrs Crimpton spoke largely to the small room. She sat back in bed as if she expected an obedient servant, black-dressed, white-aproned, to appear with the breakfast tray.

Her eyes commanded the room to increase its size. The large unwieldy furniture settled more comfortably into the new dimensions.

'I had a very good night's rest,' she addressed the wardrobe. 'Perhaps I shall pop into town later.'

Mrs Crimpton's life fell from hangers in the large, be-mirrored wardrobe. The styles suggested a short opulent span commencing in the forties and ending abruptly in the fifties.

'Tea,' she commanded; and moved to her kitchen, a large, rather common table. Her long hands wove a spell above the colourful plastic cloth, plugging in the jug, warming the worthy silver teapot, then casting the gritty black leaves within.

She caught a shadow glance of herself in one of the mirrors. 'A model figure, Norma — you have a model figure.' Someone had once said that many years ago and it would often sing in her mind. 'A model figure. . . .'

She smiled at the distant figure. Raw-boned, she had become a tall old mare, not a good doer.

Her hand grasped the teapot handle, her nails spots of blood against the white skin. She tilted the silver pot, filling her cup, the sound was comforting.

'Ah. . . .'

She pulled the curtain across and craned her neck to look at the sky. Blue. A patch of blue. She cast open the curtains upon a dark grey concrete wall.

'I shall wear the beige,' she told the wardrobe. She placed the large delicate bone china cup by the bed and returned to its warmth. She examined her wristwatch. Nine-fifteen, plenty of time. She didn't want to be there until twelve, but there was much to be accomplished before that hour.

She sighed and reached up a hand to touch one of the rollers screwing her chestnut hair tightly to her head. She began to unroll it and its companions. Each released curl sprang back to caress her head. When they were all at liberty, she shook her head and the curls danced, giving her the look of an aged Shirley Temple. She tumbled her hair happily with her fingers.

'You haven't hair, Norma. It's like a wild mane,' sang her memory.

She wiped the night cream from her face. What was today? She had 'bath rights' Tuesday, Thursday and Saturday; and sometimes she managed to sneak one on Sunday. She moved to the basin and washed carefully, powdering her body. She slipped into her padded bra, white embroidered slip, suspender belt and stockings. She could never bring herself to wearing stocking tights, they seemed to her unfeminine. She slipped on her dressing-gown.

Seated before the dressing-table mirror she examined her face — this was the one moment that shook her day. Her hand trembled as it reached for the first magic pot. Moisture cream. Her fingers tenderly smoothed her cheeks and fluttered across her brow. An olive base followed. The fingers paused, seeking colour for cheeks and finally lipstick. Her confidence returned. She smiled and nodded to herself. She trapped her eyelashes in the curler. They lay clamped, her eye bald, vulnerable. Skilfully she blacked the lashes and darkened her eyebrows. She sat quite still regarding her art. Had she made the chestnut hair too dark last time?

'No,' she assured the mirror. 'It's perfect.'

Nearly eleven. She would be late. She slipped on her white sling-back shoes and took out the beige dress. It fitted snugly at the waist; she ignored current fashion, the childish smocks and tiny skirts; they had no dignity.

She turned back to the mirror, took up her brush and attacked the tight bobbing curls. They bounced rebelliously. She tamed them with the comb. She reached up to the shelf in the wardrobe and drew out a ginger, long-furred hat. Carefully she placed it on the even-spaced curls, securing it with a hat-pin.

She smiled, almost laughed with pleasure. She opened the drawer and picked out a pair of gloves, took up her purse and a beige umbrella that was almost a parasol, paused before the long wardrobe mirror, fumbled in her bag and produced a pair of dark glasses.

'I'll be back after lunch,' she told the mirror.

She teetered down the stairs, clinging to the banister-rail. She wove her way down many levels to the street. At the door she blinked and covered her eyes with the dark glasses, which she wore, sunshine, cloud-dark.

She moved carefully through the street, switching back the years. Heads turned. The rare bird moved through the jeans and mini-skirts. It was as if a Spanish galleon had sailed into Wellington Harbour.

She enjoyed the attention. She could still turn heads. She smiled contentedly to herself and strolled on to James Smith's. She entered the doors at twelve. Took the lift.

'How are you today?' The attendant had known her for many years.

'Wonderful. It's a perfect day outside. Thank you.' She swept into her second-floor world, looked about and took a chair outside the tea-rooms.

She waited expectantly. An old woman lowered herself carefully into the chair beside her.

'How are you today?'

'Getting a bit slower all the time.'

She smiled at age. Someone took the chair on her other flank. Nicely dressed — but those short skirts were common.

'Have you the time, please?' she asked the new arrival.

'Twelve-fifteen.'

'What a very charming watch.'

'A present from my fiancé.' The young woman sounded as if this was a new situation and she wanted to test 'my fiancé', caress it with her tongue, let it hang in the air and command admiration. 'I'm waiting for him, for lunch.'

Mrs Crimpton nodded, a queen in approval.

'How wonderful for you both. I'm waiting for my husband. We've been married a very long time, most happily. I hope you will be just as happy.'

Mrs Crimpton disappeared from the girl's consciousness as she rose and moved towards the fiancé.

A woman in middle years caught Mrs Crimpton's eye. She was dressed elegantly in black. She was very smart, Mrs Crimpton had to admit. She touched her fur hat fondly and rummaged in her purse for her mirror. She bent her eyes and felt a pang of disappointment in the silvered image that looked critically back at her. Perhaps the lipstick was too heavy. The woman in black stood and moved towards a friend — taking Mrs Crimpton's sense of failure with her.

A mother with a large shopping bag and a small child sank thankfully into a chair. Her face pink, her breathing fussed.

'What a gorgeous child.' Mrs Crimpton removed her dark glasses and made her brown eyes warm. 'You have the deepest, warmest brown eyes I have ever seen,' sang memory.

'Thank you,' said the mother. 'But she is tiring to shop with.'

'Ah — but they are such companions. I do envy you. I had no children.' She replaced the dark glasses, a symbol of mourning for lack of offspring; and to hide the self-pity welling in her eyes.

The mother was too tired to deal with this confession of failure. Gratefully she perceived her husband pushing towards her, and thrust herself from the chair, almost toppling child and shopping in her desire to escape.

'Nice little woman,' said Mrs Crimpton to the old lady.

A rather military man now sat at attention in the vacant chair, looking sternly at people. Who would dare be late for him? thought Mrs Crimpton; and didn't attempt conversation.

'Darling, I'm sorry.' She was beautiful. The rigidity fell from the man as he stood beside her. He took her arm and they moved away. Mrs Crimpton was glad, and sad. She looked at her watch. One-fifteen.

'Isn't it beautiful out?' A large woman tossed the words to Mrs Crimpton like flowers.

'Just like spring,' she agreed.

'The harbour looked beautiful from the bus.'

'Yes,' said Mrs Crimpton. 'My house looks down on it and it was perfect this morning.'

'You are lucky to have a harbour view.'

Mrs Crimpton nodded: 'I've just had lunch with my husband and I'm getting my shopping list together.' She returned to the handbag and produced pen and notebook.

'I've only myself to shop for, so it's easy remembered,' said her companion.

'It is harder when you have a husband and a family,' smiled Mrs Crimpton, attacking her list. She glanced at the clock on the wall. 'I must rush. It's been delightful talking to you.' She rose and moved towards the lift.

'Ground, please.'

'Pleasant lunch?' asked her attendant.

'Lovely — the grills are always good. Thank you.'

She moved with dignity through the crowded shop and into the open air. She crossed the street in a river of people.

At the Sanitarium she bought two sandwiches and carefully placed them in her bag. She moved jauntily up Cuba Street.

Home. She paused at the door. It was good to be home, but the thought of the stairs to be climbed daunted. She took the banister-rail firmly in a gloved hand and started the ascent. Outside she paused, short-breathed, fumbled for the key and opened the door.

'I'm back,' she informed the room.

She sat at the dressing-table, stripped off the gloves and removed the fur hat, shaking her hair loose. She smiled happily at herself — the dressing-table — and the wardrobe.

'I was right to wear the beige,' she confided. 'I've had a lovely day.'

Annabel Fagan
In a Bamboo Garden

Mrs Palit was a no-nonsense type of woman with a very sprightly walk for her sixty-five years. Her grandmother had been a Kashmiri girl of middling family and lovely, lovely black eyes. Mrs Palit was Anglo-Indian with fair skin and drooped blue eyes but she was not ashamed of her inherited blood like her sister was. Her sister, who had married an Englishman and brought up white children, called it a taint and talked about *these people*, meaning Indians. Mrs Palit had married a Bengali widower and brought up his four brown children as her own. She had never given birth to any babies herself — no time, she said and besides, it wouldn't have been fair to her husband's children if she'd had any of her own. She had always been a very busy woman and she wouldn't have been able to give them the attention they deserved and needed, she might have discriminated. But like her sister she spoke English with a 'chichi' Anglo-Indian accent and the local people, *them*, the Indians, regarded them as English and foreign.

During the short cool winter Mrs Palit wore nylon stockings brought specially from London and then the servants' children would nudge each other and giggle at the strange habits of the memsahib.

— Why pull another skin over your first especially when it was the same colour and was so thin and full of tiny holes that it couldn't possibly keep you warm? Why didn't she wear a long sari like their mothers instead of short dresses like children. Didn't this white woman realize that only girls of premarriageable age showed their legs in that shameful manner? And the funny way she moved her feet must be due to the fact that she sometimes wore shoes with blocks of wood under them — heels they were called. They made her walk stiffly with her legs wide apart like a baby taking its first steps —

And the children would peep at her as she walked widely down from the house to her car, their eyes full of rude laughter, their tongues only on the latch. Then when she had driven away, they would mimic their memsahib by strutting busily up and down the path, their little bottoms sticking out and looking as gay and as bright as jungle fowl and not at all like the pallid, conservatively dressed Mrs Palit. Their parents would smile

indulgently at one another nodding in agreement and the vegetable
woman would squat by the wall of the house and call someone to help
her lift the heavy basket of carrots, potatoes and cabbages off her old
head. There she would rest comfortably in the warm winter sun and join
in the fun screeching with enjoyment at the disrespectful play. And the
children, excited by all the unusual attention would start showing off and
shouting,

— Halloa, whatisyourname . . . itissaveryfineday — to each other
in English, until a servant with a sense of dignity and respect would shoot
outraged from the house and scream furiously at them to stop.

His thin bare legs would dance angrily on the spot in time to his
words and he would wave a stick menacingly at the suddenly stilled
children,

— Badmarsh — he would shout — rascals, villains. Your little arses
wouldn't be sticking out so proudly once I had beaten them black and
blue for you! — At once the parents, in hastily donned and righteous
indignation, would leap up from the comfortable ground to run and beat
the offspring for their bad behaviour. The vegetable woman would
hurriedly start calling her wares in the midst of the scolding — (and
shouting and crying of those unfortunate children who had been caught
and slapped — ayiiiiiiii, ayiiiiiiii — they would wail).

— Gobi, arlu, piarj — the vegetable woman would shout — cabbage,
potatoes, onions, good vegetables, fresh this morning — she would lie.

Mrs Palit never noticed the ridiculing laughter of the children or
if she did she never thought it worth bothering about or commenting on.
She always was far too busy and apart from that she was used to stares
and giggles and children following her around the villages she visited in
times of famine and drought which she almost always did these years
in this particular part of India. Today she was going to a village where
relief wheat and rice were being given out, to make sure it was distributed
properly. The people there were desperately poor and emaciated — beaten
down and apathetic through lack of food and care. She knew that some
she had seen alive last week would be dead now. Horrific stories were
circulating of people selling and even eating their own children in order
to stay alive and Mrs Palit didn't discount these stories. In India she never
discounted anything. She merely made sure that her own servants and
their families had plenty to eat and did what she could for the millions
and millions and millions of others. She did a lot but it was infinitesimal
— like a stalactite dripping slowly, slowly away only to have to look down,

not far, to find it treacherously building itself up again and therefore it was all in vain — useless. Or was it? Didn't it eventually, after years and years of patient doing, achieve union with itself, a kind of orgasm when it formed itself into one perfect homogenous whole — not shaky or tenuous, but solid and sure and enduring now. Was it worth it? Was it? She thought it *was* and so she organized and nagged and shouted and journeyed until *something* was done. If her car broke down or her driver was sick, she travelled for miles over dusty, holed, uncomfortable roads by bicycle rickshaw.

As she sped along the road towards the village, driving first of all through the town, she passed a flow of cows and people. The car honked and twisted but didn't slow down, adding its own noise and menace to the bedlam of the streets. Rickshaws, buses and trucks competed for right-of-way. Beautiful brown women in bright, bright saris walked with straight, easy elegance through the unpaved streets clutched at by pantsless brown babies. Short brown men dressed in glaring white dhotis or pyjamas sat gossiping on steps or leaning on their shop counters, their huge stomachs held proud before them. Every now and then they spat juicily and betel-redly into the street adding in their own way to the colour, confusion and chaos. Mrs Palit didn't look at any of them, didn't hear or smell them. She was thinking of her bamboo.

In her garden, her riotous, flamboyant, lovely Indian garden she grew many things and had a gardener to help her. To English eyes her garden was startlingly bright, not orderly, no rows of this and that, no subdued shrubs or well behaved pale English flowers — although she did have *some* English style, her roses for example. She loved her bushes of roses and was in fact president of The Rose Society which met once a year to hold a rose flower show where the rich and fat and rose-loving of the whole area met to give speeches and to eat a lot and to arrogantly or anxiously show their superior roses. But what Mrs Palit loved best of all and was most proud of in her garden was her black bamboo. She had yellow bamboo — a whole small forest of immensely tall thick bamboos which shone bright like swords of sunshine shooting aggressively up to challenge their sun-father Suriya. Oh, they were brilliant and shocking in their unEnglish-like, radiant, eye-shattering and absolute yellowness! But they weren't so rare as the black bamboo.

It had been brought back from the jungle and given to Mrs Palit damaged and hacked down and almost totally without life. But Mrs Palit had nurtured and cherished it with determination and passion. She loved it for its rarity, its unique blackness and fought as hard for its life as she did for jobs for her grown-up crippled and blind children from the institutions she patronized. It living and not dying, it giving leaf and not withering, it overcoming and not succumbing caused Mrs Palit to admire and respect it. She was an indomitable woman, not given much to self-pity and she both approved of and understood those qualities in plants, animals and people. Her husband had died last year suddenly, while writing a letter to his wife who had been away from home. His death was completely unexpected; he had not been ill and Mrs Palit had felt stunned and depleted by the loss of the Hindu brown man she cared for so much. It was as if she had been physically brutalized — she felt dizzy and ill with bereavement — she couldn't eat or walk or energetically do anything and finally she was packed off to London to recover. But she didn't stay long although she liked London for short visits. — I'm weary — she told herself — and sad. My husband is dead but I can't stay here where there are supermarkets and laundrettes around every corner full of grey people. I can't stay here where you can buy fresh bread and milk and butter five minutes away but can pick no mangos from the non-existent mango trees. — I'm going back to India — she snapped to her friends and relations — what can I do in this cold place full of cars and traffic noises. Everything is too organized and ordered here, there is nothing for me to do — except housework and I hate housework. There, my servants do such things. And I can't do nothing! Besides I love it there. In India —

So she mourned Mr Palit in the non-privacy of India, in between visits to villages here and organizing monies for her charities there, and she was busy and happy.

The bamboo was as black, black as the yellow bamboo was yellow — it made no compromize over colour. But today, this very morning, early, early, before it had become warm, before even the dudhwalli, the milkwoman, had been, Mrs Palit, walking precariously — or so it seemed to the children — in her garden had found two, three, no *five* tiny green shoots marring the blackness of the bamboo's body. She had excitedly told her sister, then her gardener when he arrived and her neighbours. It was well that bamboo! It had spirit! It had grown roots, rare black roots. Her bamboo was living! In triumph she led the small procession to see it, with pride she boasted of its 'pulling through' under her 'nursing and supervision'. She talked about it through breakfast — the miracle, the 'agynrysing' and she thought about it in her car as she was driven to a village full of dead and dying and alive people; alive in their bodies but dead in their minds. People who could no longer even feel despair. Their babies cried — they could no longer hear them — their parents held open their mouths for water and they could no longer see them — flies sat on their lips and the corners of their eyes, darkened still further their dark nostrils and they could no longer feel them. Pathetic, apathetic, dehumanized.

Mrs Palit spoke Hindi loudly and fluently and somewhat ungrammatically. Her voice would bulldoze through a crowd of milling disorganized people, scattering them into order or at least hiding, like bits of brown earth. Then she herself would widen the furrow with her brisk presence — as she did now at the death-besieged village. She hardly looked at the body of an old man whose ribs rose up out of his body like those of a dead cow. She merely ordered that he be removed in case of disease. She didn't comment on the lack of children to follow her around, to giggle and nudge and stare as those in her own household did, thank god.

— cheeky — her sister complained.

— But healthily unbloated. Noisy little rascals. Badmarsh – said Mrs Palit thankfully. Now she shouted at the distributors and at the villagers. She intruded. She tried to ensure that everything was done, to utilize what poor resources they had as evenly and as fairly as possible.

Later, as she was about to leave a woman accosted her. The seizure was done with the eyes only — the woman stood there mute and demanding holding her baby. Mrs Palit looked at the child. It was small, undernourished but not starving and it could still cry. It appeared to be about six months old but was probably about a year, Mrs Palit guessed. She was on the point of giving some money and bananas when something moved under the woman's dirty, red and white, limp, cotton sari. It was a tiny, feeble almost unnoticeable movement and hardly caused a ripple in the cloth.

— What's that – she said arrested.

— Dusera buccha, meri bucchi, another baby, my girl baby. They are twins — the woman answered as she drew back her sari to reveal her daughter. The diminutive child hung there on her mother's hip looking much like the old dead man, reduced, only she was still alive — just. She was mangy and swollen with starvation and her skin hung thin, almost leather-like over her slight, weak baby bones. Her face had become deformed and grotesque through suffering and deterioration and barely appeared human. She was a starveling, an almost dead, deprived, small thing and seemed to be only a few weeks old. Mrs Palit looked at the woman — the mother.

— My son must live. He is a boy and must live so I feed him. She is a girl and no good to anyone. Soon she will die — the woman said dispassionately, drawing her sari and covering over the pitiful, piteous, unpitied fragment of useless, unlived life. Mrs Palit walked to her car and sat in it. While her driver was starting it up, she looked back and watched as the woman fed her boy baby pieces of banana. The woman didn't eat any herself.

— Jaldi, jaldi — she shouted impatiently at her driver, — hurry up. I don't want to sit here *all* day. What's the matter. What's wrong. Why is it that you people are so stupid, so incompetent *all* the time. Why can't you use your brains for *once*. —

The driver, without glancing at her, imperturbably started the car and drove off. He drove skilfully but with apparent abandon, manoeuvring, honking and wrestling with the wheel. And the time Mrs Palit sitting forward agitatedly on the back seat raged at him.

— Not so fast! You dolt, you idiot. We nearly hit that tree. I suppose you want to see me dead. The passenger is always the one at most risk, don't think I don't know that. Watch that child! Mind that cow! I don't know. I'll just have to get a new man to drive me. . . . By the time they arrived home she was exhausted.

— Ah — she sighed — a cup of tea. I'm too old for all this journeying —

— Memsahib — Phulo, who had been with her for twenty years came anxiously down the steps, her bare feet flip-flapping on the concrete, her ugly face yet uglier with worry and concern.

— What is it — Mrs Palit said tiredly.

Sharma pushed past Phulo. Her face was round with importance, brimming with news.

— Somebody broke into the garden and trampled the bamboo — Sharma said.

— the black bamboo Memsahib —

It was true — the bamboo was smashed, senselessly destroyed, its brittle bones ground into the soil, its once joyful, searching buds a slither of green pulp on the brown earth. Mrs Palit stared silently at the black remnants then turned her back and went into the house followed by Phulo, Sharma and the gardener. There the three stood in a group and looked on in puzzlement and awe as Mrs Palit sat carefully and neatly in a cane chair and began to lament.

Keri Hulme
Kiteflying Party at Doctors' Point

You said, write it all down, write it out, put it in writing.

Well, I will try.

It is not easy.

After years of marking essays, one is inclined to mark oneself. Teaching a craft tends to make one overly sensitive, and thus, ill at ease when handling it. One becomes a critic rather than a practitioner.

However, I will try. I will take it as it comes.

. . .

I am neither young nor old. I suppose I had a sheltered childhood, and have led a sheltered life. For as long as I can remember, I wanted to engage in an academic career. I have been a lecturer for some years, with some success. My career has not been meteoric, but it hasn't been a failure. I have been out here for three months.

. . .

You said to mention the physical details as much as possible. There isn't that much to me, physically speaking.

I am not tall, I am not beautiful, but I am not ugly. I look puffed, like swollen dough, yet my nose is sharp and my fingers are long and thin. This is a family discrepancy, I mean trait.

. . .

It had been a usual kind of night, that is disturbed. Fogged. Anaesthetized.

. . .

I will try to make it *present*.

. . .

The day is bright.

At least, outside the day is bright. In here it's the same as it is as at night, dark and stale and still.

The doorbell shrills a high continuing summons.

I have been trying to clean up, ever since I heard the car sound the horn. The horn was a challenge, the blare a knight crusading might have made, outside castle perilous.

The clamour stops.

I open the door.

Half a dozen of them, and M and K and C and D, bright in their summer clothes.

They importune,

'Come with us eh!'

and the children dart round, flashy and venomous as tropical fish.

I suppose I look furtive and sleepy-eyed, but they don't seem to notice.

They chorus,

'It's a beaut day!' 'The weather's corker!' 'We'll have a neat time!' 'C'mon! C'mon!'

I can not get used to the way they truncate, abuse, alter the language. 'What?'

'We're goin to tha beach!'

They grin collectively, they all smile, they exude friendliness.

'It'll bring you out of your moodiness,' murmurs K. 'Chase away those blues eh?'

'Moodiness? Blues?' I disclaim them, but the demon children latch on to the words and hurl them back at me, Moody blues! Moody blues! Moody blues! and their parents don't take any notice.

To stop it I say,

'I'll come, of course, I'll come.'

They cheer loudly. 'Great!' they holler.

They are laughing at me of course.

. . .

The road twists, unreels in strange ways. There is a peculiar feel to it, as though it had only just decided to turn here itself and is surprised by the direction.

It arrives at an unexpected beach.

'Where is this?'

'Doctors' Point,' says C, smiling. 'The kids love it.'

I had dreaded, crowds; noise; loud hilarious people straining for fun. But it is a bare beach, featureless, a dreary plain of sand. The wind tears at its skin.

I am afraid of the wind, and linger inside.

Everyone else surges out of the car.

They unwrap mysteries, parcels like stakes, parcels like heads. The children dance in rowdy circles and are sent to explore the sandhills for the sake of peace. Bottles are broached, fires coaxed. There is laughter and secret conversation.

It is cold, watching them.

This is the physical point: it is very cold, even though the sun is shining. I walk over to D.

'Can I help?'

He smiles, shaking his head. 'Have a glass,' he suggests.

He means, have a drink.

I try to sneer at his usage — he is a grammarian after all — but my head aches. The result must look like a lame, a timid smile. Another lie on my face.

. . .

I am tired of trying to give the lie to my face, to the mask Nature made of my face. I surge with torment inside, but to view?

Calmness. Composure. Plumply pallidly placid.

Do my eyes ever show agony? Life, even?

The dark is everywhere inside, the chase of shadows.

Nobody can see it by looking at me.

. . .

The sand on the beach is fine and white, like talcum powder. When I step on it, it squeals.

Unreal sand — for a moment I imagine I have fallen into a dream. I think there is nobody watching, so I accomplish experimental broadsides, producing crescendos of squeaks.

'It's the size and arrangement of the particles,' offers M.

She is crouched down by the sandhill to the left, ringed by avid-eyed children.

'O?'

She smiles softly. She looks down at the thing she is putting together. 'We're just going to put this kite up . . . do you want first go?'

The child horde is choiring, 'Me first! Me first! Me first!'

Shaking, I shake my head, No No No, walking away on the tormented sand.

. . .

The beach is littered with dead krill.

They appear to be the same kind here as at home, but I have never seen so many of them driven on to a beach before.

They are stranded everywhere, mounds of them heaped and ghostly, decayed to pale plastic shells.

Why have they died in this amount?

Possibly because the baleen whales kept the krill in check. The factory ships destroyed the whales. 'A whale dies every twenty seconds.' And then there were no more whales left to die. Now the krill breed to superabundance, spread an insidious red tide through the sea.

This is possible, although I don't know whether it is correct. I haven't read newspapers, watched television, listened to vain talk for many months.

The sand is squealing hideously under my moving feet.

I try to walk stealthily, silently, tiptoeing, but the sand chitters triumphantly with every movement.

I sit down in defeat amidst the holocaust of krill.

. . .

I remember thinking in one of the northern cities, just after I had arrived here, 'Courtenay Place! What a ridiculous name! Place Place!'

I chided myself immediately.

This is a new land, a new chance, a beginning. Ridicule has no place here.

. . .

I have a cousin called Courtenay.

He is presently unable to continue his research in genetics owing to nervous exhaustion. That, of course, is neither here nor there.

. . .

M has the kite aloft now.

It is a blue delta shape, batwinged. It looks like a cruel unnatural hawk as it sways on the end of its strings.

M pulls the left string. The kite dips. She pulls on the right string. The kite loops down to the sand, its white plastic tail whipping circles in the air.

The children are scrambling wildly round it. Their shrieks carry to me.

O why?

Is it triumph over the descent of the kite? Or have they found an ally? For the kite is a bird of prey. . . .

I look at the sand, my eyes filling with tears.

Through the mist I see it is not stark white. That is a trick of the sun.

It is really pale fawn, a dun colour. Though there is a mica-glitter, a light rash through it, that helps the sun's disguise.

One of the children comes trotting past.

She wears a garish T-shirt covered in scarlet and yellow blotches, and poisonous green shorts. Bare arms, bare legs, bare feet, all in defiance of the wind, the cold. She shies as she passes me, but turns to grin shyly. Small white needlepointed fangs.

My lips curl in reply. Suck off bloodimp.

Her smile wavers.

She trots away faster.

. . .

There were two things about the child; her whole air of sly friendship, defiant friendship, friendship that is not real, that snares, that entraps — that was one.

The other was the fact that she had a birthmark on her forehead, the port wine kind, and she seemed unconscious of this deformity. She did not hide it, or show herself ashamed.

I have thought about these things a lot. They troubled me: they trouble me still.

. . .

Then there was the uncomfortable feeling about the vividness and inappropriateness of her clothes.

Do people not feel the cold out here?

. . .

My dress was linen, plain, neat, covering. I felt ridiculous among the shorts and jeans and casual shirts of all of them.

But I am presently self-conscious about my clothes.

I had been sitting in my office with the door open, and I don't think they were aware of that.

D had said loudly,

'Holy Christ, have you seen her latest number? Sort of trimmed horse-blanket and the kind of necklace even my aunt Gertrude wouldn't be seen dead in!'

Throbbing laughter from them all.

I closed my door very quietly.

. . .

I am tired of living a lie, the lie that is my life. Though it is better to appear dully normal. Better to be considered old fashioned and slightly eccentric because of my sane normality.

Let them be amused. Let them laugh. Let them sneer behind my back and smile falsely to my face.

It is far better that they do this than get a glimpse of the chaos within.
But I am tired of lying.

. . .

The girl child is a long way up the beach now.

Her curling floss of hair, her thick glasses, the stain on her head,
all hidden.

Her garish clothes are easily visible however.

. . .

I have a theory about deformities. People are either fearful in the company
of a monster, or they will worship it. Any other reaction is rare.

For instance, you are familiar with the giant stone Olmec heads?

Did you know the Olmecs worshipped were-jaguars? That their race
was subject to a scourge of birth malformations, deformed children with
warped skulls and squashed-in faces? Some of these mutations may have
lived. Olmec heads seem to me to represent a deformed mutant with a
protective head-covering. A were-jaguar born to a mortal woman. A fit
subject for worship!

For my own part, I think all deformed monsters should be painlessly
destroyed at birth.

The pain they cause to those who are closest to them is unbelievable.

. . .

The wind is blowing harder. To sit still is to shiver uncontrollably.

So I walk along the sea-edge.

There are pieces of krill, of crab and weed, swinging in oozy decay
in the water's rim.

All that death . . . the sand feels unclean under my feet. It is
unthinkable to rinse it in the sea. All the oil, all the mercury and
phosphates and waste, and the brooding atomic foulness crated in leaking
concrete: no wonder the sea is dying.

And I can see huddles of krill in scarlet encrustations round the bases
of rocks in the sea. Doomed, because the tide is going out. Doomed to
join the dead masses on shore. Some are already stranded on the sand,
unmoving, cooking in their armour.

My eyes sting with tears again.

This is silly, silly.

Why cry for crustaceans? Why cry for an inevitable end? I mean,
who cries for me?

. . .

The beach is narrowing. Rocks block the end. They look rotten. Fractured dark-green rocks, knobs and specks and splinters of them, in higgledypiggledy heaps.

But they have real shade and real shadows, and the wind is thwarted by them. Even the searacket is less. And they build in unsteady blocks, higher and higher. Vaults of them. A crooked cathedral.

The floor is fine damp sand. The sea has retreated from here. It feels peculiarly clean.

The walls are greenly wet, almost translucent, like chrysoprase.

The seanoise is muted. The air is still.

I love this kind of peace.

. . .

If I could shush the voices, shush the sounds, the last whimper, the talk and recriminations and my own drawnout anguish; still the noise of the badgering living, the crying of the dead; if I could make a cathedral of peace, a retreat in my head. . . .

But I am aware that withdrawal is madness. You don't have to tell me that.

. . .

When I open my eyes, having rested a little in the cool of this cave, I see there are swarms of mussels on the wall. Crusts of them, blueblack and shiny as though varnished.

There is the occasional stranger mussel in their midst, pale green, like a wraith of a mussel. Pallid, obvious, vulnerable. There is never another palegreen mussel closeby for company.

The different, the abnormal, the alien, the malformed.

Who — or what — selects a person for the torment of difference?

. . .

Do you know the sensation of pondering deeply on something — and suddenly falling into nothingness?

. . .

Something tickles the back of my neck.

A fly?

Suddenly they are everywhere, hordes of kelpflies, a monstrous swarm rising from the walls descending from the roof swirling in humming spirals everywhere. I batter my hands against the buzzing air.

I may have yelled.

K asks,

'All well?'

His voice is deep, concerned.

My breath catches in my throat.

'Of course.'

He smiles, a ready compassionate smile, a little too smooth to have come from the heart.

'Of course,' he answers.

He draws nearer.

'I've come to see the caves. And you?'

'I had come to see the caves.'

My voice is cool and steady, a pleasure to my ears.

'Good,' he says. 'They're a neat set of caves.'

He draws back again and disappears round the seaward end of the cave. I hadn't realized the cave went further. There is a conical thrusting rib of rock, at the far end a flying buttress carved by sea and wind. Beyond it is water, stirred by the tide.

I go forward. The seanoise beats on me, and the wind pierces my smile.

. . .

There is nothing but a shallow eddy of the incoming tide in the next cave.
. . .

In the third cave, K waits.

He grins from the rock he is perched on. He looks bulky and cramped on top of the rock.

'Well, do you like our caves?'

'Is this the last of them?' My voice is still cool, still steady, despite the ache and the waves in my head.

He waves a hand vaguely south.

'There's another one beyond, same sort of thing. Besides, you can't get to it now. Tide's too high.'

He bends his head, his smile lost. He doesn't appear surprised that I didn't answer his first question. The seanoise seems somehow louder however. Then,

'Are you all right?' he asks.

Do you know that inane joke, Are you all right? No, I'm half left? It skips through my mind but I say,

'Pardon?'

'You've seemed a little, ahh a little, *tense* these few weeks you've been with us. I've been wondering if something's wrong?'

It is the inevitable. The invitation to tell. To betray.

O, I know they must have gossiped back in the staff room. I know the year gap in my record must look peculiar. I have been prepared, almost, for this question ever since I arrived. But to have it put now, not in the clean bright confines of a university office, but in a shadowed cave with the sick and dangerous sea running close by!

I cannot see any way out.

I say my lie, quickly and finally:

'A very good friend of mine died in sad circumstances. It upset me a good deal. I was under a doctor's care for some time.' It doesn't work.

'And now?' asks K.

I am silent.

'And now?' asks K.

I press my hands together as hard as they can go.

'And now?' he questions yet again.

I don't want to, Idontwanto, it blurts out, it's not me.

'Oh God I didn't mean to, it was puerperal insanity, she died by her own hand.' A small eternal silence. 'I mean, we had lived together happily for years, and then she had to go and have a baby. It was, it was, it wasn't born right. She killed it. Then she killed herself. They said it was puerperal insanity.' I am shaking again, my voice is shaking with my body. 'It was a long time ago, nearly two years, but it comes back to me. I am sorry. I try. I shall never get over it.'

The wind drops slowly, its voice moaning down to extinction.

The sea is conspiratorially silent.

His head stays bent. He remains on the rock, stolid and still.

He says at last,

'I am very sorry. We knew there was, ahh some tragedy, but we had no idea you see?'

'It is past.'

Only my hands are shaking now.

'You have had help?'

'Yes.'

'And you think you can get over it?'

'Yes.'

He climbs down from his rock and I step back. He will touch me in sympathy and I

but he says

calmly

'If you need someone to help, anyone to talk to, I am here. We are here,' softly, impulsively, compassionately. More compassionately than anything I have ever had said to me in my life.

Then he walks swiftly round the rocks into the other caves.

A wave rushes over my feet.

The tide is coming in fast.

. . .

It is nearly all lies of course.

I have been alone for most of my life.

And those nine months were horror afterwards.

Why do I tell this expedient set of lies? Why do I live a lie, portray a lie, many lies?

Because the chaos, the turbulence, the shadowhorror is too terrible a ruin and reality to inflict on anyone. To tell the truth about — NO!

If I explain with an acceptable melodrama, my frumpiness becomes an ally, my pallid composure a refuge. My alien self, a focus for pity and understanding.

. . .

UNDERSTANDING!!!

I rage. The rage shakes me harder, harder, harder, harderharderharder then convulsively to stillness.

. . .

If there had been a long period of peace and stillness after, nothing would have happened, you see.

The physical point to mention at this stage is, not only was I still very cold, but also I was so tense that if someone had dropped me I would have exploded.

. . .

There's a moon pale as gauze in the blue noon sky.

On the barbecues, the steaks drip fat. The fire smokes and sizzles and spits. Rustle and confusion as food and utensils are laid out. Clink of bottle to glass, and the laughter grows louder. The bloodstained paper that wrapped the meat lifts and shifts in the wind.

They talk casually, staff scandal and academic gossip. I am kindly included. The looks are discreet; the assumption, I will prefer pitying silence.

I am safe, for a while.

I nod, and I smile.

I know my nod is stiff, and my smile frosty and distant.

They are all sure they understand. The very air reeks of sympathy. It sifts through the talk like the burnt offering smell from the charred steak, which we are forced to inhale.

. . .

Why should I be so contemptuous?

They did their best, invited me out, invited me in. It's not their fault I don't fit.

And as for understanding . . . I don't understand.

I gave up understanding after the terrible gush of blood, after the final silence, after the weakening into darkness when all I could think was an internal gibberish.

The deed accomplished and my hands incarnadine have wreaked their mercy and all the sick sea shall fail now fail now fail now, this last pollution original sin and worst.

I gave up understanding after the wailing 'Owhydidyous?' had chanted themselves into quiet oblivion, after the slow slow settling back into a kind of normality. A normality of chaste lies. The mask face and the shadow chase of lies.

And I still don't understand.

. . .

I go for another walk on the beach after lunch, trying to feel warm, to feel at ease. I wander the high-tide line of the beach, watching the sand, gazing at the sea debris. Snail shells. Giant cockles and clams — do they call them quahogs here? Bleached bones and things so worn by time and sea they could be anything. The broken husks of crabs.

And everywhere the krill.

. . .

The laughter of the others is very far away.

. . .

I look back once.

They are gathered in a group at the far end of the beach.

I cannot see what they are doing.

I turn back to my perusal of the dead and the broken.

. . .

It began as an uneasy feeling, as though something unfriendly was watching the back of my neck.

I couldn't understand why I should feel this disturbance.

When I looked up I understood.

It was the kite.

It is the kite, high above my head, a hard electric-blue intruder. A threat.

It sways easily on the end of its strings, as though it knows it could be free of them at will, free to hunt and kill.

Did not the kites feast on the flesh of the dead?

Did not the Parsees build the Towers of Silence to invite the kites to their feast?

The sand squeals risibly, a sharper tone than I have heard from it before. I glance down. The shadow sleeks by. The tail whips past my cheek.

I have crouched, my hands shielding my head before I am aware I have done so.

Before I can rationalize it, and think, 'It's all right, it's just the kite that's fallen.'

It had stopped so fast!

And already it is back in the sky. It swings back and forth in an ominous aerial jig.

I am pinned for a moment, still crouched, like a rabbit under the scream of a hawk. Then I straighten slowly, my heart athud.

The kite above me wavers. Then it dives, striking the ground inches from my heels.

I look at the fallen thing, plastic and string. I look along the beach.

A child holds the distant ends of the strings, standing there gaudy as a toadstool, poisonous in its laughter.

The adults are laughing too, I know.

. . .

It is like being an automaton. I can approach them freely, smiling, can joke even, with equanimity.

Smiles all round, and a lot of heartiness and high laughter and back-slapping.

They invite me to take the strings, and make a game of it. And I am still smiling as they scatter up the beach, all of them, the toadstool child as well.

They rush into kite territory, eager prey.

. . .

The sun has wheeled round a little. It is late afternoon.

The sky is still a striking blue, though black clouds lower over the rim of tamed and manbarren hills.

It is the lowering clouds that make me feel that this is an arena.

I am minded of plays, of theatre. Of a starkly-set opera involving gladiators and death.

The sky is painted blue.

The hills are fake.

The wind comes from a machine.

And we are protagonists in an ancient and misunderstood drama.

. . .

Yet now, holding the kite-strings, I am exultant. I didn't know I could still feel this alive. My blood has secret fires, and they are soaring, spiring through me. The kite has a voice, and it is speaking.

I can feel the sand sinking under my feet, the hem of my dress whipping the backs of my legs, and my teeth are so chilled the fillings in them ache. But these things are immaterial. They cannot dim my rising ecstasy.

I know the lethal bird above me is really insentient plastic, frail fibreglass rods, lengths of string.

I know that, and it doesn't matter. It isn't real knowledge.

The truth and beauty is: the vibrant strings are my hands and the way I now look, out of the kite's eyes.

. . .

Down there, they are dancing, M and K and D and C, and all their mocking children. They think it is their game.

I am laughing, I am laughing, laughter that has been absent for a year. For all my life.

I am the beautiful killer. The strings are tingling sinews, and I am singing through the kite.

I know I can dive down through any one of their dancing brittle skulls.

. . .

We dip and soar and wheel and skim.

We drive them in a frantic scattering pack.

We sleek over their heads, and they dive screaming joy to the sand.

They applaud our skill wildly.

We whirl and we spiral. It is effortless. Coming near, speeding up and away amid all the gay retreating shrieks; sweeping down and brushing by with a smirking kiss of death.

With the forty-mile push of the wind, a fibreglass rod turns iron beak, and plastic and string make a griffin's skin.

And there she now runs giggling, the toadstool child. Hair an

innocent halo, shining in the sun, and below it, the dark mark flaunted
indecently . . . we swoop, and she shrieks with delighted laughter.

Ascend
steady:
and we stoop.

. . .

Struck between the shoulder blades, she falls.

And then it is black night and we are breaking apart forever.

. . .

There are shouts and cries in the distance, and people running.

The dark clouds spill over, and the air is suddenly full of fine weeping
mist.

I am numb now, so cold, so dulled.

They have grown strangely silent, along there, but I cannot let go
the dead strings.

The silence grows with the fog, blotting out even the whimpering
wind.

The sea is holding its breath.

The krill are dying, dying.

The hopelessness of the pallid mussels forever cloistered apart.

The endlessly crying sand.

And ah, my dark dark room. . . .

. . .

Have I told you anything?

Has it meant anything to you?

Or is it all just writing?

All just words?

Kathleen Crayford
Duncan

1

Whenever she heard the sound of banging coming from the vicinity of the back door, my mother would raise her head slowly and say in sepulchral tones,

'I hear a knocking at the South Entry.'

If the noise continued she would turn, throw her arms wide, and cry out in a wild, grief-stricken howl.

'Wake Duncan with thy knocking! I would thou couldst.'

In fact our back door was fitted with perfectly adequate bellchimes whose ringing could be heard all over the house. The banging my mother heard usually came from one of the neighbouring sections where somebody was busy mending a fence or chopping wood. When we did have visitors, which was not often, my mother would open the door, all bright-and-smiling like any other housewife. The perceptive visitor might have wondered at her immaculate make-up, thought the eye-shadow a little overdone, the nail varnish not entirely appropriate. The flourish with which she opened the door into her shining kitchen, her expansive gestures, and the theatrical emphasis with which she would proffer a cup of tea, might have seemed out of place in the state house and its child-loud suburban setting. But our visitors were infrequent and could rarely have been described as perceptive. My mother's make-up, like the gleaming crockery displayed on the dresser, was there for her own satisfaction. Admiration, if it came at all, came as a bonus. She lived within her own fantasy, with my brother Tahu and I serving both as audience and supporting cast. The house was her stage, and she was forever her own leading lady.

As a small child I used to wonder who Duncan was. Pondering about this, picking up bits and pieces of information not meant for my ears and supplementing these meagre scraps from my own imagination, I came to the conclusion that Duncan must have been the name of the baby brother who choked to death the night I was conceived. My mother had

had a lover, a man she had first known at Drama School in London, years ago. He'd looked her up when he was here on tour, and his stay had coincided with her husband's night-shift. On this particular night, with Tahu sleeping his sound, two-year-old sleep, she had tucked up the new baby with his bottle to keep him quiet while she had entertained her exciting red-headed lover. Next morning she had found the baby dead in a pool of vomit. Her lover took the next plane out, and was never seen again. Her Maori husband stayed until I was born, and I was registered as his child. And so I grew up with an English mother, a Maori surname, and a flaming halo of red hair. There was no way the neighbours could have overlooked the incongruity. As it was, they didn't even try.

I never knew if it was the local people who ostracized my mother, or whether it was she who cut herself off. She never spoke to them, nor they to her. We neither visited nor received visits from our neighbours. Quoting Macbeth was the nearest she ever came to acknowledging their existence. But there was never any doubt about their awareness of us. Conversation stopped when we entered a shop or passed a crowded bus-stop, and resumed with redoubled vigour as soon as we were out of earshot. Unruffled she glided by, oblivious both to their gossip and to my discomfiture. For along with his red hair, I had inherited from my father his thin, sensitive skin, skin which my mother assiduously protected from sunburn, but whose susceptibility to public opinion she apparently failed to notice. And so I would blush, and my mother seemed to be the only person in the entire neighbourhood who did not comment upon it.

As well as quoting Shakespeare, my mother used to enjoy reciting poetry and reading fairy stories. As pre-schoolers Tahu and I would listen spellbound and horrified to her rendering of the more gruesome stories of the Brothers Grimm. As we moved out of our pre-school years through the lower and middle standards, she added Greek myths and Maori legends to her repertoire, with the odd bit of Edgar Allan Poe thrown in.

Of poetry, she loved the long narrative poems of Keats, the *Pot of Basil* being her especial favourite. How she lingered over the scene where the maiden cut off the head of her dead lover and concealed it beneath the soil of a flower-pot. We even had a Pre-Raphaelite picture of the lady draped over her pot plant, mourning her dead love.

In the summertime on our immaculate lawn, or in the winter in the lounge which was furnished and lit like the set for a Noel Coward play, she would arrange us and herself in suitable theatrical positions and enmesh us in webs of horror. With her hands, her eyes, the slightest inflexion of her voice she would transport us out of our clean suburban world into lands of dungeons and giants, where men could be changed into animals, witches could cast spells, and nothing was what it seemed. With a word, a sigh, a wave of her hands, she could transform a gentle summer's day into a howling blizzard where helpless children were set impossible tasks by implacable ogres. In our bright lounge we would hear about children killing their parents, and parents devouring their children, and when at last we were released even the carpets we walked on held menace untold as we made our way to our nightmare beds.

Sometimes, for light relief, she would recite to us passages from Lewis Carroll's *Jabberwocky*:

> *'Twas brillig, and the slithy toves*
> *Did gyre and gimble in the wabe,*

she would intone, and we could practically see them, invested with terror unspeakable by the croak she put into her voice and the widening of her eyes. There were no dark corners in our house, so how did she manage to fill it with so much anxiety?

But of all the shuddering words she came out with, it was one apparently innocuous line which had the power to hold me rigid and trembling, longing to run away and yet too terrified to move.

> *And hast thou slain the Jabberwock?*
> *Come to my arms my beamish boy.*

Not even the worst excesses of Edgar Allan Poe could inspire in me the terror conjured up by that dreadful invitation.

Once I tried to find out how my brother felt about her stories.

'Do you like it when Mum reads to us?' I asked him.

'I never listen,' he said.

This reply absolutely astonished me.

'But she makes us listen,' I said.

'Well I got fed up with her carrying on. So one day I pretended I was playing football. Now I do it every time. Pretend I'm playing games, or do sums in my head. That's the best way I've found for getting away from her. Doing sums or saying tables.'

And so I lost the only comfort I ever had. Sometimes when she paused for breath I would look at my brother's face and long for eyes to meet mine and break the spell. But they never did. As he got older I lost even the reassurance of his physical presence, for my mother could not always compel him to stay home, and he took to going out more and more with his friends. He'd come in at mealtimes and then be off out again immediately. He treated her as though she didn't exist, and she didn't even notice. Except as an audience he had no meaning for her. It was a long time before I realized that the same truth applied to me.

The conversation with my brother was not, however, entirely without effect, for it drew my attention to the rewards that could be gained from school. Although I never really mastered his trick of being able to cut himself off from the present situation, I did begin to realize that school, and especially maths, could add another dimension to life. I began to appreciate the beautiful orderliness and predictability of figures. Because most of the other children fumbled and struggled through basic principles which were as clear as daylight to me, I was allowed to work my way through the maths book alone. When I surfaced between exercises it was to hear with irritation the teacher going over ground which I had left behind weeks ago. I was so desperately shy in the classroom that she had given up trying to make me read aloud. I answered questions only under duress, and then in never more than a whisper, but once I discovered mathematics the classroom held no fears for me. I was kept supplied with the appropriate books and left alone. Sometimes the teacher would look at me in a puzzled sort of way, but so long as I had my maths to do I was largely unaware of what else went on in the classroom. Nobody bothered me, and I was comfortable enough.

I suppose most children take it for granted that the way their family behaves is the way every family behaves. Our family pattern did not seem abnormal to me. It did not seem strange that apart from the readings and recitings, my mother seldom spoke. She never addressed me directly, nor called me by my name. Instructions came by way of proverbs and clichés. She had one for every occasion. 'Cleanliness is next to Godliness,' she would say, handing me a clean towel and propelling me towards the bathroom. 'A little water clears us of this deed.' I took it for granted that this was the normal means of intercourse between parent and child. I had never known anything different.

The first indication I had that all was not well was when the headmaster requested an interview with my mother following a mid-year survey in which the teacher had used words like 'withdrawn', 'self-absorbed', and 'unsociable'.

My mother made a good impression at the school. She enjoyed the role of concerned, bewildered parent. She smiled bravely as she told how her husband had left her years ago. She managed to indicate how gallantly she strove to bring us up decently, how determined she was that we should not suffer by being members of a one-parent family. Apparently the school was unaware of those facts about my origin which were common knowledge among our more immediate neighbours.

Gratifying as this interview must have been for my mother, it would have had little effect upon me had she not made a point of stressing how much time she spent reading to me and telling the stories. We had no television, which she held to be a corrupting influence, but she was quite sure, so she told the headmaster, that I had a far wider knowledge of poetry and literature than any other child of my age. I loved being read to.

In their eagerness to build a bridge between home and school, the staff assembled a collection of fairy stories which my mother had said were my absolute favourites. These were given to my teacher for classroom story-time, and she called them her Special Collection. The first time the haven of school was invaded by one of my mother's stories I think I must have fainted, though one of the other children said I'd had some sort of a fit. Whatever it was, it happened every time the teacher began to read from her Special Collection.

'Put your maths book away now Jeannie,' she would say. 'We are going to have a story.' I became so nervous that soon it was happening every time she opened a book of any kind. The slithy toves would come gimbling out from the corners of the room, I'd close my eyes and hold my breath to stop myself from screaming, and then suddenly I'd find myself flat on my back on a couch in the medical room, with one of the Teacher's Aides sitting worriedly beside me.

Later that year I was seen by the school medical officer. After examining me, he referred me to the hospital to have my hearing tested, and when it was found to be normal, my mother was asked to take me to yet another department. There, long loops of wire were stuck on to various parts of my head. The woman who did this explained to me that it wouldn't hurt, that it was simply a device to measure the electrical activity of my brain, to see if they could find out why I was having these fainting fits. But I already knew why I was having them. It was because of the slithy toves. Of course, I couldn't tell anyone that. They would have thought I was mad.

2

In contrast to the drama and alarm of being hooked up to the hospital's measuring devices, the School Psychologist entered my life quietly. He was a small man with thinning hair and bright blue eyes. When I first saw him he was talking to my teacher. She was showing him her special collection of fairy tales and folk stories. I hurried away in case she should open one of the books and let the slithy toves come out. I thought she might lend them to him, but when he turned to speak to me, he had nothing in his hands but a small folder of printed papers. He said his name was Mr Rogers and he asked me if I would go to the staffroom with him to do some written work instead of listening to a story with the other children. He made it sound as though I would be doing him a favour. In the staffroom he opened the folder and showed me the papers. He explained what he wanted me to do, and once I had got started he quietly left the room, saying he'd be back in about half-an-hour.

There were a number of maths questions on the papers, so I did them first. Then I went over the paper again to look at the other questions. They were about words, and the meaning of words. I became confused and frightened. So I checked the maths again, and having gained what comfort I could from them, I pushed the papers away and sat and waited.

Mr Rogers came back. He had more papers with him, only this time he said he'd fill in the answers if I told him what I thought they were. Then he said half a sentence and asked me to finish it, but I couldn't. He asked me to draw him a picture, but I couldn't do that either. Then he showed me some pictures on a card and asked me to tell him a story about them, and I started to feel frightened again. He piled all the cards up, gathered the papers together, glancing at the ones I had been able to tackle.

'You enjoy mathematics,' he said.

I nodded. He was quiet for a while, just sitting there looking at the papers. Then he said,

'You don't enjoy stories much, do you?'

I was so surprised that I looked quickly up at his face and whispered, 'No.'

I had been too shy to look straight at his face before, but when I did I found there what I had looked for and failed to find in my brother's. I dropped my head, and suddenly, without knowing it was going to happen, I began to cry. I went on and on, until I thought I was never going to be able to stop. He pushed a box of tissues across the table to me and said, 'It's all right. Don't worry about it,' and then he just sat and waited. No words. No fuss. Just quietly waited.

It was a funny feeling when I blew my nose, as if I'd been all cleaned up inside. I used up two or three tissues, and when I had thrown them into the rubbish bin, I glanced at him quickly again. He didn't seem to have changed. There was a feeling of rightness about him. I don't know how else to put it.

'Jeannie,' he said, as though he had come to a decision about something, 'I have to write a report for your teacher, and I want you to read it. Do you understand?'

I nodded.

'All right,' he said, 'we'll make a start right now.'

He pulled a sheet of paper towards him and wrote across it in big scrawly writing.

I looked at the note. It said, 'No more fairy stories please!' For a moment I thought I was going to cry again. Then an extraordinary thing happened. The corners of my mouth began to twitch, and a smile came on, a great big smile, and I couldn't turn it off, no matter how hard I tried.

I picked up the paper and left the room. I thought my troubles were over, which only goes to show how little I had understood my mother, and how much I had underestimated the cruelty of the other children.

It was almost home-time when I got back to the classroom. I had handed over the note, and as I returned to my place one of the boys said, 'Been to see the shrink, have you?'

I didn't know what he meant, but I felt myself blushing. There was a ripple of suppressed giggles, and I heard the word 'shrink' whispered around the room. After school they started again.

'Been to the headshrinker today, have you?'

My hands flew to my head, but it was still the same size. They laughed, and someone said they always knew I needed my brains tested.

I ran home.

At Mr Rogers' suggestion the Visiting Teacher came to see my mother next day. She brought with her a small pile of books which she told me Mr Rogers had recommended as being more suitable than fairy stories. She addressed me directly. She said, 'He asked me to tell you that you may find them a little young, but he's been thinking it over, and he thinks that as you've never had this kind of book before, you may enjoy them. You can go on to something more sophisticated when you get tired of these.'

She spoke to me as though I were a proper person. I felt very surprised.

My mother enjoyed having the Visiting Teacher call. She showed her over the house, discussing the books and pictures, and telling animated little stories about the various ornaments and mementos in the lounge. I had never realized that every one of her things had a history of its own. They were treasures that had had an existence long before I was born, in a time and place when she had been young and beautiful. I found the thought very strange.

At first, my mother seemed to enjoy reading to me from the books Mr Rogers had recommended. Certainly she gained great satisfaction from the knowledge that the school staff were interested in what she was doing. As for me, I found the stories enchanting. Some were about a little girl called Milly-molly-mandy who lived with a family of loving relatives in a farm cottage in the country. She had a friend called Susan, and another called Billy Blunt. They rode bikes, built tree houses, and went for picnics. Once they made a miniature garden in a big pie-dish and entered it for a competition where it won first prize. It was a gentle, interesting world, full of small adventures of childhood, and I loved it.

Until that time the worlds of home and school had been completely separate, so that upon entering one, the other had ceased to exist. But since my mother's visit, each began to impinge increasingly upon the other. To and from school I ran an uneasy gauntlet through the nudges and giggles of the other children. They would have forgotten it soon enough had that first interview with Mr Rogers been the only one. But regular appointments were made for me, and once a week I was sent over to the staffroom for what the teacher euphemistically referred to as Individual Tuition. The term fooled no one. My sessions with Mr Rogers were just frequent enough to maintain the children's interest. They had noticed that they could make me blush by referring to him. It almost seemed as if home and school had reversed their roles in my life. The jabberwocky nightmares receded, and I stopped having fits, but school was no longer the haven it had been. Home now became a refuge from the attentions of the other children, where I entered into the safe, consistent world of Milly-molly-mandy and her friends. It was the walk to school, and the playground, and the classroom, that became the nightmare then. Those, and the days when Mr Rogers came.

It was not Mr Rogers himself who made such an ordeal of our relationship, it was the other children's distorted evaluation of it. Any pleasure I might have gained from the anticipation of seeing him was ruined by the teasing I had to cope with before and after every interview. And there was pleasure in seeing him. When I had stumbled and blushed my way out of the classroom and into the quiet corridor, I would stand a moment, taking deep, slow breaths, and wait for my burning skin to become cool again. In the time I spent with him, I experienced myself increasingly as a real person. He accepted my nods and whispered monosyllables as valid communication, and his friendliness and courtesy were unfailing. But the price of person-hood was high. The other children's blood-lust seemed to be insatiable.

And then my mother began to tire of reading children's books. I think I must have contributed to this by my growing impatience at being read to. For the first time in my life, I wanted to read the books myself. Obviously I could read, or I'd never have coped with maths, but I had never voluntarily read a story-book: in any case, children's stories gave little scope for my mother's histrionic talents, and she decided I was ready to move on, as the Visiting Teacher had said, 'to something more sophisticated'.

And so we moved rapidly through teen-age romances to Barbara Cartland, and thence to the kind of intellectual porn that is such a feature of the drug-and-sex orientated seventies. At first I tried to cut myself off, but my own biochemistry dictated otherwise. I found things happening to my body as I listened to my mother's throaty renditions of some of the most explicit seduction scenes in the English language. How I longed for Tahu's ability to imagine himself away into a game of football. But Tahu was seldom home, and within days I was caught up in my mother's dream-world of rape and seduction, incest and adultery. The books she selected were the best of their kind, describing anatomical and physiological details I had not known existed. Sometimes it was hard to believe that they meant what they seemed to mean, and then I never knew whether it was depravity coming from within myself that held me fascinated and repelled, or whether the writer and my mother were really as depraved as they seemed to be. For now I had difficulty in distinguishing the story from the story-teller.

And once again the poison crept from home to school. The blushes that had previously spread from my face and neck, now became focused in that part of my body which had always been private and inviolable. They would start in unseen places and spread outwards like a consuming fire, throbbing and burning till I was beside myself. It seemed as if the slithy toves that had once haunted the classroom had somehow got inside me, and now there was no escape.

If the teasing I had had to put up with had been painful before, now it became intolerable. And suddenly, I didn't want to see Mr Rogers any more.

On the occasion of his next visit I was called out of the classroom as usual. I heard the familiar giggles and whispers, saw the nudges and grins, and felt the blushing fire pouring and burning out from between my legs. And then suddenly everything stopped. Ice is the antithesis of fire, and as though someone had thrown a switch my body solidified and turned to ice. There behind my desk, half sitting, half standing, the power was turned off and I was immobilized. Somewhere, like a third eye outside myself I watched my vision glaze over, heard my hearing die, and saw my body bent and rigid behind the desk that was my fortress no longer.

3

Someone must have brought me to the hospital. I have no memory of how I got there. But when I came to myself I was aware that some change had taken place in me. There was a peaceful lassitude that was unfamiliar, and I kept drifting in and out of some kind of a reverie, waking to be washed or fed, or to swallow pills, and then drifting off again. I experienced everything as though I were one step removed from myself, detached and uninvolved. I had watched myself in the classroom as I lost consciousness, and I was watching myself now as I regained it. I felt almost like two separate persons. One of me was lying on a bed, drifting. The other was becoming increasingly alert, appraising, remembering, trying to make connections.

As the days went by, the alert part of myself became irked by the ministrations of the hospital staff. I had thinking to do, and I wanted to get on with it.

Soon the nurses began to encourage me to get out of bed. They took me for walks around the hospital gardens, and into rooms where people were working or playing or talking. All I really wanted was to be left alone to think. I needed solitude, and it was the only thing they denied me.

The strange feeling of detachment continued. I saw and heard everything that was said and done as though it had no relevance to myself. I became a puppet, and yet at the same time I was an observer at the show, watching how the strings were being pulled, wanting to take charge, and yet powerless to move of my own volition. Once, a fat doctor brought a group of people to have a look at me. He told them that the acute phase had passed and I was now undergoing a period of intensive socialization training. Some of them asked questions, and he told them that the aim was always towards adjustment and discharge. I was progressing satisfactorily, he said, and would be coming up for assessment before very long.

And that brought me eventually to the Case Conference. The nurse who looked after me told me about it. This nurse had been around most of the time since I had recovered consciousness, and was said to be Specialling me. I hadn't taken much notice of her at first, because they all looked alike in their uniforms, but after a while I had noticed her voice. She talked to me and explained what she was doing. Sometimes I felt that I was her doll, and she enjoyed playing with me, brushing my hair and helping me dress, and holding conversations in which she replied to her own questions and comments with words which no doubt she thought I would have used, had I been able to speak. But I didn't always feel like her doll. Once when she took me into a room where people were busy making things, and asked me to join in, and took me away again after a little while, she put her hand under my chin and lifted my face up and said, 'Oh Jeannie, please get better.' But I didn't know how to.

Anyway, on the day of the Case Conference she was clearly excited. Excited and nervous. She helped me shower and wash my hair, which she dried with a hand-held dryer. She brushed it, playing the dryer over it as she did so, totally absorbed. Then she gave me a mirror.

'See how nice you look,' she said.

I studied the reflection in front of me. I saw a girl with clear delicate skin, wide hazel eyes and a cloud of shining red-gold hair. I had always thought I was ugly, but I could see now that I was not. I remembered the time I had cried in the staffroom at school, and I began to wish the nurse would stop being so kind to me.

We took a lift up to the Conference Room. She was carrying a folder with some notes in it. Just before we got out of the lift she said, 'This is my first Case Conference. You are my first Special. I hope everything will be all right.'

I lifted my head and glanced at her quickly. She was a girl not much older than me. She caught my glance and tried to hold it, but I dropped my head. The lift came to a halt, the doors opened and we stepped out.

I find it hard to describe my first impression of the Conference Room. The difficulty arises from my strange double awareness of every situation. I stood outside myself and watched as the nurse and I entered the room. It was full of strangers and cigarette smoke. It seemed that they had just had a coffee-break, for there were used cups on the low table, and even on the floor. White-coated men and women were standing or sitting around chatting. The fat doctor was there. We stood inside the door like two intruders. I tried to detach myself, but I was too aware of the nurse, whose hands were trembling. The fat doctor saw us and told us to come in, indicating two chairs by the window. The chatter ceased as he seated himself behind a desk and began leafing through some papers. As we sat down I risked a quick glance round the room, and I saw something that made the two parts of myself snap violently into focus. Mr Rogers was there!

Inside my head, several things seemed to happen at once. I became alert and aware of every nuance of feeling in that room. My memory for past events came back. I remembered the blushing at the same time as I became aware that it had ceased. The feeling of powerlessness had gone. The puppet-strings had been cut and I ceased to experience myself as the object of other people's manipulations.

Another glance around the room and I caught Mr Rogers' eye. He smiled, but I remained impassive. I had never seen him in other people's company before. He was the only one not wearing a white coat, and he looked out of place.

The doctor put aside his papers and began to speak. He spoke of the tragedy of schizophrenia, especially its effect on young people. He explained that its cause was still largely a mystery. Within the last fifteen years attempts had been made to trace its origin to faulty relationships between parent and child. In his opinion this was a grave mistake, as the case before us showed. This child's mother was an intelligent, cultured woman who had coped without help for years, and wanted nothing more than to have her child restored to her, cured or not. 'It is our responsibility now, to decide whether it is fair to burden the mother with this grossly disturbed child. It may be that she should remain in hospital until she is completely stabilized on the appropriate medication. Her mother is asking for her back. The question is, should we let her go?' He said this not without a touch of drama. I couldn't help wondering why he said, '*We* have to decide,' since it was clear that it was he who was the puppet-master.

He turned towards the nurse sitting beside me. I could feel her trembling.

'Now nurse,' he said. 'I understand you have been Specialling this patient for the past three weeks. What can you tell us about her?' The nurse opened her folder and began to read from her notes. The tremor transferred itself to her voice. She told them I was a good patient, quiet, showing no signs of violence. She had wondered if I might be either deaf or retarded, as I was so slow to respond when spoken to. I was totally lacking in initiative and showed no interest in other people. Here she paused and looked up from her notes, troubled.

'Well,' said the doctor. 'Was there something else?'

She replied diffidently. 'It's hard to know. It's just that when I was brushing her hair . . . I gave her a mirror to show her how nice she looked. She seemed . . . interested, sort of. . . .'

The doctor smiled kindly.

'Even schizophrenics are not entirely devoid of vanity, nurse. Was that all?'

She hesitated.

'It was just something I felt,' she said, 'in the lift coming up here. I spoke to her, and I felt. . . . It was the first time ever . . . I felt as though she'd heard me. I felt as though she wanted to reply.'

The words came tumbling out in a breathless rush, and as they did, something extraordinary happened to me. I felt myself caring about what somebody else was feeling. It was hard for her to speak as she did. She was saying something that was not in the script.

'Nurse,' the doctor said gently, 'we all have to protect ourselves against emotional involvement with our patients. I guess this girl has become pretty important to you over the past few weeks. It's natural that you should want her to respond to you. But you can hardly expect us to take seriously something you felt, fleetingly, coming up in the lift to your first Case Conference, now can you?'

'No doctor,' she said, and subsided into silence.

'However, the suggestion of retardation is an interesting one. We have among us today a guest from the Department of Education. Mr Rogers. You are a teacher I believe. You knew this girl at school.'

'I'm not a teacher. I'm an Educational Psychologist,' said Mr Rogers, 'and yes, I did know Jeannie at school.'

'A psychologist. Yes, of course. You have a B.A. in the subject I believe.'

I glanced at Mr Rogers and saw him flush slightly.

'An M.A. actually,' he said.

'Quite. But no medical training I take it? Well what can you tell us about this girl?'

The tremor I heard in Mr Rogers' voice was not that of fear, as the nurse's had been, but of suppressed anger.

'Dr Cardew,' he said, 'at your request I have provided a detailed assessment of Jeannie's potentialities. That report has been with you for several weeks, and I think you know that there is no question of retardation. I have found her above average in intelligence, distinctly gifted in mathematics, but extremely shy. I should also like to point out that she is well aware of what is going on in this room and that she probably understands every word that is being said.'

The doctor ignored the last remark and took up the question of shyness.

'You are aware, no doubt, that what you call shyness is one of the earliest symptoms of schizophrenic withdrawal?'

'Yes, I am aware of that.'

'Then why did you not refer the girl for treatment sooner?'

'Because I didn't want her labelled. I knew she was disturbed, but she was beginning to respond and I felt sure that given time, she'd come right.'

'Well you were mistaken, weren't you, Mr Rogers?'

Mr Rogers looked at him and then looked at me long and earnestly. 'No,' he said. 'I don't think I was. Something else happened. Some other factor intervened. I don't know what it was, but she was responding, and she did begin to improve. I think if you look at the test papers she did for me. . . .'

Dr Cardew looked around the room and addressed himself to the listening staff.

'I think we have here yet another example of the dangers of emotional involvement. This child is exceptionally attractive, and no one wants to believe she is mad.'

I saw Mr Rogers wince. The Doctor went on talking.

'But unless and until we accept the fact of this disease we will get nowhere in treating it. We have to decide whether, appropriately medicated, this child can survive in the outside world, and how soon we can return her to her mother. . . .'

During this exchange my eyes had returned repeatedly to Mr Rogers' face. As with the nurse, so with him, I began to find myself inexplicably concerned about somebody else's feelings. Something was going dreadfully, frighteningly wrong in that room, but it was not I who was being threatened. It was Mr Rogers. Never in my life before had I realized that I was not the only person in the world who could be frightened. But I realized it now, as I watched that small man with his thinning hair and his tired eyes, standing up to ridicule and disparagement for my sake.

Unexpectedly, he stood up and walked firmly across the room to where I was sitting. He knelt down in front of me and took both my hands in his.

'Jeannie,' he said. 'Jeannie, can you tell me what's troubling you. Can you tell me now, before it's too late?'

I felt the words inside me. I felt his longing to reach me. I felt what it had cost him to cross the room in front of all those people. The nurse beside me held her breath. There was silence as they all watched and waited, a silence only distantly broken by the voices of the other patients at their recreation outside. Someone was bouncing a ball, thump, thump, thump, and someone else was crying out, 'Here, here, over here.'

I disengaged my hands and stood up. Raising my head slowly, I opened my mouth and let the words come out.

'I hear a knocking at the South Entry!'

The tension broke. Someone giggled nervously, and the doctor smiled. 'Well Mr Rogers, you have provided us with yet another example . . . a classic example . . . of a well-known symptom. A random utterance, totally unrelated to anything. Frequently one finds such random utterances to be the only speech schizophrenics are capable of. I'm sorry Mr Rogers. It was a nice try.'

Mr Rogers looked desperate.

'How can you call it a random utterance? This is the first piece of coherent speech she has produced for over a year. You saw what the effort cost her. It cannot be without significance.'

He turned to me. The nurse too was on her feet.

'Please, Jeannie,' he said.

Once more I felt words inside me. I lifted my eyes to his face, and though it cost me my soul I was determined to tell him exactly where the trouble lay. And so I said, in a loud voice whose urgency nobody could mistake.

'Wake Duncan with thy knocking. I would thou couldst.'

And then I think I fainted, for the next thing I was aware of was that I was back on my bed, drifting, separated into two parts again, one self watching the other, waiting to see what would happen next.

4

In fact, very little happened. The hospital resumed its inexorable routine. I had a different nurse looking after me, and after a period of rest she started trying to get me to join in games and discussion with the other patients, but I was not interested. Two things remained with me from the Case Conference. One was the memory of the fat doctor saying I was exceptionally attractive and no one wanted to believe I was mad. The other was that, given the strength, the puppet-master could be resisted. I had seen the nurse do it, and I had seen Mr Rogers do it. I began to see that my lack of interest in the hospital's games was my own way of refusing to be bound by the script.

My mother visited sometimes, but she was more interested in impressing the staff than in paying attention to me. She brought me clothes and sweets, which later she took away almost at once and began sharing around the ward with the other patients. So I didn't take very much notice of her. I didn't care whether she came or not.

At least, I didn't until the day she came looking very different from her usual self. The make-up was missing. Her nails were their natural colour. And instead of sweeping into the ward with a flourish and greeting staff and patients alike as though she were some kind of Lady Bountiful, she walked in quietly and came straight over to where I was sitting.

'Hello Jeannie,' she said. It was the first time she had called me by my name. She sat down beside me. There was a long silence, and then she said awkwardly,

'Would you like me to read to you?'

I said nothing. She pulled a book out of her bag and held it out to me.

'It's one of the Milly-molly-mandy books. Would you like to choose a story?'

This was something new. Never before had she offered me a choice of what stories I would listen to. That had always been her decision. I took the book and opened it at random. She read the story. I don't remember what it was, I remember only that her voice had changed. She was no longer acting. She was trying to communicate.

When the story was finished she said, 'Would you like to sit in the sun for a while?' and stood up. I followed her out into the garden and we sat down on a bench. There was another silence. My mind took off and became absorbed watching the antics of a bumble-bee on a nearby flower-bed, and I forgot she was there. She cleared her throat and I felt her preparing to speak.

'Mr Rogers rang me up,' she said.

My mind scrambled back into my body so fast that I almost laughed out loud, but I said nothing. I continued watching the bumble-bee, and I waited.

'He asked me to go into his office and see him. He said you'd said something.' She stopped, and then went on again with an effort. 'He told me you'd said something about . . . about Duncan. He asked me if I knew what it meant.'

She stopped again. I began to feel frightened, brittle and precariously balanced, as though the least movement would knock me over and shatter me into a million pieces.

'I told him. I told him about how the baby died, and all about . . . everything.'

She leaned forward and put her elbows on her knees, clasping her hands in front of her and looking at the ground.

'He asked me if you knew. He said I should tell you. He said I should talk to you about. . . .' Her voice dropped and became husky.

'About Duncan.'

We sat there a long time, saying nothing. Slowly the brittle feeling went away. At last she stood up.

'I can't talk about it now. He says I have to be honest with you, and tell you about real things. He says it's important for both of us. Perhaps next time. Will you walk with me to the gate?'

My mind did not leave my body again. That night I refused to take my medication. There was no fuss about it. I just lifted my head and said, 'No!' and pushed it away. A doctor came to see me, a young man I had not noticed before.

'You don't want to take your medication?' he said.

Again I lifted my head and said, 'No!'

He turned to the nurse.

'It's the first time she's shown any initiative since she's been here. There must be a reason. Scrub it for tonight and just keep an eye on her. She may be coming right.'

I continued steadfastly to refuse to take any more tablets or pills. By the time my mother came back again, the feeling of detachment had almost gone. I slept badly, but that gave me time to think.

The nurse who had accompanied me to the Case Conference came back on the ward, and when I saw her the edges of my mouth began to twitch, and a tiny little smile came on. She saw it, and came rushing over to me absolutely beaming, but before she reached me she stopped dead and looked upset, remembering no doubt, about the dangers of emotional involvement. Then she came on more slowly, composing her face.

'I'm so glad you are feeling better,' she said primly.

I have heard about people's eyes twinkling, though I had never understood what it meant. But if eyes can really twinkle, I'm sure that mine did then. The smile stretched my mouth a bit more. It felt most strange. We stood grinning at each other like a couple of idiots, and then she turned abruptly and left the room. Later, I heard her singing.

Although I no longer needed to be Specialled by any particular nurse, this nurse became very special to me. She was unable to conceal her pleasure in my continuing recovery, and it was for her sake that I finally agreed to join the group of patients who went to the Occupational Therapy workshop every afternoon.

My mother came to see me twice a week. She brought books to read, and soon a pattern began to develop. It almost seemed as if she could not get her voice going unless she read to me first. Then she'd put the book away and start to talk. On the first few occasions she prefaced her conversation by some reference to Mr Rogers.

'I was telling Mr Rogers,' she'd say, 'about the time when. . . .'

But after a while it came more easily to her. She told me about her life in London, and about the drama school where she had first met my father. She told me about the places they went to and the things they did; about the London river-buses, and Kew Gardens, and Buckingham Palace where they had seen The Queen come out onto the balcony. It wasn't anything like the awful magical spell-weaving she used to do. She was just a lonely woman, talking about times when she had been happy.

And so the weeks went by. In the hospital garden, the dayroom or the corridor, or anywhere that was quiet and private, she picked up the pieces of her life and began to put them together again. I used to go down to the gate to meet her, and we'd walk up the drive together, and she'd talk to me. The possibility of my going home came up. I could see she was nervous about it, because she started referring to Mr Rogers again. It was, 'Mr Rogers says . . .', or 'Mr Rogers thinks. . . .' One day she said it and I looked at her and grinned. She laughed. 'Oh well. *I* think . . .' she said, and went on to say what she had to say. And that was the last reference she made to him.

And then one day, slowly and painfully, with many pauses and long silences, she began to talk about the occasion of my conception. As though it had happened only the day before, she went through the whole awful agony again. I had picked up a good deal from around the neighbourhood when I had been too young to understand it, and I had woven my own fantasies around the event. But no fantasy of mine could have been as bad as what she went through, both at the time, and in the telling. There had been an inquest on the baby, and the coroner had had some hard things to say. It had been in all the newspapers. Everybody knew.

And yet, when she had told all this, she was still not at an end. There was something else that, strangely, had never got into the newspapers, nor come to the neighbours' ears. Or rather, the accident which killed my father had been to them no more than a distant event in the history of aviation. A plane had crashed upon landing at Singapore Airport. There had been no survivors. There was no reason for the neighbours to connect that news with the departure of my mother's lover. Nor was there any reason why the airport authorities should know that one of those mangled bodies they managed to identify held any interest for one obscure family in a State Housing area in New Zealand.

Telling the story with tears, with pain, but with infinite relief, my mother produced an old press-cutting about the crash. Although she had kept no memento of the baby who had died, no newspaper reports of the event which had haunted my childhood, she had kept this tattered account of an aviation disaster that seemed to have no bearing on my life. And yet she showed it to me, complete with a list of the casualties, and a blurred photograph of an actor with a touring company, an actor who, the newspaper reported, would never have been on that flight had he not been called to return home urgently, because of a family crisis.

And that was how I learned what perhaps I should have guessed
right from the start. I had been mistaken about the name of the baby
who died. I had been mistaken about the origin of my mother's continuing
grief. And more than anything, I had been mistaken about its relationship
to myself. The baby had not been called Duncan.

Duncan was my father's name.

Jean Watson
Princess!

I've always been embarrassed by Darien. Sometimes I'd even go as far as to say I wish she didn't exist . . . a pointless wish, she'll be here as long as I am here, so Gareth tells me.

He doesn't seem to mind her. He accepts her coarseness as readily as he accepts Fay's fussing. The more I try to ignore Darien the worse she seems to get.

I blush when I recall how she carried on at breakfast time this morning; 'Gawd! . . . is *this* all we're getting to eat!' she said. Then fidgeted uncomfortably when Fay fixed her with a cold prim stare. Nothing was said for the rest of the meal, the atmosphere could've been cut with a knife.

I know that she has to live in this house with us but I wish she'd stay down in the basement where she belongs. Gareth says she wouldn't be nearly so troublesome if Fay didn't hate her so. We don't quite know where Fay lives. I think she belongs down in the basement with Darien and that Old Man.

I spend my days in the reference library. The others are usually with me. Frequently they argue over who is to read aloud to me, usually I find myself listening to the one who is most determined at the time. There are so many books . . . they are stacked from the floor to the ceiling all round the walls. I think there must be two or three layers of shelves by now because we keep collecting more. It's all Gareth can do to open the window. A lot of the time we don't bother with the window. The continuance of the world outside reaches our ears as a muffled hum, cacophony, chatter of voices, clatter and roar.

We've all lived in this house together for as long as I can remember. I don't even recall any of us ever going outside.

Actually there's so much to do downstairs here, around the living-room, basement and library, that none of us have even been upstairs. The staircase might as well not be there for all the notice we take of it.

As usual I've had to listen to the constant bickering that goes on between Darien and Fay. This time it started over a book that Darien was reading aloud to me, a very large, frequently read book titled *The Fun We Had That Summer* . . . like many of the books in the library it has changing contents; every time one reads it the story is a bit different. Well, that carry-on was common enough until Darien impatiently threw the book to the floor and said: 'Gawd! aren't there any men around the place?' Fay was shocked and frightened. 'Oh, Darien — how could you! How could you!' She waited as helpless tears rolled down her pale, fastidious face.

Darien laughed scornfully.

Then Gareth came to the rescue with a distraction . . . he moved some books just enough to open the window so we could hear the noise from a party the next door neighbours were having. We all listened with rapt attention for the rest of the day.

One is always safest to listen to Gareth explaining the facts about Darien and Fay. Also he tactfully distracts me when I get frightened by that Old Man who's always talking about earthquakes and how this house we all live in might fall down one day.

Sometimes when the window is open Gareth hears interesting things which we all discuss . . . also we usually find relevant books in the library.

As a matter of fact, just today he heard something interesting which concerns this house. It is that there is a Princess living up in our attic under the peaked roof. Apparently she has always been there.

We discussed this information in our usual considered balanced way. Gareth, humorously sceptical but at the same time conscious of being open-minded. Myself, incredulous, very interested and wanting to believe it yet, somehow not surprised.

We went through as many of the books as we could to find references to both Princesses and attics.

It would make this house so much more worth living in if there was a Princess in the attic. Surely it would have a good effect on Darien . . . it could silence her forever. It is interesting to note that all the time Gareth and I were talking of the Princess, those wretches were quiet for once. I think they must have left the room. How peaceful without them!

We read up a little bit about attics today, it is this; if one creeps quietly to the bottom of the stairs and listens ever so quietly . . . one can hear the resident Princess singing!

I intend to try it.

There wasn't a single footprint nor a mark of any sort in the thick dust on the stairs . . . no one had trodden them for years, nor so much looked at them, not even a brief glance as during the day we pass them to get from the living-room to the library.

For a few minutes this morning while the others were asleep I stood on the bottom step tensing every muscle in my body to listen. Yes . . . yes . . . I'm sure I heard something! The echo of a whisper . . . a haunting far-away refrain . . . was this the Princess singing? I held my breath . . . but just then a clatter from the kitchen reached my ears instead. The others were preparing breakfast.

All day we've been in the library discussing the Princess and whether or not I actually heard her singing. There is something really new and exciting about all this and yet at the same time . . . familiar, as if we'd always known it. Gareth read out a poem which says that to hear even the faintest distant echo of the Princess singing is to love her forever. He spoke and read as always, with a smile, an interested, intelligent, considering smile — he suggests that it is possible I imagined the singing. But no, I don't believe he is right, I am growing in the conviction that what I heard *was* Her song. . . .

I *must* hear Her again, I *must* climb further up the stairs!

If only the others wouldn't keep following me. I can't hear a thing with their inane chatter going on!

Twice today I crept to the foot of the stairs but they heard me and followed. Curious interfering meddlers!

'Shut up Darien! Shut up Fay! Shut up Old Man!' I said, 'Can't you see that I want to hear the Princess singing. . . .' Darien laughed insolently and flounced off with a voluptuous swish of her raven curls. Fay wept and wrung her hands saying that I needed her help if I was ever to hear the Princess.

'You wait!' The Old Man grated through his teeth. Then Gareth came out of the library and told me that I should ignore them altogether and perhaps they might give up and leave me alone . . . but then on the other hand they may well get worse in a bid for attention. Darien in particular is likely to eat more and start putting on weight. I gave up and went to set the table for the evening meal.

I heard! I heard!

There *is* a Princess!

I listened at the foot of the stairs early this morning while the others still slept.

Never could I have imagined such a beautiful sound. Just one sweet wild breath of song.

So sweet but alas so fleeting and so fragile, my listening.

There *is* a Princess! I know . . . and although I've never seen her I know how beautiful she is.

I know her breath is sweeter than the scent of violets, that only a white gown wraps her silken flesh and her fine hands and feet need no adornment and her hair falls like sunlight on rippling water and she sings forever. I am stricken with love for her, for the vision in my mind of her, for the memory of that one breath of song!

How can I meet her?

Is there some way I can attract her attention?

Gareth is still sorting through the library for any information relating to Princesses. As well as that he decided that we would keep the window open more often, in case we get some news from passers-by. Gareth says I will have to get further up the stairs if I want to hear Her better.

Fay has taken it upon herself to read out to me a book called *Purity of Purpose*. She has frequent fits of weeping during which she insists that I will never meet the Princess as long as Darien lives with us. Darien has been strangely quiet these last few days . . . but she seems to be putting on weight. I wouldn't be surprised if she's been sneaking stuff from the kitchen while the rest of us talk about the Princess.

She lives, she lives forever!

The Princess, I'm so happy to know that she is there in our attic!

Oh black despair!

Will I *never* hear Her again?

Today I set foot on the first creaky step of the stairs and stood for a minute there holding my breath . . . then another step, another minute's breathless wait. . . .

Yet another step, my fingers gripped the dusty banister. . . . All was silent.

'Princess . . . Princess . . . I love you.' I called.

When Darien, Darien that evil, cruel, malevolent wretch! She let the kitchen door slam causing the whole house to shake.

How I despise her!

She spoilt any chance I had of hearing the Princess that day. Then Fay came rushing out of the library and began to scold her. Of course Gareth tried to placate them both.

I'm beginning to see how little control Gareth has over those others. As for the Old Man, I think Gareth is actually scared of him.

I know I've relied on Gareth for years and I know he's doing his level best to help me meet the Princess.

But I must say I'm getting sick of the sound of his voice. I can see that if I want to meet the Princess I will have to dodge them ALL.

I know one day I'll see her!

She lives! the radiance of her beauty imprisoned in her attic.

I want to set her free to rule us all.

I know she is there and that she is more beautiful than the first early morning ray of sunlight shining through the window. Her song sweeter than the first bird's song at dawn.

Joy Cowley
God Loves You, Miss Rosewater

He had planted barely half a row of potatoes when the preaching lady came round the back of the house with her bag of brochures and her terribly bright smile.

'Mr Bennett, isn't it? Lovely morning to be gardening.'

'Indeed, indeed.' He put down the bucket of seed potatoes and glanced behind him at the tool-shed. It was much too late to hide.

'What a marvellous garden!'

He knew the woman by sight. She came at the same time nearly every Sunday morning, at an hour when he was usually in bed surrounded by papers, the wreckage of breakfast and screaming kids who had to be hushed for the doorbell. Not that he ever went to the door. He made Hazel go. 'For your own good,' he'd tell her, pinching her on the backside until she was off her side of the bed, furious; and then, while she called him names and the children looked on, hoping for a real fight, he'd say, 'It takes a woman to deal with a woman.'

He believed that, believed it with all his being. He was not a liberated man. He still suffered from a debilitating code of chivalry which made him a doormat for any saleswoman.

The preaching lady's heels clicked on the brick path between the rows of red-currant bushes. Her dress, years out of fashion, stopped an inch above her knees and she wore white gloves that were curled like fern fronds, one at her chest, the other round the strap of her bag. Her face was very plain.

'I trust I'm not disturbing you.' She was out of breath as though she'd been exercising. 'We haven't met yet but I know your wife. My name's Gilwater, Mrs Esther Gilwater. I'm sorry. I have interrupted you, haven't I?'

'No, no, it's all right.'

He wondered why she deliberately held her voice at child's pitch. The sound was thin and delicate and it fluttered urgently like wings in a cobweb. Yet there was nothing frail or timid about her eyes. They shone with an aggressive kind of joy.

He winced without sound and wiped his hands on his trousers.

'I went to the front door and your little boy answered. He said you were in the garden.'

So it was Hazel's doing. He looked at the kitchen windows and imagined her watching in dressing-gown, head large with curlers, doubled over and choking ha-bloody-ha on cigarette smoke.

'I was wondering, Mr Bennett, if you've read any of the material I've given your wife.'

He blinked. 'Well, no. No, I haven't. Actually, I've got my own church. I'm Presbyterian. I don't have the time. . . .' But the word church had extended his hearing and he suddenly realized that his sad, little excuse was being exposed all over town. They were ringing everywhere, big bells, little bells, tattle tongues all, tintinnabulation — poetically speaking. He was being judged by dozens of blasted church bells.

Ah, Miss Drainwater, you are an exceedingly clever woman. Like the professional thief, you choose your moment well.

She was smiling at him, but her expression was too simple, too open for triumph. She opened her bag. 'As a concerned parent, you might be interested in one of these articles about aggressive tendencies in the young.' She was quoting now and her voice was strong. 'I'm sure all parents are worried about the young people today who seem to be involved with drugs and violence at an increasingly early age. Where will it end? we ask ourselves. The answers are in the Scriptures, Mr Bennett. As this article points out, we can hardly blame our children. In the last days the forces of evil will be let loose on the Earth. Families will be divided and nations will rise against themselves.'

'I haven't got money with me,' he said. 'If you go back to the house. . . .'

'I can get the money next time.' She was flicking pages. 'God has prophesied in his book of Revelations: "Babylon has fallen and become the habitation of devils and the hold of every foul spirit." This means that our children have to face all sorts of appalling abominations. It's a very disturbing thought, isn't it?'

He wanted to scratch himself. When I go back there I'll shoot the lot of them, he thought, and I shall bury Hazel in the garden with a tomato stake through her heart. He felt depressed. The sun on his woollen shirt had started trickles of sweat which itched under his arms and on his chest like swarms of ants. If the world was going to end, it had better get a move on.

When he thought about it, he had to admit it wasn't so much the

itch that made him miserable as his inability to scratch in front of this
— this Dullwater, Drainwater. He looked down at her shoes, mere scraps
of leather, then at his boots, size 10 encased in wads of mud, and he was
amazed at the extent of his cowardice. She went on about earthquakes,
blood from heaven and falling stars. He said nothing. He gently scraped
his boots on top of the spade and let her talk while the sweat ran inside
his corduroys and bumble-bees growled in the rows of broad-bean flowers
behind him.

'God is going to make all things new,' she said. 'He that overcomes
shall inherit everything, but the others, those not written in the Book
of Life, they'll be cast in the pit of fire.'

He rubbed the back of his neck. The trench he'd dug was dusted
with a mixture of superphosphate and blood-and-bone, and the seed
potatoes, hardened to greenness, were in line to the half-way mark where
he stood. 'OK. Well, I'll take a copy. I don't want to rush you but I do
have to finish this.'

'There's another short article on page 26.'

'No. Look, I'm sorry, but there's a lot to be done, Miss, Miss. . . .'

'Gilwater,' she said. 'It's Mrs, Mrs Gilwater.' And her voice was thin
again, so translucent that he saw clear through it to pink hair ribbons
and long white socks. Curiosity stilled him. What kind of marriage could
make a woman lose all the years between nine and 40? he wondered as
he studied her face. Her mouth was small, you would call it undeveloped,
but it wasn't an embittered mouth. Her grey eyes were round, clear and
entirely without knowledge.

'You have children?' he asked.

She smiled. 'We haven't been blessed that way.'

'Your husband then — he's still alive?'

She hesitated long enough for him to think, ah, so that's it, that
explains it all, then she said, 'Oh yes. My husband is very well, thank you.'

'And does he also — is he involved in this sort of work?'

'I'm afraid not, Mr Bennett. My husband is not one of us yet. But
he will be. The day will come, I know it. It must come. In the meantime
he's in God's care.'

Her smile had the chill of total conviction and her voice — it was
fine, all right, fine as piano wire — cut him to the extent that he was
defending himself when he said, 'What about your husband's attitudes?
Don't they count?'

'They will change,' she said. 'He's a good man, my husband, and many a good man has fallen prey to the woman of Babylon. He'll come back. When the scales fall from his eyes he'll leave her and come back to me and God's mercy. Seven years may have seemed a long time, but it's not long in God's reckoning. Jacob waited twice that for Rachel. He will be returned to me, oh yes.' Her white-gloved hand tapped between her breasts. 'I know it here for certain.'

He shut his mouth and thought, well now, that would teach him to mind his own business. Poor old thing. The discomfort of his discovery shifted him until he no longer had to look at her. So that's what it was about, eh? Poor old Stormwater, too ignorant for heaven, too innocent for hell, and the odds were against her ever attaining either.

He turned to her. 'Would you like a lettuce?' he asked.

'Oh.' Her smile wavered and she didn't seem to know. 'Only if — I mean, you're quite sure you've got one to spare — '

'Look at them.' He pointed at a row, spring green and every one fat-hearted.

'Oh yes. I see. Thank you, that would be nice.' She walked across the wet earth, at each step sinking to the depth of her heels and leaving small holes that looked as though they had been made for seedlings. She stopped beside the lettuces and said, 'Aren't they terribly early?'

He crossed the garden and stood next to her. 'It's an early season,' he said, looking down on her hair, which really wasn't too bad — not much colour to it but a lot of shine and a clean smell. 'Everything's come away like wildfire,' he said.

He unfolded his pocket-knife and bent over the row, feeling the leaves for the most solid heart. He cut it and held it out to her. But she was unprepared for the weight of it, and she let it drop on the ground between them. They both reached out, leaning forward at the same time. Her arm brushed against his, a quick, live touch, and she drew back so abruptly that she lost her balance and would have fallen had he not grabbed her hand. She gasped as though she had gone under cold water and tried to pull away, but he tightened his grip on her wrist and held on for longer than was necessary. The glove made her hand feel like a small animal, smooth pelt over bones that were hard with alarm.

'It's these shoes,' she said. 'The others are being repaired. The heels, see? See how silly? I shouldn't have put them on this morning — quite ridiculous.'

As he let her go he thought, well, well, it's still there, all right, it's still very much there. Not so much of the lost soul, after all. He gave her a long, understanding look and she turned away in panic. 'I should be more careful. Did I break that? That plant? Oh yes, I have, I've broken it. Will it grow again?'

'Don't worry,' he said.

'I'm so clumsy. I always have been clumsy. I hope it's nothing important.'

He shook his head at the damaged tomato plant and thought that later, when he had time to extend the metaphor, he'd be able to construct a parable from it, a sermon for Miss Rosewater. You mean you don't recognize this bit of green? It's a love-apple, that's what it is. It's broken and it will die. All things are meant to die, Miss Rosewater. Come away, come away. Spend your time with the living.

'No,' he said. 'It's not important.'

Her cheeks were flushed and she seemed about to cry. 'I — I'd better let you get on with your work.'

He wanted to reassure her about the plant, but she was ready to leave and it would have been cruel to try to stop her. 'Your lettuce,' he said, and bowed.

'Thank you very much.' She bundled the lettuce into her bag and started down the path, but after a few steps she turned and, although she was still pink with embarrassment, she was able to look him in the eye. She moved her fingers in a small wave.

'Goodbye, Mr Bennett.'

He waved back. 'God loves you, Miss Rosewater,' he said.

His words came out as a complete surprise to him. He stood facing her, unable to tell her what he'd meant. She was silent and waiting, her smile fluttering on and off, but he had nothing more to say to her.

What was there to say?

She went round the side of the house and he returned to his potatoes.

A few minutes later Hazel came out from the kitchen. She'd got dressed and combed her hair around her shoulders.

'You're a fine one,' he said. 'I could have wrung your neck.'

She didn't answer. She walked round the garden, arms folded, inspecting the seedlings, then came back to him and said, 'You didn't buy one of her little books.'

He stood up straight. 'No, by George, I didn't! I told her I would and then she went away with it.' He laughed. 'How did I get off the hook so easily?'

Hazel wasn't laughing. She moved up close, put her arms around his neck and deliberately leaned against him.

Her perception appalled him. 'What do you think you're doing?'

She grinned then, and kissed him on the neck, but her eyes were still as watchful as a cat's. 'What did that woman put in her bag?' she said.

'A lettuce. I gave her a lettuce. Do you have any objections?'

'No, none at all.' She rested her face on the front of his shirt. 'You know, you stink,' she said.

'All right, all right.' He put his arms around her and asked, 'What are the boys doing?'

'Tearing the house apart.'

He turned her by the shoulders and steered her towards the path. 'Let's have a look in the shed,' he said.

Janet Frame
Insulation

In the summer days when the lizards come out and the old ewes, a rare generation, a gift of the sun, gloat at us from the television screen, and the country, skull in hand, recites To kill or not to kill, and tomatoes and grapes ripen in places unused to such lingering light and warmth, then the people of Stratford, unlike the 'too happy happy tree' of the poem, do remember the 'drear-nighted' winter. They order coal and firewood, they mend leaks in the spouting and roof, they plant winter savoys, swedes, a last row of parsnips.

The country is not as rich as it used to be. The furniture in the furniture store spills out on the footpath and stays unsold. The seven varieties of curtain rail with their seven matching fittings stay on display, useless extras in the new education of discernment and necessity. The dazzling bathroom ware, the chrome and fur and imitation marble are no longer coveted and bought. For some, though, the time is not just a denial of gluttony, of the filling of that worthy space in the heart and the imagination with assorted satisfied cravings. Some have lost their jobs, their life-work, a process described by one factory-manager as 'shedding'.

'Yes, we have been shedding some of our workers.'

'Too happy happy tree'?

The leaves fall as if from other places, only they fall here. They are brittle in the sun. Shedding, severing, pruning. God's country, the garden of Eden and the conscientious gardeners.

Some find work again. Some who have never had work advertise in the local newspaper. There was that advertisement which appeared every day for two weeks, full of the hope of youth, sweet and sad with unreal assumptions about the world.

'Sixteen-year-old girl with one thousand hours training at hairdressing College seeks work.' The *one thousand hours* was in big dark print. It made the reader gasp as if with a sudden visitation of years so numerous they could scarcely be imagined, as if the young girl had undergone, like an operation, a temporal insertion which made her in some way older and more experienced than anyone else. And there was the air of pride with which she flaunted her thousand hours. She was pleading, using her richness of time as her bargain. In another age she might have recorded such time in her Book of Hours.

And then there was the boy, just left school. 'Boy, sixteen, would like to join pop group as vocalist fulltime' — the guileless advertisement of a dream. Did anyone answer either advertisement? Sometimes I imagine they did (I too have unreal assumptions about the world), that the young girl has found a place in the local Salon Paris, next to the Manhattan Takeaway, where she is looked at with admiration and awe (one thousand hours!) and I think that somewhere, maybe, say, in Hamilton (which is to other cities what round numbers are to numbers burdened by decimal points), there's a pop group with a new young vocalist fulltime, appearing, perhaps, on *Opportunity Knocks*, the group playing their instruments, the young man running up and down the stairs, being sexy with his microphone and singing in the agony style.

But my real story is just an incident, a passing glance at insulation and one of those who were pruned, shed, severed, and in the curious mixture of political metaphor, irrationally rationalized, with a sinking lid fitted over his sinking heart. I don't know his name. I only know he lost his job and he couldn't get other work and he was a man used to working with never a thought of finding himself jobless. Like the others he had ambled among the seven varieties of curtain rail and matching fittings, and the fancy suites with showwood arms and turned legs, and the second circular saw. He was into wrought iron, too, and there was a wishing well in his garden and his wife had leaflets about a swimming-pool. And somewhere, at the back of his mind, he had an internal stairway to the basement rumpus. Then one day, suddenly, although there had been rumours, he was pruned from the dollar-flowering tree.

He tried to get other work but there was nothing. Then he thought of spending his remaining money on a franchise to sell insulation. It was a promising district with the winters wet and cold and frosty. The price of electricity had gone up, the government was giving interest-free loans — why, everyone would be insulating. At first, having had a number of leaflets printed, he was content to distribute them in letter boxes, his two school-age children helping. His friends were sympathetic and optimistic. They too said, Everyone will be wanting insulation. And after this drought you can bet on a cold winter. Another thing, there was snow on Egmont at Christmas, and that's a sign.

He sat at home waiting for the orders to come in. None came. He tried random telephoning, still with no success. Finally, he decided to sell from door to door.

'I'm going from door to door,' he told his wife.

She was young and able. She had lost her job in the local clothing factory, and was thinking of buying a knitting-machine and taking orders. On TV when they demonstrated knitting-machines the knitter (it was always a she, with the he demonstrating) simply moved her hands to and fro as if casting a magic spell and the machine did the rest. To and fro, to and fro, a fair-isle sweater knitted in five hours, and fair-isle was coming back, people said. Many of her friends had knitting-machines, in the front room, near the window, to catch the light, where, in her mother's day, the piano always stood, and when she walked by her friends' houses she could see them sitting in the light moving their hands magically to and fro, making fair-isle and bulky knit, intently reading the pattern.

'Yes, door to door.'

The words horrified her. Not in her family, surely! Not door to door. Her father, a builder, had once said that if a man had to go door to door to advertise his work there was something wrong with it.

'If you're reputable,' he said, 'you don't advertise. People just come to you through word of mouth, through your own work standing up to the test.' Well, it wasn't like that now, she knew. Even Smart and Rogers had a full-page advertisement in the latest edition of the local paper. All the same, door to door!

'Oh no,' she said plaintively.

'It can't be helped. I have to look for custom.'

He put on his work clothes, a red checkered shirt, jeans, and he carried a bundle of leaflets, and even before he had finished both sides of one street he was tired and he had begun to look worried and shabby.

This is how I perceived him when he came to my door. I saw a man in his thirties wearing a work-used shirt and jeans yet himself looking the picture of disuse, that is, severed, shed, rationalized, with a great lid sinking over his life, putting out the flame.

'I thought you might like to insulate your house,' he said, thrusting a leaflet into my hand.

I was angry. Interrupted in my work, brought to the door for nothing! Why, the electrician had said my house was well insulated with

its double ceilings. Besides, I'd had experience of that stuff they blow into
the ceiling and every time there's a wind it all comes out making snowfall
in the garden, drifting over to the neighbours too.

'No, I'm not interested,' I said. 'I tried that loose-fill stuff once and
it snowed everywhere, every time the wind blew.'

'There's a government loan, you know.'

'I'm really not interested,' I said.

'But it's new. New. Improved.'

'Can't afford it, anyway.'

'Read about it, then, and let me know.'

'Sorry,' I said.

My voice was brisk and dismissing. He looked as if he were about
to plead with me, then he changed his mind. He pointed to the red print
stamped on the leaflet. There was pride in his pointing, like that of the
girl with the thousand hours.

'That's my name and phone number, if you change your mind.'

'Thank you, but I don't think I will.'

He walked away and I shut the door quickly. Insulation, I said to
myself with no special meaning or tone. How lovely the summer is, how
cosy this house is. The people here before me had carpets that will last
for ever, the ceiling is double, there are no cracks in the corners, that
is, unless the place decides to shift again on its shaky foundations. How
well insulated I am! How solid the resistance of this house against the
searching penetrating winds of Stratford. The hunted safe from the
hunter, the fleeing from the pursuer, the harmed from the harmer.

'How well insulated I am!'

That night I had a curious ridiculous dream. I dreamed of a land like
a vast forest 'in green felicity' where the leaves had started to fall, not
by nature, for the forest was evergreen, but under the influence of a season
that came to the land from within it and had scarcely been recognized,
and certainly not ruled against. Now how could that have been? At first
I thought I was trapped in a legend of far away and long ago, for the
characters of long ago were there. I could see a beggar walking among
the fallen leaves. He was the beggar of other times and other countries,
and yet he was not, he was new, and he was ashamed. I saw a cottage
in the forest and a young woman at the window combing her hair and
— a young man with a — lute? No, a guitar — surely that was the prince?
— and with the guitar plugged in to nowhere he began to play and

sing and as he sang he sparkled — why, it was Doug Dazzle — and he was singing,

> *One thousand hours of cut and set*
> *my showwood arms will hold you yet*
> *baby baby insulate,*
> *apprentice and certificate*
> *God of nations at thy feet*
> *in our bonus bonds we meet*
> *lest we forget lest we forget*
> *one thousand hours of cut and set. . . .*

The girl at the window listened and smiled and then she turned to the knitting-machine by the window and began to play it as if from a 90 per cent worsted, 10 per cent acrylic score. I could see the light falling on her hands as they moved to and fro, to and fro in a leisurely saraband of fair-isle. Then the beggar appeared. He was carrying a sack that had torn and was leaking insulation, faster and faster, until it became a blizzard, vermiculite falling like snow, endlessly, burying everything, the trees and their shed leaves, the cottage, the beggar, the prince, and the princess of the thousand hours.

The next morning I found the leaflet and telephoned the number on it.

'I'd like to be insulated,' I said.

The man was clearly delighted.

'I'll come at once and measure.'

We both knew we were playing a game, he trying to sell what he didn't possess, and I imagining I could ever install it, to deaden the world. All the same, he measured the house and he put in the loose-fill insulation, and following the Stratford custom, although it was summer, I ordered my firewood against that other 'drear-nighted' winter.

Violet Coalhouse
The Mask

I'm walking along a road.

Ahead of me walk two fat quail.

On the right toitoi rustles in the faint breath of wind. On the left cows are grazing. The pasture dips down to a raupo swamp.

Above, at three o'clock in the afternoon, saunters a warm winter sun. Birds fly. A rag dangles from a bare tree. The tree's branches are the colour of amber.

There's a grey road winding in front of me. I suck the piece of chocolate fudge bar in my mouth. A fatnosed aeroplane drones behind my head like a fly.

The road winds on and on.

A dead bird lies smeared across the asphalt. Crickets sing. A green car zooms past. I glimpse the people inside, the people who sell wine on the island.

Cows graze. Toitoi whispers. I'm walking along a road.

***

I come to the crossroads. I read the signpost earnestly (or so it might appear to anyone watching but the baches appear shut up for the winter, their windows dead eyes).

It's three thirty in the afternoon. Which would be the quickest way home? There's a park with a swing and slide and jungle gym.

In my mouth, the chocolate fudge bar's melted, every sweet morsel, a long time ago.

There's a doctor's house, a butcher's shop, a TAB, and here's a dairy. Have I got enough money for some chippies? A dollar in small change is in my purse.

'Twennytwo,' says the little man behind the counter.

Onion flavoured. I rip the packet open as I walk down the path to the beach. From above the changing sheds is a child's folded paper toy. A fantasy in grey. There are three people sitting on a concrete bench gazing out to sea. A duffel-coated father, a permed middle-aged mum, and a bored daughter with dark hair rippling down her back. The man looks round at me. He looks familiar but I look away quickly. I walk past them crunching up the chippies as fast as I can go.

I come to two swings on the grass verge. Behind them is a red house with trellises and bric-à-brac picked out in white.

I sit on the left-hand swing and lazily push myself back and forth. The chippies are all gone. But my mouth still tastes of onion flavour. My jeans bite into my stomach. Pinching the skin.

* * *

I'm thinking about the man and the child. They've been visiting me for the long weekend. I've been to the wharf to see them off. The child had some pebbles she'd picked up from the side of the road. They were in the pockets of her red overalls. There was a wait for the ferry, so we finished up the last of my peppermints. We spent the last minutes squeezing the pebbles into the empty peppermint container. On the boat, the man found a seat next to a guy smoking a cigarette beside a window. I passed the child to her father and kissed them both. I didn't want them to go. The child's face was impassive. The man looked old and vulnerable. I stumbled back up the boat steps and leapt ashore just in time. But I had missed the bus that was going to Whakarite Bay. So I sat down on an upturned dinghy, took out my sketchpad, and began to draw the ferry alongside the wharf. But at that point it steamed off into the afternoon, back to the mainland. So I drew the wharf without the boat. It would make a nice postcard, I thought. Then I bought a chocolate fudge bar at the shop-made-out-of-a-bus. Then I began to walk along the road.

* * *

For quite a while I sit on the swing. The beach is a great white crescent from where I sit. I wonder if my new burgundy shoes aren't starting to give me blisters. Wriggling my feet round I admire the cut of leather, the neat stitching. I wonder if the husband of the woman raking the lawn of the red and white house is watching me from behind lace curtains. Along the beach sit the three people gazing out to sea.

There's a pinkbreasted bird flying across the headland. Shall I go up the road over the hill in case there's another bus soon? Or I could go round the rocks to the next beach and get a drink at the shop there.

Round the rocks the tide is out. Rocks squat in slides of shining sand. My feet are tired and drag through the scrabbles of shells and heaps of kelp. A boy appears from the opposite direction.

Good. That means there must be a way round. Doesn't it? The boy's scratching wriggly lines in the sand with a big stick.

An old man comes round the headland, holding the hand of a small girl in a blue dress. I pass them with my head down so I won't have to nod and smile at them. And then I'm round the headland.

There's a tiny version of the crescent-shaped beach I've just left. A delta with myriads of forks must be crossed. It's very shallow and my shoes don't let the water in thank god. But the shop is closed. A handwritten notice hangs inside the closed door.

Back at 4. Surely it must be that by now. I peer hopelessly in the window. Bloody chippies have made me so *thirsty*. But. Will I wait in this cold valley where the sun is blotted out by huge macrocarpa trees? Will the shop open? Will a bus come?

I plod up the winding hill. I suspect there won't be any more buses till the next boat comes in.

Sometimes there is sun on my back. Warming me.

Other times, a frost seems ready to settle on the steep banks. Gorse is in fragrant flower.

***

I hear a bus lumbering up the hill! But it doesn't appear and I realize it must be going up the other hill. I practise how I'll flag down the bus if one comes my way and I'm between stops. But here the houses have an air of being lived in so maybe I'm being watched! Maybe the people behind the little wistaria patios think I'm just another loony. Of which there are plenty on the island.

The Island of Cascading Waters, they call it in English. Except I haven't yet come across any cascading waters. Only been here two months though.

My back's aching. I'm walking up the road like a pregnant lady. Hands pressed in the hollow of my back to ease it. I suppose the ache comes from having to hold the child all the time on the wharf. She was struggling to get down and watch the water through the planks, all sparkly. But I hadn't wanted to let go of her.

I've arrived at the top of the hill.

A concrete seat still partly in the sunlight. From it, a marvel of sky, sea, islands. I place my cloth bag on a part of the seat free from birdshit. That can be my cushion. I sit down, realizing that I *have* got blisters on my heels. But if I take the shoes off, I won't want to put them on again. A taxi drives up the hill. The driver glances at me. He has squinty eyes. Pity I couldn't afford a taxi now but I spent too much money on food for my visitors over the weekend. And I wonder if I should go back. Back to the endless circles. Back to the suburban street, the man, the child, the big house, my study full of books, paints, dead flowers, junk? Back to the concrete yard, the fruit trees, the traffic roaring by? And away from the blueblack sea.

Do they need me. The man and the girl, do they? Ah how complicated it is! And yet, it's quite simple really. I always do go back and it always does begin again. And I will not be free.

I feel sad. Tears spring to my eyes and I'm startled by the tears. Because it's been so long since I felt like crying. Because now it seems like a luxury when it *used* to be a necessity. I let the hot salty tears slide into my mouth. And feel perfectly contented. So the tears must be tears of joy or something.

. . . and clouds and islands trembling in your eyes . . .

Wasn't that the poem about the cave by the poet who was so tall he had to stoop coming through our kitchen door and he gave us cherry brandy to taste out of a funny old bottle and us kids got all giggly and afterwards I hid under the table and there was another writer who had a wooden leg and the kitchen was warm with talk and laughter?

And where was the warmth now that they were all dead?

But birds wheel in the clear sky. Sun sparkles on water where boats skim. The hills are covered with bush and the valleys are moist. I want to put my arms around somebody and make love. I throb with wanting it.

Sighing, I begin to walk along the winding ridge road.

***

Another shop. Another bus stop. A woman with a black dog. She's got a red spotty scarf tied round her head like a bandage. She stares at me when I ask her. 'No more buses till the boat comes in dear,' she says, sympathetic. 'Might as well walk, it's not far now, take the right fork, it's quicker!'

Thanking her I trudge on. Round the next bend I'm pleased to see that she's right! There's just one more hollow, one more ridge, and down the hill will be my cottage.

Suddenly I notice things. Bare trees alive with chattering birds. Goldfinches, I think. They are fat and take no notice of my passing. On gates are painted names. Shangri La, Waiwurri, Dunroamin, Mon Desir. You'd think people. . . . But no. Let them be. You can see into their living-rooms and kitchens. You can see where they while away their lives.

A man is building a pole house. I notice his lean tanned body (he's wearing only tatty shorts) until he stares at me. Then I ignore him. Another man's mowing his lawn with a motormower. The noise sears the afternoon.

Up on this ridge there's some wind. It's blowing my hair into my eyes. A taxi passes going the other way. A bearded man waves to me from the taxi, do I know him?

Suddenly the sun sinks. The earth goes chill. Going down the last hill, everything becomes awfully clear. Each twig, berry, flower, pebble, leaf, stands out razor-sharp to my eyes.

I shiver.

I cross my arms against my chest, hugging myself to keep warm.

Yes I shall have to go back, but not yet, I decide. Back to the man, the child, the house. But not yet.

Down below my cottage nestles. The pine trees stand straight and tall, sheltering it. It's a little white box, black trimmings, red iron roof. Next door a tiny man is cutting down a tree with a power saw. The noise vibrates menacingly across the valley.

I'm walking down the road. Smoke curls softly from chimneys. The blue flickering square of television glares through windows. A burst of gunfire here. A whinny of horses there. From a place down the road, the blast of a pop song. Rod Stewart, I think. I pass the bus shelter on the corner. The phone booth. Up the road a sheep is tethered, and I say hello to it, but it just goes on nibbling.

I'm walking up my path. I unlock the door of my cottage. I enter.

I hang up my mask behind the bedroom door. Kick off my shoes. Pour myself a big glass of white wine. The rest of the night's mine.

***

There's no moon tonight. From the back door I watch the sky. Its black is laced through with diamonds. I see the mainland where the man and child will be. A faint glow. Inside the cottage, Mozart is bright and warm. Ginger flowers climb up the curtains, intertwined with green leaves, brown curlicues. Scrabble, and a jam jar of geraniums picked for me by the child yesterday, sit on the table.

Later, I take a glass of wine into the bedroom, hop into bed. Propped up on pillows I read for a while. The book is *The Ascent of Man*. It has nice pictures. My eyes are closing. I turn the electric blanket off, the light off. And snuggle into the warm bed.

My mask hangs behind the door.

Patricia Grace
Kepa

Girls against boys today, and so there were the girls with their dresses tucked into their pants, waiting. The boys came out of their huddle and called, 'Ana.'

'We call Ana.'

'Ana Banana.'

Ana could run it straight or try trickery. Straight she decided, and committed now with a toe over the line. Away with hair rippling, eyes fixed on the far corner, that far far corner, the corner far. . . .

Boys bearing down, slapping thighs and yodelling. And confident. If Denny Boy didn't get her Macky would.

'Ana Banana.'

'Anabanana.'

'Banana Ana,' Denny Boy leaving the bunch in a fast sprint, slowing down and lingering for the show of it, then diving for the ankle slap. But not quite. Not quite. Ana was ready for him. She side-stepped and kicked him in the knee, then she was off again.

Infield. No hope of a straight run now, nearly all on top of her. Facing her. Spreading out and facing. Back at the line the girls all screamed, 'Run Ana.'

'Run.'

'Ana run.'

'Runana,' over the humps and cracks, plops and thistles. Not far to go, but they all knew someone would . . . Macky. She hit like a slammed door while the other girls all yelled at her to get up Ana.

'Get up.'

'Up Ana.'

'Come on, gee.'

'Gee, come on Ana, get up.'

'Up.'

Macky's fingers were clamped to her ankle but he hadn't got her yet. He hadn't got her three times in the middle of the back and those were the rules. She kicked out with her free foot, but he wouldn't let go, and now the other boys were sitting on her. Thumping One, taking their time for the show of it, Two, caught Three. Howzat?

'Howzat?' The boys were doing some sort of dance, an arms and legs dance, a face dance, a bum dance, and the girls were wild. Sukeys they called.

'Pick a fast runner next time sukeys.'

'Cheats.'

'Sukeys and cheats.'

Not that the boys cared, getting together for their next conference. They decided to call Charlotte, just to prove they weren't sukeys. Or cheats.

'Cha-arlotte.'

'Ba-anjoes.'

'Charlotte Banjoes,' they weren't scared.

Charlotte leapt forward and three of the boys ran ahead to help from the front because they knew it would take a united effort. Macky was coming from behind, but suddenly Charlotte halted and put her foot out and he somersaulted over it. 'Go Charlotte, go Charlotte,' the girls screamed. She went off at another angle with only three boys to beat. She charged straight for them, stopped and buckled her knees at them, then changed direction again and went for the line. Safe, with Macky throwing dung at her and the girls yelling, 'All over, all over,' running out into the bunch of angry boys.

Two more of the girls ran across safely while those who were caught went to the sideline to recuperate, and to await the revenge time.

'How's that you fullas?'

'Only three of you fullas left.'

'Shut up you cheats.'

'Just only three.'

'Who do you call?'

Erana ran out with fists flying. She saw a little gap between Jack and Denny Boy that could be big enough for a side-step foot-change and through, but not quite. She was quickly caught, held and tagged, and so was Becky. That left Charlotte.

'Banjoes.'

'Cha-arlotte.'

'Ba-anjoes.'

Charlotte ran out on to the field and swerved round two of the boys. She knocked another down knowing there was still a long way to go.

Knowing Macky had it in for her and that the foot trip wouldn't work a second time. He was gaining on her and wasn't put off by her sudden balk tactic. Still gaining, and with a strong group up front, Charlotte knew her chances were not good. She tried a change of direction but Macky stayed with her. He was close enough now but seemed to be delaying, and Charlotte didn't know why. Then suddenly she knew. She saw the thistle as Macky brought her down on top of it. Macky wisely held tightly on to both of her legs until help came. It came swiftly. 'One, Two, Three.'

'All out, all out.'

'Howzat?'

'Howzat you fullas?' but the girls were already conferring and Charlotte was enraged. 'Macky-Blacky,' she called, and she was going to throw that Macky in the tutae for sure.

After him. The slipperiest, the ugliest. . . . Charlotte was running alongside and they all knew she would have to do something quick because Macky-Blacky was faster than she was. She kicked his legs from under him and swiped him in the back with her fist. Macky was down with Charlotte on top of him. He wriggled on to his back so that she couldn't tag him; after all he was not only the fastest but also slipperiest so he wasn't caught yet. But Charlotte wasn't so interested in tagging him because there was a big round, soft plop not far away. She dug her knees into Macky's thighs, pinned his arms down and rolled. Now he was on top but still quite helpless. Another heave and roll . . . a splash and his back was right in it, good job. 'Good job Blacky.'

Macky bounced up, and suddenly there was blood pouring out of Charlotte's nose. Then the two of them were down again punching and kicking, while all the others shouted at them to get up.

'Come on, gee.'

'Gee-ee you're spoiling the game.'

'Gees you fullas spoil everything.'

And Denny Boy was really mad. He was still *in*. He hadn't been caught yet and these fullas must fight. He got through the fence and had a drink at the creek, then he sat on the stile to wait. Gee those two fighting, and the rest of them hopping about and shouting, and he was still *in*. He hadn't had his turn yet. A-ack they made him sick.

He stood up on the stile . . . and it was from there that he noticed, far away at the end of the beach where the road began, a little speck which seemed to roll from side to side. He'd seen that same speck doing that same thing more than two years ago. And he knew what it was if only he could remember — Now he remembered. He knew what it was, who it was. It was Uncle Kepa, home from the sea, lifting his feet high as he walked so as not to get dust on his shoes. Uncle Kepa who had been to all the countries in the world and who was bringing them back a monkey. Denny Boy began to run. Across the paddock, down to the beach and over the stones.

Back in mid-field Lizzie noticed him going for his life, he was cunning that Denny Boy. You had to watch Denny Boy, running off in the middle of a fight like that. He was up to something. Look at him, running like a porangi. . . .

'Uncle Kepa,' Lizzie screamed, and began to run too. The others were only seconds behind her, calling.

'Come back here Denny Boy.'

'Cheat.'

'Liar.'

'Stink bum.'

Charlotte, still running, ripped the bottom off her dress and wiped the blood from her face. Then she handed the rag to Macky who wiped all round his mouth where his teeth had come through his lip. 'You wait smarty,' she was yelling, 'Come back tutae face.' But Denny Boy was way ahead. Not even Macky or Charlotte could catch him now. And if Uncle Kepa gave that monkey to Denny Boy well watch out.

For some years now, whenever they had thought about Uncle Kepa who had been round the world thousands of times, millions of times and overcounting times, they would discuss claims on the pet monkey that their uncle would one day bring.

Charlotte said she should have it because she was the eldest, but she would let them all come and see it whenever they wanted to. Denny Boy thought that he should be able to keep the monkey because he helped Uncle Kepa a lot. He cleaned Uncle's tank out, chopped his wood, and looked after his fishing lines while he was away. Becky and Lizzie backed Charlotte's claim because she was their sister and that would make them second in charge. One day Mereana had said that Uncle would be sure to give her the monkey because she was the youngest, and they all stared at her wondering if this could happen. No. Charlotte decided that Mereana was too small to look after a monkey.

Yes. The others were relieved. Mereana wasn't big enough but they would let her — and just then, Macky, who was stretched out on his back looking at the sky said, 'Uncle Kepa, he's going to give that monkey to me.'

'You?' they all yelled.

'You?'

'You don't even know Uncle Kepa.'

'You haven't even seen Uncle Kepa.'

'Aunty Connie, she only got you last year.'

'Uncle Kepa, he's not your real uncle.'

Macky closed his eyes, 'Uncle Kepa, I bet he'll give that monkey to me.'

'What for?'

'Yeah. What for? He never told you he was bringing a monkey.'

'You weren't here.'

'Aunty Connie, she only got you last year.'

'Uncle Kepa, he'll give that monkey to me."

'What for?"

'Because I look like a monkey that's what for. And the monkey will like me the best.'

They all stared at Macky angrily, wondering. 'You always say that's what I look like, a monkey, so that means I do.' Macky got up and started running around on his hands and feet. Then he stood up, stuck his bottom teeth out up over his top lip and began scratching under his armpits. When he could see that they were really worried he ran up a tree and hung from a branch by one hand making noises like Tarzan's ape.

They watched him without speaking for a long time. Then Charlotte said, 'You don't look like a monkey any more.'

'No,' they all agreed. 'You don't look like a monkey at all.'

'Only when Aunty Connie first got you you did.'

But they were worried.

'I think Aunty Connie might give you back soon.' And after that they'd spent the rest of the morning swinging in the trees and gibbering.

Later that day someone had put forward the idea that if they made a house for the monkey and kept it in the orchard then that would be fair, because the orchard belonged to everyone. They had all agreed, each thinking he would find a way out if Uncle Kepa gave the monkey to him.

But now, there was Denny Boy hugging Uncle Kepa. And while it was one thing to be the eldest, or the youngest, or to be lucky and look like a monkey, it was another thing to be first and *smart*. Uncle Kepa was sitting himself down in the lupins at the side of the road to wait for them. He put his arms out and they all fell in. 'Ah my babies, my babies,' he kept saying.

His babies all hugged him then moved back so the monkey wouldn't get squashed. Where would Uncle keep a monkey? So far they couldn't see a monkey anywhere. All Uncle's pockets were flat and he wasn't carrying any boxes. There was only his bag. Charlotte dug her elbow into Mereana and whispered, 'You ask, you're the youngest.' So Mereana hid behind Lizzie. And Denny Boy, making sure to keep the upper hand said, 'Uncle you got us a monkey?'

'Ah no my babies. Not this time. The monkey, he got away. That monkey, he's too quick for this funny old uncle. Next time my babies.'

Ah well.

They walked along the beach with their uncle who rolled from side to side as though he was still on board. Uncle was a big strong man, and he had chased a monkey the length and breadth of some faraway jungle, climbing trees and swinging from branch to branch, but the monkey had got away. It shows you how quick and clever monkeys are.

That evening when Uncle Kepa was sitting in a chair by the stove at Aunty Connie's place with all the kids hanging round, he said, 'Ah that's good. Good to be a landlubber for a while. Good to see all my babies again. All my babies. These the only babies I got.' Then the kids heard Aunty Connie say, 'What about that drop kick of yours over in Aussie?' and Aunty Connie was laughing.

Then Uncle looked at the ceiling and started to laugh too, 'Ee hee, ee hee, ee hee hee.' Uncle Kepa was a great big man but his laugh was high and skinny like a seagull noise. And gee they all had a lot of things to talk about when it was time to go back to school. All about their uncle who was a great big man who went everywhere in the world in a big ship. And who was bringing them a monkey one day. As well as that they'd just found out that uncle was a famous footballer too, and it made him laugh like anything.

Shonagh Koea
Meat

After the murder I always said the seeds of that carve-up were sown right back when the council decided to build a new gymnasium.

When I say the council decided I really mean that a few bright boys decided and they out-voted the older ones. One thing about age is that it teaches you that this year's new doesn't stay new. The bright boys weren't that bright.

In a town like this there isn't much besides the main street, Carter's Wholesalers, the pub and the picture theatre. The old gym was where everybody went, even people who never climbed a rope in their lives. It was like a club.

Bill Arthur was the caretaker and he kept the place going right through the war, and afterwards when there were all the shortages.

In those days people lived with their in-laws, or they knocked themselves up a garage to live in if they could afford a section. The housing shortage got everyone. A lot of people lived in the transit camp down by the railway-line.

For a lot of them the old gym was the only place they could go at a weekend to talk without the relatives hearing. There was always a big crowd but you can be very private in the middle of a lot of people.

Bill lived at the back in a big flat that ran right along the building behind the kitchen where the ladies' committee used to make cups of tea on a Saturday night. Everyone knew it was Bring a Plate, Please, and it used to be quite a spread.

There were the changing-rooms, the showers, the kitchen and then there was Bill's flat, as big as a house, right along the back. He needed the room. His wife was what my wife called a messer and she always said a messer needs more space than a tidy person. Bill's two boys were at high school when the war broke out. They used to make those aeroplane models, I remember, with size and tissue-paper and bits of balsa wood all over the place.

They were both nearly grown up when Marigold was born towards the end of 1944. My wife said that you could just bet on a messer like

Mavis Arthur, to have another baby at her age. She said it was just plain undiluted untidiness, and she could have been right.

Right from the start Marigold was a beautiful child, but there was something wrong. You lifted her little arm up, it stayed up. She was no bother, they said, and everyone thought that was a bad sign. Nobody said Marigold wasn't quite right. After a while there was no need to. Even old Dr Hellaby only said, 'So you've noticed,' when Bill asked him. Sometimes you could swear she was all there, and then she'd get that blank look. She was a beautiful child, though, and my wife was very fond of her.

We lived next door to the gym and when we worked in the garden Marigold used to come to the hedge and call through to my wife. She was a child that was very fond of flowers and any little living creature. I've known the time when we'd have ten or twelve jars in a row on the veranda, and each one would have a spider with a broken leg or a fly with one wing.

Marigold used to get very upset over those broken creatures and often after dark we would be out with the torch trying to find another one the same. We used to let the damaged one go and replace it with a good one ready for the morning when she came over. You couldn't have the heart to disappoint her.

I've tried telling them how she likes insects and little creatures and they were quite nice about it but they said the problem is the jars. Even plastic can get quite an edge on it, they said, and they couldn't take the responsibility.

In the beginning, years before all the trouble, when Marigold was just a little thing she used to sing out to us over the hedge. Then there was the day I got home from the shop and there was my wife waiting for me with the clippers. She wanted me to cut through the phenalbium towards the back of the section, where it always grew thinner than the rest. I could tell she was set on it, otherwise she'd never have bothered me on a Thursday. She knew Thursday was my busy day getting all the mince and sausages done ready for the Friday.

I cut through the hedge and at the weekend I put in a couple of old fence posts and swung a little gate in the gap so it looked neat and tidy. The trouble about having no children is that you get too tidy. Everything has to be just so.

Marigold liked flowers. My wife had a lovely garden in those days — all lilies round the back, and roses too. If I got home from the shop and found the house empty I always knew I'd find the pair of them out in the garden. My wife bought Marigold a little set of garden tools and made her a frilly pinafore all patterned with pansies so she kept clean. Not that her mother bothered but my wife liked everything proper and in its place. Nothing must do but Marigold must wear her pinafore in the garden.

My wife loved lilies. She used to take all the prizes in the show every year — Best Lily, Best Arum, Open Lily, Best in Show. I've got all her cups in the china cabinet.

Lilies multiply wonderfully but I've let them spread too far. There are even some coming up through the front lawn but I don't like to dig them up. They remind me of my wife and the old times, before all the troubles next door, and before she got too sick to look after them. Even right at the end when she could only take diluted orange juice and the doctor said it could be a day or a week, she used to like me to lift her up so she could see the flowers.

I was home all the time then, retired. The boy I had in the shop turned out quite a good lad and he bought me out later on. Mind you, the shop's not what it was. It's gone very modern now. They have smoked duck and schnitzel and slices of pork done so thin you could see through them if you held them up. It's not like when I started off in the business and you had your sausages and your roasts and a nice bit of lamb, the cheaper cuts for stews all trimmed up, and something a bit different for a Friday like Spanish roll. I did a very nice window too with a parsley trim round the edge like a miniature hedge, but you don't want me to be telling you about the shop. I was telling you about the lilies and the garden and the old days, before the murder.

I take Marigold a bunch of lilies every Christmas when I go to see her. It's a long drive and I'm not getting any younger but I make it my holiday for the year. I stay a few days near where she is. She doesn't take the interest in things that she used to. It's being kept like that.

Every day I go to see her and she always asks me about my wife. Aunty Muriel, she calls her. I'm Uncle Athol. I haven't the heart to tell her so I always say Aunty Muriel's gone shopping and she'll be coming tomorrow. Then she forgets. She's much blanker than she used to be but, like I said, she doesn't feel the interest.

Her father was a marvellous handyman and in the old days at the gym we used to hear him belting up new sheets of iron on the roof or mixing up a barrowload of concrete to patch the walls. He was a great chap for getting what he wanted, even with all the shortages. If that place needed a sleeve put in the roof to cure a leak or a bit of mortar over a crack in a wall he'd be out round the town begging a bit here and there. He had a real nose for smelling out who had a bag of cement hidden away or a few four-by-twos.

The place looked like a piebald horse after the war, with all the patches here and there and no paint to cover them up. But he'd kept the place going. The town had kept going and a lot of things that kept it going were started off right there, at the gym. I remember the night we introduced Neville Bailey who had the men's outfitters down at the corner to Pam Stacey whose husband was killed in the Western Desert the year before. It stopped her crying over spilt milk and it stopped him making such a mess of bringing up that little boy of his after his wife drowned in the dam. A lot of things were settled at the gym, one way and another.

Bill never thought of any other job. That was why when the bright boys decided to build a new gym he hadn't an idea in the world he'd be passed over. It turned out they wanted someone who knew about gymnastics so he could train a team, something to make a splash for the town.

The next thing was they gave Bill a golden handshake to make up for the three years' work he'd miss retiring early and they advertised in the cities for a replacement.

He used to sit in his chair in the house he bought behind us holding the letter he got from the council when the new gymnasium was first mentioned. The letter said in all probability his employment would continue. He read that letter every day and he showed it to anyone who would look. About a year later he nodded off in that very chair and he didn't wake up. My wife said he died of a broken heart.

I had made a gateway for Marigold in the back hedge by that time. The old posts had rotted but I could use the gate again. It didn't seem any more than a year or two since I'd swung it on its hinges the first time though by now Marigold was coming up to fifteen. She could read a bit — just simple things like *The Everyday and Nowaday Fairy Book* — and she could write a few things like her name and address.

I told you before that Mavis Arthur was a messer. Bill used to keep her at things, 'What about cooking a nice pie with these windfalls,' he'd say. Or, 'What about finishing cleaning the windows, May?' He used to do all the shopping, managed the money. She couldn't even get the hang of driving a car so Bill drove her everywhere.

We all thought when Bill died she'd do all the things widows do but we were in for a shock. My wife tried to get her interested in the Women's Institute and the Ladies' Guild but she just laughed. She was out here, there and everywhere. Three nights after Bill's funeral she was out dancing at the timberyard fancy-dress ball dressed as a panda. She even used to go down to the lounge bar of the pub on a Saturday night, and that's where she met Wally Carmichael.

Six months to the day that we buried poor old Bill she upped and married him. He wasn't a bad workman if you could keep him off the booze, but he could be nasty-tempered. His first wife ran off with an American during the war and everyone said that all the free nylons would be a change from Wally's black eyes.

He won a prize once at the winter show for wood-chopping. The only thing he took a pride in was his axe and if you asked him to show you how sharp it was he used to shave the hairs off his arm. . . .

You could tell when Wally got home from the pub by the noise. When he first went to live over the back you'd hear crashes as he hit the fence or the gate posts with his old truck but he knocked them right down after a while. Then it was a straight, clear run into Bill's shed. The posts and part of the fence stayed where they lay on the lawn and after a while the long grass grew over them. Bill would have had a fit at the condition that place was in, and if he hadn't already died it would have killed him to hear what went on.

We used to ring young Barney Marks when it got too bad. He was old Barney Marks's youngest boy, the big one that went into the Police and married the red-headed girl from the Tip-Top. But, as he said, if you go into a place and they tell you to bugger off you've got to go, even the police.

It all happened just before Marigold's seventeenth birthday. I remember the moon was on the wane because it looked just like a lamb chop thrown up into the sky. I was out late that night digging the garden ready for the spring sowing and the turfs were curling off the shovel a treat, just like the best slices of sirloin. The ground was in such good heart that I stayed and stayed digging till in the end I had to go and open the kitchen door so the light shone out across the garden.

That was when I saw her standing in her little gateway in a splashy print dress. She didn't speak or move so I walked right up to her, to see what the matter was, and after that I called my wife.

'What's been going on, my darling?' my wife said, and took her hand.

Without a word Marigold walked back through the hedge with us after her.

We found them inside. I wasn't upset, really. You get used to making the brawn and sausage meat out of all the bits, but if anyone had to find it I'm glad it was me.

I often put one in the window on a Friday when I had the shop. It used to amuse the kids, with a hat on and a pipe in its mouth. If you think of it just as the top end of something, a pig's head or a man's head are just top ends. In my trade you get used to meat.

My wife took Marigold outside and they went down through the gap in the hedge again, where the lilies were coming through the ground.

She said later she was sorry there was nothing in the garden for Marigold but daisies. Marigold just stood there, in the light from the kitchen, holding the flowers till they took her away. My wife always said the only things that make misery and heartbreak bearable are the flowers and the singing of the birds.

I remember standing there with them and thinking so many things all at once that it seemed I was thinking about the whole world. I remembered when she was born and when Bill and I were at school in old Miss Tucker's class and she gave us six of the best for writing on the desk with a pin and I couldn't help thinking, over and over again, that in all my years in the trade I'd never seen a better set of neck chops. He'd always been such a bull-necked fellow.

Jennifer Compton
One of my families

I was walking in a forest of broom flowers. The city was humming under sunlight. A vapour of broom scent clouded the air. The earth was ochre brown and silky. The sky was lightest clearest blue. And my heart and my thoughts were my own. My Father was idly throwing wood onto the back of a truck. My Mother was sunnily shopping for a tin of Nescafé and a packet of frozen peas. My red-headed sisters were bent over their books in dreamy classrooms. My brother with the harelip was racing across a rugby field, always a bit behind the other boys and condescended to because, although I never could, the world thought he was a cripple.

Somehow what the world thought never quite sunk in. I could see other people did strange things but that was just their little way. One of their little ways was to touch and finger with their muddy hands beautiful moments in the sun with masquerades of gross and vicious nature. That was one of their little ways, and any pain it caused me was for the fields of broom flowers that they would rather not see.

And when my Father put on his wooden leg I knew that he could still wriggle his toes. He told me so. And I believed him. He thought he could. I posted sixpences in the little hole just below his kneecap. My uncle, years back from the trenches, let me poke daisies into his wooden leg. My sister and my cousin and I picked wreaths of flowers and asked him why they took away his leg? He didn't tell us. I don't think he knew.

My beautiful aunt with the Italian face married a very dull man. I could see he was dull. I never asked her why. She didn't want me to know anything about that. I wish she'd told me. She took me to see my great aunt Beryl sitting in her chair, looking out at Kirk Green wondering why it's still there. She had given my aunt a delicate dinner set and she gave me my great great uncle's silver chain.

My brother carried my Father's coffin on one shoulder. Just behind him was our next door neighbour who had tried to do nasty things to me behind the woodshed. That was a very strange thing I thought. Why does he want to do that? But now I know. His wife had lumps on her leg and didn't want to know. He was very clever. Won prizes at school. For Literature. And read. Had rows and rows of *Reader's Digest*s.

My cousin's husband stayed one night with me when he was in town for the Royal Show. But he missed my cousin. She had five children before the doctors would tie her tubes. She just sighed. The second girl talked to animals. You could see she did. She wouldn't talk to humans though until they took her to the city and ther he was quite all right. I wonder if she still talks to the pigs? She'd be ten or so now.

I saw my cousin Jack on my Father's side last week. He was passing through town with his woman. He wants to teach mentally retarded children but doesn't want any of his own. Children, that is. He looks like Cliff Richard but he fell off his motorbike in England and has a scar on his chin, so he wears a beard. He didn't write to his Mother till he got out of hospital. She'd married her first cousin and was so scared of monster children she went to pieces with each of them. Three of them.

Well, that's some of my family. There's great uncle Albert who was given six months and a pension in 1918 and died in 1971. They gave him something to live for my Father always said. And there's Stanley, who's a cubmaster, and Cheryl who has a voice like a corncrake and a pillowy bosom, and Sandra who skates, and my brother, who used to play table tennis like a panther, but got married. I don't quite know what to say, except — that's a few of them

Daphne de Jong
Vagabundus Vinea

The open window delivered the scents of jasmine and the sea into the room. Harvey went to close it, getting up from the sagging armchair to grapple with the unfamiliar catch.

'Don't shut it.' Elizabeth came in from the kitchen, carrying their two coffees on a tray. 'Can't you smell the sea?'

'Moths,' Harvey said, slamming the window decisively and turning the catch to lock it. And indeed there were moths, small and fluttering, flirting with the bright bulb under the white plastic halo in the centre of the room.

Harvey subsided into his chair again as Elizabeth placed the tray on the small coffee table. The table looked as though it had been knocked up from packing-case wood, and it shone with cheap yellow varnish. Elizabeth pushed his cup over and sat down. Her chair was higher than Harvey's, not a match. It had a firm, humped seat and wooden arms and was upholstered in harsh-textured red moquette. Harvey's was more comfortable, but the heavy brown velvet covering had a particularly large and ugly mustard yellow fleur-de-lis pattern. The owners must have furnished the place from second-hand shops. She could picture them arriving weekend after weekend towing a trailer behind their car — a station-wagon, of course, with rowdy, wriggling children in the back seat — carrying odd pieces of furniture tied down by convoluted bits of thin knotted rope. The four dining chairs round the extending oak table with the heavy turned legs were covered in orange vinyl. Everything had the temporary, second-best look of the typical beach house, a place for weekends, rented out in summer to cover rates and maintenance costs.

'Did you put sugar in?' Harvey asked, reaching for the cup nearest him.

'Yes.' She always put his three teaspoons in. The room seemed stuffy with the window closed. The jasmine scent lingered vaguely, and the boom of the waves, but the wet salt tang of the sea had been shut out.

'The jasmine's nice,' she said, 'around the porch.'

'Needs trimming.' Harvey sipped his coffee, grimaced because it was hot, and put the cup down on the table. 'Gone right along the front of the house. It'll be climbing in the windows if they're not careful.'

Elizabeth imagined the jasmine climbing in the windows, pushing inquisitive tendrils over the sills, through the half-opened casements, perhaps into the bedroom where their two brown suitcases and Harvey's navy canvas holdall and her smart overnighter with the two zipped outer pockets sat on the pink candlewick bedspread. She saw the jasmine waving its green pointed ends as though sniffing something out, slithering down the wall to caterpillar itself across the floor and up onto the bed, prising open the cases and finding Harvey's maroon pyjamas with the white piping and her lace-trimmed cream satin nightie. The jasmine lifted them and made them dance about each other in an empty, flopping way and then dropped them and began twitching other garments out, examining and abandoning them, tossed on the floor. Harvey's white Y-fronts, her pretty pink and blue panties and matching bras, Harvey's striped open-necked shirt, his brown bermuda shorts and nylon socks, and her sundress with the lined cups and the shirred back.

Elizabeth giggled and Harvey said, 'What's so funny?'

'The jasmine,' she said. 'Climbing in the windows.'

'Plants,' Harvey said sternly, 'are stronger than people realize. If it gets under the weatherboards it could tear them off.'

A thin finger of green wriggled under one of the boards on the outside of the house, pushed, prised, until the nails creaked and the board gaped away from the corner. Another tough, green, wriggling tendril grasped the next board and pulled. Two boards tore away from the wall and crashed to the ground.

'What was that?' Harvey said.

'What?'

'That noise.'

Elizabeth's blue eyes were guileless. 'I didn't hear a thing.'

Harvey stared hard at the dark window, the narrow pale moths crawling frantically up the glass. Only the sea's subdued thundering reached them. Harvey picked up his coffee, leaning forward. Elizabeth could see the coinspot of thinning hair at the crown of his head.

'A tonsure,' she said, 'used to be a symbol of chastity.'

'What?'

'Nothing.'

He sipped his coffee irritably. Elizabeth didn't blame him. She thought he would look rather distinguished with a bald, shiny crown, rather important. Solid and responsible — a good credit risk. She sighed.

'What's that for?' Harvey seemed to regard the sigh as a criticism.

Elizabeth smiled angelically. 'Nothing.'

Harvey shifted in the swaybacked chair, looking suspicious. 'I wish you wouldn't keep saying that.'

'Saying what?'

' "Nothing", the way you do.'

'Oh. Well, perhaps it's because I have nothing to say.'

'Now you're just playing with words.'

Elizabeth played with words, tossing them idly from one hand to the other, letting some slip through her fingers and fall — splat! — onto the floor.

'What are you doing now?' Harvey asked, wearily belligerent.

Nothing, she could have said. 'Playing,' she told him, 'with words.'

Harvey closed his eyes. 'Oh, do stop being silly.'

'Othello,' Elizabeth said mournfully, 'strangled his wife. Don't you ever want to do anything silly?'

'Like you?' He opened his eyes again and looked at her accusingly.

'Why not? Or like Othello.'

'Strangling his wife? That wasn't silly, that was criminal.'

'It was silly. He was jealous because he thought she was sleeping with someone else. And she wasn't.'

'It's only a story, anyway.' He put down his cup again and sat back, his hands hanging slackly over the arms of the chair.

'Would you strangle me if you thought I was sleeping with someone else?' she asked him with interest.

His fingers grew thinner and thinner and longer, until they snaked greenly on tough wire-like stems out from the cuffs of his shirt and reached for her across the coffee table, hovering about her throat, curving inwards. 'No, of course I wouldn't,' he said. The long curving tendrils withered and drooped dispiritedly, shrinking back into his sleeves and becoming hands again.

'You wouldn't?'

'You haven't, have you?'

She contemplated saying yes. She shook her head.

'I've thought about it.'

Harvey shrugged. His smile said, Why should you want anyone else when you've got me?

'Have *you*?' she asked him curiously.

'Thought about it?' he said, still smiling. 'Of course. Now and then.'

Elizabeth looked at him very hard. Outside the jasmine rustled in the dark. The window rattled faintly.

Harvey glanced at it. 'There's a wind getting up,' he said. 'I hope the weather isn't going to break now.'

He got up and went to the door and opened it and the smell of the sea rushed into the room and snuffled damply at the corners and settled itself on the furniture. 'You've got something on your shoe,' Elizabeth told him. It was a word, squished beyond recognition, soft and oozing. Harvey wiped the sole of his shoe on the coir mat outside the door, finishing off by turning his foot edgewise and rubbing it against the harsh fibres.

'Shut the door,' Elizabeth said, 'before the jasmine gets in.'

He cast a deprecating glance at her. He shut the door.

Elizabeth jumped up. 'Let's go for a walk.'

'In the dark?'

'Why not? In the moonlight.'

'There's no moon.'

'What, none at all?'

Firmly, he said, 'None.'

'Well, let's go for a walk anyway.'

Harvey looked long-suffering. 'All right. Hold on while I find a torch.'

She waited on the porch, talking to the jasmine while he went into the bedroom and opened his holdall and found the torch. 'Who were you talking to?' he asked as he switched off the room light and closed the door behind him.

'The jasmine,' she said, tucking her arm cosily into his. 'Its name is Jasminum Polyanthum. It came from China.'

Harvey didn't comment on that. The circle of light ahead of them broke over humps of buffalo grass pushing up the sand beside the uneven pathway to the beach, jumped to a clump of spinifex, and shimmied its way through a colony of furred hares-tails.

Following the light, they stumbled silently across the cool, moon-coloured sand until it became dark and firm and the torch was picking out glimmers of broken white shells and twists of black, shiny seaweed discarded by the receding tide.

Elizabeth let go of Harvey's arm and wandered closer to the water, across the lingering, scalloped aftermath of a spent wave, the hissing bubbles disintegrating before her bare toes. She lifted her skirt above her knees and ran into the next froth-tongued wave as it approached, feeling its salty slap against her legs, the swell that followed tugging at her thighs. She turned when the wave retreated from the beach, looking into the eye of the torch as Harvey shone it on her. She put up a hand to shield her eyes, and her dress dipped into the water, soaking the hem.

Behind the dazzle of the beam she couldn't see Harvey at all, but further back were the dark huddled houses spread along the beach front, and some of them had lights on, glowing squares of yellow, or dimmer, luminous lines between drawn curtains.

'I want to swim,' she said. 'It's lovely.' It was actually very cold, and when she glanced behind her she could see nothing but black, with a sinister thickness and a kind of sullen, secretive lubricity about it.

The torchlight wavered. 'Don't be an idiot!' Harvey called. 'There could be rocks or holes, and you've got your clothes on.'

'I can take them off!' she said gaily, as a wave buffeted her from behind. She dropped the handful of her dress that she still held, and the water dragged the wet fabric between her knees, almost pushing her off balance. She planted her feet firmly apart and lifted her hands to the zipper at the back of her dress.

'There've been sharks here this summer,' Harvey told her. 'You can't see them in the dark.'

A slippery, sinuous pale shape brushed between her calves and caught its triangulate fin in her skirt, making her stagger and cry out with fright. She fell forward onto the shark's back and straddled it for a few moments, felt its smooth skin slipping against her palms, the straining muscular undulations of its body twisting under hers before it tossed her off in the shallows and headed out to sea, the white fin quickly fading into the inky night.

Harvey splashed into the water and helped her up. 'There, you see?' he said triumphantly. 'I told you not to be so silly.'

'Yes, Harvey,' she said meekly. 'I didn't know about the sharks.'

'They have patrols in the daytime,' he said. 'You'll be all right tomorrow if you want to swim.'

'Oh, Harvey,' she said. 'You are kind.'

'Look what you've done,' Harvey said. 'You're all wet and sandy.'

'So are you. Your trousers — '

'Yes, well, never mind,' he said somewhat crossly. 'We'd better go back to the house.'

'Oh, do we have to?'

'For heaven's sake, Elizabeth, you're all wet! And shivering.'

She was shivering, her dress had gone clammy, and her hair dripped.

'Yes, all right,' she said. 'Let's go back, then.'

It wasn't far, they had only walked a little way along the beach. But they seemed to take forever to traverse the deep dry sand of the upper beach, and the low, grass-tufted dunes. The hares-tails danced against her ankles, and she walked with care to avoid stepping on a warm furred body hidden in the hollows. She didn't like to take Harvey's arm again, but he held her hand all the way back to the house. The jasmine rustled in some amusement as they mounted the steps. She grasped a starry cluster of blossom by its scrawny green neck and said severely, 'It's all very well for you to laugh. I wasn't to know there were sharks, was I?'

'Come inside,' Harvey admonished her, 'and get out of those wet. things.'

She released the jasmine, and it tearfully dropped a few wan petals on the step. 'Sorry,' she muttered guiltily and stalked into the house.

'You'd better have a shower,' Harvey ordered. 'And then get into bed and I'll bring you a hot drink.'

He was kind. She had always known him kind.

She showered until she was pink and flushed like a hothouse rose, and then put on the cream nightie rescued from the scattered clothing on the bedroom floor, and got into bed, sitting up expectantly when Harvey came in carefully carrying a steaming cup. He almost tripped over his pyjama top as it tangled his foot, and she said, 'I'm sorry. I should have put them away.'

'I'll do it.' He set about tidying up while she sipped at the drink. It was warm and milky and sweet and she hated the taste, but drank it to please him. He was, after all, doing his best.

'Finished?' he asked as she drained the cup.

'Nearly.' She hid it with her hand curved around it. 'Sit and talk to me while I finish it.'

He sat down on the bed, by her feet. She said, 'You've changed your trousers. And your shoes.'

'Yes, while you were in the shower. I rinsed my feet under the tap outside.'

He looked newly cleaned and pressed. 'I'll wash your trousers tomorrow,' she promised.

'Drink up,' he said, with great patience.

She pretended to drink. 'It's warm in here. Can't we have the window open?'

'When I've turned the light out, I'll open it.'

'You're not afraid of the jasmine?'

'Are you?'

'It's only curious,' she said comfortingly. 'Only it doesn't know its own strength.'

He glanced at the cup in her hand and she hastily raised it to her lips.

When she brought it down he held out his hand. 'Finished?' he said again.

Elizabeth reluctantly surrendered the empty cup with the soggy bit of discoloured sugar in the bottom. He took it and stood up. He put a hand on the bedclothes and pulled them over her as she slid down the pillow. 'Goodnight, Elizabeth,' he said, and kissed her brow.

'You never call me Liz,' she told him, as he straightened. He looked taller from this angle, and somewhat forbidding.

'Does anybody?' he asked, apparently startled.

'Not since school.'

'Well, then. I knew you didn't like it.'

'Didn't I?' She couldn't remember if she had liked it or not, but he seemed positive.

'It doesn't suit you.'

'Oh.' She was disappointed. 'Sometimes,' she said wistfully, 'I feel like Liz.'

'Do you?' He looked at her with more positive attention than he had all day. 'I always thought I'd like to be called Harry.'

'Oh!' she said, delighted. 'Did you really? But you never told me!'

'Well,' Harvey looked down into the cup he held in his hand, 'you never asked, did you?'

'Oh,' she said softly. 'Oh, Harvey, I never asked.' Tears filled her eyes quite unexpectedly and poured down her cheeks.

'Hey, hey!' he said, dismayed by this. He put the cup on the floor, for there was no table by the bed, and knelt beside her to gather her into his arms. 'There now,' he said, rocking her gently. 'No need for that. Shh, shh. What is it? What's the matter?'

She stopped crying quite suddenly and lifted her head away from his shoulder to wipe her eyes with the back of her hand. 'Nothing,' she said. 'I'm being silly again, I'm afraid.'

'Never mind,' he said, not contradicting her. 'Try to sleep, now.'

He eased her back onto the pillow.

'I'm sorry,' she sniffed. 'It's probably reaction — I don't meet a shark every night.'

'Go to sleep,' he said, and she closed her eyes. He stood by the bed for a while, until she turned her head a little and sighed, and slept. Then he switched off the light and went to the window and opened it. The scent of jasmine leaped into the room and filled it, and a spray of the tiny flowers dropped down to the inside of the casement and hung there, quivering.

He reached up his hand and broke off the stalk and said to the dark-leaved night, 'You don't mind, do you? Only, I think she'd like the company.' And he placed the cool white constellation on the pillow next to her cheek before he picked up the cup and went out.

Jessie Feeney
A Married Woman

It was Northland in the early 1930s and New Zealand was still in the gloomy grip of the Depression, but our hearts were light and free this sunny crisp early February morning as my brother and I walked through the gate and into Adolph Zomers' paddock. We felt the sun warm on our shoulders and we felt the unaccustomed luxury of a total sward of clover and other soft grass under our bare feet. There wasn't much total grass in our patch of Northland in those days. Forty years before the bushmen had shaved the land to the bone and burned off all the remains of the trees. Then the gumdiggers had come and gone leaving gaping holes in the white dry clay scarp.

Sure, the paspalum grass grew new and long and sweet in clumps along the water courses and in the places the cows knew. After rain, light slim danthonia shoots would appear on the open places and the cows would crop them fast and joyously. But this was a whole paddock of well-established grass, short cropped but thick and green and on this cool autumn morning heavy dew lay on the clover in light filled drops wet and soft and luxurious between our toes.

This was an established farm and the paddock was surrounded by Australian gum trees planted for shelter by an earlier settler. At the very far end of the paddock on the rise stood a small wooden cottage with a corrugated iron roof and a corrugated iron tank on a stand beside it. This was the rented dwelling place of Adolph Zomers. He was our neighbour and he had been here when we arrived seven years before. He was something of a mystery in the neighbourhood. He was different. He did not farm the land he lived on, he did not garden, he did not go out to work, he did not visit, and he spoke with a Continental accent, Danish probably. He wore a tweed jacket and pants, not dungarees or serge as the others did.

My father wore a felt hat, Adolph Zomers wore a cloth cap. He was a big well-built man in his late thirties. His cheeks were ruddy, his face was healthy, his eyes were bright blue and he always walked quickly. Once a week he walked into the township and bought and paid for his stores, collected his mail, and walked back with them, passing our gate on the way to his place a mile further on. He did not speak much to anyone but when he did his voice was bright and clear. It was known that he read widely and received the *People's Voice* in the mail.

My mother was also a reader and occasionally she would be working near the road, moving the calves which were kept on ropes staked to the ground because we had no fences yet, or putting the cream can out at the gate as he passed by. He would call out in his foreign accent:

'Good morning. Good morning, Mrs McMann', and my mother would reply, 'Good day to you Mr Zomers', and sometimes he might pause and mention an article in the *People's Voice* under his arm and say, 'I'll leave it in your box as I go by next time Mrs McMann, so you can read it for yourself.'

'Thank you Mr Zomers,' my mother would reply formally as he went on.

Today as my brother Jim and I walked through the grass I was very much aware of the adventure and privilege we were being allowed. I had asked my mother that Jim and I go to Mr Zomers' paddock in the early morning to look for mushrooms. Mushrooms only grow on established fields and it was possible that at this time of the year there would be some there, and at any rate there was the adventure of looking for them.

My mother considered my request gravely. As was her practice she did not immediately give a decision, but she gave the matter her full and serious attention. She looked me directly in the face. She was dressing her youngest, aged two, in clean little boy cotton pants and shirt made by her own hands, but when I asked her she stopped, put her arms around the child and held him in front of her as she looked at me.

I tried to look winning. She herself did not eat mushrooms but she knew I liked them. I knew that in asking to go away from home territory I was asking something unusual. I was the eldest child, eleven years old, and I knew our family ways.

Early, my mother had established with her children a clear pattern of conduct, and inherent to this was that we did not go away from home except to school or to the township on a message and nowhere else unless accompanied by her or my father. She did not visit neighbours and did not allow us to do so unless for a specific purpose and then we were expected right back. Although she had a firmness about her and her rules were clear and strict, I knew from past experiences that she would take my wish into consideration and that her openmindedness would allow her to change the rules if the occasion warranted it.

She asked what made me think there would be mushrooms there, agreed there could be some, and what time would I leave and would I watch over Jim. She then thought again looking at me warmly, then she gave her permission adding that we were to go nowhere near Mr Zomers' house as she knew he would not mind us looking for mushrooms but we must remember that his privacy must be respected.

So here we were. Mr brother Jim was nine years old, a dark, intense, interested, scudding boy. Sometimes he would be hooting on ahead, sometimes up a high bank, balanced peering into a kingfisher's tunnel, sometimes far back up a tree fast like a monkey and down with a terrifying leap onto the ground or off to the side looking deep into the cracks of fence posts for trapdoor spiders. He was everywhere, and I barely thought of him as I saw, but did not look for, the many colours on the eucalyptus trunks where the summer heat had stripped the tree bark back, and the marvellous glistening spider webs on the fence wire. Always a little further on we might see some mushrooms round and white in their gorgeous rings of seeding patterns. But there were none to be seen this morning and then I topped another rise and found myself close to Mr Zomers' cottage.

My brother had fallen back and I was alone as I stared at the building, the first time I had seen it close up. There was a tin dish on the tank stand and the curtains were drawn right across the one small window. Suddenly, as I stood there, around the corner from the back of the house came Mr Zomers.

He was stark naked. His body was big and gleaming white in the clear light and his pubic hair was the same colour as the hair on his head. He walked towards the wash bowl and in that instant he saw me. He started violently, his face moved with concern, he clapped his hands over the private part of his body and swiftly wheeled and vanished behind the house.

I was not unmoved at this first glimpse of a naked male body, but nor was I in any way disturbed. I was aware that I should not have been there. I also felt secure and protected by his manner and actions in the same way as I felt at home by the family pattern of decent modesty which my mother and father and all of us observed.

I was disappointed that there were no mushrooms to be found today so we went on home. My mother had rolled-oats porridge ready for us in the pot and she gave it to us with brown sugar and rich milk. Of the mushrooms she put me at ease by saying easily that maybe it was a bit early for mushrooms. I did not mention Mr Zomers, simply because I was not supposed to have been near his house.

My mother was thirty-three, in the full flush of healthy womanhood. She had married young and had five children. She loved her children and had turned our small spare barn of a house into a real home. She loved her babies dearly and breastfed each one. For the past seven years she had lived on our own land.

It had been a poor buy and it was poor, difficult country but capable of being brought into production and she had wanted her very own house and land and she set into it with her full strong will. She planted seeds and now she had flowers around the house and fruit trees growing up and a vegetable garden which shielded us from the worst impact of those hard years.

She had planted trees as soon as we arrived and they were now growing tall enough for shade. She brought some cows with her and reared the calves, she cleared scrub and hakea and my father did too and burned it off and scattered the grass seed.

The valley had begun to look more covered but it was a hard life and particularly for her. The soil nourished grudgingly and water was short and there was no electricity or telephone. She gave herself fervently to providing for her family, her home and her animals and she did it with a flourish of will and with good humour.

My father was a working man, a bush man in his youthful days, he had married late in life and now he was approaching sixty. He looked much younger than that, active, humorous, vigorous but, don't ask me how I knew, I knew that nature had given him an unkind blow. He had been married twelve years and he had five children. I knew he loved all of us and I knew it must have been clear to him that he must limit his family.

We were Catholics and fertility meant abstinence. He was an affectionate person and lately I had become aware that a cloud had come over both my parents.

My mother was always busy, too busy. Sometimes in the evening in the house my father seemed bemused, ill at ease with himself and her. I missed seeing him brush her long brown hair as he used to do in the evening when she let it down. He worked hard, manual work on contract, and now he was away from home a lot.

The next time I saw Mr Zomers it was late spring. The hillside teatree was growing strong and the pine trees too and late one afternoon my mother went up the valley along the boundary fence line to look at a cow up there. While she was gone Mr Zomers came down our path, a letter had been given to him by mistake and he came to give it to us. As he talked to my father in the living-room of our cottage I could see my mother coming back, walking with her loose, easy stride fast down the hillside. Then she passed out of my range of vision and I forgot her as I listened to the two men talking.

All of a sudden she swept into the room. She came with a rush, exhilarated. She wore a light cotton skirt coming to well below her knees and a long-sleeved blouse and her long hair was knotted loosely, in disarray at the back of her head. In her arms she carried a full-grown grey-and-white rabbit. The gum holes on the property provided ideal places for rabbits to burrow and there were rabbits aplenty about, but they were wild creatures, one quick sight or sound of humans and they'd be away like the wind.

'It jumped straight into my arms!' she cried out in wonderment. 'It was feeding and I didn't see it until I was on it. It jumped right into my arms!'

Her face was alight. She was Eve, all wonder and innocence at the beauty of the garden and Creation, she was Eve aware, all woman at her find.

I was mesmerized by her face. It was aglow and alive, her cheeks flushed pink, her eyebrows strong and dark and under them her eyes alight, the whites very white and the pupils bright green, luminous, flashing sparks. She was beautiful and my eyes never left her face as she flung herself down on the stairs. She was completely unaware of herself.

The two men stared at her in wonderment as she sat there loose-limbed and relaxed, holding the rabbit triumphantly in her arms and her eyes flashing with excitement. The creature was motionless, petrified with fear, or safe for the moment, hiding its face in the crook of her arm.

'It jumped straight into my arms!' she said again, looking still at the two men. I felt the wonder of the moment and of her appearance and I knew my father felt it too.

His face went Irish-soft and his lips looked fuller. I was an onlooker aware of each of the others and myself, but the feelings of the others were stronger, and each one of them was alone in a brilliant bubble of individual reaction. From the corner of my eye I could see Mr Zomers' face. His mouth was half opened and his face was almost vacant, idiotic; his eyes looked glazed.

Now I seemed to see more of Mr Zomers. He was walking past more often. He put the *People's Voice* in the box every single week. Sometimes he would leave a book with it, a hard-covered book, or a small pine seedling or a eucalyptus for my mother to plant in her groves. I would collect from the box and bring the articles to her and invariably she would receive them half humorously.

'What's 'Dolph Zomers sending me now?' she would say and later she would give me the book and the *People's Voice* newspaper to leave in the box for him to pick up.

The time went on — spring left, summer over, and winter came on. My father took a job digging drains and stayed away, coming home only at weekends. The stream alongside our house flooded and the torrent washed away my mother's winter garden and the polyanthus along the path to the door.

My mother loved to hear plays on the radio, real voices late in the evening telling a story, lifting the mind and imagination, but often the battery of the radio was flat and the sound so weak she would sit with her ear pressed against the radio speaker and her expression would be strained and isolated. But in the morning she would call the cows and milk them and feed the baby and she would look at the valley and remark to me on the lovely sweep of the knoll here or there and the fine line of that ridge as it swept down the valley and that one day it would all be covered in good grass and show these contours to their best.

We had watched her plant an acorn and she called us to see the first green shoots of an oak tree break through the soil, so I knew she had plans and hopes as I watched her swing down the hillside with her light flowing step, or clear the table, or make butter, her movements quick and decisive. The winter was cold and wet and one day my brother came running in — 'Brownie's stuck in the swamp!'

The cow was stuck in the mud, an old gum hole mudded over. This was a job for a team. My father was away but we all set to with a will to pull the cow out before the cold and wet overcame her. Animals often died bogged in a gum hole and sometimes they had to be destroyed there. We could not lose a valuable cow. We attached a rope to her horns and tried pulling and pushing. She heaved and struggled but sank deeper and her eyes rolled back in her head. We tried again and again.

My mother, always compassionate to animals, was desperate and racked with anxiety for the poor animal, and it was winter and Brownie was also our only milking cow. On the road above Mr Zomers hurried along. My mother's hair had straggled down and her face was drawn and tired when we looked up to see Mr Zomers there beside us. He set to with vigour.

'Come now. Come now, my girl,' he called, encouraging the exhausted cow, and we strung another rope around her hindquarters and dug in trying to free her back legs. It was arduous and gruelling, but, eventually, with a long drawn-out bellow of fear and relief she floundered out onto dry ground and stood there on her legs, shaking and wet and caked with swamp mud, with pieces of dry rushes clinging to the mud on her body.

My mother and Mr Zomers took water in a bucket and together they washed off the mud and rinsed and dried the cow's body until her hair lay clean, wet and wavy along her flanks and neck and her nostrils and eyes were clear. Then my mother gave her a hot bran mash.

The two of them led and pushed her to drier ground and the exhausted animal lay down. My mother's relief was immense. She said 'Mr Zomers you have done me a very neighbourly turn today'. They both stood there with mud on their clothes and splattered all over with mud and grime from the cow's struggles and their own struggles to help her.

'Some water, and I will wash some of this off me in the cowshed before I walk home,' Mr Zomers said.

We were very late with our evening chores and they still waited for us so I went straight to the separator shed which was part of the cowshed, for it was my daily job to put the cream separator together. It was a hand separator of course and each time it was used it had to be taken apart and each individual piece of it washed and aired. Next milking it had to be put together again. I stood looking at the clean, gleaming aluminium cups and arranging the other pieces of the separator ready to assemble.

I heard Mr Zomers leave the cow and walk over to the cowshed and I watched my mother go into the kitchen and take the kettle of hot water off the stove. She poured some hot water into a dish and then filled it with cold water from the tap outside. She went inside the house again and came out with a cloth and towel and then carried the dish in her hands over to the cowshed to Mr Zomers.

Neither of them noticed me. Mr Zomers grasped the dish and towel from my mother's hands and put it down. Then, moving with quick, determined motions he undid his shirt buttons, he pulled off his shirt, he pulled his singlet off over his head, he undid the buckle of his leather belt and pulled down his trousers and his underpants with one quick deliberate movement, and in a minute he stood there naked before my mother, his body white and aroused in the fading light.

He stood proudly, showing himself without shyness and my mother stared at him, wordless. Then his words came out in a quick tumble.

'I want love,' he said. 'I want love. I want to be touched. I want to be touched everywhere, here and here, by the woman I love. It is always in my mind. I need love.'

His arms and face were still mud splattered but his body was clean and impressive in its show of strength and virility. The words spoken, he stood there with his eyes wide and clear and his arms hanging loosely at his sides. He had no tan but the very whiteness and the fine skin of his body emphasized the masculine beauty of it. My mother stood still, and she gave him a long full look. She had moved back a step or two and she looked at him candidly.

Her face was very grave, but warm as when she had said I could go for the mushrooms, compassionate and comprehending, and I felt proud of the sight of her. She stepped over and put her hand on him, it was dark, dark brown against the pink-white flesh.

'Mr Zomers,' she said kindly and with absolute finality. 'You forget Mr Zomers, I am a married woman.'

With that she turned without hesitation and left the shed and called to the children to go in for the night and took her bucket and stool to milk the cow. Mr Zomers dressed quickly and went out up the road and away.

I was excited and at peace. Our cow was safe and I was safe. I wanted to dance and sing. I wanted to kiss my father and welcome him back home tomorrow. I wanted to roll around in long grass. I wanted to run to my mother and tell her what she had given me and how real and sure she looked and tell her I felt secure in an intact world. But it was all feeling and there seemed no need to say any of it. So I put the separator together and went through the darkness to the other children in the house. She had lit the lamp on her way to the cow and soon she came in with the bucket of warm milk.

After that when necessary, and this is not often, my mother would refer to Mr Zomers formally as before, perhaps with an inflexion of the voice that brought a little more formality into it, or did I imagine that? But always with respect in her tone and words, and this recognition of him seemed perfectly right to me, and added to my safeness. He did not come again and when the war started he left the district.

Margaret Sutherland
Loving

This morning the priest spoke on *apartheid* and the Springbok tour. Aroha wriggled about, as children do during sermons, and I gave her the holy cards from my Mass book. As I flipped the pages a pressed violet fell out. Eric gave it to me the first week after Lent, 1955 — our honeymoon. There are violets out now. But buying them yourself, it's not the same.

The pictures distracted Aroha for a while. Children seem to like grisly things. When I was small I was fascinated, too, by those images of cross and skull; saint's accessories. She poked me, pointing to a painting of Jesus nailed to the cross.

'Why does it say that, Gran?'

'Ssh. Don't talk in church.'

The inscription on the card read *God is Love*. I have wondered about their connection; love and suffering.

Just the other day Gay said, 'It's wonderful what you do for Eric. You must love him, Leah.' And I just looked at her.

Father was summing up. *The question us freedom, not sport — every man's right to own land, work, travel in the country of his birth. In Christ's name, stand up and be counted. Stand up for dignity.* He turned and left the pulpit.

'Is it finished, Gran?'

'Ssh. No, it isn't finished.'

She wriggled and sighed and the cards fell on the floor. I helped her pick them up. The lessons of patience are a trial for us all!

After Mass, Aroha went dancing down the aisle. One woman touched her dark curls; her expression saying to me, Just let anyone call me racist. I felt annoyed but Aroha just smiled at her and skipped on, out into the frost.

'Father gave a sermon on *apartheid*.' I keep Eric up to date though he doesn't go to Mass now, hates anyone to see him in the wheelchair.

'Blaming the rugby players?'

'He said you can't separate religion from sport.'

'Funny, I managed.'

Eric was very keen on the game, played for Waikato around the time we were courting. I remember him, young, confident, running out on to the field.

Holding the warm towel, I knelt in front of him. Sunday, Foot Day.He has his Radox soak before I check for any injury which, untreated, could become infected. There is a risk of gangrene because of his diabetes and poor circulation. Sunday, Eric's in a bad mood with me. He hates the procedure, finds it humiliating. We always start with the right foot. That's the routine. If one day I said, We'll start with the left, what would happen? I feel, something terrible.

I took the weight of his leg and lowered his foot gently. Poor foot; purple, swollen. He was such an active man, would work overtime to make up urgent prescriptions and deliver them to the door himself. He'd have liked to be a doctor, he said, if he'd had the brains and money. He read up medical books and he had a healing touch. Terry wouldn't let me remove his splinters — always had to have his father. Eric played down his skill but I used to tell him, 'There's plenty of countries where they'd welcome your knowledge.'

I think Eric knew before any of us what his symptoms meant. Just the odd bout of weakness at first. He didn't seem sick. Not having heard of multiple sclerosis myself, I asked, 'What exactly is it, Eric?' 'A gentle, treacherous disintegration, my dear.'

He said it like some silly joke and I took no notice. But it's turned out to be a fair description of what is happening; what he's letting happen. I think he gave up when the doctor discovered diabetes as well. That was treatable, with the diet and insulin. He learned to inject himself, and joked about that too. Straightaway he sold up the pharmacy, long before he needed to. I'd never given a thought to retirement, wives don't retire. But Eric did.

I tried to chivvy him along, interest him in this and that. His look said, Yes dear, anything you say dear.

Of course Eric doesn't hate me. Not often. And I cope, I have my tricks. Once I made a list of everything Eric's lost, and all I have to be grateful for.

I dried his foot, taking good care between the toes. The nails didn't need trimming. I was pleased. That means a longer session, and my knees complain. I started on the other foot.

'Actually I missed part of the sermon. Aroha was fidgeting. Father was in good form — he said at the end, "Stand up for dignity".'

'Dignity, eh?' said Eric.

Terry wandered in as I was powdering his feet. I'd heard him come in at some ungodly hour, and I wished he'd taken another five minutes in bed. Eric detests anyone to see me fussing over him.

'Well!' Eric started. 'His lordship has finally arisen.' Terry didn't look at him.

'You were late last night,' I said.

'Keeping your mother awake.'

'I was awake anyway.' Two hooks, baited — choose me; no, me. So alike, the two of them, they can't see just how similar they are. I put Eric's feet into his slippers and stood up, my knees cracking.

'Nice evening, Terry?'

'The meeting went on a bit.'

'Whose meeting? The ranks of the unemployed?'

'We took a vote, Mum, about the tour.'

'Oh Terry, I hope there won't be violence.'

'Isn't it marvellous, Leah? Eighteen, and he can solve the problems of South Africa.'

I followed Terry to the kitchen.

'Why is he like that?'

'He's sick. Anyway, I don't want you in trouble.'

'I'm joining a peaceful demonstration. I happen to care about the oppression of black people, is that all right?'

'Please don't talk down to me, Terry. I have enough of that.'

'I hate to see you that way.'

'What way?'

'On your knees.'

'Have your breakfast now.'

I weighed up Eric's allowance and carried the tray through. I started to cut the toast into fingers. He knocked my hand aside I handed him the knife and went to eat with Terry. Later I picked up the knife from under Eric's chair. There were crumbs and a clot of scrambled egg on his chin.

'Eric.' I tapped my chin and offered a serviette. He dabbed his face angrily.

'Will that do?'

'I thought you'd want to know.'

I did the dishes. Eric's not always like this. He's hit a bad patch. I know he needs me. It may be a bleak need, but it would comfort me, hearing him express it. I might be able to say, I need you too.'

But as it stands, he'd laugh if I said that. He'd laugh out loud.

It's an early start on Mondays. Gay takes me shopping soon after nine, and Eric has to be attended to before I go. Fortunately he's regular. At least in that way he's made his body bow to his will.

At eight-thirty he wheeled his chair into the bathroom. It's easier for us since we had handrails fitted. Sometimes he can manage with very little help. The muscles are unreliable, that's the problem.

'Right,' he shouted, and I went in. He had his feet on the floor and his fly undone. While he pulled on the rails I levered him upright, worked down the trousers and underpants as quick as possible and helped him swivel and sit down. The I left him in privacy. He would call when he wanted me.

It was a good day. All I had to do was help him swing up, fix his clothes, tuck him in and help him sit back in the chair. He snapped off the brake and manoeuvred to the handbasin.

'You could easily manage that chair in the street.'

'Yes; and win the Grand Prix.' He was smiling as he washed his hands.

Gay invited me to go up to Auckland to see the Henry Moore tapestries and *As You Like It*.

'I'd love to, but it wouldn't be possible.'

'Someone from the church would see to Eric.'

'I know. Thanks anyway.'

'You look tired, Leah.'

'It's winter. Everybody feels the winter.'

I shopped in the usual supermarket. Phyllis, my regular check-out girl, greeted me. 'Going to the march?' she asked, clattering the buttons, and sending foodstuffs flying along the counter.

'The Springbok demonstration? No, I'm not going.'

'Well I am. Things are pretty bad if people can't forget politics and play a friendly game, I reckon. Why don't you come? It's for anyone, kids to senior citizens.'

'Is that what I am? Excuse me, I didn't put that chocolate in.' I looked for Aroha — disappeared.

'Do you want a refund?'

'Leave it. I'll ration it out.'

'Got your grand-daughter with you again?'

'I don't mind. She brings some life into the house.'

'See you Wednesday!'

I smiled and shook my head.

At teatime Eric and Terry started to argue about the tour. Like flies in jam, the words buzzed on and on; an excuse to score points, I thought, for neither one was listening to the other. I carried my dinner away and scraped it into the sink tidy. Terry sensed I was angry and offered to help with the dishes. Aroha stayed beside Eric, watching television.

'What's up Mum? I thought racism was one issue you'd care about.'

I didn't answer.

Eric waved to the set as I carried in the coffee. 'Muldoon's just said his piece. The tour's still on.'

He looked alert and I thought, That's something.

'You might have sung out, Dad.'

'Better you give your mother a hand. The gist of it was, why pick on individual South Africans.'

'That's not the issue. . . .'

'It's very much the issue. . . .'

I left them to it. They can blame their conflict on sport or politics or *apartheid* as they please. Their war isn't over a game of rugby.

Tuesday I saw Eric reading the paper carefully. Sunday, feet; Monday, groceries; Tuesday, rubbish. I stapled up the bag. It's a race between the collectors and the dogs.

Eric announced he wanted to hear Rowling and Beetham make their replies to the Prime Minister's decision so I served his dinner in the lounge. Terry wasn't home, thank goodness. But he came in after Eric had gone to bed and I was glad of a few minutes alone with him. Away from his father he's a gentle boy. I worry for him. He hasn't much ambition, takes temporary jobs. He smiles when people say he ought to know by now what he wants to do in life. It's as though he doesn't quite believe in the affluence we've tried to give our children. Eric doesn't try to understand him. He judges a man by his work; as he judges himself now. It's why he feels so bitter.

'Terry? Please. I want to ask a favour of you.'

'Sure.'

'Tonight, Eric said he'd like to see the Springboks play. A year since he left the house and he comes out with this. Oh I don't know, the crowds, we'd have to take the chair, I don't know if it's wise — but, would you drive us to the game?'

He said he couldn't do it. I wasn't surprised. Eric has always tried to live by his conscience, too.

'Mum?' He sounded worried.

'It's all right, Terry.' There was no point in arguing. I was too tired, and angry — but not with him. Human helplessness may stand out more sharply in countries like South Africa; but I am helpless, Eric is, and Terry. And I pity us, each one.

Eric had an accident on Wednesday. He was in the bathroom; the usual morning routine. He called. The tone of his voice told me something was wrong. He gets the shakes sometimes; an involuntary spasm. He had one there, sitting on the lavatory, his face dumbly asking for help. Lord, I'd never had to get him back into the chair in that state. He's fourteen stone, even now.

Oh, there are life scenes that imprint themselves and that is one I will always bear — Eric suffering that indignity, showing desperate need; and myself, desperate inadequacy.

'The wheelchair,' I said.

That was our routine. We could surely cope once Eric was decently dressed and back in that chair. It wasn't far. A step or two. I tried. He did. In distraught embrace we pulled and dragged.

'I can't! Wait, Eric — I'll get Terry.'

'No.'

I tried again. He slipped, overbalanced, slid to the floor and lay there shaking shaking and the smell in the room the smear recording that horrible slide from manhood to infancy his face weeping his words to me Ah Leah, God, how long?

I wanted to be on the floor with him, cradle him and say, I know.

I just said, 'Are you hurt?' He shook his head.

'Pull the chain.' He knew I'd have to bring Terry.

I woke Terry and explained. We got Eric up between us. The spasm was easing. He even managed to hold the handrails with Terry's support, while I washed him and got his trousers up. We got him settled in the chair.

Oh, the morning went on as usual, like any Wednesday. Eric wasn't physically injured and neither was I.

Sometimes I know I have to go apart if I am to go on at all. When I am empty, a way of seeing can come into the space.

'Terry, I'm going for a walk. Please attend to whatever your father needs.'

He nodded and said, 'O.K. Mum.'

Our land — what used to be ours — runs down to the river. An acre; imagine it now! Prime real estate a stone's throw from Hamilton. Perceptions of distance change. Then, people said, Fancy buying out there! Eric and I loved the peace, the country touch. We planted chestnuts, elders, citrus. As they grew the area kept pace and we gained neighbours who complained our leaves blocked their gutters, and untidied their lawns. But we protected our trees and they returned a rich crop. Their changing beauty never failed to astonish me. It broke my heart when costs kept going up and the land became too much for us. We had to subdivide. The chainsaws rip up our week-ends and home units clutter the paddocks where our goats were tethered.

But they haven't taken all the trees. I can walk here beside the river and they speak to me, the willows. Their trunks are stark. The golden rods dive down. Winter elucidates a truth — a spare one to be sure.

Feel, say the willows, tipping the water.

Wait, say the seedpods of the elders on the bank.

The ducks honk, hidden in the reeds. The birds have gone. It is that season. Life is like this, here.

For once Terry and Eric weren't arguing when I got back.

'I peeled the spuds, Mum. You haven't forgotten?'

'Your demonstration? I remembered.'

'Can we have tea early?'

'Wouldn't it be better to go with an empty stomach?'

'What good would that do?'

'None at all.'

He went off after the meal and I watched TV with Eric.

'Your feet,' I reminded him. He had them on top of the radiator, courting trouble. He changed position, then did something I wasn't expecting. He reached over and took my hand.

'Had a bit of a chat with Terry while you were out.'

'Oh?'

'Asked him why he was going to this thing tonight.'

'I'm glad. I hope there's no violence. What can it achieve?'

'He'll be all right.'

'Well I'm not waiting up — those days are past.'

But I was awake anyway. Sleep matters less to me now. I read and think. So I knew it was late when I heard Terry creep in. How intrusive that cautious noise can be! I pulled on my dressing-gown and went out to the kitchen. He was at the biscuit tin. I smiled.

'I'll join you in a cuppa.'

'Don't you ever sleep?'

'Enough. How was it, dear?'

Terry told me. He'd been posted with a group whose purpose was to block the assembly point and disrupt the start of the march. It sounded chaotic, what with home-bound traffic, and people shouting abuse at one another, and the police expecting trouble. Certain members of parliament were rumoured to be joining the march. Terry's group spotted an official car and surged forward. Instead of stopping, the car accelerated and one of Terry's friends was caught and dragged a little way before he managed to roll aside. The car didn't stop. The boy lay there, in pain. When he saw Terry he said to him, 'You bastard. I felt you push me.' Someone called an ambulance and Terry went with him to the hospital. That's why he was so late.

'You missed the whole march then?'

'We thought his leg was broken. Lucky it wasn't. I didn't push him.'

'Of course not.'

'They were all pushing. I couldn't do anything.'

'I know ' So he's eighteen. I hugged him anyway. We went our separate ways to bed.

Thursday morning, Eric asked me where I stored old clothes. I pointed to the drawer and went off to draw up his insulin. When I came back with the syringe, he faced me, smiling.

'Eric! That old thing!' It was the scarf I'd knitted him when he was still playing rugby. The wolf in sheep's clothing, he called it, it devoured so many skeins of wool. 'I'm surprized it's not full of moth.'

'It's been in naphthalene.' Eric the pharmacist, who always likes things to be called by their proper name . . . *the scarf flapping in the keen wind and Eric impatient to lead his team on to the field. The crowd-feeling, that strange passion building as muddied men attack and battle for the line. Winners and losers coming off the field together. Eric loved the game, that was enough for me. . . .*

Let him see me, I decided: I stood there and I felt the tears run down my face and he wheeled the chair to me and drew me down to him.

'You know me, Leah. I don't say much. But I'm grateful. I love you, Leah.'

I stayed, kneeling beside him, letting him comfort me.

I stood up, nose running, knees cracking — happier. We'd forgotten all about the insulin. I passed him the syringe. He checked the dosage and injected himself. I handed him the swab. He rubbed the spot.

'Did Terry tell you he's taking me out today?'

'No, he didn't mention that,' I said.

Eric wheeled the chair to the doorway. 'It's getting the hang of these things that takes the time.' He swivelled expertly into the passage. 'After that, it's a piece of cake.'

Fiona Farrell Poole
Airmen

. . . this afternoon, sitting under a silver birch in early summer, I decide I shall write about three things I do not understand: a man, a motorbike, and an aeroplane. Why? It will be a challenge (think of Ibsen with Nora at his elbow in her blue dress, Hardy and his secret red-lipped Tess). It will be an adventure. No guidebook, only a smattering of the lingo, up and over the border into foreign territory. . . .

I'll begin with two boys. Those square-faced, white haired boys with pink cheeks who went to country schools and wore cut-down trousers and striped handknitted jerseys. A barn, grey wooden slabs pulling this way and that letting in zigzag streaks of dust-laden light. Harrow, dray, wire in exploding coils, bags, some full, some empty and flung down. Straw tumbling, nest for mice and rats and the narrow grey farm cats. And behind the harrow, leaning against the wall, a Harley Davidson 989cc motorcycle.

'That's Jim's bike,' says one white haired boy who is Graham to the other who is Eddie. Jim is in France. Jim is with the Royal Flying Corps. Jim is 'Anzac Atkins'.

'We got a letter today, from Jim,' says Graham.
'Oh,' says Eddie, sitting astride the bike, leaning forward nyerrowwmm into the long invisible straight.
'He shot down a Hun four weeks ago.'
'Mmmm,' says Eddie.
'The newspapers call the Flying Corps the "Knights of the Air".'
'My uncle's in France,' says Eddie, taking a fast corner.
'What's he do?' says Graham. 'It's my turn. Get off.'
'He's a sapper,' and Eddie climbs down slowly.
'What's a sapper do?'
'I think he blows up things.'
(You couldn't compete with a Knight of the Air.)

Another afternoon, rain beating on the barn roof, dripping onto the straw and the sacks, trickling along a muddy furrow in the floor.

'His plane's called Annie,' says Graham. 'After our cousin.' Curious. Annie is small and sharp with freckles. 'What did he want to go and call it after her for?'

Graham shrugs. 'It's painted brown, his plane. But all the German planes are different colours, like in a circus so that's what they call them, the circus. They're red and yellow and black and all colours.' Eddie sits on a sack picking at bits of chaff and red, black and yellow splinters scatter in a grey French sky.

Under Graham's bed and well hidden, knees tucked up away from brothers and sisters. There's an applebox filled with treasure, his plane collection cut carefully from magazines '. . . and that's a Sopwith Scout . . . and this is a Fokker Eindecker EIII . . . a Handley Page 0/400 but it's not a real fighter they just use it to drop bombs . . . a Le Rhone Nieuport Scout . . . an SE5. And this is a Sopwith Camel,' which was the best because it had two guns and could climb high and it was the fastest.

'What does Jim fly?'

'A Sopwith Camel, of course.'

Of course.

It was a thin black metal cross, punctured by two neat holes. Graham brought it to school in a toffee tin lined with cotton wool. It had been torn by Jim off one of those bright little planes.

'He's bagged six. This was off the sixth.'

'Are those bullet holes?' tracing the rough metal edge with your little finger.

'Yep.'

The uncle who is a sapper is in hospital in Kent. You couldn't compete with a Knight of the Air.

. . . Sopwith Scout . . . umm, Fokker Eindecker EIII . . . Albatross . . . SE5 no Handley Page 0/400 . . . Nieuport Scout and Sopwith Camel, the fastest and the best . . .

> 'Just think of it, Graham (the handwriting thick, black and sloping) we taxi out in the early morning, the whole flight, and wait wingtip to wingtip, till we get the order. Then it's open throttles and off

we go with a whoop and roar you can probably hear all the way back at home. We head out towards the lines, keeping a sharp look out all the time. The Hun is very cheeky and very clever. He'll wait up in the eye of the sun where he can't be seen then swoop down like a hawk on a mouse — so you must always watch and keep your wits about you. We give chase to any Huns we meet, rattling away at them and they go like stink. Then back to base when we've cleared the sky, stunting and spinning. Our chaps are A1 Hun-getters. We have a hit roll in the mess and the list grows daily. P.S. I have a little dog, a terrier cross. I call him Bert because I found him on the road near Bertangles. He is a scallywag, but good company and he keeps my toes warm on these cold French mornings. . . .'

'Those cold French mornings.' So clear. You lift up through mist and cloud into autumn sunlight. At 13,000 feet it's cold and ice forms round your nose and mouth under your mask. The plane you've named after your cousin shudders under your hand and you climb up over the lines through puffs of smoke white for ours, black for theirs, watch for gunfire flash, count, change course, zigzag towards the enemy, sunlight on wings and wind driving full in your face. . . . No. Nothing could compare with it, being a Knight of the Air.

Nyerrowwwmmmm. Dadadadadat.

Mrs Everitt is small and round and soft as a bun. She has to stretch to reach the top of the board, so Eddie stays behind sometimes to help her dust off words and sums to leave a clear black space for the morning. That's when they talk. That's when he tells her about the bike. That's where the experiment takes shape.

It was one Saturday. Graham was away but Eddie had gone over to play and while he waited there was this bike, Jim's bike, a Harley Davidson 989cc. Really fast. He'd ridden it up and down the road and no, Graham's mother didn't seem to notice or mind, so he was looking at it and suddenly he thought why couldn't it fly? Because it would be simple if you put some poles on the sides and tied a sheet or something over the top, if you got up enough speed. (The mountain clear and white overhead, the paddock stretching away towards the house.)

'And how would you steer it, Eddie?'

'With a kite, Mrs Everitt. You just put the kite on the back, then you sit on the seat and lean on the handlebars with your chest like this' (leaning over a chair while Mrs Everitt prints carefully 'Today is Thursday, March 3, 1918' on the board) 'and it goes wherever you want.'

So he made the wings from bamboo and sheet and flew the Harley Davidson round the paddock first, just to try it out. Mrs Everitt said, 'That's very interesting, Eddie.'

A week later the Harley Davidson flew round Egmont. Eddie rode alone, leaning against the handlebars, bending this way and that, sunlight on bamboo and sheet and the Tasman wind full in his face. He recalled quite clearly how the bike had at first bumped over rabbit holes and gorse as they raced down the paddock and then the clean lift into the air. There was no question. No doubt. Mrs Everitt wrote Qq Qq Qq in a row and said, 'You're a very clever boy, Eddie. That must have been thrilling.' And it was.

Nyerrowwwmmmm. Dadadadadadat.

And that could be the end of the story. But I like him, this boy I've made. I like especially the way his thin little-boy legs press firm against the triple comforts of metal and power and speed. I like the way he bends forward, eyes streaming in the wind. So I shall put him aside, keeping just the corner of one eye upon him. And I shall think more about Jim. . . .

Jim is a tougher assignment. See him as Eddie sees him first that summer, at the welcome home. He sees Anzac Atkins with 13 Huns torn and burning somewhere in the air about him. And he sees a tall man with Graham's white hair and wary eyes who dances carefully heel toe one two three with all the girls and sharp-faced Annie. Eddie slick as a new pup drinks his lemonade with the other boys by the door and twists the button in his hand: it is a button from the uniform of Anzac Atkins who is also it seems just Jim and for which he has contributed two Indian rupees and a fossilized shark's tooth to Graham's toffee tin.

Jim says little, but the whole district hears him often enough for the two months he is home. The Harley Davidson roars into life up and down the road to town a dozen times a day at least, skidding into corners and a great streamer of dust rising. Jim rides like the devil, as though all the Huns in the world were screaming down out of the eye of the sun after him. Bent low over the bike in goggles and flying jacket, coaxing every stroke from the engine. Then silence and Jim is away again, to a resettlement farm up the Papaoiea valley. The road is suddenly quiet and the bike is back in the barn.

The Papaoiea valley. It closed around Jim as though a door had shut. No more letters to Graham, just odd scraps from grownup conversation. It was rough country, heavy scrub, steep. Jim had driven some stock up the track in 1920 and he was 'trying to make a go of it,' they said. Then he'd married, not Annie after all, but 'a girl from Stratford.' They had two kids. And in 1925 they came back down the track. No stock. No farm. No money. Beaten. She moved back into town near her parents' place with the kids, and he kept right on going. He did some fencing here, scrub cutting there. Droving. He was over on the east coast for a bit. Then up north. Just once he came home.

The boy Eddie has grown, well past playing on the Harley. He has discovered capitalism, and is earning money rabbit shooting. The skins don't fetch much but it is easy enough to get them, the rabbits that year practically lining up to be potted. He goes out with Graham and returns with a sack stiff with blood and dirt over one arm. So here they are, one July afternoon, coming down the gully behind Atkins' place, sacks full, mimicking the easy stride of older men. The gully is dark, thick with overgrown pines and poroporo and near the house they hear it, a howl and a sudden smash. Graham drops his sack and is up the gully and scrambling through the rank green leaves and Eddie is two seconds behind. There's a caravan behind the wash house, completely dark. No movement. They walk round it, not breaking a single twig. Open the door. The van gasps smoke, booze, body reek. The crash they'd heard was a bottle hitting the stove, glass shattered and whisky dribbling to the floor. Jim sits on the bed, smoking. He doesn't look up as they come in so they stand, a little foolish, uncertain, and watch while the Knight of the Air struggles to light a cigarette, striking matches with stiff fingers. Who had waited wingtip to wingtip in the early morning, who had headed out across the lines, spun and looped and zigzagged through detonating anti-aircraft fire and expected death to knife down on him clean from the sun. Whisky drip drip drips from the stove.

'You all right?' says Graham.

'Eh?' says Jim, cupping the cigarette like a flower.

'You all right?'

'A1,' says Jim.

Graham takes some kindling and makes up the fire in the stove while Jim sits. As they leave he turns, rolls over onto the bed and drags a blanket round him, lying like a long grey bag someone had flung in a corner. 'We'd better get these skinned before dark,' says Graham, and they talk loudly about decent football boots, a watch and a bike as the light goes.

And the story could end there, but I can't let him creep away like that. He must pull up out of it and through to clear air again. Let's say Jim teamed up with an old Air Corps mate, that they began flying, making deliveries, offering rides, stunting up and down the country. You read about him in the papers. He'd work from a park or a paddock, take people up for rides at 10/- a time, spin them round the town for a bit, loop the loop if they looked like they could take it; he'd buzz the church, the main street and upside down over the showgrounds to finish — all the evasive tactics he'd learned during the war. And let's say that one afternoon Graham comes over to Eddie's place. They see each other less often now. Graham has left school and works for his father who believes in getting his money's worth but it's pay just the same, so Graham runs a bike and sometimes Eddie in cap and shorts sees him at the station in the morning, waiting for some delivery, nonchalantly astride his Indian, feet planted on the gravel. It's a barrier. But Graham has come to say that Jim plans to fly under the Awanui bridge that afternoon as part of an aerial display. 'You're kidding,' says Eddie, and Graham says no, his father thinks Jim is going to kill himself and Eddie says he's probably right. 'Come on,' says Graham. 'Let's watch him try.' So they ride Graham's bike into town.

And let's say the showgrounds by the river are packed. They stand shoulder to shoulder with the crowd peering up into the sun. The faintest buzzing at first above the murmur of voices, then there they are, the aeronauts, swooping over the clock tower. The crowd sighs watching them skim the trees and grandstand, two little grey Moths looping, twisting, tumbling and rolling. Gusts of applause blow up from the crowd and the planes zigzag above it. The showgrounds overlook the bridge on the main North Road. From where the crowd stands the arch looks impossibly narrow, but at last one of the planes circles and lands, and Jim draws back alone up the river. The crowd, in the words of the local paper, went quiet. The noise of the engine drums up the river, closer, louder, a flash of sunlight on wing and it's all over. The little plane is through the arch as neat as a pin and gaining height quickly before the river narrows at the gorge. Graham takes off his jacket and swings it over his head. The crowd, one voice now, roars. They have watched death slide through the eye of the needle. So they yell and cheer and (as the paper said) give Jim a hero's welcome.

'Come on, young Eddie,' says the Knight of the Air late that afternoon. 'Hop in. Give yourself a thrill.' So Eddie hops and feels the plane bouncing over the rough turf before lifting as a swan does, easy after much flailing, into unimpeded air. Through the air piece he hears Jim call from behind 'Hang on' and the plane lifts. A roll. Eddie's body sags against the narrow straps while the flat plate of the earth turns over his head. Then up again and it switches into sharp focus. Trees, hill, buildings, the mountain. You have never seen them so clear before. You will never see them so clear again. You are God on the seventh day, beating slowly over a new earth.

Two weeks later, Jim tried the bridge stunt near Auckland. He hit the river at 110 mph, bounced and flipped for a quarter of a mile and smashed into rocks.

And the story could end there.

But I want to return to the barn, to the Harley Davidson draped with a sack or two behind the tractor. When Eddie drags it away from the wall chaff flies in the sunlight zigzagging through the cracks. He wipes the dust from the seat, tears cobwebs from the wheels, and pulls it heavy against his side out in to the afternoon. Behind the barn the track falls away down the hill towards the creek, rutted and channelled by the winter's heavy rain. He steadies the bike and puts a leg over the saddle settling into its wide leather curve. Egmont stands over them, so white it slices the air. He looks up testing the wind, hearing sheep and trees and the creek and pushes off. The bike lurches over the ruts at first and he swings his legs taking giant strides to drive her down, hold her straight. As the track steepens she gathers speed. Egmont shudders and the bike thuds so on flat tyres and rough ground that he can hear nothing but his body shaking apart and wind drumming in his ears as the Harley Davidson, earthbound, careers down the hill and over the bridge teetering from side to side through pothole and puddle until on the flat it leaps under his hand and they fall. Into a sudden smooth quiet so total he could have died and slipped under the mountain. Or perhaps they'd begun to fly.

The Women's Press is a feminist publishing house. We aim to publish a wide range of lively, provocative books by women, chiefly in the areas of fiction, literary and art history, physical and mental health and politics.

To receive our complete list of titles, send a stamped addressed envelope. We can supply books direct to readers. Orders must be pre-paid with 60p added per title for postage and packing. We do, however, prefer you to support our efforts to have our books available in all bookshops.

The Women's Press, 34 Great Sutton Street, London EC1V 0DX

Grace Bartram
Peeling

Ally and Rowley have been married for thirty years. Now Rowley is going away with another woman, and Ally, too much of a lady all her life to swear even mildly, has been screaming filth at him.

Peeling describes how Ally gradually and painfully peels away the layers of her sedate, protected and deeply conventional life to discover a person she has never suspected. Mainly it is the women at the refuge for battered women who set her off; they frighten her, depress her. But she finds in them, and in herself, reserves of strength that surprise and revive her.

Grace Bartram, journalist and author of two previous books published in her native Australia, draws on her own experiences of working in a women's refuge for this powerful novel.

ISBN: 0 7043 3994 3
0 7043 2878 X (hardcover)   Fiction £3.95

Janet Frame
Scented Gardens for the Blind

'A brilliant outburst of a book' *Kirkus Reviews*

In this haunting novel Janet Frame leads us to inhabit in turn Vera Glace, the mother who has willed herself sightless; Erlene, the daughter who has ceased to speak; and Edward, the husband and father who has taken refuge in a distant land. She bids us consider the pain – impossibility? – of closeness, of love, among human beings; and the beauty, and danger, in the world of the senses. Then, behind this parable of human relationships, she springs another level of meaning upon us: a study of a mind that has burst the confines of everyday individual consciousness and invented its own colourful and tormented reality.

ISBN: 0 7043 3899 8   Fiction £3.95

Living in the Maniototo

Winner of the Fiction Prize, New Zealand Book Awards, 1980

Janet Frame again offers us a richly imagined exploration of uncharted lands. The path is through the Maniototo, that 'bloody plain' of the imagination which crouches beneath the colour and movement of the living world. The theme of the novel is the process of writing fiction, the power, interruptions and avoidances that the writer feels as she grapples with a deceptive and elusive reality. We move with our guide, a woman of manifold personalities, through a physical journey which is revealed to be a metaphor for the creative process – on which our own survival depends.

'Puts everything else that has come my way this year right in the shade' *Guardian*

ISBN: 0 7043 3867 X   Fiction £3.95

Janet Frame
You Are Now Entering the Human Heart

'My life had been for many years in the power of words. It was driven now by a constant search and need for what was, after all, only a word – imagination' Janet Frame in *To The Is-Land*

This selection of Janet Frame's stories, written over a period of forty years, gives the reader a chance to rediscover the imaginative power and brilliance of language of one of the world's finest writers of fiction. The subjects range from impressions of a New Zealand childhood to sardonic accounts of life in a great city: London, Philadelphia, New York.

The selection has been made by the author herself, from her three published collections *The Lagoon* (1951), *The Reservoir* (1962) and *Snowman Snowman* (1962), as well as from more recent, uncollected, stories.

ISBN: 0 7043 3938 2   Fiction £3.95

Faces in the Water

'I will write about the season of peril . . . a great gap opened in the ice floe between myself and the other people whom I watched, with their world, drifting away through a violet-coloured sea where hammer-head sharks in tropical ease swam side by side with the seals and the polar bears. I was alone on the ice . . . I traded my safety for the glass beads of fantasy'

Faces in the Water is about confinement in mental institutions, about the fear the sensible and sane of this world have of the so-called mad, the uncontrolled. Banished to an institution, Istani Mavet lives a life dominated by the vagaries of her keepers as much as by her own inner world.

'Lyrical, touching and deeply entertaining' John Mortimer, *Observer*

ISBN: 0 7043 3861 0   Fiction £3.95

Janet Frame's Autobiography
To the Is-Land

To the Is-Land is a haunting account of Janet Frame's childhood and adolescence in the New Zealand of the 1920s and 30s. Its simple yet highly crafted language brings alive in vividly remembered detail her materially impoverished but emotionally intense railway family home, her first encounters with love, and death, her first explorations into the worlds of words and poetry.

ISBN: 0 7043 3904 8   £4.95

An Angel At My Table

An Angel At My Table, the second volume of Janet Frame's autobiography, records her struggle from childhood into the public world of adults.

While the framework of this book is that of a traditional 'success story', with the painfully shy teenager eventually gaining self-knowledge and self-respect as a writer, the devastating truthfulness of the observations and language make it also a unique work of art.

ISBN: 0 7043 2844 5   £7.95 (hardcover)

The Envoy from Mirror City

The Envoy from Mirror City tells how the young woman, free at last of the nightmare years in mental hospitals, makes her break with home to embark on the journey to Europe, where all 'real' writers of course must go. She shivers in a damp garden shed in Clapham; dreams of publication with pale poets in cafés in Soho; and travels to Ibiza, where she finds sexual love and haunts the outskirts of the artists' colony.

The book is a brilliant and moving evocation of thirty years ago, and of the process by which an uncertain but somehow determined young woman became a writer and an artist.

ISBN: 0 7043 2875 5   £8.95 (hardcover)

Caeia March
Three Ply Yarn

'The blitz on the London docks got my mum. My dad died in Burma. That's when Dora and me first took to cuddling. Behind the hay barn, while Nellie collected eggs.'

This passionate story is narrated by three women, Dee, Lotte and Esther, as they struggle to take command of their own lives in a world they have not made.

The three choose different paths. Lotte marries for money, Esther seeks education and politics, Dee loves women and learns, through her relationship with her lover's black daughter, about an oppression different from her own. Yet their lives increasingly intertwine, and their realisation grows of the importance of other women to each of them.

Full of the realities of working-class lesbian experience, *Three Ply Yarn* is an absorbing read from an important new writer.

ISBN: 0 7043 4007 0

Fiction £3.95

Tove Ditlevsen
Early Spring

Translated by Tiina Nunnally

'Childhood is long and narrow like a coffin, and you can't get out
on your own'

Tove Ditlevsen is one of Denmark's best loved writers, and the
author of over thirty books of poetry and prose. Yet her
childhood, as a clumsy and ungainly child in a working class area of
Copenhagen in the 1930s, was one of incredible loneliness and
deprivation. Poor to the point of starvation, her family showed
little interest in her. Despite this, Tove never lost sight of her
dream and one aim in life – to become a poet. *Early Spring* is
poignant, funny and unforgettable. It is a story of immense courage
and hope.

ISBN: 0 7043 4004 6   Fiction £4.95

Padma Perera
**Birthday Deathday
and Other Stories**

'Hers is a gift to treasure' Tille Olsen

A stubborn old woman vows to stay silent one day a week, until her death becomes her loudest silence; two dubious holy men wake a child to the irony of belief; an unjustly dismissed schoolmaster demonstrates the uselessness of hindsight . . .

Padma Perera's is a dazzling new talent. She has a faultless sense of language, and the ability to draw her reader into her world within a single paragraph. Her stories, most of them set in India, have been published in the *New Yorker, Saturday Evening Post, Horizon, Iowa Review* and elsewhere.

ISBN: 0 7043 3984 6

Fiction £3.95